My Remarkable
Little
MONKEY

MARK LAGES

authorHOUSE®

AuthorHouse™
1663 Liberty Drive
Bloomington, IN 47403
www.authorhouse.com
Phone: 1 (800) 839-8640

Published by AuthorHouse   05/09/2017

ISBN: 978-1-5246-9002-1 (sc)
ISBN: 978-1-5246-9001-4 (e)

Library of Congress Control Number: 2017906617

Print information available on the last page.

This book is printed on acid-free paper.

William Shakespeare

Surely you've heard of it. It has a name; they call it the Infinite Monkey Theorem. If you don't believe me, you can check it out on the Internet. You'll find it described on Wikipedia, where they say one of the first known references to the idea was by a French mathematician named Emile Borel back in 1913. I first heard about the theorem when I was a kid in grade school, from my fourth-grade teacher, Miss Blaine. She told us that if you were to put a single monkey in a room with a computer and a word-processing program for an infinite period of time, the monkey would eventually type all the works of William Shakespeare, without a single spelling mistake. Fourteen years after Miss Blaine told us this story, I would have a monkey of my own, and I would name him after the theorem. Yes, I named him William Shakespeare. What a great name for a monkey, no? He was a capuchin whom I purchased from a man in Riverside, about an hour's drive from my home. Before I tell you about the day I purchased Shakespeare, let me tell you a little about myself.

My name is Marty Anderson, and I'm now thirty-eight years old. This story starts when I was twenty-three, on the day I purchased Shakespeare. When I made the purchase, I'd recently graduated from the University of California at Berkeley, where I majored in business administration. It's not that I had a burning interest in business, but at that time, I had no real passions in my life—not the way some kids do with music, art, literature, medicine, engineering, or whatever. My father had suggested business as an ideal choice of major. It was my father's opinion that everything in life was a business of one kind or the other, so if I didn't know exactly what I wanted to do with my life, a business degree would always come in handy. This made sense to me, so I followed my father's advice and spent four years of college concentrating on accounting, economics, and the management of people. I took a lot of other classes as well, getting a well-rounded education. I have no complaints about college, and I think I got a lot out of my four years.

It wasn't imperative for me to have a job lined up when I graduated. My father had made a fortune in the real estate industry developing office buildings all over Southern California, and he had left me a substantial inheritance when he died during my junior year in college. Both he and my mother died the same night, hit head-on by a drunk teenager on the Pacific Coast Highway while they were on their way home from a restaurant in Huntington Beach. The teenager also died. It was a horrific accident, and there were pictures of it on the eleven o'clock news. That's how I found out about it—by watching the evening news. I was at my parents' home in Newport Beach on the night of the accident, visiting for spring break. The reporter didn't say who'd died in the wreck, pending notification of the families, but seeing what was left of the car, I knew it was theirs. It was a 1957 red and white Corvette, the car my dad liked to take out on weekend evenings. My dad had quite a few cars, but the Corvette was his favorite. I checked the garage after watching the story on the news, and sure enough, the car was gone. I got a visit from several police officers a short time later, giving me the awful news that both my parents had just been killed in the accident. It was a terrible tragedy, and it affected me deeply.

I am an only child, with no brothers or sisters. When Mom and Dad died, I was left alone—well, except for Uncle George, Aunt Margaret, and my two cousins. I seldom saw these people, though, since they lived back east in Vermont. I graduated from Berkeley when I was twenty-two and now live about five miles from my parents' old house in a place my father bought for me before he died. It's a typical little dwelling in a little beach community. I'm probably making it sound more humble than it actually is. Corona del Mar, the town I live in, is a desirable place to live, and the homes here are quite expensive. My dad purchased the place when I was eighteen and rented it out while I was in Berkeley. It was his intention for me to move into the house when I was done with college. He told me the place would be mine if I wanted it. Well, of course I wanted it. What kid in his early twenties wouldn't like to live near the beach in such a perfect little house? When I graduated and moved back to Southern California, I asked the tenants to move out, and I moved in. It has three bedrooms,

2

three bathrooms, and a small backyard. It has lots of brick and wood siding and several mature cypress trees in the front yard. I use one side of the two-car garage to park my car, and on the other side, I store the boxes of stuff I kept after clearing out and selling my parents' house.

Dad left me a ton of money when he passed away. I had no need to get a job, so I didn't. I spent a lot of my time playing tennis, reading, going to parties, working in the yard, and improving the house Dad had bought for me. I remodeled and renovated every room, doing most of the work myself, learning the trades as I went along. It was a lot of fun and kept me busy. With the money Dad left me, I could've bought something a lot nicer and a lot larger, but I knew Dad had wanted me to live in this particular house. So I stayed, and I kept myself hopping with activities. Not everything I did was about me, for I found a charity to which I could give a good chunk of my time. They needed someone with the talents I had, and my business degree from Berkeley proved helpful. I kept their books, did their tax returns, and helped them manage their financial affairs. It was a scholarship fund founded by one of my father's oldest friends, Vince Atkins, and we were helping a lot of disadvantaged kids go to college. Except for the fact that I didn't have a job, I lived a normal life. And it was a satisfying life, on the surface anyway. Deep down, I felt I was missing something.

So is this why I wanted to purchase a monkey? I don't know; maybe you can tell me. You know, all people wish they could be rich, until they actually are. Once you're rich, it's funny what happens to you. You don't want to give up a dime of your fortune, yet you complain about being wealthy as though it's a curse. So what was I complaining about? I found myself complaining especially about other people, about the way they looked at me, and about the way they treated me. There's no denying the fact that you're different when you have a lot of money, and not necessarily in a good way. You aren't especially talented or humorous or witty or intelligent, but everyone tries to make you feel as though you are. They want to chum up to you, to feel closer to your wealth. They all want a piece of the action. Women are the worst of the lot, and dating can be a real nightmare. I don't know that I'd met a single sincere woman since coming back to Southern California and moving into my house in Corona del Mar. Things had been so much different in college. While living in Berkeley, I had been just another ordinary student, and girls weren't exactly fawning over me. In fact, if I hadn't gone out of my way to know them, I doubt any of them ever would have even said hi.

When I purchased Shakespeare, I was dating a young woman named Kimberly Koch. She was typical of the sort of females I was meeting. She was an attractive brunette with big brown eyes and a charming smile. She could fool you with her smile, fool you into thinking she really cared about you as a person. That was what she was good at—making you think there was a special place in her heart just for you. But the truth was that my bank account and all its zeros were of a lot more interest to her than I ever would be. Slowly but surely, the telltale signs began to appear, just as they had with all the other girls I'd dated. "Why do you live in this little house?" she finally asked. "With your money you could afford a place three times this size." Whenever we went anywhere in my car, she always wanted to know why I didn't trade it in for something more in keeping with my net worth. And when we went out to dinner, it always had to be at a restaurant that charged an arm and a leg for its pretentious, miniscule portions of food, not enough to feed a flea. Have you ever been to one of these restaurants? I don't know about you, but I like to feel like I'm actually getting something for my money. No, I didn't like these restaurants, and I was very fond of my rusty old car. With women like Kimberly on my scent, I was getting nowhere with my love life. True, I knew lots of people and went to lots of parties, and Kimberly and I went out often, yet I felt so alone. I needed something different. I wanted a companion without all the pretense and perfume, and that's when I decided I needed a monkey.

Well, I didn't decide on a monkey immediately. At first I considered a dog or a cat, the usual and more acceptable route to go. But what would I do with a dog or a cat? They were too subservient for my taste and too docile. I needed a companion who would stand up for himself, be reasonably independent, and desire to do something other than hang around the house all day, waiting to be fed and hoping to be petted. I read up on monkeys and learned that they were truly a handful to take care of. Much of what I read said that they actually made terrible pets, that they were not at all like dogs or cats, that they were wild animals who actually didn't belong cooped up in a house with human owners. I read all these warnings, and the more I read, the more I wanted a monkey. I needed some kind of challenge in my humdrum life, something to keep me on my toes. And I needed a real companion, not someone or something that was just after food and money. I wanted a wild animal, trained to behave himself and keep me company. The animal would be wonderfully independent yet also willing to be my friend. And I knew after further research the exact type of monkey to get: a capuchin, the same little monkeys they used to dress up and train to collect money for old-fashioned organ-grinders, taking coins and dollar bills from the hands of onlookers and dropping the booty into their little tin cups. Yes, an organ-grinder's monkey. I'd seen an organ-grinder and his capuchin once when I was a child. It was a wonderfully intelligent, long-tailed living being with perfect little hands and feet and a delightful, bright-eyed face.

So where would I find this monkey? Certainly not in a pet store. Going on the Internet, I found a guy in Riverside who had several capuchins, one of whom was up for sale. It was a baby, and according to the posting, the man already had too many monkeys in his house. Another baby monkey was the last thing he needed, and he was looking for a buyer. I did some more research on the Internet and learned that one had to have a special license to own such an animal and that the government gave out licenses only to those who actually needed a monkey, such as paraplegics who used trained capuchins to perform certain tasks. Since it was unlikely that I could get an actual license, being that I had no special need other than my desire to own one, I asked the man in Riverside if he'd sell to me anyway, even knowing I had no plan to get a proper license. He told me that he needed to get rid of the creature as soon as possible and that if I had the cash, the monkey was mine—to heck with the licensing. "Just don't let it get around that you have a monkey in your house," he said.

So I met the man at his house the next day. He lived on several acres out in the middle of nowhere, in the dry rolling hills of Riverside County, in a house that looked like it hadn't been painted or repaired for many years. I pulled into the driveway, and he came out through his front door, expecting me. "You must be Marty," he said.

"I am," I replied. "You must be Vern."

"That's me. Come on in."

I followed Vern into his house. He was an older guy, probably in his sixties, dressed in a plaid shirt and jeans. He had a head full of uncombed gray hair and a face lined with wrinkles. His eyes sparkled, the pale blue color of a clear sky. I liked his eyes, and they made me feel comfortable with him and our transaction. "Sorry if I'm a little late," I said. "I ran into a lot of traffic on the way here."

"Here he is," Vern said. He was now holding a tiny monkey in his hands. "Go ahead and hold him yourself."

"Oh yes," I said.

He handed the monkey to me. As I held the monkey, he looked up at me with the most amazing expression on his face. There's just something so special you get out of a monkey's face, a feeling you don't get looking at a dog or cat.

"Cute little bugger, isn't he?"

"Yes, he's very cute."

"Just a year old."

"Where are his parents?"

"I locked them up in the bedroom. I didn't want them to see their baby being taken away."

"He seems to like me." I said this because he was so docile. He just sat in my hands, looking at me with his remarkable eyes.

"He's a smart little bugger."

"Capuchins are supposed to be smart, aren't they?"

"I mean, this one is really clever."

"Why do you say that?"

"Do you notice anything unusual about him?"

"No, should I?"

"He isn't wearing a diaper."

"No, I guess he isn't."

"His mom and dad are still in diapers. Capuchins have to wear diapers; otherwise, you know, the house would be a mess. They'd be pooping and peeing all over the place."

"Of course."

"But not this one."

"Why not?"

"He toilet trained himself."

"He did?" He wasn't even mine yet, and already I was proud of the little guy.

"I didn't have to teach him a thing. He just figured it out for himself. He saw me using the toilet one day. I had happened to leave the door open, and he picked up on what to do right away. Hasn't worn a diaper since. He sits on the seat, balancing himself with his tail, and does his business like a trooper, wipes himself with the paper, and flushes the toilet. No fuss, no muss."

"Wow," I said.

"Never had a monkey do that before. I'd keep the little bugger, but like I told you over the phone, I've already got three of them, his mom and dad and a third. They're all I can handle."

"I think he likes me." I was looking again at the monkey's face.

"Did you bring your checkbook? Are we still okay on the price?"

"It's an awful lot to pay for a pet."

"A monkey's much more than a pet."

"I guess so."

"You'll find out. Do you know how to take care of him once you get him home?"

"I've done a lot of research on the Internet."

"That's good."

"Yes, I think I'm ready for him. Can you hold him for me a second? I'll write you a check." I suddenly heard some banging on one of Vern's bedroom doors. "What's all that?" I asked.

"It must be his parents. They probably know something's up."

"That you're selling their baby?"

"Something like that. These animals are pretty smart."

"Should we even be doing this?"

"Do you want the monkey or not?" Vern asked firmly. He didn't want me changing my mind or wasting his time.

I thought about it and then looked at the little monkey in Vern's hands. He was still looking at me. "Yes, I want him," I said.

"Then write the check and take him away. By this time tomorrow, his parents will have forgotten they even had a baby."

I doubted this was true and figured Vern was saying this to make me feel better about taking their baby away. I wrote the check and handed it to Vern. I then took my monkey from Vern's hands, and Vern accompanied me out of the old house. When we got to my car, I asked Vern if he thought it was safe for me to drive with a loose monkey in the car, and Vern said he did it all the time. I had the impression Vern would've said anything to get me out of there; he just wanted me to go. As we backed out, Vern was waving to us. I doubted he was waving to me; I think he was waving to his baby monkey. I think it broke the poor guy's heart, seeing the little guy leave. The monkey just sat on the passenger seat of my car, quietly and without making a scene, still staring at me.

"I'll take good care of you," I said. "I don't know what Vern's been calling you, but I have a name in mind. I'd like to call you Shakespeare, if that's okay with you."

Obviously, there was no response from Shakespeare, for he was only a monkey, and it would've been hard to believe he had any idea what I was talking about.

When we arrived home, I let Shakespeare explore the house. He checked out all the rooms, and although I had no way of knowing this for sure, I felt everything was to his liking. When he was done checking out the house, he went to the kitchen and stood in front of the refrigerator. I took this to mean that he was hungry. Of course, he knew what a refrigerator was, having lived for a year with Vern and having seen him open his own refrigerator door again and again for food. I opened the refrigerator door and removed a fruit platter I'd purchased earlier in the day from the grocery store and also grabbed a banana from the counter. I put the items on the breakfast table, and Shakespeare jumped up on the table to check the stuff out. The banana seemed especially to his liking, and he picked it up, peeled it open, and took a bite. He was so small that he nibbled off only the end of the banana. He also tried the other fruit, including a piece of watermelon and a chunk of cantaloupe. He even tried a grape. It was funny watching him eat, and he didn't seem to mind my staring at him. When he was done eating, I put the fruit back in the refrigerator and got him a glass of water from the faucet. He knew how to use the glass right away, holding it to his lips with both hands as he drank. Vern must have taught him how to do this. When he was done, he jumped to the kitchen counter and put the empty glass in the sink. "That's a good boy," I said. "Vern has taught you well. So how would you like to watch a little TV with me? There's a Lakers game on this afternoon. It should be starting soon."

I didn't know why I was talking to Shakespeare about watching a

Lakers game. He'd have no idea what I was talking about. It was funny how people talked to their animals, I thought, as if they were actually listening and could understand anything they were saying. I stepped over to the sofa and grabbed the remote, turning on the TV. Shakespeare stayed at the kitchen sink for a moment, seemingly wondering what he should do, and then jumped down to the floor and ran over to join me at the sofa. I sat on one end, and Shakespeare got comfortable on the other. I put my hands behind my head, leaning back, and Shakespeare did the same, putting his tiny hands behind his own head and leaning back. I then crossed my legs, and he crossed his too. He was mimicking me, and I laughed at this. After I laughed, Shakespeare made a similar sound that I supposed could be misunderstood as his own laugh. It was weird having a furry little monkey on my sofa, copying everything I did. But it wasn't at all disconcerting. It made me feel like the two of us were going to be great pals. For the rest of the afternoon, we watched the basketball game.

Around dinnertime I got a call from Kimberly. Apparently, she still thought the two of us had a future together, and when I answered the phone, she was cheerful, nearly giddy. "What are we doing tonight?" she asked.

"Nothing that I know of," I said.

"Do you want to come over?"

"I can't right now."

"Well, should I come over to your place?"

"Oh no," I said. "Don't come over here."

"Why not?"

"I'm kind of busy."

"Busy doing what?"

"I kind of have a guest over."

"Is it someone I know?"

"No," I said.

"Who is it?"

"I can't tell you."

"What do you mean you can't tell me?"

"I just can't."

"Oh, I see," Kimberly said, as if she'd figured me out, thinking that I had another woman over.

"It's not what you think."

"Well, what else could it be?"

"Something different."

There was a long pause on the phone as Kimberly thought about this. "If you didn't want to see me anymore, all you had to do was say so."

"You're right," I said. Seeing this as an opportunity to get her out of my life once and for all, I added, without lying, "I should've told you about my new friend."

I knew she would interpret this to mean I was with a new woman friend. She knew nothing about my monkey, and I needed to keep it that way. Then I told her I was sorry if I'd hurt her feelings. There was another pause on the phone and then a click; she had hung up on me.

"Good job," I said to Shakespeare, who was still on the sofa, minding his own business and watching the TV with his hands behind his head. Already the little guy was proving to be handy. I'd been wondering for weeks how I was going to get Kimberly out of my life, and with Shakespeare at my side, we'd done it in just a matter of minutes.

What a great idea this had been, bringing home this little monkey. Even if he was rather expensive, he was worth every cent. In the months that followed, we got along famously. He followed me around the house wherever I went, watching me, learning from me. He didn't tear the house apart, knocking things over or throwing objects the way some monkeys might; he was very well behaved. And he'd been growing. He was large enough now to open the refrigerator door on his own. He'd jump up and grab the handle with both hands, and then planting his feet against the kitchen cabinet, he'd pull the door open easily. He'd get his food out of the refrigerator and place it on the breakfast table to eat. He also knew how to get himself a glass from the cupboard and fill it with water at the faucet. Vern was right—he was smart. What was most interesting about Shakespeare, however, was how he liked to watch TV. I knew he didn't have any idea what the people were doing or what they were saying, but he'd spend hours glued to the tube, watching show after show. He'd seen me using the TV remote, and several times I saw him pick it up and aim it, pressing random buttons, trying to make the device work for him. So I finally sat down with him one day and tried to teach him how to use it, showing him which button to push to turn the set on and off. I taught him how to change channels and how to adjust the volume. It didn't take him long to learn these commands, and in no time he was controlling the TV all by himself.

Then the most remarkable thing happened. One afternoon I walked into the room while he was watching a talk show, and he had the remote in his lap. He sat up, set the remote down on the coffee table, and jumped off the sofa. He went over to the television and put his little hand on it, as if showing it to me. He then looked at me. "TV," he said.

"What?" I said. "Say that again."

"TV," he said again. There was no question as to whether he had spoken or what he had said. His voice was high-pitched, like some silly cartoon character, but it was clear and emphatic. "TV, TV, TV," he said.

"Yes!" I exclaimed.

He jumped up and down, clicking his tongue. He was very excited.

"That's the TV," I said. "You're right, that's our TV."

Me Like Sarah

O kay, so he had said a word. But it was just a fluke, wasn't it? Everyone knew that monkeys couldn't talk, and since he didn't say another word for months, I put the incident out of my head. But listen, even if he wasn't a talking monkey, he was still very smart. There was no question about that. And I felt sorry for him, sitting on the sofa and watching TV day after day, with nothing constructive to do. I had to do something to keep his mind and hands busy, to prevent him from becoming a pathetic little couch potato, trapped under the roof of my home. So I went to Walmart and then Target and bought him hundreds of dollars of different toys and kids' games, the sort of stuff preschool children get to fiddle around with: Legos, building blocks, some simple puzzles, a toy xylophone, a little drum, and a lot of other similar kid's aisle stuff. I also bought some coloring books and a couple boxes of crayons, along with a plastic table and chair at which he could sit and draw. I then went to a children's furniture store and purchased a small bed and miniature rocking chair, both just the right size for his little monkey body. When I brought all the purchases home, he watched wide-eyed as I carried everything into the house. I put the items in the spare bedroom, making the room his. "This is all for you," I said. "I want you to feel at home here."

He seemed to understand what I meant, and he immediately jumped into the room to play with all his new belongings. He knew exactly what to do with everything, except for the coloring books. So I kneeled down with him at the little table and showed him how to use crayons, how to color the pictures within the lines, without scribbling all over the pages. He quickly learned how to do that too. This was such a great idea, giving him this roomful of things to play with, his own chair and table, and his own bed to sleep in. I could tell he was pleased. So was I just being anthropomorphic? I don't think so. He truly seemed happy.

There were four rooms in the house that Shakespeare now used daily. First there was the kitchen, where he got his food from the fridge and his glass of water from the faucet. Second was the hall bathroom, where he used the toilet and groomed himself in front of the mirror. Third was the family room, where he relaxed and watched TV, and fourth was his bedroom, where he played with all his toys or just curled up and slept. He was a busy and happy little monkey, always doing this or that. I think he felt at home inside my house, especially in his bedroom. I'd sit in his room for hours and watch him play with the stuff I'd bought for him, marveling at how creative he was and how fast he was learning. I discovered he especially liked music, for often when he watched TV, he turned on shows where bands were playing or people were singing. And in his room, he loved banging out notes on his toy xylophone, not just at random like you'd expect a monkey to do, but carefully and thoughtfully, as though searching for an intelligent melody. So I bought him a CD player and an assortment of music CDs. I brought home some rock, country, jazz, and classical CDs and taught him how to insert them into the player. Then I showed him the play button, after which he'd put on the music and try to keep up with it by tapping on his toy drum. At first it sounded dreadful, all this drumming, but gradually he got the hang of it, keeping pretty decent time with the music he played.

During these months I was able to go on with my life, business as usual. I continued to play tennis every day at the club, and I was still helping out with Vince Atkins's college scholarship fund. And I worked in the yard, usually on weekends. I was no longer working on the inside of the house, for things were just the way I wanted them, and there was no remodeling or renovating left for me to do. And I was able to leave Shakespeare alone in the house, without having to worry about him taking the place apart. He was always busy doing something he liked, and he stayed out of trouble. Everything I'd read on the Internet about monkeys was wrong, at least when it came to Shakespeare. I could tell he didn't like it when I left the house, but I'd left and returned enough times for him to know I'd always be back eventually. He was smart that way; he caught on to things quickly.

It was during these days that I first met Sarah Tyler. She worked at a Starbucks on the Pacific Coast Highway, and she took my order one morning for a medium latte and an old-fashioned glazed doughnut. I tell you, I liked the girl from the minute I saw her. She had thick, long brown hair tied back in a ponytail and deep, intelligent brown eyes. You can tell a lot about a woman by looking into her eyes, and Sarah's eyes told me she was different from all those other girls I'd been meeting at parties or at the tennis club or by way of mutual friends. Her eyes told me she was bright, kind, and gracious. After I gave her my order, she caught me staring at her, and I blushed and tried to look away. But I couldn't keep my eyes off her, and I looked at her again. I handed her a twenty, and she gave me my change. Then I got up the nerve to ask her name, and she told me it was Sarah.

"Sarah," I said, trying to smile nicely. "I like that name. Sarah, would you be willing to go out with me?"

"Go out with you?" she asked. "You mean, as on a date?"

"Something like that," I said. Now I couldn't believe I'd asked her, and I was embarrassed for perhaps having been too forward. All she had done was take my order, and there I was, asking her to go out with me.

"I don't even know you."

"No, you don't."

"What's your name?"

"Marty," I said. "If we went out to dinner or something, you'd get a chance to talk to me. Then you could say you know me."

"I don't know."

"I'm not a bad guy."

"No, you seem nice."

"Let's do it this way," I said, picking up a napkin. Since she hadn't flat refused me, I was getting up more nerve. "I'll write down my name and phone number, and you can think it over. Do you have a pen?"

"Here," she said. She handed me a ballpoint pen she found beside the cash register.

I carefully wrote my name and number on the napkin. In the meantime, the man behind me was clearing his throat, making himself obvious. Apparently, he didn't appreciate my clumsy date arranging being done on his time. Maybe he was in a hurry. I turned to look at him.

"Please, I'll be just another second," I said. Then turning back to Sarah, I said, "Here, take this napkin. I hope you'll give me a call. Please say you'll at least think about it. This is my cell phone number, so you can reach me easily. Please say you'll call me."

"Okay," she said.

"So you'll call?"

"I'll think about it. You need to move on. You're holding up the line."

So that's how we met. I got out of the way, and the man behind me finally got to place his order. Sarah didn't call me that night, but a couple nights later, she decided to give me a ring. It just goes to show that if you want something in life, you've got to speak up. True, I'd made kind of a dope of myself at the Starbucks that morning, writing my name and number on that napkin and holding up the line, but she did call. And we decided to go out to dinner that night. I let her pick the restaurant, and she chose a pleasant place—nothing fancy, just some good food and decent portions for a very reasonable price. I could tell she wasn't used to paying top dollar at restaurants. She wasn't after me for my money, and that was refreshing.

"So tell me about yourself," I said once we were seated at a table.

"You first."

"You want me to go first?"

"Yes, tell me something about Marty Anderson. I don't usually go out on dates with guys I don't know, or at least know something about. So unless you want me to get up right now and leave, you're going to need to tell me just who you think you are." She was kidding, of course. I didn't think she had any plan to really get up and leave. She seemed comfortable with me, comfortable enough to kid around.

"Well, I'm twenty-four years old."

"I'm eighteen. You're older than me."

"Is that a problem?"

"No, not at all."

"I graduated from Berkeley a couple years ago. I was a business major."

"I'm going to UC Irvine. I'm an English lit major. I work at Starbucks to pay for my food and rent. My parents are paying for my tuition."

"My parents paid mine too."

"And what are you doing now? Are you running some sort of business with your business degree?" She smiled. I got the impression that she didn't think too much of my business studies. I've found that business majors at universities aren't thought of very highly by most others. I don't know why this is. It's just something I've noticed.

"I work for a nonprofit."

"Oh?" she said. This seemed to interest her, the idea of my doing something meaningful. "Which nonprofit do you work for?"

"It's a scholarship fund. It was started by a friend of my dad's years ago. We collect donations from wealthy people and provide college scholarships to disadvantaged kids all over Southern California. I was hired to handle all their money and business affairs."

"Well, you're not going to get rich doing that sort of work."

"No, I'm not. But I don't need to get rich."

"Wow, you're unusual."

"Unusual?"

"Yes, like one of a kind. It seems like every guy I've met here in Orange County just wants to get rich as soon as possible. I mean, everyone around here wants to be rich, don't they? A girl doesn't often meet a guy your age who's happy just working for a nonprofit, who isn't obsessed with driving a Mercedes and buying a big house in Newport Beach."

I laughed. She had no idea that the reason I wasn't obsessed with earning lots of money was that I already had well more than I needed. But I let it go at that. I liked the idea of her liking me. And I liked her thinking that I was a man of modest means. I certainly didn't want her thinking I was wealthy. Money had a way of ruining my relationships with women, and I didn't want it to have that same effect on this one. Well, it wasn't exactly a relationship yet, but it did have a chance of becoming one.

"Are you from around here?" I asked.

"I'm from Nebraska. How about you?"

"I was born and raised here."

"Do your parents live nearby?"

"My parents are both dead."

"Oh, I'm sorry."

"They were killed in a car accident while I was going to Berkeley. Actually, I was visiting here for spring break when it happened."

"Do you have any other family?"

"An aunt and uncle in Vermont. And some cousins, but I seldom see any of them."

"So you're sort of on your own."

"Yes, I am." This wasn't exactly true. I did have Shakespeare. He was kind of like a family member, but I didn't figure Sarah was referring to animals when she described me as being alone. I decided not to tell Sarah anything about Shakespeare, not on our first date. She might think I was kind of weird, living with a monkey.

Sarah and I went on several dates after that first dinner, and I never mentioned Shakespeare once. I enjoyed our dates, and she seemed to as well. I took her to the beach, and we lay in the sun and swam a little in the cold ocean water. I took her to Disneyland because she said that she'd never been there and that she'd always wanted to see it. I also took her to Hollywood Boulevard, for the same reason we had gone to Disneyland—just to see it for the sake of seeing it—but she said she thought Hollywood was awful and had no desire to return there ever. Months passed. Sometimes we'd just take walks together, sometimes we'd see more sights, and sometimes we'd just hang out at her apartment. She lived in Costa Mesa, just a fifteen-minute drive from my place in Corona del Mar. Her apartment building was kind of run-down and seedy, but she kept the inside nice. She had a big sofa we would sit on to watch old movies together. Sometimes I would stay at her place until the early morning hours watching movies. I had to be careful not to be gone with her for too long, though, because I had Shakespeare waiting for me back at my house. We never went to my house at all, and Sarah still knew nothing about Shakespeare. In fact, no one, with the sole exception of Vern in Riverside, knew I owned a monkey.

So now there were two things that Sarah didn't know about me, that I was keeping secret. The first was my wealth—that I didn't need to hold a paying job, that I could basically do whatever I wanted. And the second was that I lived with a capuchin monkey. Now certainly the wealth wouldn't be something she'd hold against me if she ever found out about it, for what woman in her right mind would turn away a man with lots of money? Realizing that I'd kept it from her might make her mad at me for a moment, but I was sure she'd forgive me after I explained the trouble I'd had with other women. But the second secret was much trickier. It's not that there was anything wrong about living with a monkey, but capuchins live to be almost forty years old when in captivity, meaning my relationship with Shakespeare could go on until I was in my sixties. It was a long-term commitment I'd established, and depending on how Sarah felt about living with a monkey, it could prove to be a deal breaker. I needed to be honest with her, not just about Shakespeare, but about everything. I needed to get the cards on the table. So I told her I had two secrets and said I'd fill her in on both. I decided to invite her to my house, something I had avoided so far, and yes, I would introduce her to Shakespeare.

"So this is it?" Sarah asked, standing at the sidewalk in front of my house. It was a beautiful day. The sun was filtering through the cypress trees and casting shadows on the front lawn. My house looked like the perfect home. "It doesn't look so bad to me."

"No," I said. "It's not so bad."

"So why have you always been so hesitant to bring me over here?"

"Just come inside." I opened the front door and went in first, in case Shakespeare came running to greet me. I didn't want his enthusiasm to scare Sarah away. We both stepped into the house.

"It looks as nice inside as it does on the outside," Sarah said, looking around at the front room, taking everything in.

"Here's the thing," I said. "I live with someone. I don't live by myself."

"You live with someone?"

"I have a roommate."

"What's her name?" Sarah asked, assuming my roommate was a girl. Otherwise, why would I have been so reticent to have her over? It's funny how, when you're acting in any way suspicious, women always think there's another female in the picture.

"It's not a she."

"So your roommate is a man?"

"No, not exactly."

"I don't get it."

"He must be in his room," I said. Shakespeare wasn't on the sofa, and he wasn't in the kitchen. The hall bathroom door was wide open, and he wasn't in there either. "Follow me."

"This is so mysterious."

"You might think it's kind of weird."

Sarah followed me, and we came to Shakespeare's room, where his door was shut. So I opened the door, and there was Shakespeare, on the floor playing with his Legos. He looked up at me with his bright eyes as if to say hello.

"I live with a monkey," I said. "This is Shakespeare."

"Oh my," Sarah said.

Shakespeare put down his Legos and looked at her.

"Don't make any sudden moves. You're the first person I've brought into the house since bringing him home. He might be afraid of you. He might even bite. Capuchins are known to bite when they get spooked."

"He bites?"

"I don't think he will. Let's give him a moment to take this in and see how he reacts." Then to Shakespeare I said, "I want you to meet a friend of mine. This is Sarah. I like her very much, and I'd like you to like her too."

Shakespeare stood up from the floor and approached us slowly. He stopped in front of Sarah and grasped one of her fingers. He was looking up at her, and she was looking down at him. "Sarah," he said.

"He said my name!"

"He does that sometimes."

"He says your name?"

"He mimics words. I don't think he actually knows what they mean. You know what they say—monkey see, monkey do. He's like a myna bird, repeating what he hears."

"I see."

"Sarah," Shakespeare said again, and he tugged at her finger. "Sarah, Sarah."

"He knows that's my name," Sarah said. "He keeps saying it like it means something to him. Monkeys aren't supposed to be able to talk, Marty. Not at all."

"No?" I said. I'll admit I wasn't as surprised as Sarah, having lived all these months with Shakespeare. I knew my monkey was particularly clever. He wasn't just your average capuchin. I mean, what monkey plays with toys the way Shakespeare did, solving simple puzzles, making things out of his Legos? You should see the different things he made. And what monkey colors in coloring books, keeping inside the lines? He was an amazing little animal, to be sure. I didn't know that much about monkeys, and maybe some other monkeys did these kinds of things as well. What did I really know about monkeys other than what I'd read on the Internet? I knew a lot about Shakespeare, but little about monkeys in general. I guess it had never occurred to me just how unusual his behavior might be. "You should see him open the refrigerator," I said. "Or see him get a glass of water."

"Did you train him?"

"No, he just picks this stuff up on his own. He's even toilet trained."

"He uses a bathroom?"

"Yep," I said.

Finally, Shakespeare let go of Sarah's finger and went back to work on his Lego project. He appeared to be building a crude monkey version of a castle.

"I think he wants to be left alone," I said.

"Okay."

"He likes his playtime. Sometimes, he just likes to be by himself. If he wants to interact with us, he'll come out of his room." We stepped out and closed the door, leaving Shakespeare by himself.

"Why didn't you tell me about your monkey? We've been dating all these months, and you've never said anything. Did you think I'd have a problem with it? I love monkeys, and I think Shakespeare is wonderful."

"You do?"

"So why so secretive?"

"I had to be sure I could trust you."

"Trust me?"

"I had to be sure you wouldn't tell anyone."

"But why?"

"Because I think I'm supposed to have some sort of special license to keep a monkey in my house, and I never bothered to get one. If the authorities were to find out he's here with me, they could take him away from me. It would break my heart. So you have to give me your word you won't tell anyone."

"You have my word, Marty."

"I believe you," I said.

"Now what's your second secret?"

"My second secret?"

"You told me you had two. The first is clearly Shakespeare, that you live with a monkey. But what could the second secret possibly be?"

I thought a moment before answering. "That can wait for another day."

"Tell me now."

"No, later," I said. "Don't worry, it's nothing bad. And it's not weird, like the fact that I have a monkey in my life. It's a good secret, actually. I think you'll like it."

"Then tell me."

"I've got a better idea."

"What's that?"

"Let's have a pizza delivered."

"A pizza?"

"Sure, we can watch TV and eat a pizza. Shakespeare will join us. He loves pizza."

Just then Sarah's cell phone rang, and she removed it from her purse. She looked at it and told me, "It's my mother."

"Well, answer it," I said.

"Hi, Mom," Sarah said into the phone. From then on she just listened. I could hear her mom talking. I mean, I could hear her voice coming out of the phone, but I couldn't understand anything she was saying. Sarah had a serious expression on her face the entire time she was on the call. Finally, she said, "I'll be there on the first flight." Then she ended the call.

"What is it?" I asked.

"Daddy's had a stroke. He's in the hospital."

"Is he going to be okay?"

"My mom doesn't know. She just said I need to get out there as soon as possible. She sounded very flustered. I didn't understand much of what she was saying."

"Do you need a ride to the airport? Do you want me to take you?"

"Would you?"

"Of course I will," I said. "Call and get your tickets. I'll take you when you're ready."

"What about Shakespeare?"

"He does fine by himself."

"Are you sure?"

"Just call and get your tickets."

Sarah got back on the phone and arranged her flight. I went to Shakespeare's room and told him that I was leaving again but that I'd be back soon. Don't ask me why I always did this, explaining things to him like he understood English, but I did it anyway. I liked to think he got what I was saying, and even if he didn't understand me, at least he felt like I was trying to communicate. At least he didn't get the idea that I was ignoring him whenever I left the house. I said good-bye to Shakespeare and then took Sarah to her apartment so she could pack some clothes and toiletries into her suitcase. From there we went straight to the airport, and I saw Sarah off.

"Give me a call when you get there," I said. "Let me know how things are going."

"I will."

"Do you want me to go to Starbucks tomorrow morning and tell them what happened?"

"No, I'll call them from Nebraska."

"You sure you have everything you need?"

"I'm good, Marty. I'll talk to you soon." And with that, Sarah gave me a quick kiss and then rushed into the airport, her purse strap falling off her shoulder and her wheeled suitcase dragging along behind her. I felt like I was going to cry, not because I was worried about her dad, but because I was going to miss having Sarah around. I'd grown so used to her, doing things with her, going places together. It was then that I first realized I might be falling in love with her, the pretty girl who worked the cash register at Starbucks, the girl who had no idea how wealthy I was, the girl who'd just discovered I lived with a monkey. She had said she liked Shakespeare, hadn't she? She said she thought it was wonderful that I had a pet monkey. Most people wouldn't be that open-minded. Did she love me? She'd never actually said the words, but it wouldn't surprise me to hear them come out of her mouth. No, it wouldn't surprise me at all.

I drove home and parked my car in the garage. When I walked into the house, Shakespeare was there on the sofa, leaning backward on a throw pillow, his little hands behind his head, watching a reality show about lumberjacks on one of the cable channels.

"It looks like it's just you and me again," I said, sitting down next to him. "Is there anything on besides this stupid lumberjack show? I'm not really in the mood to watch ill-tempered lumberjacks. Why do you even watch this nonsense?"

Shakespeare handed me the remote, apparently sensing that I wanted to change the channel. I grabbed it from him and flipped through the stations, one after the other. There was nothing worth watching, not a single interesting show, and I turned back to the lumberjacks.

Shakespeare then reached over and grabbed my finger, the way he did when he wanted my attention. "Me like Sarah," he said.

"So do I," I said, not looking up from the TV. Then I turned quickly to look at him. He seemed to be smiling. "Did you just say what I think you said?"

"Me like Sarah," he said again.

One Plus One

I t had now been a little over a year since I brought Shakespeare home from Vern's house, separating him from his natural parents and replacing them with me. It was the afternoon of my twenty-fourth birthday, and I found myself sitting on the front-room sofa reading a book about astronomy. Shakespeare was busy in his room, banging out his monkey tunes on his colorful toy xylophone. Sarah was in my kitchen, making a mess, preparing cake and ice cream for my birthday party. I say party, but it was really just the three of us. I felt so content on this day, in such a good place. I lowered my book to my lap, counting my blessings—or in this case, just taking stock of my single and most important blessing of all, Sarah. She was good for me, nothing like the other girls I'd been going out with, and the two of us were getting along so well. Neither of us had said the actual words "I love you" to the other, but I think both of us knew how we felt, and it was just a matter of time before one of us spoke up. I could see this happening soon.

Before I describe this little birthday gathering, let me update you on what happened after Sarah took her trip to Nebraska. Her father recovered from his stroke, and though he was still having a little difficulty with his speech, he was making good progress. The doctors said that it could have turned out a lot worse, that he was lucky Sarah's mom found him when she did, getting him prompt medical attention. They figured the speech problem would probably go away in a few months, and in no time he'd be good as new. It's funny how an event like this sort of speeds up life, creating a sense of urgency for everyone involved. Sarah, for example, now wanted me to meet her parents right away—I suppose before one of them actually died. But there was no way we could go visit them in Nebraska because Sarah was too busy with her college courses, and the manager at Starbucks

24

said if she took off another day, he'd find someone to replace her, not just while she was gone but permanently. So she tried to talk her parents into coming to California, and they finally agreed. They'd never been here before, and they wanted to see the sights and meet Sarah's friends. They especially wanted to meet me, they said, this mysterious man who had captured their daughter's heart. Sarah laughed and said her dad wanted to be sure I was good enough for his little girl. The way things were looking, they would visit in several months.

I still hadn't told Sarah about all my inherited money. She seemed to have forgotten that I was keeping a second secret, for she never brought it up or asked me about it. Not once did she mention the secret after returning from her trip. Had she just forgotten about it? Or maybe she remembered but had just decided to leave the subject alone, figuring I'd tell her when the time was right. Either way, this was fine with me because I liked things just the way they were. I had absolutely no complaints about us and wanted to keep it that way. And I felt no need to hurry anything along, for we had plenty of time. My money wasn't going anywhere, and if something were to happen in the meantime to wipe out my fortune, we'd still be happy. Having never been told about it, Sarah wouldn't even know the difference.

Sarah had been working hard on my birthday cake this morning. She'd been at my house since around ten, having stopped for ice cream and cake ingredients at the grocery store on the way over. Who knew she could be so domestic? I mean, actually baking a cake from scratch? She said she'd gotten the recipe from her mother, who had e-mailed it to her last night when Sarah told her about my birthday. When everything was ready, Shakespeare and I went to the dining room. Sarah dimmed the lights so the candles would glow brighter and then brought the cake to the table while singing "Happy Birthday." It was like a scene right out of a Norman Rockwell painting—well, except for Shakespeare. I don't remember ever seeing a monkey as an integral part of any Norman Rockwell scene.

Shakespeare was watching all this, fascinated. He'd never seen a birthday celebration before, and I could tell he found it very amusing. He was especially in awe of all the candles on the cake. "I don't think he's ever seen fire like this before," I said. "I mean, he's seen it in the fireplace, when we burn a few logs, but he's never seen anything like this, twenty-four individual flames."

"Hot, hot," Shakespeare said, looking at all the burning candles. He'd learned this word when I lit fires in the fireplace, at which point I had explained to him that fire was hot.

"Yes, it's hot," I agreed. "Fire is hot." I picked up one of the candles and held it toward him, not so that he'd be threatened by the fire but just so he could get a closer look at what it was, and he reached for the candle cautiously. "You want to hold it?"

Shakespeare nodded his head, as if to say yes, and I handed it over to him.   He held the candle in his little hand, watching it flicker. The yellow light from the candle wriggled and danced in his curious eyes. Then he stuck a finger into the flame. He let out a little yelp and pulled the finger back.

"Don't let him do that," Sarah said.

"That's how he learns," I said. "He needs to learn. Now he knows not to stick his hand in a fire. Now he knows that fire burns."

"Seriously, Marty? Just make a wish and blow out the candles," she said.

"So what should I wish for?"

"Wish for money. I know you don't think money is that important, but we could always use more. Everyone can use more money."

"Okay," I said. "I'll do that." I took the candle away from Shakespeare and stuck it back in its place on the cake. Then with all my might, I blew and blew until all the candles were extinguished. "There, that should make us especially rich. I wished for millions."

"Good," Sarah laughed.

"No more hot," Shakespeare said.

"You're right," I said. "No more hot. The candles are all out. No more hot."

Now I know it's remarkable for a monkey to converse like this with human beings, and you might be thinking that Sarah and I should still have been astonished, still sitting on the edge of our chairs. But Shakespeare had been doing a lot of this lately. He wasn't speaking fluent English, but he was speaking, trying hard to vocalize his thoughts. And yes, we were growing used to it. How do I best explain this? It's like how when you see a magic trick performed for the first time, it can make your jaw drop. But when you see the same trick performed over and over, it just becomes an everyday event, nothing to jump up and down about. I think we both knew how special Shakespeare was, but we no longer made a big deal of it every time he said a word or attempted to string together a sentence. Like I said, we'd grown used to it. It was a routine occurrence in my house.

Sarah was cutting the cake, and I said, "I'll take the biggest piece."

Shakespeare was focused on the candles that Sarah had removed and placed to the side. "No more hot," he said. He picked up one of the candles, holding it with one hand and touching its tip where the flame once had been. Once it had been on fire, and now it was not. This transformation from a glowing flame to a burned-out candle was interesting to him.

Sarah handed out plates of cake and ice cream, and the three of us began to eat. It was Shakespeare's first experience with a cake, and he approached it carefully, at first scooping some icing with his small finger and tasting it and then deciding that it was to his liking, stabbing the cake with his fork to get a bigger piece.

"We should open your presents now," Sarah said. There were three gifts on the table, and Sarah handed one to me. "Here, open this one first. You'll like it."

It was a nicely wrapped gift that felt like a book, or books, and I tore off the paper eagerly. Shakespeare watched me tear the paper away with great interest. Inside the wrapping were three Dr. Seuss books, and I laughed. "My mom used to read these to me when I was a kid," I said. "I had all of them."

"You can read them to Shakespeare."

"Yes, I can. What a great idea."

"He likes to talk, so maybe you can teach him to read as well."

I handed one of the books to Shakespeare, and he looked it over, first checking out the cover and then looking at the back. Then he opened it up, flipping through the pages with his sticky fingers.

"One fish, two fish," I said.

"Fish, fish," Shakespeare said, looking at the cover again, at the fish. He then set the book down, and with his fork he stabbed at his cake again.

These would prove to be important gifts, for during the weeks that followed, I would read the Dr. Seuss books to him every single day. He seemed fascinated by the crazy, colorful drawings, but he was even more intrigued with the words. He would repeat what I said from each page, and he seemed to be making a connection between written and spoken words. He would say the words in his funny, high-pitched simian voice, while at the same time touching the words on the page with his finger. Some words he pronounced with greater clarity than others, but he was speaking better with each reading. It was obvious that this book-reading thing really struck a chord with him, so I ordered more children's books from Amazon. I ordered a lot of them, and Shakespeare and I spent hours on the sofa, with him in my lap and a book in our hands, reading simple stories together. Of all the books we had, however, the Dr. Seuss books Sarah had bought remained his favorites. Sometimes I'd hear him in his room, playing with his toys, reciting the lines. "One fish, two fish," he'd say, playing his xylophone or beating on his little drum. "One fish, two fish, red fish, blue fish!"

When Sarah's parents, Tom and Judy, finally came to visit, they stayed in a hotel in Newport Beach. Sarah's apartment was too small, or she would have had them stay with her. They had decided to visit for one full week. Since they'd never been to California, Sarah took them all over, showing them the sights. They also spent a lot of time on their own, checking things out while Sarah was in school or working at Starbucks. I didn't see Sarah much during this week since she was so busy, but we did arrange to have dinner together, the four of us. This was to be my chance to meet her parents and prove what a worthy boyfriend I was. We went to a place that Sarah picked, a restaurant the two of us often visited. It was the perfect place, not too fancy and not expensive. I got there first, a little early, and waited for them to show up. When they arrived, Sarah introduced us, and we shook each other's hands. Tom and Judy said how happy they were to meet me, and I told them that I was likewise glad to meet them. Then we were taken to a booth by the hostess, and we sat down with our menus.

"Our daughter tells us you were born and raised here in California," Tom said.

"Yes," I said.

"Do your parents still live around here?"

"They died in a car accident several years ago."

"Oh, I'm sorry."

28

"Thanks," I said. I was never quite sure what to say to people when they said they were sorry my parents had died. I just figured "thanks" was the appropriate response, and "thanks" is what I always said.

"What did your dad do for a living?"

"He was in real estate. He was a real estate developer. He built office buildings."

"So he made good money?"

"He did well for himself."

"Did your mom work?"

"No, she was a stay-at-home mom."

"Sarah tells us you work for a nonprofit."

"That's true," I said.

"I don't imagine there's much money in that."

"Daddy," Sarah said.

"I'm just asking some questions."

"I don't mind," I said. "No, my job doesn't pay a lot, but it's very rewarding. We help send a lot of kids to college who wouldn't be able to afford it otherwise. What we do is important."

"We're sure it is," Judy said. Up until now, she'd been quiet. "We think what you do is very commendable, don't we, Tom?"

Tom ignored his wife and said, "But will you be able to support a family? I mean, it's a fine life for a bachelor, not having to worry about money. But what will you do when you decide to get married and you have children and a wife to support?"

"I guess I'll cross that bridge when I come to it. I haven't given it a lot of thought. I don't have any immediate plans to get married or to have kids."

"How old are you?"

"I'm twenty-four."

"He's just a child," Judy said. "Why don't you leave him alone?"

"I'm just curious. He is, after all, dating our daughter."

"So what were you doing when you were twenty-four that was so impressive?" Judy asked her husband. Then she laughed at the thought of it. "I'll tell you what you were doing—you were playing that silly guitar of yours and singing. Do you remember? You were playing that guitar and singing at bars and weddings. You thought you were going to be a country star. Oh, the silly dreams you had. Do you remember what your father used to say?"

"He told me to get real and find an actual job, and he was right."

"You didn't think he was right back then."

"Well, I was a kid."

"You played the guitar?" Sarah asked.

"Yes," Tom said.

"I wish I'd seen that."

"And he had long hair. That was back when he did have hair. And he had a beard. He looked just like Grizzly Adams."

"Who's Grizzly Adams?"

"A character on TV," Judy said. "He had his own show. It was before your time."

"Jesus, Judy, I didn't look like Grizzly Adams at all. You're exaggerating, as usual."

"Your dad used to write songs," Judy said.

"You were a songwriter?" asked Sarah.

"I wrote a few."

"So how'd you wind up owning a hardware store?"

"I finally wised up."

"There's nothing wrong with owning a hardware store," I said. "I think it'd be fun to own a hardware store. I like that sort of stuff."

"It isn't fun and games," Tom said. "It's a lot of hard work. People don't realize all the effort it takes, keeping the shelves stocked, figuring out what people want to buy, dealing with the public, and keeping tabs on your inventory."

"We all appreciate what you do," Judy said.

"Kids these days think life is easy. But it isn't at all easy, earning a living, making enough money to live a decent life. There are things a person needs."

"I don't need much," Sarah said.

"You'll need a lot more than you think."

"I doubt it."

"This is such a nice restaurant," Judy said, changing the subject.

Just then, the waitress came to our table, and we ordered our food. Then we talked about Nebraska for a while, and Judy told me what Sarah had been like in high school, describing some of the boys she dated, telling me about some of her teenage antics, even recalling Sarah's brief stint as a high school cheerleader for the football team. "She had her eyes on that handsome Billy Braddock, the team's quarterback, but when Billy got Monica Powers pregnant, she lost interest in him, and a week later she quit the squad. Then she got a crush on that other boy—what was his name? His father had his own floor-covering company."

"You were a cheerleader?" I asked.

"Mom's just trying to embarrass me."

"Billy Braddock is now playing at Purdue," Tom said. "He's their backup quarterback."

"How do you know that?"

"I follow college football. Do you follow football, Marty?"

"Not really," I said.

"Ever play any sports at college?"

"No, I never did."

"Sarah told us you went to Berkeley."

"Yes, that's right."

"That's a very liberal college, isn't it?"

"I guess it is. Yes, I guess you could say that, but not everyone there was a liberal."

"Liberals are ruining this country."

"You know where I'd like to go while we're here in California?" Judy asked. She was changing the subject again, trying to keep Tom from ranting about liberals. "I'd like to see the San Diego Zoo. It's supposed to be one of the best in the world."

"I'd like to go there too," Sarah said.

"I guess that'd be okay," Tom said. "Do they have lots of monkeys?"

"I'm sure they do."

"I love monkeys. They seem so bright, yet they're so hilariously stupid."

"Some are smarter than you think," I said.

"You know something about monkeys?"

"Not a lot."

"Tell them about your parents' monkey, Marty," Sarah said, and I looked at her in confusion, wondering what the heck she was talking about. "Marty's parents had a monkey in their family for years when Marty was a child," she continued. "What kind of monkey did they have? You told me the name, but I forget."

I realized that Sarah was giving me an opportunity to talk about Shakespeare without having to admit I currently had a monkey. So I went along with her idea. "It was a capuchin."

"A what?" Tom asked.

"An organ-grinder's monkey."

"Oh yes, an organ-grinder. I've seen those monkeys."

"Ours was pretty smart."

"Could he do math?"

"I'm not sure he could do math."

"That's how you tell how smart an animal is, by whether it can do math. I once saw a horse at the county fair that could do math. They'd ask it what this number plus that was, and the horse would stomp out the correct sum with its right front foot. Could your parents' monkey do that?"

"I don't know. I don't remember ever asking him to do a math problem."

"The horse could do subtraction too."

"It was probably a trick," Judy said.

"How could it be a trick? The guy asked the horse a question, and it answered, just like that. There was no trick to it. The horse obviously knew exactly what it was doing."

"I always liked the trained elephants at the circus," Judy said. "How did they get those animals to do all those things? I love it when they stand up on two legs or hold each other's tails and walk around in circles."

"Tell them about your parents' monkey," Sarah said.

"Tell them what?"

"How it could talk."

"Well, yes, he could sort of talk." I couldn't believe Sarah had gotten me to say this, and I was hoping Judy would change the subject again.

"A talking monkey?" Tom had a good laugh. "You must have had quite an imagination, Marty. Everyone knows monkeys can't talk."

"You're probably right," I said. "I was just a kid at the time." I wasn't going to pursue this any further. After all, Tom was right. Everyone knew monkeys couldn't talk. Sarah looked at me, now smiling sympathetically. I think she realized how pointless it was to argue about the possibility of a talking monkey without having Shakespeare on hand to prove our case.

And introducing Sarah's parents to Shakespeare was out of the question. Tom was the sort of guy who would blab our little secret all over the planet, and I still most definitely didn't want anyone knowing about him.

So that's how things went, this dinner with Sarah's parents, but I did get something out of it, all this silly talk about animals, for it got me to wondering, could Shakespeare do math? Could he be taught to add and subtract numbers like Tom's county fair horse? The idea of this was intriguing, and when I returned home that night, I found Shakespeare in his room, playing with his building blocks. "Stop what you're doing for a minute," I said.

Shakespeare stopped playing with the blocks and looked up at me with his marvelous, inquisitive face. He liked it when I talked to him and was always curious to hear what I had to say.

I picked up two blocks. Then, one by one, I set them down on the floor, counting them out. I said, "One plus one makes two." I pointed to the two blocks on the floor. "We have two blocks, Shakespeare. Do you see what I mean? There are two of them." I didn't think he understood, so I then held his hand and did the same thing with his fingers, first closing his fist and then raising two fingers, one at a time. "One plus one makes two," I said.

He looked at me, seemingly wondering what I was talking about.

Then I grabbed two Lego pieces and put them into his hand, one by one, and asked him, "How many do you now have in your hand?" I pointed to the Lego pieces.

"My Legos," he said.

He wasn't getting it, so I said, "Yes, but how many?"

Again he looked in his hand and said, "My Legos."

I wasn't going to give up this easily. So I did it over and over, with blocks, fingers, and Legos, until he finally gave in and said the word "two." When I expressed my pleasure with his answer, he too was delighted, and he jumped up and down. He then pointed to his xylophone and said the word "two." He pointed to his drum and said "two" again. Now everything was a two, and though this made no sense to me, it made perfect sense to him. He felt like we were communicating, although what exactly I'd communicated to him, I had no idea.

"No, no, no," I said. "That's a xylophone, and that's a drum. Those are Legos, and these are blocks. I'm trying to teach you math. Don't you understand what I'm trying to say? It's very simple; I'm saying one plus one makes two."

He could tell I was getting upset with him, and he tossed one of the Lego pieces across the room. "Not two!" he said, and then he shrieked, the way he did when he was frustrated.

I sighed and said, "I guess we'll work on this later."

Shakespeare went back to working on his blocks, stacking them on top of each other. He liked stacking the blocks but had no conception of the number of blocks he was stacking. He was not catching on to my math lesson.

But I would not be discouraged. At least once a day for months, we would go through this same exercise, counting out Lego pieces, blocks, and fingers. I wasn't going to give up. This was something I was sure he could master. I mean, if he could express thoughts in words, which was a pretty complicated intellectual feat for any monkey to tackle, certainly he could understand that one plus one made two. How could he not understand this? Then, like a beam of light shining down from the heavens, the breakthrough came. Shakespeare and I were eating lunch at the breakfast table. I'd put some fruit pieces on his plate, along with a single chocolate chip cookie for dessert. He reached over and pointed at the cookie on my own plate and said, "Me want too."

I showed him that I'd already put one on his plate.

He shook his head no, and again he said, "Me want too."

Again, I told him he already had one.

Then he shrieked and said, "Me want too, me want too!"

This is when I figured it out. I suddenly realized exactly what he was trying to tell me. He wasn't saying, "Me want too." He was saying, "Me want two!" He wanted two cookies rather than the one I'd given him. "Wow, you've got it," I said. "One plus one makes two, right?" I went to the cookie jar and got his second cookie, placing it on his plate.

"Two, two, two," he said. "One plus one makes two!"

Dr. Barney

Months had passed since our memorable mathematical breakthrough with the chocolate chip cookies. It was now a warm weekday afternoon at the tennis club, and I was sitting at the bar, sweaty and exhausted. I'd been playing a spirited match with a man I'd just met earlier in the day named Phil Bosh, and the two of us were now enjoying a couple cold beers and killing time. Phil was an attorney who was about ten years older than me, and he was married with three children, one boy and two girls. The girls were doing fine, but Phil said the boy had been a problem for as far back as he could remember. The eight-year-old had some severe anger and self-restraint issues that made it impossible for him to attend either a public or a private school. They'd tried several of them, but not matter where he went, he constantly got into verbal and physical altercations with the other students. He also disobeyed his teachers, cussing at them and defying them. He had even gotten in trouble for spitting in a principal's face.

The boy was now staying at home with his mother, Phil's wife. They did their best to manage the boy, and he was better off at home than he was at school, being that he was now away from all the students and teachers who seemed to annoy him. But there was a problem getting the boy educated, for he would have to be taught at home, a task that was more than Phil's wife could handle. She was completely over her head dealing with the boy and had no idea what to do. From a friend of a friend, they had been given the name of Dr. Barney Hepburn, a man who liked to be called Dr. Barney, a local psychologist and educator who specialized in helping children who, for whatever reason, couldn't deal with being in a school environment. Phil told me the doctor was a virtual miracle worker.

"I don't know what we would've done without him," Phil said. "He has a real way with kids, and our boy is finally beginning to make progress."

I asked him for the doctor's phone number. Phil asked me if I had my own children, and I said no, but I told him I had a buddy with a troubled youngster of his own, and this friend would certainly be interested in contacting the doctor. This, of course, was a lie. I had no such friend.

The truth was that I knew nothing about how to educate Shakespeare. He was only a monkey, but he was a very special monkey, like a child. He needed someone who knew what he or she was doing to teach him and give him a formal education. I mean, who knew how intelligent this monkey actually was? Was it possible he could learn to read something other than his Dr. Seuss books? Could he learn to perform more advanced math problems? Was he musically or artistically inclined? I knew nothing about any of this stuff, and I needed some professional help. Of course, if I got the doctor involved, there was the risk of our being discovered. There was always the chance that he'd tell others about Shakespeare. But psychologists were bound by confidentiality laws, weren't they? Whatever I told this psychologist would have to be kept between us. And whatever he did with Shakespeare as a psychologist, assuming he agreed to do anything, would remain a secret. So it occurred to me that this might be a perfect opportunity, and after Phil wrote it down for me, I stuck the doctor's phone number in my pants pocket, planning to get a hold of him later.

When I returned home, I gave the doctor a call but reached only his voice mail. I hung up at first but then called him back and left a long and meandering message. "Hello, Dr. Barney. My name is Marty Anderson. I live in Corona del Mar. I have a child … well, he's sort of a child. He's a child to me, and I need someone who can help me give him an education. You see, he can't go to any school system. It's not that he's a troublemaker or that he has any serious behavioral issues, but he just can't go to school. If you were to meet him, you would immediately see why I say this. You would agree with me that his only hope of getting a decent education would be if it took place at our home, away from other kids, and you would agree also that I'm just not the right person to be teaching him. It's true, I'm sort of his father, but then again, I'm not his father at all. To tell you the truth, I don't know if he thinks of me as a father or not. His biological parents are now out of the picture, for reasons you will also understand.

"I am only twenty-four, unmarried, and unemployed yet charged with the responsibility of raising and educating this boy of mine. He is, after all, mine, and I paid good money for him. And he is a boy; he certainly isn't a girl. As his owner, I'm obligated to give him the best possible life I can. Though I may be unemployed, I am also a man of substantial means, and I am willing and able to pay whatever fee you charge. I understand from a friend I recently met that you can work miracles, and that's what I need, a miracle. By now you're probably thoroughly confused by this message, but a simple visit to my house will clear everything up and make my needs obvious. So I'm asking if you can come over here to my home as soon as possible. I'll leave my cell phone number. Call me any day, and at any hour. I look forward to speaking with you."

Well, Dr. Barney didn't call back that evening, but he did call the next day. Apparently, my cryptic message had gotten his attention. He sounded very curious to find out what the heck I was talking about and asked me for more information. I told him that he needed to meet with us in person, to see the situation for himself, that this wasn't something I could explain well over the phone. He agreed to pay me a visit that night, and he arrived at around seven, knocking on my front door.

I let him in and looked him over. I was a little surprised at his appearance since he wasn't quite what I had expected. For some reason I'd thought he would be a lot younger, vibrant, and handsome. I don't know where I ever got this idea, perhaps from the outgoing message on his voice mail. He had a very youthful voice, charming and energetic. But he was actually well into his sixties, gray-haired, and slightly overweight. He wore a scruffy hedge of a beard that could have used some serious trimming, and his clothes were wrinkled, as though he'd slept in them.

"Thanks so much for coming over," I said.

"Your message was most unusual," he said. "To tell you the truth, I couldn't make heads or tails of it."

"Sorry about that, but it couldn't be helped. I have a very unusual situation on my hands. You'll soon see what I mean. I truly hope you can help us."

"I like unusual cases," Dr. Barney said. "They keep me on my toes. At my age, it's very important to keep on one's toes."

"Follow me," I said. I led the doctor down the hall and to Shakespeare's door. The door was shut tight, and I reached to open it, but right before I pushed it open, I turned to the doctor and said, "Please don't laugh when you see him. He can be a little touchy."

"I would never laugh."

"Good, good," I said. I opened the door, and Shakespeare was on his bed looking at one of his Dr. Seuss books. The room was a mess, toys strewn from one end to the other.

The doctor followed me in, stepping over the toys on the floor, and asked, "Where's your boy?"

"You're looking at him."

"He's a monkey?"

"Yes," I said.

"You're kidding me, right?"

"His name is Shakespeare."

The doctor laughed, not gently but loudly and obviously. "You want me to help you with a monkey?"

"You said you wouldn't do that."

"Do what?"

"Laugh at him."

"I wasn't laughing at your monkey. I was laughing at the whole idea of this. You brought me over here to assist you with educating your monkey? What exactly do you think I do for a living? I'm a psychologist."

"But Shakespeare is special."

The doctor stared at me a moment and then said, "I think I should probably leave."

"Please, just hear us out."

He then looked at his watch, as though he had to be somewhere else. He sighed and said, "Very well. I'll give you ten minutes."

"Just talk to him."

"You want me to talk to your monkey?"

"Yes, ask him a question."

"This is silly," the doctor said. But he approached Shakespeare anyway, so that the two of them were within several feet of each other. Shakespeare looked up from his book. "What's your name?" the doctor asked. I could tell he felt like he was being hoodwinked, being asked to talk to a monkey.

Shakespeare just stared back at him, not saying a word. "Ask him something else," I said.

"Very well. What's the name of that book you're reading?"

Again, Shakespeare did not reply.

"This is just dumb," the doctor said.

I couldn't let the doctor leave, not now that I had him here. I figured perhaps if I did this questioning myself, Shakespeare might feel more inclined to respond, so I said, "Please, Shakespeare, tell us the title of the book you're reading."

Again, no answer. He just ignored me and looked back down at his book.

"He doesn't seem too interested in talking to you either," said the doctor.

"I'm not sure what the problem is. I don't know why he's ignoring us."

"He isn't saying anything because monkeys don't know how to talk. I could've told you that over the phone and saved myself a trip." I could tell the doctor was a little miffed and about to leave the room.

Suddenly, Shakespeare dropped the book to his lap, and looking at me, he said angrily, "Your man, he laugh at me. Shakespeare no like man laugh at me."

Well, I thought the doctor was going to have a heart attack right then and there. You should have seen the expression on his face, like he was about keel over, holding his chest with both hands. He looked at me and then back over at Shakespeare. "What did you just say?" he asked.

Shakespeare said, "You laugh at me. I no like man who laugh."

"I told you not to laugh like that," I said. "I warned you he could be sensitive."

"Good Lord," the doctor said. "He actually did talk to me."

"Do I have your interest now?"

"Oh yes," he said. "You most certainly do."

"Do you think you can help us?" I knew this was something the doctor had never seen in his life, a talking monkey.

"I would very much like to try."

"But you have to promise me something."

"Promise you what?"

"That you won't speak of Shakespeare to anyone else, not a soul. Doctor–patient confidentiality—isn't that what you psychologists call it? Everything you see and hear in this house, and everything to do with my little friend, is to be kept completely between us. You must promise not to utter to a single person even the smallest of details about what we're doing here. Do I have your word as his doctor?"

Dr. Barney thought about this for a moment and then said, "I can give you my word."

"I'm serious about this. You can't even tell your wife."

"I'm not married."

"So much the better."

"No one will hear anything from me."

"So now that we're on the same page, I'd like to have you start as soon as possible."

"And my fee?"

"What exactly do you charge?"

"I bill the same hourly fee to all my clients, no matter who they are—or in this case, no matter what they are. I'm not cheap, but I'm worth every penny I charge. I'm very good at what I do." The doctor then told me his hourly rate, and I agreed to pay it.

"I'll write you a check at the end of each week," I said, "if that's okay with you."

"That'll be fine. I'll have to juggle my schedule around. I've been very busy lately. I'll need to make room for this project."

"Shakespeare must be your top priority."

"Oh, trust me, he will be."

"Shall we shake on it?"

"Yes, we shall." The doctor extended his hand, and I shook it.

So the deal was struck. I gave Dr. Barney a week to make room for Shakespeare in his schedule, doing whatever it was he had to do with his existing obligations. As promised, he set up his work life so that Shakespeare would be his primary client, and he agreed to visit my house every afternoon of every weekday. Each session would last for five hours. I told him this sounded fine. Had I made the right decision? I tell you, I had a very good feeling about Dr. Barney and felt I had now placed Shakespeare in a pair of very capable hands.

Of course, the proof was in the pudding. And I was not disappointed with the pudding. As the weeks went by, Sarah and I saw an immediate change in Shakespeare's ability to communicate. His vocabulary was improving in leaps and bounds, and he was using accurate words to convey his thoughts and ideas. He was also putting these words together in grammatically correct phrases and sentences, something he had previously had a lot of trouble with. And Shakespeare's initial dislike of the doctor had rapidly transformed into a warm friendship. I think Shakespeare genuinely liked the guy and loved his daily lessons. It must have been a huge relief for Shakespeare to finally be able to express himself clearly. It was no longer such a struggle for him to make things known to Sarah and me. In addition, he now understood what others were saying. This too was a huge step for him, just as important as being able to talk clearly. By the sixth month, I'd say he was much like an eager young boy of five or six, able to talk, able to understand, and overflowing with youth and energy. He was a delight to be with, and there were times I wished I could end all the secrecy and share him with the rest of the world. People would be so amazed. But I knew better.

For Shakespeare, one big advantage to this education was being able to watch TV and actually understand what people were saying. He'd stay up late at night and watch old movies; how he loved to do this. He especially liked old pirate films or anything about sailing ships at sea. It wasn't the ocean that intrigued him; rather, it was the amazing men who climbed all around on the masts and ship rigging. He thought he would make an excellent sailor, crawling upward, sideways, and down and swinging around in the air high above the ships' decks as though he was in his natural habitat, in a jungle of broad-leafed trees and their branches. I guess it was only natural for a monkey to yearn for this, but it was interesting just how strong the urge was for Shakespeare. When he watched these movies, he paid little attention to the plots or the acting or even the music. He told me that when he grew up, he wanted to join a ship's crew, that he was sure he would be hired. I explained to him that these old ships were a thing of the past, that men no longer built or sailed these kinds of vessels. He was so disappointed. He just looked down at the floor and said, "Oh, then I guess I'll have to do something else for a living."

Shakespeare also loved old Tarzan movies. These weren't on often, but he did get to watch a couple of them. The films made him sort of crazy. I'd be sleeping, minding my own business, when I'd suddenly hear the TV at full volume, blaring Tarzan's voice as he howled his famous cry, swinging on vines from tree to tree. Edgar Rice Burroughs couldn't have dreamed up a more devoted fan than Shakespeare. While the movie was on, sometimes Shakespeare would leap up on the dining room chandelier and swing to and fro, hanging by one arm. The dining room was adjacent to the front room, so he could see the TV from the light fixture. I caught him doing this once, dangling from the chandelier and watching his Tarzan movie while eating a banana. I didn't scold him. I could only laugh and just hope the chandelier was securely fastened to the ceiling.   "What's the story behind Cheeta?" he asked me the next day. "Why doesn't he ever talk?"

"Most monkeys don't talk," I said.

"Why not?"

"They just don't."

"That doesn't make sense. It seems they'd have a lot to say. I like to talk."

"You're not an average monkey, Shakespeare."

"I'm not?"

"You're very special."

"Do any monkeys talk?"

"You're the only one I know of."

"In the whole world?"

"Yes, in the whole world."

Shakespeare turned quiet, not saying anything further. I couldn't tell if I'd made him proud of his ability or just very lonely.

As he grew up, he also became naturally curious about his ancestry. He'd heard Sarah and me talking about our own parents at times, but we never talked about his. He knew Sarah's parents lived far away, and he knew my parents had died. One day he brought the subject up while we were all on the sofa, reading. He wanted to know where his mother and father were and why they were no longer a part of his life. "Did they die like your parents?" he asked me.

"No," I said. "They didn't die."

"Then where are they?"

"They live with someone else," Sarah said.

"A man named Vern," I said.

"And who's Vern?"

"He's the man who sold you to me."

"So he still has my mom and dad?"

"Yes, he does."

"Can we go see them?"

"I don't know," I said. I thought about this. "Are you sure you want to do that?"

"They're my parents, aren't they?"

"They're different from you," Sarah said.

"Quite a bit different," I added.

"I understand. They don't talk. Everyone tells me monkeys don't talk, but I'd still like to see them. I think they'd like to see me too."

"Possibly."

"Maybe you can give Vern a call," Sarah said.

"Can you?" Shakespeare asked enthusiastically. "I'd like to see them."

"I guess I can call. But it'll be up to Vern, whether you can see them. He might say no."

"Call him anyway."

"If he does say yes, you'll need to promise me something."

"What do you want me to promise?"

"That you won't talk in front of Vern."

"Why not?"

"Vern doesn't know about you. You have to promise you won't say a word."

"I can do that."

So I called Vern, and he agreed to have us over to his house. I don't think he understood why I wanted to reunite Shakespeare with his parents, but he didn't argue with me about it. He said he'd be surprised if any of the monkeys recognized each other; as humans we tended to attribute more memory and intelligence to our monkeys than they actually had, he said. "Sometimes they seem human to us, but the fact is that they're just monkeys. You'll see what I mean." We set up a date for several days after our phone call, and I told Shakespeare he'd soon be meeting his parents. This seemed to make him happy, and he was in a very good mood for the rest of the week, looking forward to the trip to Vern's house.

In the meantime, Sarah and I were still getting along like champs. After my parents passed away, I had felt so alone. I'd had a difficult time getting over their deaths, but having both Shakespeare and Sarah in my life pushed away this loneliness. And now I had Dr. Barney as well. My life was full and bustling with activity. Each day I had a full schedule, starting off with breakfast together with Shakespeare. I would then read the morning paper and catch up on all the news. Then I'd shower, shave, and leave for work. By work, I mean the time I spent at the scholarship fund, where I'd put in around four hours every morning, helping out however I could. At noon I'd come home and have lunch with Shakespeare, after which Dr. Barney would come over to give Shakespeare his lesson. In the afternoons, I'd leave the doctor and Shakespeare alone in the house and go to the club to play tennis. Upon returning home from playing tennis, I'd do my chores or maybe some reading, or maybe I'd go out and run errands. By dinnertime Sarah would be at the house. Sometimes she made dinner for us, and sometimes Sarah and I would go out to a restaurant, just the two of us. Later, when late evening rolled around, you could usually find the three of us watching TV or reading on the sofa before going to bed. I know it probably sounds routine and mundane, my very predictable life, but it was so fulfilling. I was never bored, and I enjoyed every waking hour.

I think Sarah was the key to my contentment. It was the way she made me feel. There was no longer any question about my feelings: I was deeply in love with her. It made me feel so amazingly happy, having this wonderful girl in my life. I finally got up the nerve to tell her I was in love with her, and she said she felt the same about me. It's funny what happens when you tell someone you love her, how suddenly everything completely changes. We weren't married yet, but I no longer felt like a bachelor. We did discuss marriage, not as a possible option but as an inevitability. It was no longer a question of whether it would happen, but rather when. It was a given that we'd spend the rest of our lives together, for better or for worse, and we hadn't even said our vows yet. We both wanted this to happen sooner rather than later and knew the day wasn't far away.

So now I decided it was time to come clean with the girl. I still hadn't told Sarah about the inheritance my father had left me. She knew I had some money because I was using it to pay for Dr. Barney's time with Shakespeare, but she had no idea of the extent of my wealth. It was time for me to be honest, so I went to Starbucks while Sarah was working. As I stepped into the building, I saw a long line of people waiting to place their orders and Sarah busy working the cash register. I crept behind the counter, out of Sarah's view, and walked up behind her, putting my hands over her eyes. "Guess who?" I said.

"Marty," she replied.

"Stop what you're doing."

"What is it?"

"I need to ask you a question."

"What is it, Marty? I'm very busy."

"I want to know if you'll marry me."

"Yes, you know I will. We've already discussed this." She was smiling but trying to get back to work.

"If you say yes, you have to quit this job."

"I said yes, but I'm not going anywhere."

"But you have to quit."

"What are you talking about?"

"My wife isn't working at Starbucks. Neither is my fiancée."

"We need the money, Marty."

"We don't need it."

"Of course we do. Let me get back to work."

"I'm trying to tell you, you don't have to work here. Trust me. Take off your apron and come with me. You no longer have to work here." I untied Sarah's apron and began to take it off her.

"What are you doing?"

"Just come with me."

"I'll get fired."

"They can't fire you if you've already quit."

"But I haven't quit."

"You have now."

"What's going on here?" the manager said. It was like he'd appeared from nowhere. Sarah had told me about him, and I knew he was kind of a jerk. He was staring at me, his hands on his hips, wondering what the heck I was doing to his employee.

"Sarah quits," I said.

"Please, Marty."

"Is this true?"

"Here's your apron, sir." I handed the manager the apron and said, "Put this on and serve these customers yourself. Sarah has much more important things to be doing with her time."

"Oh, does she now?"

I grabbed Sarah by the arm and pulled her away from the cash register. "She's going to be my wife, and my wife no longer works for you."

"Do you know what you're doing?" Sarah asked me.

"I know exactly what I'm doing."

"Well, you're fired," the manager said.

"She quit," I said, correcting him. "She quit before you fired her."

"Whatever."

"Come with me," I said to Sarah. She was half-confused and half-furious with me. I got her to follow me out to my car. I opened the door for her, and she climbed in. Stepping around the car, I opened my door and got comfortable in my own seat.

"I hope you're satisfied," she said. "What's come over you?"

I started the engine and said, "There's something you need to know about me, and I need to tell you now."

Reunion

So how'd she take the news? I'll tell you exactly what Sarah had to say about my inheritance, but first let me tell you about our trip out to Vern's house. We left in the early afternoon, hoping to miss the work traffic. Sarah came with us because she too wanted to see Shakespeare's parents. Even though we were well ahead of the work traffic, the freeways were filled with cars, and Shakespeare was astonished that there were so many people. This was the first time he'd been out of the house since I brought him home from Vern's. "Where are all these people going?" he asked.

"Who knows?" I said.

"Where are the monkeys?"

"There aren't any," Sarah said.

"Monkeys don't live around here," I explained. "This isn't exactly their natural habitat."

"But Vern has monkeys?"

"Yes, Vern has monkeys. The last time I saw him, he had three of them. He had your mom and dad and a third. They were capuchins like you."

"Capuchins?"

"That's your type. There are lots of different types of monkeys, and you're a capuchin."

Shakespeare was standing up, looking out his window, still in awe of all the vehicles and drivers. "When do I get to drive a car?" he asked.

"You don't," I said.

"You won't let me drive a car?"

"You're too small."

"What if they made a special car for me, one that I could operate?"

"You still can't drive."

"Why not?"

"The government won't let you. You have to be a human being to get a driver's license."

"What's a driver's license?"

"It's a little card that allows you to drive a car. The Department of Motor Vehicles issues them. In order to get a license, you have to be human, and you have to pass a driver's test."

"You need their permission, just to drive a car?"

"I'm afraid so."

"So how am I supposed to get around if I'm not allowed to drive?"

"You get a ride from Sarah or me, like you're doing now. Or Dr. Barney can drive you."

"What if I need to go somewhere, and you guys are busy doing something else?"

"Where is it you think you'll need to go?" Sarah asked.

"I don't know. I'm just asking."

"You'll be fine, Shakespeare. I don't mind driving you around. If it's urgent, I'll drop what I'm doing and take you. My car is your car."

Shakespeare thought for a moment and then asked, "Can we drive to South America?"

"South America?"

"That's where Dr. Barney says monkeys like me come from. I'd like to see South America."

"No, we can't drive to South America."

"Why not?"

"It's too far. We'd have to fly. Do you know what an airplane is?"

"Of course I do. I've seen people fly them in the movies. They're like big birds, except they're stiff and have no feathers." Shakespeare was still looking out his window, but now upward toward the sky. "Do you think I'll get to see an airplane today?"

"You might, if you keep your eyes open."

"Can you tell me how airplanes fly? It doesn't make any sense to me. How do they do they stay in the air without moving their wings? Birds have to flap their wings, don't they? So why not airplanes?"

"Airplanes are propelled by engines."

"Like cars?"

"Something like that."

"Why aren't we flying to Vern's house? Wouldn't it be a lot faster to fly?"

"We don't need to fly there. We can drive there just fine. Some places you need to fly to, and some places you don't."

"I'd like to fly in an airplane sometime. Are monkeys allowed to fly in airplanes, or do they need a license for that too?"

"No, they don't need a license. We'd be allowed as passengers in an airplane, but they'd probably have me put you in a cage."

"In a cage?"

"They wouldn't let you just run loose in the cabin."

"What's a cabin?"

"The inside of the airplane."

"Sometimes I just wish I was human."

"Well, that's funny because some people wish they were animals."

"Why would they wish for that?"

"Because being a human can be very complicated and frustrating."

"Well, it's no cake walk being a monkey."

"No cake walk?"

"That's what Dr. Barney calls something when it's very easy: a cake walk."

"I think you should step back and count your blessings."

"What's a blessing?"

I laughed. This conversation just seemed to keep going on and on. I said, "You're asking an awful lot of questions today."

"Dr. Barney says it's good for me to ask questions. He says the more questions I ask, the smarter I'll get. You do want me to be smart, don't you?"

"Of course I do."

"Wait!" Shakespeare exclaimed.

"What is it?"

"I think I see an airplane." He was looking up through his window. Sure enough, there was a big silver plane flying out of a patch of clouds and into the blue sky. "Do you see it? It's right over there!"

"Yes, I can see it. It's a big one."

"It looks so small from here. And it looks like it's barely moving."

"That's because it's so far away."

"I wonder where it's going," Sarah said. "Whenever I see an airplane, I always wonder where it's going."

"Maybe it's going to South America."

"Maybe," Sarah said.

"Are we almost at Vern's house?"

"It's up ahead," I said. We had pulled off the freeway a minute or so ago and were now driving on a two-lane highway through a run-down rural area. "Just a mile or so, and we'll be there."

"Are those horses?" Shakespeare asked. There were several horses standing in a field we were passing, grazing on the dry grass.

"Yes, those are horses," Sarah said.

"I suppose they can't talk?"

"No, horses can't talk."

"Can any animals talk? I mean, besides me."

"Myna birds can talk," I said. "They can say words, but they don't know what they mean."

"Then why do they bother to say them?"

"I honestly don't know."

Shakespeare was now jumping up and down. He was getting excited. "Are we almost there?" he asked.

"You just asked me that."

"Well, are we?"

"The house is up ahead."

A minute later, I steered the car into Vern's gravel driveway and drove through the open gate. I then parked in front of the old, dilapidated house and noticed Vern standing in the doorway, waiting for us. We got out of the car, and I told Shakespeare to hop up in my arms so I could carry him. I didn't want him running around loose because I had no idea how the other monkeys would react when they saw him. I'd spent a lot of time with Shakespeare, and I knew him pretty well, but I still didn't know that much about other monkeys and how they behaved.

"Well, hello," Vern said.

"Hi," I said.

"Let me take a gander at the little bugger," he said, looking at Shakespeare. "He's all grown-up. He's no longer a baby."

"I brought along my fiancée," I said. "I'd like you to meet her. This is Sarah."

"Nice to meet you, Sarah. Come on in, all of you, and meet the family." By "family," Vern meant his other monkeys. To the best of my knowledge, Vern and his monkeys were the only ones who lived in the house.

We stepped in, and I felt Shakespeare's body tense up. He was holding on tightly to me, his fingers digging into my shoulders, not sure what to expect of this reunion. Vern's monkeys were all slouched on the sofa like three lazy old men, watching the TV. They were still wearing diapers, and from the way the place smelled, one or more of the diapers could have used changing. When they saw us, they didn't move an inch.

"From left to right, this is Matilda, Ernie, and Amy," said Vern. "They're usually pretty tame this time of day. Matilda and Ernie are your fella's parents. By the way, what did you name him?"

"His name is Shakespeare."

"Shakespeare, eh? Well, that's an odd name. But to each their own, no?"

"Yes," I said.

"Put him down and let's see what they do. Like I said, my monkeys are pretty tame right now. I don't think they'll go after him. They'll probably just sit there and do nothing at all. If you'd arrived earlier, you would've seen them a lot more active."

I set Shakespeare down on the floor, and he didn't seem to want to let go of me. I had to pry his hands off my shoulders in order to set him down. He seemed scared of the other monkeys and stayed close by me. Vern's monkeys noticed him and gave him a lazy glance, but they were more interested in the TV than they were in him.

"Go on," I said to Shakespeare. "Go meet your parents."

He looked up at me, as though wanting me to help him. It's funny how he'd been so energetic and talkative in the car on the way over here, and now he was so shy and cautious. I held his little hand and slowly walked him over toward the three monkeys on the sofa. When we were within a few feet of them, Shakespeare stopped walking. He just stood there and stared. I let go of his hand and walked back toward Sarah, leaving Shakespeare on his own. He stepped a little closer to the sofa. Slowly, he reached out and touched the leg of Matilda, his mother. Matilda looked at him with a slightly annoyed expression and then swatted his hand away.

He jumped back. She apparently didn't feel like being bothered, not even by her own son. The truth was, she probably had no idea that he was her son, and if she did know, she certainly had no interest in him, not even a little curiosity. Then she suddenly jumped up to her feet. She leaped off the sofa and ran to the nearby kitchen, where she grabbed a banana from a bunch on the countertop. She returned to her spot on the couch and proceeded to peel it. Ernie reached in, wanting a piece, but she made an awful ear-piercing shriek, indicating she had no intention of sharing. She then looked at Shakespeare. She leaned forward toward him and shrieked again, baring her teeth.

Shakespeare ran to my side and grabbed hold of my leg. He looked up at me with the strangest look on his face, and if I hadn't known better, I would have thought he was going to cry. I patted him on the head, and then I turned to Vern. I said, "His mother seems to be more interested in watching her TV show and eating a banana than she does in reuniting with Shakespeare. This is probably not a good time to bother her."

"It is her TV time," Vern said.

"You say they do this every day, sit down and watch TV like this?"

"They like seeing the pictures move. I tried to teach them how to use the remote control, but all they do is press the buttons willy-nilly. They don't care which channel is on, and they don't care how loud it is. I don't know why they even bother watching, but they do it anyway. Doesn't your little fella watch TV?"

"Yes, he likes the TV."

"He likes old movies," Sarah said.

"You mean he has a preference?"

"He seems to," I said nonchalantly.

"I always knew he was smart," Vern said. "Smarter than his mom and dad, that's for sure. Ever since the day he toilet trained himself, I said to myself, 'Vern, this little bugger is special.'"

"Yes, he's special."

"Have you taught him to do any tricks?"

"I've taught him a few."

"Such as?"

"I taught him to get the morning paper from the front yard."

"Heck, a dog can do that."

"Well, I also taught him to sweep the kitchen floor. He knows how to use a broom and a dustpan."

"Say, that's good. I taught Matilda to take out the kitchen trash, but I never thought of teaching her to sweep the floor."

I looked down at Shakespeare, and I could tell he just wanted to leave. His own mother had wanted nothing to do with him, and he probably thought this Vern fellow was an idiot. The reunion was over.

"I guess we should be going."

"You just got here."

"I was hoping Shakespeare's parents would recognize him, or at least that his mom would, but they don't seem to have any idea who he is."

"I told you to expect that when we talked over the phone."

"You did," I agreed. "I should've listened."

Then to Shakespeare, Vern said, "It's been great to see you, little fella. I'm glad you came by."

Shakespeare ignored him and grabbed my finger. He pulled on it, trying to lead me out the front door.

"It was nice to meet you," Sarah said, following Shakespeare and me.

The three of us walked out of the house, and Vern stayed in the doorway, watching us climb into the car. As we backed out of the driveway, Vern waved in a friendly manner. I felt kind of sorry for him, living alone without any human companions, alone with those monkeys.

"So what did you think?" I asked.

"Are you asking me or asking Shakespeare?" Sarah said.

"Either of you."

"This was a big mistake," Shakespeare said. "I don't ever want to come here again." That was all he had to say for the entire ride home. He sat looking down at his lap while Sarah and I talked. We tried to get him to join in our conversation, but he wouldn't say anything.

When we arrived at our house, Shakespeare went straight to his room. He sat down at his table and opened one of the books Dr. Barney had brought over. It was a book about volcanoes, part of Shakespeare's science studies. When I checked on him later, I asked if he was okay. He was still looking at his book, and he said, "I'm going to be the world's smartest monkey." Then he looked up at me. "Sweeping the kitchen floor, really?"

"I had to come up with something," I said.

Shakespeare was still staring at me, and I couldn't tell if he was hurt or angry. "Matilda didn't even know who I was."

"I know."

"What a stupid monkey."

"She just is what she is, Shakespeare. I wouldn't call her stupid."

"She was stupid," he said.

Although the trip to Vern's house had been a disappointment for Shakespeare, I think it also inspired and motivated him. He took his lessons with Dr. Barney a lot more seriously; in fact, he studied all the time, taking breaks only to eat or watch an occasional old movie on TV. He no longer spent hours playing with all those children's toys I'd purchased, and he put them away in his closet. I think the toys represented for him a phase in his life that was now over: his childhood. This was not to say that he was no longer playful or that he'd lost his sense of humor. He was, after all, still a monkey. He was fun to talk to and a joy to be around. He just no longer wanted to be seen as a baby. He wanted to be happy, but he also wanted to grow up.

Something else came out of our trip to Vern's. We decided from that day forward to go on more outings with Shakespeare, away from the house. He enjoyed being out in the real world, seeing all the activity, expanding his horizons. There were so many places to see and experience that we had no trouble coming up with new and fun ideas. Every weekend the three of us took an excursion, driving around Southern California and getting out of the car whenever possible. I grew less paranoid about people seeing me with Shakespeare. The odds of anyone complaining to the authorities were slim. So what if we had a monkey with us? Since when did anyone actually check to see if you had a proper license? Most people probably didn't even know I was supposed to have one.

Shakespeare's favorite place to go turned out to be the beach, which was a good thing because it was just several minutes from our house. It didn't require miles of driving through traffic and sitting in the car. I didn't take him to the local beach in Corona del Mar because it was too crowded, and his presence might have created a scene. But there were beaches on the Newport Peninsula that had very few people, and we'd go there and take long walks along the shore. Sometimes he'd go into the water up to his knees and kick and splash. He also liked to pick up shells and seagull feathers with his little hands and put them in a plastic bucket I'd bought for him. He'd then dump the bucket out when we were done with our walk and choose his favorites, bringing them home. He kept these special shells and feathers in our backyard, in a wooden box. Some days he'd take these out, look them over, and put them back in again. I saw him do this several times. I think he knew every shell and feather he'd collected by heart.

It was during a day at the beach that Shakespeare first became interested in wearing clothing. We were walking along the water's edge and passed a group of children. One of the kids pointed at Shakespeare, and they all began to giggle. "Look at the naked monkey," the kid said.

Prior to this, Shakespeare had never given a second thought to walking around unclothed, but suddenly he was embarrassed of his naked body. When we got home that day, he wrapped a washcloth around his waist and told me he wanted to wear clothes. I had no idea where in the world I'd find them for a monkey, but Sarah had the perfect idea. She'd heard there were people who made custom clothes for dolls, and she said we ought to find one of these people to sew for Shakespeare. I searched the Internet and found a lady in Buena Park who said she made doll clothes for any type of doll. I e-mailed the lady and told her I was looking for someone to make some clothes for my monkey, and she called back and told me to bring him right over to be sized. She had him stand on a chair as she took all his measurements, and long story short, we had a whole wardrobe of miniature clothes made for Shakespeare. His naked monkey days were over. Not only was Shakespeare going to be well educated, but he was also going to be well dressed. Indeed, he was growing up.

I still haven't told you about Sarah and what she said when I revealed the details of my large inheritance. I told her on the way home from Starbucks, on that day I caused her to lose her job. I wasn't looking at her. I was driving, paying close attention to the road, so I can't tell you the expression on her face. But I can tell you what she said. Well, at first she didn't say anything at all. I think she was letting it sink in, and then she said, "Are you kidding me, Marty? Because if you're kidding me, I'm not going to think it's funny."

"I'm telling you the truth," I said.

"So you're rich?"

"Yes, I truly am."

"You certainly don't act rich."

"How does a rich person act?"

"Well, you certainly won't find one of them driving around in a crummy little car like this."

"But I like this car."

"I know you do."

"Don't you believe me?"

"I'm trying to. It's just hard to digest."

"Well, digest it."

Sarah was quiet again. I think she was trying to get a handle on what this wealth would mean for her. "So no more Starbucks for me?"

"No more Starbucks."

"Good. Let's go home. To our home."

"I'm on it, like white on rice."

A Few Little Secrets

Planning the wedding was way more complicated than I'd ever imagined, but fortunately, Sarah was willing and able to do all the work. If it'd been up to me, we would have just gone to Las Vegas and gotten hitched in one of those little chapels off the strip, but Sarah wanted a complete wedding ceremony and reception, with all the nuptial bells and whistles. She chose a church in Newport at which we would be married and a restaurant in Laguna where we'd all dance and party afterward. Her parents had wanted her to do everything in Nebraska, but Sarah insisted on California, where we lived and where all our friends were. Before meeting each other, both Sarah and I had made a lot of friends, and we wanted all of them to come to our wedding without having to fly out of state. When we added our friends to all Sarah's relatives in Nebraska and my few from Vermont, we wound up with a fair-sized guest list. Sarah's dad insisted on paying for the entire affair, but I offered to contribute my own funds if the price became overwhelming. I think he appreciated my offer to help out; however, he said it wouldn't be necessary.

Sarah's parents both now knew I had a lot of money, and I have to tell you the truth: this knowledge changed their attitude toward me—well, not so much the attitude of her mother, who had always been nice even before she knew of the inheritance. But it definitely changed the attitude of her father, who previously had seen me as both idealistic and naïve and maybe even a little lazy. Now he treated me with respect, almost as an equal. I didn't dislike him for having this new perspective, and it didn't make me think less of him. It's just the way it is when it comes to people and money, and it's why I didn't like people knowing I was wealthy. Honestly, it changes the way they see you, and it's kind of annoying to be treated with respect just because you have a substantial net worth. It's not like I had done anything to deserve my wealth; my dad was the one who had toiled for it, not me. I had just wound up with it because I happened to be his son.

Now that I was getting married, a choice had to be made. I had to pick someone to be my best man, and this posed a problem. I actually had two friends who would have fit the bill, and by asking one, I would surely offend the other. The first was Jackson Wilson. I had gone to high school with Jackson, and we had remained good friends after high school. Jackson didn't go to college because unlike most kids his age, he didn't need to. His career path was all set up for him in advance: his father owned a chain of Jack in the Box restaurants, and he wanted Jackson to join him in managing them as soon as he graduated. Eventually, Jackson would inherit and run the entire little fast-food empire, and he was fine with all this. It was a lucrative business, and there was no reason to let it fall into another's hands. His father had been grooming him to take over the position for years. During high school, he'd had Jackson take food orders at one of the local restaurants and then work as a cook, wanting him to get some hands on experience and learn the ropes. I remember that one of the high school teachers, Mr. Phelps, would stop at this restaurant every day after school for a hamburger, fries, and a Coke. Jackson didn't like this teacher, and he told me that when no one was looking, he'd spit on the teacher's beef patty and then place it between the buns. He told me he didn't just spit a little, but a lot, providing a big puddle of his hidden saliva for the teacher to eat. I don't know if he really did this or if he just made the story up to make himself sound cool. That was years ago.

Now that Jackson was a twenty-five-year-old man like me, he was working with his father in their offices, wearing a jacket and tie, helping to manage the entire chain. He was not really a bad guy, and except for the doctored hamburgers he had supposedly fed to Mr. Phelps, he had been a well-behaved kid. When we were in high school, we did a lot of stuff together, but we seldom got in trouble. He was a very good friend, and we had remained close even while I was in college. I have to say, looking back, he was one of the closest friends I had.

My second candidate for best man was Jeff Sanchez. I had met Jeff in Berkeley, where he was a business major like me. We were dormitory roommates our first year, but Jeff had taken off a couple years to work after graduating from high school, so he was a little older than me. It was a rule in the dorm that if you were lucky enough to have convinced a young girl to come to your room, you were to put a sock on your doorknob so that your roommate would know not to come in and disturb you. Well, Jeff had a sock on our doorknob probably more times than the rest of us combined. He always seemed to have a girl in our room. I honestly didn't know how he did it, for he wasn't especially handsome or charming, but something about him was apparently irresistible to females on the campus. I can't even count the number of times I had to avoid my own room, just because one of Jeff's socks was on our doorknob.

Once, when it was late and I had nowhere else to go, I sat on the hallway floor, reading one of my schoolbooks and waiting for the girl to leave. Finally, our door opened a crack, and Jeff's hand appeared to remove the sock. Then the door closed. So the coast was clear? I stood up and went to the door, opening it and looking inside. Jeff was by himself, and there was no girl at all. I asked Jeff what he thought he was doing, and he broke down and admitted that there never had been any girls. It turned out Jeff had been putting his sock on the door as a ruse to make us all think he was popular with the opposite sex. Wow, I suddenly felt for the guy, and the two of us had a heart-to-heart talk about his insecurities. It took me by surprise, how honest he was with me, but I guess he needed someone he could talk to. I never did expose his secret to anyone else, and somehow after that night, the two of us became close friends. I always felt I could tell Jeff anything, and I think he felt the same with me. Jeff graduated from business school the same year I did, and now he was working for an accounting firm in Los Angeles. Every several months, we'd meet and have lunch. The last time we met, he said he still had no girlfriend. There was a gal he liked in his office, but he couldn't get up the nerve to ask her out.

So that was my best-man dilemma, choosing between Jackson and Jeff. I asked Sarah whom I should pick, and her solution was simple. She said to get my two friends together and flip a coin. So that's exactly what I did. I had both of them meet me for lunch at a restaurant, where I explained the situation. I said that I liked them both equally and that they'd both been very good friends. Then I said, "I don't want to have any hurt feelings, so I'm going to flip a coin. This is the fairest way I could come up with to handle this predicament. Who wants to call it?"

Jackson said he'd call it, and he picked heads. I tossed a quarter up in the air, and it landed on the table. Heads it was, and Jackson was my best man. Jeff would be one of my ushers. That was one of my problems solved, simple as that.

But that was only my first problem. It turned out that writing my vows was to be a second, for Sarah didn't want us to read from some pat list of vows written by someone else. She wanted each of us to write our own vows. I'm not much of a writer, so I asked her if she'd please write mine for me. I didn't think it was fair that I was being asked to write my own, since Sarah was an English major and had a far better command of the language. If I wrote my own vows, they would seem so childish compared to hers, wouldn't they? But no matter how much I objected, she kept insisting that I do my own writing. "Only you know exactly what you want to say to me," she said. "The words should come from your heart, not from mine."

When I finally realized that she wasn't going to give up on the idea, I searched the Internet for examples, and I found a few vows others had used that I liked, more or less. But even these didn't seem appropriate. It was like wearing someone else's clothes. No, I needed something original. Then the thought came to me like a clap of thunder. Why should I write the vows at all? Why not have Shakespeare write them for me? He was doing well with his writing lessons, and if anyone knew how I felt about Sarah, he certainly did. He'd spent more time with the two of us than anyone. So I approached Shakespeare while Sarah was out of the house and secretly pitched the idea to him. At first, he didn't think he could do it, but I was able to change his mind. Finally, he agreed to write the vows, and he completed them in a week, working on them late at night rather than watching old movies on the TV. When he showed them to me, I thought they were great, with the exception of a few lines that sounded too weird, like they'd been written by a simian. But it was easy to delete these lines and make adjustments, and that's what I did. Then I corrected some minor spelling errors, transcribed the entire thing into my own handwriting, and submitted the vows to Sarah for her approval.

Needless to say, she loved them. "See what you can do when you're inspired and put forth a little effort?" she said. It's funny, isn't it? Our wedding was probably the first in human history where the groom's vows had been written by a monkey.

I have no idea how much Sarah's father spent on this wedding. Sarah's dress alone must have cost the poor guy a fortune. But to his credit, he never asked me for a cent, despite my offer to help out. It was important to him that he pay for everything, being the bride's father. He even agreed to pay for Shakespeare's tuxedo. Yes, Shakespeare was in the wedding ceremony. Did you think we'd have it any other way? We decided he would be the ring bearer and assured everyone that we could train him to do this. Of course, training him was easy; all we had to do was tell him what to do. You should've seen him, dressed up in his little tuxedo and walking up the aisle, taking his place beside us. When the minister asked for the rings, Shakespeare raised his little pillow just as we'd practiced during rehearsal, and we removed the rings, placing them on each other's fingers. When we kissed, everyone applauded, especially Shakespeare. He jumped up and down, clapping his hands together as loudly as he could.

I wish my parents had lived to see me get married. I think they would've liked Sarah a lot, and I think they would've gotten along with her family. The only relatives I had at the wedding were my aunt and uncle and my two cousins. Aunt Margaret and Uncle George lived in Vermont on a former farm, having bought the land with money Uncle George had made in the stock market while they lived in New York. They had moved into the farmhouse twelve years ago, with the intention of turning the property into a retreat. They planned to have cabins, a clubhouse, and a swimming pool. They were also going to bring in a yoga instructor, an acupuncturist, a hairdresser, and several masseuses from Switzerland. Uncle George said they were going to have a world-class chef to prepare guests' meals in their own restaurant. I knew about all this because I had heard them talking about it when they visited my parents, when I was thirteen years old. I remember how exciting it all sounded, opening up this retreat.

Unfortunately, they spent all their cash on the property, and they couldn't find anyone to finance the rest of their project. No one was interested in risking money on their big idea. When my aunt and uncle finally decided to put the property up for sale, to live somewhere else, they couldn't find a single interested buyer for the price they were asking, which was even less than they'd paid. So for twelve years they'd been living in the farmhouse with all that land. They both had to get jobs to pay the bills. Aunt Margaret worked as a waitress in a little restaurant in town, and Uncle George worked as a real estate salesman for a local broker. Their children, Frank and Stephanie, my two cousins, also lived in Vermont but not in the old farmhouse. I hadn't seen either of them for years and knew little about them. I barely recognized them when they came to the wedding. I hardly knew any of these people, but they sat in the first row because they were my family. I don't even know why I invited them. I guess I just felt they should be at my wedding since they were related to my mother.

The wedding was nice. The minister said his words, and then Sarah and I said our vows. We put on our rings as provided by Shakespeare, and I lifted Sarah's veil to give her a kiss. When we walked out of the church, everyone threw rice at us, just like you see in the movies. Then a limo that Sarah's dad had arranged took us to the restaurant for the reception. During all of this hoopla, Shakespeare was with us, by our side. At the reception, we kept him close to us. It's not that I didn't trust him being out of my sight, but he was, after all, a monkey. I didn't want him doing anything crazy with the guests. With him at our side, we could keep an eye on him. It was funny—all the guests wanted to meet the little monkey in the tuxedo, and they all wanted to know more about him. They wanted to know why I'd named him Shakespeare and whether he could do any tricks. They wanted to know where in the world we had ever found a tuxedo his size, and several people asked where I'd gotten him. I could tell all the questions were driving Shakespeare crazy, but he did a good job behaving himself. There were plenty of times he could've said something clever to shock everyone, but he held his tongue and kept silent.

After the reception we were off to our honeymoon, and Shakespeare came along with us. The three of us hopped in the car and drove away from the crowd at the reception, with the people all waving and cheering. For our honeymoon we had decided to spend five days at the famous Coronado Hotel near San Diego. Sneaking Shakespeare into the hotel was tricky. We got two rooms, one for ourselves and one for Shakespeare. The bellboy carried up our luggage except for a large blanket, inside of which we secretly hid Shakespeare. Sarah carried the blanket, and I registered us at the front desk. Several times Shakespeare's tail came out from the blanket, and Sarah had to stuff it back in before anyone noticed. When we finally got Shakespeare to his room, he didn't want to be alone. He wanted to be in our room, with Sarah and me, so we let him join us. We called room service and had our dinners delivered to the room. Shakespeare ordered a fruit salad, and Sarah and I each had a hamburger. We also ordered a bottle of champagne. Neither Sarah nor I was a big drinker, but the champagne seemed appropriate. Then the three of us got into our pajamas and got comfortable on the bed watching TV. Shakespeare wanted to watch an old movie, but midway through the movie he fell asleep, between Sarah and me. Neither of us wanted to wake him, since he seemed so content. So that's how we went to sleep on our wedding night, no wild lovemaking or romping around in bed, just Sarah and me with our capuchin monkey snoring between us.

I guess you can imagine what the rest of our honeymoon was like, the three of us. I'm glad Sarah wasn't an insecure or self-centered person, or she probably would have had a problem sharing these special days with a monkey. Shakespeare considered us to be his family, and it would've hurt his feelings to be nudged out of the picture.

When we got home from the trip to Coronado, we unpacked and called Dr. Barney. During the time we were gone, the doctor had done a lot of thinking. He had a couple of ideas, the first of which was to buy Shakespeare his own computer. He wanted me to buy him a laptop. I asked him if he thought Shakespeare would actually be able to operate such a thing, and the doctor was sure of it. "He may have difficulty typing at first, but he'll make it work for him. I think he'll catch on quickly, and I think it will facilitate his learning."

So at the doctor's urging, I went out and bought Shakespeare his first computer. When I brought it home, Shakespeare was very excited. He jumped up and down and shrieked and then sat down to figure the thing out. I showed him how to use Google to perform simple searches and was amazed at how fast he caught on. From that point on, I couldn't pull Shakespeare away from the thing. Dr. Barney had been right; the computer was an excellent idea.

The doctor's second idea was even more interesting: he wanted us to have Shakespeare's IQ tested. I laughed when he first said this. "You honestly want to test the IQ of a monkey?" I said.

But the doctor didn't think the idea was strange at all. He'd been working closely with Shakespeare for months, and he felt Shakespeare might be brighter than we realized. The doctor said he could administer the test himself, so that no others would be involved. Like I've said before, if others learned about Shakespeare, they might try to take him away from me. Who knew what people would try to do? So I agreed to let the doctor administer this test in secret at our house, after which he would score the test himself. We agreed that we would keep the results between the three of us, between the doctor, Sarah, and me. We would not tell Shakespeare the purpose of the test; we would just tell him it was a general exam. If the results came in low, we didn't want him to think less of himself and get discouraged. I knew from my own experience that learning of a low score might damage his self-esteem and make him less inclined to continue working hard at his lessons.

In between the time we agreed to test his IQ and the afternoon we actually did it, Shakespeare's knowledge of the world grew in leaps and bounds. I attributed this to his computer, which he was using night and day. The TV no longer interested him. He researched all sorts of topics, but he was still especially interested in airplanes and found several websites that explained how airplanes were able to fly. Then he found another website that described how he could make a model airplane out of tissue paper and balsa wood. More than anything, he wanted to make one of these model planes. We found a hobby shop, and I went in and bought the tools and supplies he would need. He then went to work on the table in his room, and within a few days he had constructed an entire model airplane. It didn't have an engine—so it was actually a glider—but according to the website, it would fly just like the real thing. So we took it to a public park early one morning when there weren't any people, and Shakespeare climbed up to the top of a tree with his plane. "Ready," I said, and he tossed it. It took to flight and must have gone fifty or sixty feet before it finally came to a landing on the lawn. Shakespeare was delighted, and we did it again and again, until a family finally arrived at the park to have lunch at one of the picnic tables. I decided it would be best for us to leave.

"Can we do this again tomorrow morning?" he asked

"Sure," I said.

I knew from talking to him that Shakespeare wanted more than anything to fly in a real plane. A commercial jet would be out of the question since it would probably have prohibitive rules about animals, especially monkeys, but why not a private plane? I did have a friend who had access to his father's Cessna. Ted Ambrose and I had been friends since high school, and he and his father had always been into flying. Ted had attended our wedding, and he still seemed like a nice guy. So why not call Ted? Why not see if he'd take Shakespeare and me for a short flight in his plane? This would be the perfect outing, I thought, and I gave Ted a call. He worked these days for an advertising agency in Santa Ana, and I had the business's number. I called, and the receptionist answered. I asked for Ted, and she put me through to him.

"Hey, Ted. It's Marty Anderson."

"Hi, Marty," he said. "How was the honeymoon?"

"It was great."

"So what's up?"

"I'm calling to see if you're still flying around in your father's plane."

"I go up once in a while."

"I'm calling to ask you a favor."

"What is it?"

"Do you think you could take me up with you? Me and a friend of mine?"

"Where do you want to go?"

"Nowhere special, just up in the air."

"I'm flying this weekend. You can come along if you want. Who is it you're bringing?"

"A friend of mine. You would've seen him at my wedding."

"What's his name?"

"You'd laugh if I told you. He isn't really a person, but he's very interested in flying."

"He what?"

"You'll understand when you meet him."

"Okay," Ted said. He sounded busy, like he wasn't listening carefully. But he said he'd be happy to take us with him. He then told me where to meet him Saturday morning, and I jotted down the address.

Later that day, I told Shakespeare what I'd arranged. His eyes lit up, and he gave me a great big smile. "We're going in a real airplane?"

"Yes," I said.

"This Saturday?"

"Yes, this Saturday. You need to be on your best behavior. Ted probably isn't used to having monkeys fly with him."

"I'll be good," Shakespeare promised. "And I won't say a word."

When Saturday came, we drove to the airport and met Ted as planned. Ted laughed when he saw Shakespeare. "You brought your monkey? You've got to be kidding. It's your monkey who wants to fly?"

"Yes," I said.

"How do you know he wants to fly? Did he tell you he wanted to go up in a plane? Can he talk?"

"No, of course not."

"Well?"

"He plays with toy airplanes in his room, and he always looks up toward the sky when real planes fly over our house. I just know he'd love this. If he could talk, I'm sure he'd tell me."

"What's his name again?"

"Shakespeare."

"Oh yes, Shakespeare the monkey. How could I forget your monkey ring bearer? Shouldn't he be wearing a diaper? I don't want him making a mess in the plane."

"He's toilet trained."

Ted rolled his eyes and said, "Oh, my dad would kill me if he knew about this."

"Honest, it won't be a problem."

Ted stared at me for a moment, with a twinkle in his eye. He seemed amused. Finally, he smiled and said, "Well, what the heck. Let's get going."

You should've seen the look on Shakespeare's face; he was like a kid who'd just been handed his first ice cream cone. I don't think I'd ever seen him as happy as he was when we all climbed into the plane. Ted and I sat up front, and Shakespeare sat in the back. Ted started the engine, and we rolled toward the runway. When we took off, I was gripping my seat with both hands, but Shakespeare was standing, watching over Ted's shoulder, taking a mental note of everything he did. There were probably a hundred questions he wanted to ask, but he kept his mouth closed, just as he'd been told. When we got high into the air, he looked down through his window at the streets and buildings below, in awe of the bird's-eye view. Then I had an idea.

"Do you think he could steer your plane for a minute?" I asked.

"Steer the plane?"

"He could sit in your lap. You could let him hold the steering wheel, just for a minute."

"You want your monkey to fly my plane?"

"Just for a minute."

"I don't know."

"He won't do anything dangerous. He'll do what I tell him. He'll just hold the wheel steady."

"I guess for a minute," Ted said. I could tell he was wondering what he was getting himself into, allowing a monkey to sit in his lap and take the wheel.

"I really appreciate this," I said.

"Okay, okay."

"Shakespeare, come up and sit in Ted's lap. You can steer the plane. It's your job to keep us steady, so don't make any sudden turns."

"Does he understand what you're saying?"

"More than you realize."

At first Shakespeare hesitated, but I told him not to be afraid—that Ted would be right there with him to help if needed. He crawled between our seats and up onto Ted's lap, and with both his little hands, he took hold of the steering wheel.

"No sudden moves," Ted said.

"He knows."

"Yes, he's doing it."

"Good job, Shakespeare."

"Yes," Ted said. "Good job." Ted now seemed to be getting a kick out of Shakespeare holding his steering wheel, flying the plane.

After about a minute of this, I told Shakespeare that was enough and asked him to hop back to his seat, which he did.

"He does seem to understand you."

"He's a smart little monkey."

"What kind is he?"

"He's a capuchin. He's the same kind of monkey organ-grinders used to use to collect money from people. They also use them to assist paraplegics."

"A capuchin, you say?"

"Yes," I said.

"Well, how about that? I guess you learn something new every day."

When Ted landed the plane, we all climbed out to the tarmac, and Shakespeare jumped up in my arms and hugged me, kissing my cheek. He then climbed down from my arms and walked over to Ted, holding his hand out to him.

Ted looked at me. "What does he want?"

"I think he wants to shake your hand. He's trying to say thank you."

"So he is," Ted said, and he shook Shakespeare's little hand. "You were a fine copilot. But don't ever let it get to my father that I let you fly his plane. This will have to be our secret. My dad would have a heart attack if he knew."

"We can keep a secret," I said. Then I looked to Shakespeare and asked, "Can we keep a secret?" He clapped his hands and nodded his head.

Two days later, Dr. Barney gave Shakespeare his test. Shakespeare took the test in his room with the door closed and spent a couple of hours on it. I have no idea where the doctor got the test, but he assured me the results would be accurate. I still had some personal reservations about giving Shakespeare this exam. When I was in grade school, my dad had wanted me to take such a test. He arranged for it with a child psychologist, and I can still remember what it was like, struggling through the questions, being nervous about what my father would think. When the testing was over, I was never told my IQ, but I assumed it was not spectacular because after my dad got the results, he no longer pushed me so hard to excel in school. It was like he saw my IQ and just said to himself, *Oh, what's the use?* I think it's a mistake to treat kids differently just because you know their IQ. I wish my father would have kept pushing me to do well in school, instead of backing off. To be honest, it made me feel like he didn't love me as much. I knew this wasn't true, but it sometimes felt that way. And I didn't want Shakespeare to feel like less just because he didn't score high. He was, after all, just a monkey. What were we really expecting from him, testing his IQ like this? If we found out he was just very average, which he probably was, or even below average, would we be less inclined to spend time with him? Honestly, would we be disappointed?

The morning after the test, the doctor called me with the results. "I thought you'd want to know as soon as possible," he said.

"Yes," I said. "Tell me."

Also a Monkey

When you owned a monkey such as Shakespeare who had so many human characteristics, it was easy to forget a fact of great importance, and that's that he was first and foremost a live monkey. Sometimes I got to thinking of him as a little human being, and in a way he sort of was. But he was also a monkey, and though he might often think and behave like the rest of us, he still had primal and instinctive needs. I discovered that one of these strong needs was to climb and swing in trees. It sounds sort of like a cliché, a monkey swinging from the branches of a tree, but it was a very real desire he had. I learned out about this one night when I was having difficulty sleeping and found myself looking for him. I don't know why I was so wide awake, maybe too much coffee or maybe too much sleep the previous night. Whatever it was, I just couldn't doze off, so I climbed out of bed and headed toward the kitchen for something to eat. The TV was off, and the front room was dark, so I figured Shakespeare must have gone to bed. I stepped to his room and opened his door to check on him. But Shakespeare was not in his bed. I looked all around the room and then all around the house, and I couldn't locate him anywhere. He was gone. It was about two in the morning, and I began to panic, wondering where in the world he might be. Then I noticed an open window in the front room. Had he run off?

I opened the front door and stepped outside into the night air. It was dark but not pitch-black. There was nearly a full moon, and plenty of moonlight was shining down into the front yard. My eyes adjusted quickly to the semidarkness. I stepped out further, looking around and hoping to see him, hoping he had not run off too far. Then I heard a rustling overhead, and I looked upward into the trees. Was it him? I could see what seemed to be the silhouette of a small animal, hanging from a high branch by one arm, its tail dangling below. Were my eyes playing tricks on me, or was it really him? He seemed to be up toward the top of the tree, and not wanting to wake anyone in the neighborhood, I whispered, "Shakespeare, is that you?" The silhouette remained motionless, and I whispered his name again. "Is that you?" I repeated. "Come down from there."

The silhouette then came to life, swinging from the branches and leaping from tree to tree, as though he hadn't heard me.

"Come down from there," I said again. This time I put a little voice into my whisper, to be sure he could hear me.

He stopped swinging and whispered back, "Is that you, Marty?"

"Yes, it's me. What the heck are you doing up there? You need to come down."

"You'll need to close your eyes."

"Why?" I asked.

"I'm not wearing any clothes."

"Okay, I'll close my eyes."

"Are they closed?"

"Yes, they are."

"Okay, I'm coming down. Promise you'll keep them closed."

I heard Shakespeare climb down, leap to the front lawn, and run to the open window. After I heard him climb through the window, I opened my eyes and stepped back toward the door. He had gone to his bedroom to put on his pajamas, and as I entered the house, Shakespeare appeared in the hallway, now dressed.

"What are you doing up so late?" he asked.

"I could ask you the same thing," I said.

"I was just, you know, climbing."

"At two in the morning?"

"I'm sorry," he said.

"You don't have to be sorry. It just frightened me. I didn't know where you went."

"I'm sorry," he said again.

It probably wasn't the first time he'd done this, and it wouldn't be the last. Several times after this incident, I checked on him late at night, just out of curiosity. His room was empty, and the window was open again. I decided not to make a big deal of it, and I didn't make him come out of the trees. It was highly unlikely anyone would ever see him outside at this late hour, and this routine, climbing around naked in the trees, seemed to be something he needed to do. Actually, I wished I'd never caught him doing this, for it was sort of an invasion of his privacy. I'd embarrassed him that night, and I believed that everyone, including my monkey, deserved a little time for himself or herself.

Following the IQ test we gave to Shakespeare, Dr. Barney asked if he could work with Shakespeare full-time, from first thing in the morning right up until dinnertime. I agreed to this, and the doctor got rid of his other clients, now working with Shakespeare exclusively. His IQ had come in at 156, which was ridiculous for a monkey and even quite high for a human being. It was hard to believe, but this monkey was actually smarter than any of the rest of us, and we wanted to do everything possible to help him reach his full potential. As the months went by, he was actually beginning to do some high school–level work with the doctor. I didn't know Shakespeare's exact age since I didn't know the precise day he was born, but I figured he was now a little over four years old.

One thing Shakespeare loved each morning was his breakfast. The food, of course, was essential, but even more important was the morning paper. Shakespeare read the paper from cover to cover, from the headline news to the sports section, even through to the comics. He asked me if I thought the paper might be interested in publishing an article from him, and I thought about this. I mean, the idea was a possibility. Of course, he would have to write his article as though he were a human. Or would he? This was certainly a curious idea, an article being submitted by a monkey, with the byline of Shakespeare. No one would think a monkey actually had written the article, but it would still be written from a monkey's perspective, sort of as a joke, people would wrongly assume. Perhaps the paper would accept it as a bit of creative writing and actually publish it. And the byline? Well, people did get away with naming themselves after famous people, didn't they? There was Madonna, of course. Everyone knew she wasn't actually the Madonna, but they all accepted her silly name. So I began to like this idea of Shakespeare submitting an article, for there was a certain anonymity to it. Of course, those who knew me and knew about my monkey would think I'd written the article under his name. But most people knew nothing about me, and they'd have no idea what to think.

I suggested to Shakespeare that he start with a simple letter to the editor, and he agreed this would be a good idea. His first letter surprised me. It wasn't the kind of topic I had expected him to be thinking about. He wrote the following:

> I am a monkey—a capuchin, to be precise. I read your newspaper every morning, and I have a simple question to ask of your readers. Why do humans kill each other? They are the most intelligent animal on the planet, yet they kill each other constantly. It makes no sense to me. You don't see animals killing their own kind the way humans do. Is there something about their intelligence that makes humans more prone to murder and war? Wouldn't you think it would be just the opposite? Wouldn't you think the smarter an animal is, the more capable of living peacefully it would be? Yet the opposite seems to be true. I ask this simple question of your human readers and look forward to reading their responses.

That was Shakespeare's letter, a question to human beings, short and to the point. I told him that if he wanted the letter to be published, he ought to drop the part about his being a monkey, warning that the newspaper probably wouldn't take him seriously. But he e-mailed the letter just as he had written it, and sure enough, a week later it appeared in the paper. In the days that followed, the paper published pages full of letters from readers in response to his question. Not one of these letters challenged the letter writer's claim to be a monkey, for I think they all assumed he was taking on this identity to be entertaining, exercising a little poetic license for the sake of humor. And also, none of the responses complained about his name. They accepted his name and played along like they were just responding to a curious monkey who happened to be named Shakespeare. He was thrilled with all the replies, and I could tell we were onto something—a public forum in which Shakespeare could communicate with other humans, telling them that he was a monkey but not actually risking being found out for what he was: an actual monkey. Does that make sense? In the months that followed, he wrote several more letters, and the paper published all of them. And people responded to them enthusiastically. Then Shakespeare received an e-mail from one of the editors at the paper, asking if he was interested in writing a piece for their opinion section. It was just what he'd hoped for, and Shakespeare wrote the editor back, asking what subject they wanted him to write about. The editor told him to pick any subject that interested him, and Shakespeare was thrilled.

"What are you going to write about?" I asked.

"I don't know."

"It has to be an opinion, not a question. Do you have an opinion?"

"I have lots of opinions."

"Do you have an opinion that readers would find compelling?"

"How about drugs and alcohol?"

"What in the world do you know about drugs and alcohol?"

"Nothing, yet everything."

"I guess it would be interesting."

"Wouldn't it? Picture me writing about drugs and alcohol. I could tackle the issue from a monkey's perspective."

I thought for a moment and then said, "Yes, I think you should do it." Why not?

So Shakespeare wrote his first newspaper article, and he showed it to me before e-mailing it to the editor. It was an interesting piece of writing to say the least. I actually liked it. Considering that he was only four years old and taking into account that he was just a monkey, it was surprisingly insightful. It wasn't condescending, yet it also wasn't overly sympathetic. It was clear why people liked Shakespeare's previous letters and why they were probably going to like this article. He had a way with words and a way of seeing solutions where there were problems. To his credit, and to his way of thinking, there wasn't a problem on earth that didn't have some sort of practical solution. It's the sort of optimism that comes with youth— and, I suppose, that also comes with being a monkey—and the responses Shakespeare got to this article were very encouraging. I think everyone appreciated getting a good old-fashioned breath of fresh air. And that is what Shakespeare's writing was: a breath of fresh air, a breath of lively and encouraging thinking from a self-proclaimed monkey and observer of the human condition.

This monkey thing was funny. I mean, it was funny in that no one ever questioned Shakespeare's claim to be a monkey. I don't think anyone actually believed a monkey was behind anything Shakespeare wrote, but no one ever came out and challenged it, not a single time. It was like people wanted to pretend, like they were playing along because it was fun to do so. And play along they did. It was a huge boost to Shakespeare's self-esteem, knowing people were willing to give credence to his thoughts and ideas as if he were human. Before the paper started publishing his writing, the only people he had gotten any feedback from were Sarah, Dr. Barney, and me, but now he was virtually conversing with people all over the county. And they seemed to like him as much as we did.

After the piece about drugs and alcohol, he wrote others, a handful of editorials about terrorism, the economy, our health care system, child rearing, and other topics that stirred his interest. Then things started getting serious. It had never occurred to me that these readers were suddenly going to get serious about my monkey's writing, but they did. They truly wanted to find out just who the heck this writer was; everyone knew he wasn't a monkey, and they wanted to know what clever human being was writing all these articles under the nom de plume of Shakespeare, pretending to be a monkey. Every day there was a letter or two published in the paper imploring the man behind the Shakespeare articles to come forward and reveal himself. It was becoming a public obsession. The paper easily could have traced the articles to me through my e-mail address and printed my name, but they kept it a mystery and let their readers continue to wonder and take wild guesses.

"What should we do?" Shakespeare finally asked me. "Should we just tell them the truth?"

"No one would believe us," I said.

"They would if they met me. They would believe it if they talked to me."

"It would be a fiasco."

"I don't see why."

"The world isn't ready for an intelligent monkey. The world is barely ready for intelligent men."

"But they like what I write."

"Only because they think a human has been writing your articles. If they learn a monkey has actually been doing this, they'll go right off the deep end."

"So you say."

"I think you should send one last letter to the paper and tell them you're done. Tell them you're not writing any more articles. We need to put an end to all this curiosity and speculation. In fact, I'm not suggesting it; I'm telling you to do it." I said this as firmly as I knew how, without sounding too harsh.

You should have seen the look of disappointment on Shakespeare's face. I was demanding that we end the one thing that connected him to the rest of the world. It wasn't fair, I'll admit this. I felt awful, but I was right that revealing his true identity was out of the question. If we were to do this, everything in his life would change, and not for the better. It would be a freak show, and there was no telling what people would do. So reluctantly, Shakespeare wrote the letter to the paper as I had instructed him. Like a faucet that was suddenly turned off, the movement to discover his true identity ceased. It turned out the public had a very short attention span, which worked in our favor.

Things went back to normal in the paper, and there were no more letters about Shakespeare. I'd be lying if I said he wasn't angry with me. For several weeks he ignored me and gave me the cold shoulder, and when I asked if he was going to be okay, he just said, "I'll be fine, so stop asking me that." I must have apologized to him a hundred times. This was the first time, I think, that he had been genuinely mad at me, but like I said, this lasted only a few weeks, and then the anger gradually went away. Soon he was his old self, seemingly happy with our close-knit group at my home. I think he'd given the matter some thought and realized I had been right to have him stop writing for the paper when he did. I think he realized I had his best interests at heart, and rather than being mad at me, he now seemed to appreciate me more than ever.

"You were just looking out for me," he said, and I told him that was true. "You love me, right?" he asked, and I told him yes, I loved him. And this was true. I was very fond of him. It was shortly after we had this conversation that Dr. Barney came to me with yet another one of his ideas, and idea that would eventually allow Shakespeare to get his literary juices flowing again.

I had just come home from a tennis match, and I was about to hop in the shower. The doctor grabbed me by the arm and said we needed to speak in private. We sat down on the sofa while Shakespeare was reading in his room.

"I need help," the doctor said.

"With what?" I asked.

"With your monkey."

"Why? What's the problem?"

"I'm a smart and well-educated man, but I have my limitations. Obviously, I haven't taught Shakespeare everything I know, but with each day that passes, I find myself getting closer and closer to being ineffective. Shakespeare is very bright, as you know, and his hunger to learn is coming very close to exceeding my ability to feed it. I'm accustomed to helping grade school and early high school students, but Shakespeare will soon be surpassing those levels. I guess what I'm trying to say is that I need to make a recruitment. I'd like to bring in someone to assist me with Shakespeare, someone who is a level or two above me. Your monkey needs to be challenged, and soon I won't be able to do this. He's going to lose interest in his studies. I'm trying to be honest with you, Marty, and I'd love to stay involved in Shakespeare's life. I'm just saying that I need to bring someone else into the picture, someone smarter than me."

"Do you have someone in mind?"

"Yes, I do."

"Do you think he'd be interested?"

"I'm sure he would be."

"Is he trustworthy?"

"I think he can be trusted."

"What's his name?"

"Professor Julius Wild."

"Where is he now?"

"He's teaching at a community college."

"So he's already busy?"

"He'd drop everything, I'm sure of it."

"And you think he knows more than you?"

"He's a true polymath."

"What's a polymath?"

"Someone who knows a lot about many subjects. We need him. And the sooner we get him involved in Shakespeare's life, the better."

"Is this man a friend of yours?"

"I've known him for years."

"Have you already told him about Shakespeare?"

"I've told him nothing."

"How do we go about asking him if he's interested, without risking him telling others?"

"Do you have an attorney?"

"Yes, our family attorney."

"Have him draw up a confidentiality agreement binding the professor to absolute silence. Get the professor to sign the agreement. Then we can introduce him to Shakespeare."

"I suppose it could work."

"It's in Shakespeare's best interest to make this work."

"Yes," I agreed.

"You'll like the professor. He's a very likable guy. A little eccentric, but very smart. Once he meets Shakespeare, I'm sure he'll be on board."

I made an appointment with my attorney for the following afternoon. I refer to him as my attorney, but he was really my father's attorney. Dad had used him for all sorts of things, and I'd met him here and there over my lifetime, the last time being the reading of my father's will. He said he was glad to hear I was doing well and asked what he could do for me. This posed a slight problem since there was no way I could have him draw up the proper agreement for the professor without telling him about Shakespeare. I knew he had to keep my situation confidential, being my attorney, but more and more people were now learning about my monkey's remarkable abilities, which was not good. But what else could I do? We needed the professor, and to get him, we needed my attorney on board. There was no way around this.

The attorney's name was Patrick Casey, but he liked to be called Danny. He was in his sixties and had gray hair but a youthful face, and he took good care of himself, being trim and athletic for his age. I mean, he wasn't fit as a fiddle, but he wasn't weak-armed and overweight like a lot of other men his age. He had a slight Irish accent, which he could have lost if he'd wanted, but I think he felt it gave him personality. Because of this accent, it was fun to listen to him talk.

When I walked into his office, he stood up and greeted me with a big smile. His teeth left a little to be desired, crooked and stained with some decay and a few missing molars. You'd think with all the money he made as an attorney, he'd be able to afford some decent dental work. Anyway, he happily shook my hand. "It's great to see you, Marty," he said. Then he saw my companion and said, "Well, who do we have here?"

"This is Shakespeare," I said.

"You brought a monkey?"

"He's a capuchin."

"Yes, of course, a capuchin."

"He's the reason we're meeting."

"You told me over the phone that you needed help with a venture."

"In a way, Shakespeare is a venture."

"I see," Danny said. He then looked down at Shakespeare, who had approached him. Danny was still standing, and Shakespeare reached out his little hand. Danny shook it gently, obviously enjoying my monkey's display of good manners.

"It's nice to meet you," Shakespeare said, and Danny's jaw nearly hit the floor. I mean, you should've seen the look on Danny's face. It was like he'd just heard a monkey talk, and yes, that's exactly what had happened.

"A talking monkey?" he asked.

"He's much more than that."

"He spoke to me. Can he say anything else?"

"He can say a lot."

"Like what?"

"Like anything he wants. He's like you or me. He's like a little person."

"That's impossible," Danny said.

"Then test him."

"Like how?"

"Ask him a question."

"Such as?"

"Ask him anything."

Danny kneeled down and looked at my monkey. He chose a question that would be easy to answer. "What color is the sky?"

Shakespeare smiled at this. Then he said, "To our eyes, most of the time the sky appears blue. This is the result of light scattering off tiny oxygen and nitrogen molecules. These molecules tend to scatter short wavelengths of light, which are seen as blue. This phenomenon is referred to as Rayleigh scattering, named after the British physicist Lord Rayleigh, who studied and wrote about it back in the 1800s."

"What the heck?" Danny said, standing back up.

"Amazing, isn't it?"

"It can't be."

"Ah, but it is. Shakespeare is a very bright little fellow."

"I think I need to sit down." Danny took a seat behind his desk, still staring at my remarkable monkey, probably trying to figure out how I'd been able to pull off such a trick. Surely, Shakespeare hadn't said what he'd just heard.

"I need you to draw up an agreement," I said, ignoring Danny's astonishment and getting on with the business at hand.

"What sort of agreement?"

"A confidentiality agreement."

"For whom?"

"For a certain professor. We're going to approach this guy about helping us teach Shakespeare. I've been working with a psychologist, and we've been teaching Shakespeare all we know, but Shakespeare's ability to learn is soon going to exceed our ability to teach. The doctor recommended that we seek help from a professor friend of his. He says the guy is a polymath. Do you know what a polymath is?"

"Yes, of course."

"Listen, I'm sure he's trustworthy. He's a friend of Dr. Barney's. But I don't want to let him in on our little secret without first having him sign an agreement. You can imagine the problems we'd have if Shakespeare's special talents suddenly became public knowledge."

"Yes, I can imagine."

"So you can do this?"

"Yes, I think I can."

"And you'll keep what you've seen and heard this afternoon between you and me? You won't divulge this information to anyone, no matter what?"

"Yes, I can do that too."

"Good. Here's the professor's name, address, and phone number." I handed Danny a slip of paper with all the information, and he placed it before him on his desk. "You'll need to type this up and print it out yourself. I don't want your secretary knowing anything about it. When it's ready to be signed, give me a call, and I'll come pick it up in person."

There was a pause in our conversation while Danny seemed to be thinking. Then he asked, "Where did you find him?"

"You mean Shakespeare?"

"Yes," Danny said.

"I went out a few years ago to get myself a monkey. I was just looking for an interesting animal companion. I had no idea I was bringing home a long-tailed Albert Einstein. I was as surprised by this as you are now. But as you can see, here he is, as big as life, and it's my responsibility to take care of him. I owe the little guy the best education possible."

While I wasn't looking, Shakespeare had stepped over to Danny's bookshelves on the other side of the room. Something had caught his attention high up on the shelves. Before I could stop him, he had climbed up to the top of the bookcase and grabbed one of Danny's shiny golfing trophies. "Can I have this?" Shakespeare asked.

"No, you can't have it," I said. "And get down from there. You're going to break something."

"But what is it?"

"It belongs to Danny," I said. "It's his trophy. Put it back where you found it." Turning to Danny, I said, "Sorry about that. But while Shakespeare is many things, he's also a monkey. And he never lets me forget it."

Enter the Polymath

S arah's parents flew out to California for her twenty-first birthday. It was a milestone occasion, and they wanted to be with her to celebrate. We decided we'd all go out to eat that evening, and Sarah wanted Shakespeare to come with us. Her parents knew we had a monkey, but they didn't really know anything about Shakespeare's special gifts. They just thought he was a regular chittering and branch-to-branch-swinging monkey. For our dinner, Sarah picked an Italian restaurant we had been to many times before, where we had come to know the owner. It was a small establishment located in Mission Viejo, in a strip shopping center. The restaurant owner knew Shakespeare and let us bring him inside to eat with us. We always got the strangest looks from the other patrons, but no one ever complained about Shakespeare. He was always well behaved, minding his manners and keeping his mouth shut except to eat. His favorite dish was the eggplant parmigiana, and for a drink he always had a Coke. He used his silverware just like everyone else and would dab his mouth with his napkin, making sure none of the marinara sauce was showing on his lips. Usually, someone eating in the restaurant would come over to our table and comment on the excellent manners of our monkey, saying something to the effect that they were impressed at how well trained he was. It was funny to watch Shakespeare's face when they did this, the mild look of disdain he would have, for he had never thought of himself as trained. Stupid monkeys were trained, but Shakespeare was, well, civilized.

When we arrived at the restaurant, the place was busy, but Jerry the owner had kept a table open just for us. It was a big round table, probably bigger than we needed, but it was nice to not be cramped around one of the smaller ones. Jerry came to us and handed out the menus so that we could look over the offerings. Everyone lifted their menus and began reading, including Shakespeare, and Sarah's mom noticed this. "Isn't it funny how he holds up the menu and pretends to read?" she said.

"Monkey see, monkey do," Tom said.

"Look at him concentrate," Judy said. "If you didn't know better, you'd think he was actually reading."

"Sometimes we wonder if he can," Sarah said. "He's a very bright little monkey."

"Bah," Tom said. "Monkeys are monkeys."

Shakespeare lowered his menu to his lap for a second and gave Tom a stern look.

"What does he eat?"

"He likes the eggplant," I said.

"I was thinking of getting that," said Judy.

"Eggplant is monkey food," Tom said. "Order something with some meat in it."

"Well," Judy said, "I was also thinking about getting the spaghetti and meatballs."

"Well, that's original," Sarah said.

"I don't know what any of this other stuff is. We never eat Italian back home."

"It's all pasta," Tom said. "It's all the same thing, just different shapes and sauces."

"So our little girl is twenty-one," Judy said, changing the subject. Judy was a master at changing the subject. I didn't know if she did this on purpose or if it was just the way her mind worked, jumping from one topic to the other.

"Yes, I'm finally twenty-one," Sarah said.

"Are you going to order a drink?" Tom asked. "You have to order a drink."

"Maybe I'll get a glass of wine."

"You Californians and your wine," Tom said.

"Why? What are you going to get?" Sarah asked.

"A beer, of course."

"I think I'll try a glass of wine too," Judy said. "We never have wine back home."

"We don't drink much," I said.

"Does your monkey ever drink?"

"He likes Coke."

"Have you ever ordered him a glass of beer?"

"No," I said. "I don't think he'd like it. Besides, he's only four years old, definitely underage."

"Ha," Tom laughed.

"How old will he get to be?" Judy asked.

"In captivity they live about forty years."

"He's going to be living with you until you're in your fifties or sixties?" Tom asked. It wasn't really a question. It was more an exclamation.

"That's how it appears."

Then Tom said, "I hear when they get older, monkeys can be very difficult to put up with."

Shakespeare lowered his menu to his lap again, just for a second, and gave Tom another disapproving look.

"Do you see how he does that?" Tom asked. "It's like he understands what I'm saying."

"He probably understands more than you think," Sarah said.

"If only monkeys could talk," Judy said. "It would be so interesting to learn what they have on their little monkey minds."

"Yes," I said. "Can you imagine?"

"I think I like the sound of this one," Judy said, now looking back at her menu, her finger on one of the items. "Fettuccini Alfredo. It sort of rolls off the tongue. What exactly is it?"

Sarah described the dish to her, and Judy said that it sounded great and she was going to order it.

"I'm going to get the spaghetti and meatballs," Tom said. "I haven't had a good plate of spaghetti and meatballs for years, not since I was a teenager when my mom used to make it."

When the waitress came to our table, we placed our orders, and she scribbled the items on a pad of paper. Sarah did the ordering for Shakespeare, and the waitress then retrieved all the menus. We continued to talk for a while, mostly about Tom's hardware store back in Nebraska, and then the waitress brought out our food. Tom said he liked his spaghetti; this seemed to be a very good restaurant, he noted, but he was especially impressed to see Shakespeare using his silverware to eat. Shakespeare wasn't seated, for he was too small for the table, so he ate while standing. If you weren't used to seeing this, as Sarah and I were, it could be very amusing. "You should build a booster seat for him," Tom said. "That's what I'd do. I'd build a booster seat."

"That's not a bad idea," I said.

"So when am I going to get my little grandchild?" Judy asked, changing the subject again. She said this sweetly and not in a demanding way, but the question embarrassed Sarah.

"Oh, Mother," Sarah said.

"Actually, I've been wondering the same thing," Tom said. "Your mom and I aren't getting any younger."

"Marty and I haven't even talked about it."

"You're kidding, right?" Tom said.

"Shakespeare keeps us very busy. Think of him as your grandchild for now."

"A monkey for a grandchild?" Tom looked over at Shakespeare, and Shakespeare smiled.

"For now, yes, he's your grandchild."

"Do you even hear yourself?"

"I was hoping for a little boy or a girl," Judy said, looking at her food. It was obvious she was very disappointed.

Something suddenly occurred to me as I watched Judy looking sadly at her food. Sarah was right: not once had we even discussed having children. Didn't normal married couples at least talk about this once in a while, the possibility of having kids? Had Shakespeare actually become our own version of a child? This seemed to be the case in our household. Maybe Sarah's parents would have had a better understanding of the situation had they known more about Shakespeare, had they been told the truth about his special talents. Shakespeare wasn't just a monkey or some facsimile of a child; he was the real deal, so dependent on us, always overflowing with questions, just as confounding, and certainly no less loving. And we were parents, weren't we? We fed and clothed him, disciplined him, taught him how to behave around others, and had him properly schooled. And we loved him as our own and felt pride whenever he succeeded at his endeavors. When he was writing those articles for the newspaper, it had made me nervous, but I was very proud of him, the same way I would be proud of my own son. And when we took him out to eat with Sarah's parents, I felt that same pride, watching him use his silverware, pat his lips with his napkin, and eat his eggplant parmigiana like a grown-up human being, as civilized and well behaved as the rest of us.

Why would Sarah and I ever need to have children at all when we already had Shakespeare in our lives? Was this weird? And was it shortsighted? I mean, were we going to wake up someday and suddenly realize we'd missed out by not having a human baby, a little human child to call our own? And what about Sarah's parents? Were we being unfair to them? Don't all grandparents deserve little grandchildren to call their own and spoil, to bounce on their knee and tell their stories to? A mischievous little banana-eating monkey was hardly a proper substitute for a grandchild. Or maybe Shakespeare would just have to do. And maybe the day would come when we'd allow him to talk to others, to talk to Sarah's parents, showing them just how special he was and why he was all we needed. No, I didn't see any children in our future. Sarah's parents would understand. Someday the world would understand. Then it hit me that Shakespeare would not remain a secret forever. The time would come when we would share him with the world. It was a sad thought, knowing that one day we'd lose control. Out into the real world he would go, into the big, bad, dangerous, and sometimes very cruel world.

"What are you thinking?" Sarah asked.

"What do you mean?"

"You look kind of sad."

"I don't know. I was just thinking."

"Whenever I get sad, I try to think of something in my past that made me happy," Judy said. "Sometimes I'll think about my first high school dance and the first time a boy asked me to go with him. I remember that boy like it was yesterday. His name was Bobby Taylor, and he was very cute. Or I'll think of how it felt when Tom and I got married, what it was like to kiss him in front of all those people. It felt so good to be starting our lives together. Or better yet, I'll recall what it was like when we first brought Sarah home from the hospital. We went there, just the two of us, and came home the next day as a family of three, Sarah sitting in the little brand-new car seat we'd purchased for her just a week earlier. We had our little bundle of joy. I was so excited."

I know Judy was trying to make me feel better, but she only made me feel worse by talking about bringing Sarah home from the hospital. It was sort of sad, knowing that our child was a monkey, knowing that Sarah would probably never give birth to a son or daughter, that we'd never bring our own little bundle of joy home for the first time.

When Sarah's parents hopped back on the airplane to return to Nebraska, things got back to normal in Corona del Mar. We no longer had to pretend Shakespeare was just a run-of-the-mill monkey, and so long as we were in our home, we could talk to him freely. And with Sarah's parents gone, we could now have Dr. Barney contact his professor friend and bring him over to the house.

Dr. Barney got the professor to sign the confidentiality agreement, and the pair visited us on a Saturday afternoon. I answered the front door and was a little surprised by what I saw. Dr. Barney had told me that Professor Julius Wild was a little eccentric, but he hadn't told me he was an outright nut. You don't have to take my word for it; I'll describe him for you. He was a little older than the doctor but not by much, probably in his late sixties. He had red hair, but not like a normal redhead; his hair was brilliant, flaming, and uncombed, as though he'd messed it up on purpose. He also wore a bushy moustache, which was the same shade of red and so large it nearly covered his entire mouth. I'd describe the rest of his face to you, except that it was just background music to this big moustache of his. He did have on a pair of wire-rimmed glasses that sat crooked, one side higher than the other, not by a little but by a lot. And oh yes, there were his ears, which were quite large, sort of comical in appearance, like a feature you'd see drawn on a cartoon character for comic effect. He had on a T-shirt, jeans, and sneakers. He was skinny as a twig, and I noticed that his arms were hairy, the same brilliant color of red hair he had on his head and moustache. Holding up his baggy jeans were a pair of suspenders, and pinned to his suspenders were several buttons. One button was an old-fashioned peace sign, and another said in colorful letters, "Make love, not war." A third called for the freeing of someone named Huey. Standing next to the professor was Dr. Barney.

"You must be Professor Wild," I said.

"That would be me," he replied.

Sarah appeared behind me, also curious to see the professor.

"Here's the paperwork," the doctor said, handing me the signed confidentiality agreement.

I looked it over and then opened the door wider so the two men could come in.

"Nice pad," the professor said.

"Thanks. We like it here."

"Marty remodeled everything himself," Sarah said.

"That's groovy, to be so handy with a hammer and a paint brush. So where's the student?"

"Follow me," I said.

We all walked to the hallway, where I opened the door to Shakespeare's room. He was seated at his table, using his laptop. He turned to look at us. The doctor said hi to him.

"Hi, Doc," Shakespeare said.

"There's someone I'd like you to meet," I said.

Shakespeare climbed out of his chair and looked confused for a moment, likely wondering if he should've spoken.

"It's okay," I said. "This is someone you can talk to. This is Professor Wild. We brought him here to see about him helping out Dr. Barney with your lessons. Go ahead and say hi to him."

Shakespeare greeted the professor and extended his hand.

The professor kneeled down and shook his little hand, laughing. "Hi, little dude," the professor said. "That's a nice grip you've got there."

Shakespeare smiled, and from the way he was looking at the professor, I had a feeling the two of them were going to get along great. Of course, this was assuming that the professor agreed to work with us. Right now, he was just checking Shakespeare out, to see if the doctor's claims were for real.

"Are you another teacher?" Shakespeare asked.

"I'm a college professor."

"A college professor?"

"I'm like a substitute teacher, actually. It's a good gig. They use me to cover for the other teachers when they can't show up for class. I'm kind of a jack-of-all-trades, master of none. They call me a polymath."

"A polymath?"

"Do you know what that is?"

"No," Shakespeare said.

"What's your favorite subject so far? I mean, of all the things Dr. Barney has been teaching you, which really turns you on?"

"I like everything."

"Then you're just like me. Maybe you'll be a polymath too. How old are you?"

"I'm almost five."

"I'm sixty-eight. I've been around a long time, and there's a lot I can teach you, if you'll let me. Are you hip?"

"Am I what?"

"Hip, man—do you dig it?"

"He means, do you want him to teach you?" Dr. Barney explained.

"Yes," Shakespeare said. "I think I'm hip."

"When do you want to start?"

"It's up to Marty," Shakespeare said.

Everyone looked at me.

"Marty is the boss around here," Shakespeare said. "He makes all the decisions."

"We haven't discussed your salary or your hours," I said to the professor. "We need to get straight on these things before you can begin work."

"Listen, I'm not in this for the money," he said. "When Dr. Barney told me about Shakespeare, I told him if he was on the level, I'd teach the little guy for free. I mean, how often does one get to work with an intelligent monkey? Like never, right? This is a once-in-a-lifetime gig. I guess all I ask is that you pay me the same as I was making at the college, enough to cover my bills."

The professor told me how much he'd been making at the college, and I agreed to pay that amount. If he was as good as Dr. Barney claimed, this was a bargain. The only thing that concerned me about the professor was the way he dressed and talked, kind of like an old throwback, like an old hippie or beatnik. But I had grown to respect Dr. Barney, and I truly trusted his judgment. If he said this professor was the right man for the job, then he was the right man. We decided that the professor would start with Shakespeare the coming Monday, and both he and the doctor would work with him simultaneously. I think Shakespeare was excited that someone new was coming aboard. You have to realize that Shakespeare got to talk to so few people, so bringing in someone new with whom he could converse was probably a very big deal to him.

"I'll see you cats on Monday," the professor said. He shook Shakespeare's hand again and said so long.

Shakespeare went back to work on his laptop, and I shut his bedroom door. Sarah and I walked the two men to the front door and saw them off.

Once they were gone, Sarah said, "He's kind of odd, isn't he?"

"Yes, he is."

"What's the deal with the buttons and suspenders?"

"I don't know."

"Are you sure you want him here?"

"If Dr. Barney says he's okay, then I'm okay with the idea. We can always fire him if he doesn't work out. It's not like we signed a long-term contract for his services."

When Monday came, Shakespeare had just finished his breakfast and read the paper when the doctor and professor arrived. They all went into Shakespeare's room and closed the door. I could hear them talking and laughing. Things seemed to be going well, so I went off to my job at the foundation. Sarah had already left for school earlier that morning, and she wouldn't be home until dinner. I had my job and then a tennis match scheduled for the afternoon, so Shakespeare and his teachers would have hours of uninterrupted time together. I arrived home at about five, and Shakespeare's door was still closed. I knocked on the door, and Shakespeare opened it.

"Are you guys about done for the day?" I asked.

The two men stood up and stretched, looking ready to leave. "You have a remarkable little monkey here," the professor said.

"We're very fond of him."

"He's going to learn a lot from me."

"That's good," I said.

"He picks up on things very quickly. He has a very agile mind."

"Yes," I said. "We've noticed that."

"I've assigned some homework."

"Homework?"

"I want him to start reading Plato's dialogues. He doesn't need a book.

It's available on the Internet, and he can read it on his laptop. We'll rap about what he's read tomorrow."

"Okay," I said.

"If I have him working on anything you object to, just let me know. There are mountains of topics we can cover, and even if I might think one is important, you might disagree. I'm fine with that."

"No, we'll let you decide. We'll leave the curriculum up to you."

The professor gave me a thumbs-up and smiled. Then he and the doctor stepped out of Shakespeare's room, and the three of us walked toward the front door. I opened the door for them, and they left the house. When I went back to the room and checked on Shakespeare, he was already working on his reading assignment. I closed his door so he'd have some privacy and then went upstairs to shower.

When I returned downstairs, Sarah was home, preparing dinner in the kitchen. "How'd Shakespeare's lesson go?" she asked. "What did you think of the professor?"

"I think it went well."

"Did you watch them at all?"

"No, I just let them be."

"So what are they working on?"

"Shakespeare is reading Plato's dialogues. They're going to rap about it tomorrow."

"Rap about it?"

"That's what the professor said."

"Do you ever wonder if we're doing the right thing?"

"What do you mean?"

"Keeping Shakespeare's abilities a secret."

"Sure, I've wondered."

"And?"

"We're doing the right thing. Exposing him to the public would be a disaster at this age. Maybe it'll be okay when he's older; in fact, maybe it's inevitable. But not now. No, not yet."

Shakespeare suddenly walked into the kitchen and jumped onto the counter so that he was at eye level with us. Speaking to both of us yet primarily to me, he said, "I want to know what my IQ is."

"What brings this up?" I asked.

"The professor says we should have it tested."

"Does he?"

"I asked him how I would get it tested, and he said all I had to do was take a simple exam."

"That's true."

"When I asked him what the exam was like, he described the kinds of questions they asked. And you know what? The questions he described to me were exactly like the ones on the test you and the doctor gave me last year. Do you remember? Of course you do. That was an IQ test, wasn't it? You and the doctor tested my IQ."

"And if we did?"

"Then you both know what it is. Will you tell me what it is?"

"It's very high. Is that enough to satisfy you?"

"What's the number?"

"It was over 150."

"I mean exactly. What was the exact number?"

"I think it was 156."

"Wow, 156."

"Does that make you feel better?"

"It makes me feel like I'm smart. I mean, I always knew I was smart, and I can tell by the way I can figure out things, but to put a number on it, that means a lot. Can I tell the professor what my IQ is?"

"I suppose it won't do any harm."

"That's groovy."

"Groovy?"

"That's what the professor says when he likes something. And I like the professor. He's groovy too. He's going to teach me a lot."

Sword and Shield

Three months after I hired the professor, he came to me with a plan. I thought it was kind of crazy at first, but then the more I thought about it, the more I liked it. He wanted to take Shakespeare to a classical music concert, but he needed me to approve of his idea before he set the wheels in motion. Of course, as an animal, Shakespeare surely wouldn't be allowed into any respectable performing arts center. Can you imagine a monkey sitting in an audience between two nicely dressed patrons, listening politely to a symphony? The very idea of it was absurd and a little funny, but this wasn't exactly what the professor had in mind. His idea was to rent a wheelchair and sit in it, pretending to be a music-loving paraplegic going to a concert. He would bring Shakespeare along as his trained service animal, for he knew trained service animals had to be allowed in public places along with their owners. It was the law, a requirement of the Americans with Disabilities Act. The right to bring a service animal with you was written into the act, in black and white. There was no way a concert hall could turn them away, and Shakespeare would be allowed entry.

The professor picked a concert hall and then selected a night on which they were performing a Mozart piano concerto, a piece he thought Shakespeare would especially like. I told him that Sarah and I would like to come along, and he had no problem with this. When we all arrived at the center on the night of the performance, the professor rolled up in his wheelchair to the old lady at the entrance. Shakespeare was sitting on his lap, holding out his ticket, and she gave them the strangest look. She didn't take the ticket, instead saying, "I don't think we allow animals in the concert hall."

"This isn't just any animal," the professor said. "His name is

Shakespeare, and he's been specially trained to assist me. He's my service animal."

"But he's a monkey."

"Yes, you're very observant."

"I can't allow a monkey in here."

"Actually, you can, and you will. You can't turn away a service animal. It's against the law."

"Against the law?"

"That's what I said. It's against the Americans with Disabilities Act. Have you even heard of it?"

"Is there a problem here?" a man asked as he approached. He appeared to be a supervisor.

"This woman won't let us in."

"He wants to come in with his monkey," the woman explained.

"His name is Shakespeare. You can at least call him by his name."

"Is this a service animal?"

"I can't believe you're asking me that. Why else would I be sitting here in a wheelchair with a monkey on my lap? Do you think I'm sneaking him in so he can enjoy a little Mozart?"

"Calm down," the man said.

"Can we hurry things along?" I said. I was standing behind the professor with Sarah, pretending to be there on my own, acting like I was growing impatient. It was funny watching these people trying to sort out the situation.

Shakespeare held out the professor's ticket to the lady again. She looked at her supervisor, wanting to know whether she should take it.

"We have to let him in," the supervisor said.

"So you want me to take his ticket?"

"Yes, take it." Then to the professor, the man said, "I'm sorry for this misunderstanding, sir."

"It's cool," the professor said.

The lady took the ticket from Shakespeare's hand, and she scanned it and handed it back to him. It was a sight to behold. And that's how Shakespeare got to see his first classical music concert. Shakespeare turned his head to look at me after they'd been allowed in, and he had a smile on his face and a little twinkle in his eye. I think he enjoyed the professor's scheme to get him into the place as much as he was going to enjoy actual Mozart performance. Shakespeare liked the idea of having the professor as his advocate, always doing things like this for him. And I liked the professor too and the lengths to which he would go to educate my monkey. The professor was a good man.

After six months under the professor's thoughtful tutelage, Shakespeare was growing up and changing. I was impressed with the progress he was making in more ways than one. It wasn't just that he was learning facts, formulas, and concepts; he was also becoming more mature. He acted less like a mischievous monkey and more like a thoughtful adult. We still took walks along the beach together, but he no longer spent his time picking up shells and feathers or splashing in the water like a kid. Instead, he spent our time together talking to me about all he'd been learning and about subjects he'd been pondering. Yes, there was definitely a more serious air about him.

Then came the day of his great idea, his desire to write a book; he told me about it while we strolled along the sand. He said he missed that time when he had been allowed to submit articles for the newspaper; he enjoyed writing, and he had liked seeing his work published. He'd now like to write a book, he said, and see if he could get it published too. I asked him what he'd like to write about, and he made me promise not to laugh. Why would I laugh? Of course, I promised not to laugh, and he told me in some detail what he had in mind. I was impressed with the subject matter of his book and asked if he'd discussed any of it with Dr. Barney or the professor. He said that he had talked to both of them and that they had told him to ask me. Everyone knew how sensitive I was to the idea of Shakespeare going public in any way. I had been dead set against this idea for years and had done little to veil my concerns and feelings. Shakespeare was very eager to write this book, and he said, "It would be an immediate best seller, but only if everyone out there knew it was written by a monkey. I'd have to come clean with the public. They'd need to learn all about me."

Well, I guess I had known this day was coming. It was inevitable, wasn't it? How long had I thought I'd be able to keep Shakespeare's talents under wraps? He wanted to publish this book, and he wanted everyone to know precisely who had written it. Shakespeare seemed mature now, like a level-headed adult, but would he really be able to handle the pressures of taking himself public? It would be a three-ring circus, and it wouldn't affect just Shakespeare; it would change my life and Sarah's as well. I had no desire to be famous, yet I too would be in the spotlight as the owner of the monkey with the 156 IQ. Everyone would want to know about me and my monkey who'd just written a best-selling book. They'd want to talk to me, sticking their stupid microphones in my face and asking me to comment. They'd all want a piece of my monkey, following him like bloodhounds on a scent. News reporters would pester us at home, at restaurants, and at grocery stores. We'd be dodging the paparazzi night and day. Our names and faces would be plastered all over newspapers and magazines, and we'd be on the evening news. Was I overestimating the fallout? I don't think so. Shakespeare and his book would be big news all over the world, no matter how you looked at it, no matter what we did to play it down. Shakespeare would be an overnight sensation. These are the concerns that bounced around in my head like angry bees in a jar. As we continued to walk along the beach, the sun began to drop.

Shakespeare was growing impatient, and he wanted an answer from me. "Well?" he asked. "What do you think?"

"Let me talk to Sarah about it," I said.

"Can you talk to her tonight?"

"Yes, we'll talk tonight."

"You can decide before we go to bed?"

"Maybe."

"It's important to me."

"I know it is."

"I'm tired of pretending to be an ordinary monkey. I really am. I'm tired of keeping quiet. Think of how you'd feel if you were me, being required to keep all your thoughts and feelings to yourself. I love you, Marty, and I'll do what you say. But I want you to put yourself in my shoes. I truly want to write this book, and I want to publish it under my name, Shakespeare. And I want everyone in the world to know who I am."

So what was I supposed to do? I couldn't very well say no to him. I would talk to Sarah, but I already knew what our decision would be. We would stand behind Shakespeare's desire to write his book and let him take full credit for it. And in doing so, we would finally be letting the proverbial cat out of the bag, and the world would be introduced to its first genuinely intelligent capuchin monkey. And things would never be the same.

So Shakespeare went to work on his writing project. Are you curious to know what this book was about? The title was *Sword and Shield*. It took Shakespeare only three months to write the entire thing. He maintained his lessons with Dr. Barney and the professor during the day and wrote the book at night. When he handed me the manuscript, I was stunned. "You're done already?" I asked, and he nodded his head and grinned.

He told me he wanted me to be the first to read it, and I felt honored. I went into my home office, and setting the manuscript on my desk, I read every word. I was fascinated by his ideas, but honestly, I was terrified about what was going to happen when we found a publisher. Finding a publisher would be easy, for what publisher wouldn't jump at the chance to print the world's first book conceived and written by a monkey? But what exactly would happen to us? I've already told you some of my specific concerns. So would our little family of three be obliterated? Would Shakespeare survive the onslaught? Would Sarah and I make it through unscathed? Would there be anything left to salvage? There were so many questions to be answered, but enough about my concerns and worries; I still need to tell you what Shakespeare wrote.

Shakespeare was an observer of human beings. Monkeys and other animals didn't interest him at all, but he found humans fascinating. I think because of his intelligence, he identified with us. He'd done a lot of thinking on human-related subjects and had come to some conclusions, one of them being the subject matter of this book.

According to Shakespeare, humans—men specifically—were creatures of war. To his way of thinking, there was nothing more important to men than starting up and trying to win wars. War was more important than eating or breathing, more important than procreation. Men would give up everything just to fight their enemies, and they'd kill other men in every way imaginable. Sometimes they'd claim to hate what they were doing, yet the truth was that they loved every minute of it, every bloody second. This, according to Shakespeare, had always been the great preoccupation of humankind: taking sides, drawing lines in the sand. "So whose side are you on?" Isn't that the great question men always have to answer? Pick a side and fight for it, or be ridiculed as a scoundrel or weakling. It isn't a matter of right and wrong. There hasn't been a reason known to man that he hasn't used as an excuse to wage war against the other side. Men fight for freedom, and they fight to oppress. They wage war to take land away or get it back. They fight against other races or other states or other cultures. Always, it's the other side who started it and the other side who has been unreasonable, untrustworthy, overbearing, or just plain uncivilized. Have you ever seen a side in a war that thought it was wrong? If it wasn't such a bloody and destructive business, it would be hilarious, all this crazy finger-pointing. And the funny thing is that in the great scope of things, the viewpoints of the sides don't even matter. It isn't bad blood, history, greed, or religion that has caused wars. They occur because men love to fight, and they love to take sides. The truth is that it's the act of taking sides that matters to men, not what the sides themselves represent.

Shakespeare went on to explain how this longing to take sides permeates nearly every aspect of what humans do. "Just think about it," he wrote in his manuscript. "Think of how humans are expected to behave. They're to be either pro-this or anti-that, either a Democrat or a Republican, either a liberal or a conservative, either a communist or a capitalist, either a prosecutor or a defendant. There never seems to be any direct path toward constructive human behavior." Shakespeare said that most often there's no sensible, unbiased route toward any mutually beneficial goal, only opposing forces doing battle.

It's this splitting into factions and ideologies that causes humans so much grief when they try to solve problems. Everything becomes a fight, sides pitted against each other, men and women all raising their swords and shields to do battle with the opposition. But who exactly is this opposition, if not fellow humans? It's all one giant false dichotomy. If only people could see this, so many things could change for the better. The world could improve in leaps and bounds, for we all basically want the same things, don't we? We all want justice, peace, good health, morality, and prosperity. We want our laws to be fair, and we want everyone to follow them. There are so many things we agree on, yet the world is filled with so many opposing sides. Our problems are laughing at us, over the absurdity of the fact that we spend more time fighting ourselves than we do finding solutions. Shakespeare said we needed to learn that this business of taking sides is all wrong, that it's pointless and often destructive. If we really want to behave like the most intelligent animal on the planet, we need to stop inventing forces to fight each other and create forces that go more directly to the hearts of our problems. Despite what many say, it isn't more altruism or love we need. What we need is to put down our pitchforks and torches and actually work together using the brains God gave us.

I'm probably not doing Shakespeare's book justice with my summary here. I mean, it took Shakespeare hundreds of pages to get his point across, and I'm giving you only a couple of paragraphs of my own clumsy prose. And I am not a monkey, so unlike Shakespeare, I am not writing this from a monkey's point of view. I am a human, trying to explain how a monkey thinks, trying to describe what I read the day Shakespeare handed his manuscript to me.

Anyway, I did tell him that I thought it was amazing, that it should definitely be published. The question now wasn't whether we should get it published, but which publisher we should go to. I told Shakespeare we should meet with the largest, most respected publisher we could find; there was no way they'd reject a manuscript written by a monkey, especially one as interesting as his. So I got the address of Fisher & Sons in New York City and chartered a private jet. The jet was expensive, but it was better than dealing with the hassle and humiliation of subjecting Shakespeare to a commercial flight. I had called the publisher and set up a meeting with one of the editors. The person I spoke with sounded very skeptical and didn't exactly emote enthusiasm about the potential of the manuscript. But the idea of a monkey author was just too intriguing to ignore, so the publisher agreed to our meeting. I was sure the person they were having me see was low on the company's totem pole. But that was fine for now. At this point in time, anyone would do. Once they'd had a chance to meet with Shakespeare and talk to him, and once they had given his manuscript a reading, they'd be climbing all over each other to sign him up. I was sure of this.

The man we were to meet at Fisher & Sons was named Jason Trimble. When we arrived at the company's offices, I told the receptionist who we were, and she asked us to take a seat in the waiting area. We must have waited there an hour before Mr. Trimble finally came out to get us. "This must be the monkey," he said.

"This is Shakespeare."

"And that must be his manuscript." Trimble pointed to the papers I held in my hands.

"Yes, this is the manuscript," I said, and he asked that we follow him to his office.

He didn't seem exactly thrilled to see us, to have been given this strange assignment and told to see the man with the monkey who supposedly had written a book. "I don't have a lot of time," he said. "So we'll have to make this meeting brief."

"Okay," I said. I knew the meeting wouldn't be as brief as he thought, but I didn't argue with him. We just followed him into his little office. As I had figured, they'd handed us off to one of the company's lower-level editors. His office was small, tiny even. It was cramped and stuffed with a desk, a few old chairs, and several bookshelves. The desk was covered with other manuscripts, and there were Post-it notes stuck all over his walls. It was the sort of office you'd expect of someone who did the grunt work for the company and who met with writers the other editors didn't want to waste their time with. But this was okay, for we were getting our foot in the door. When this guy actually talked to Shakespeare and learned just what he had on his hands, everything would change. "You probably think I'm some kind of nut," I said.

Trimble wasn't paying attention to me, so I stopped talking. He was thinking about something else, but then finally he gave me his attention. "So this is the book-writing monkey," he said.

"Yes, this is Shakespeare."

"Of course his name is Shakespeare. Did you give him the name?"

"Yes, I did."

"Can he talk as well as write?"

"Of course he can talk."

Trimble looked at my monkey and decided to test him out. "Well, good afternoon, Shakespeare."

"Good afternoon," Shakespeare said.

"So you really can talk!"

"He's very intelligent," I said.

"So you wrote this manuscript?"

"Yes, I did."

Trimble looked at me curiously, maybe to be sure it wasn't a trick, to be sure I wasn't a ventriloquist throwing my voice. Then he looked back at Shakespeare. "You wrote this entire thing?"

"It took me about three months."

"Three months?"

"But it's a very interesting book."

"I read it myself," I said. "I think it's worth publishing."

You should have seen the look on the poor guy's face. "Just a minute," he said. He got on his phone and pressed a couple of buttons. "Get me Mr. Hayden," he said. "Tell him to come to my office right away." He hung up his phone. Then to Shakespeare he said, "So what kind of monkey are you?"

"I'm a capuchin."

"A capuchin?"

"An organ-grinder's monkey."

"So you were trained by an organ-grinder?"

"No, I haven't been trained by anyone."

"How'd you learn to talk?"

"I've been educated."

"Educated?"

"I have two teachers, Dr. Barney and the professor. They come over to our house."

"How old are you?"

"I'm five."

"Only five years old? And you've written a book?"

"He's very bright," I said.

"So he is," Trimble said, just as his office door suddenly swung open. A man stood in the doorway. "So this is the monkey?" he said.

"Listen to him talk, Mr. Hayden," said Trimble. "Ask him a question."

"You want me to talk to a monkey?"

"Just ask him a question."

"Okay, how are you?" Hayden asked Shakespeare, speaking very slowly, apparently assuming this was necessary for Shakespeare to understand.

"I'm doing great," Shakespeare said. "How are you doing?"

For a moment Hayden just stared. Then he turned to Trimble. "How does he do that?"

"He talks."

"You men have barely scratched the surface," I said. "Ask him something challenging."

"Like what?"

"Like anything."

"Okay," Hayden said. "What's the square root of nine?"

"It's three," Shakespeare said.

"And the square root of sixteen?"

"Four."

"Well, I'll be damned."

"Ask him something else."

Hayden thought for a moment and then asked, "Where is the Great Wall? I just got done reading a manuscript about the Great Wall."

"You mean the Great Wall of China?"

"Yes!" Hayden said.

"It's in China, of course. It was built to protect China from foreign invaders. It took around eighteen hundred years to put up, and it's about thirteen thousand miles long. And I'll bet I know something about the wall that you don't."

"Which is?"

"The recipe for the mortar they used included rice. Many experts believe that rice is one of the reasons for the wall's strength and longevity."

"Where the heck did you learn that?"

"I've learned a lot of things."

Trimble looked to Hayden. "What do you think?"

"Is this some kind of trick?"

"It's no trick at all," I said. "I told you guys over the phone that Shakespeare was special."

"Jesus, this is unbelievable. I mean, this is really stupendous," said Hayden.

"And he's written a book," Trimble said.

"Where is it?"

"Right here." Trimble showed his boss the manuscript.

"Can I read this?" Hayden asked.

"That's why we brought it," I said.

"Give me a few hours. Let me read what you have here. Then let's talk."

"Okay," I said.

"Come back tonight at five."

"So you're interested?"

"Oh yeah, I'm interested. Just give me a chance to read this manuscript. Have you talked to any other publishers?"

"No," I said.

"Good, let's keep it that way. We can talk in depth tonight."

A Star Is Born

Everything changed. I don't even know where to begin. Well, actually, yes, I do. I'll start at our meeting with Mr. Hayden, who now considered me a friend and wanted me to call him by his first name, Rudy. Shakespeare and I met him in his conference room. He'd just finished reading the manuscript and was all smiles and handshakes; in fact, I'd go so far as to say he was giddy. Rudy brought several others from Fisher & Sons with him in a show of force, including the publisher's attorney, Jefferson Pratt, who wanted us to call him Sonny. He was from the south and had an accent to go along with his heritage. There was also a stodgy older man with a bow tie named Henry Gilchrist and a middle-aged, well-dressed woman named Mollie Gum. Jason Trimble was there too, but apparently he no longer had much of a role in our project. It seemed the senior employees had taken over for him and Jason was just there to be quiet and learn. Jason sat off to the side, sipping a cup of coffee, while Rudy introduced his senior team to Shakespeare and me. It was funny watching these people shake Shakespeare's little hand, not knowing what to expect from him. When we were done shaking hands, Rudy sat down and said to Shakespeare, "We're very interested in your book."

"That's good to hear," Shakespeare said. I think Mollie actually gasped upon hearing him speak. I'm sure she'd been told that Shakespeare talked, but actually hearing him in person was surprising.

"We want to be your publisher."

"That's good to hear."

"So what exactly are you offering?" I asked. I was trying to remain businesslike and not overly enthusiastic. I didn't want any of them thinking they could take advantage of us. This was a reputable publishing company, but I still felt it best to stay on my guard.

"Yes, of course you want to know what we can do for you," Rudy said. "That's why I brought the others here to this meeting. They can explain the services our company offers. Mollie, for example, heads our marketing efforts, and Henry here is our chief editor. Sonny, of course, handles all our legal and contract issues. I think between the three of them and me, we'll be able to answer all your questions."

"This is good," I said. I then turned to Shakespeare and asked, "What do you think?"

"I think I'm hungry," he said.

"What time is it?"

"It's a little after five," Rudy said, checking his watch. "Do you two want something to eat? This meeting could take a while. Do you like Chinese food? There's a great little takeout place down the street, and we can send Jason to pick us up some dinner."

"That sounds good," I said.

"That works for me too," Shakespeare said. "I like Chinese food."

"Jason," Rudy said, "can you run down and pick up some dinner for us? Get enough for everyone."

Jason stood up to leave, and Rudy handed him several twenty-dollar bills. "Thanks, Jason," he said.

"I like spicy chicken," Shakespeare said. "Spicy chicken with peanuts. And I like fortune cookies. I don't like eating the actual cookies, but I like reading my fortune."

Rudy laughed at this and then said to Jason, "Be sure they give us some fortune cookies."

"Got it," Jason said, and he left the room.

Much of the meeting that followed wasn't very exciting, so I'll spare you most of the details. I will, however, tell you about a couple of interesting topics we covered. First, we discussed the editing, something Henry would be responsible for. Rudy said he'd briefly discussed the book with Henry, and both of them agreed that in this case it would be best to limit the editing and to make typo and spelling corrections only, leaving the rest of the text exactly as Shakespeare had written it. He said normally Henry would have suggestions regarding grammar, form, and content, but the fun in reading this book was going to be experiencing the voice of a monkey, not necessarily the polished product of an experienced editor. The rough patches in the book would give the writing its unique character and texture, and they didn't want to interfere with this. I said this made sense, but I also pointed out that Shakespeare was actually an excellent writer. Shakespeare nodded his head when I said this; he knew that he wasn't just some monkey playing around in his room with a word processor, that he was actually a talented writer who had produced a thoughtful and well-crafted book. And I knew he didn't like the implication that there were rough patches in his writing. Rudy quickly said that he had never meant to say Shakespeare wasn't a good writer. The others all nodded in agreement, even though none of them had even read the manuscript and had no idea what they were nodding their heads for. It was funny watching them try to deal with a monkey, trying to be so agreeable. The last thing they wanted to do was insult Shakespeare and lose his book to another publisher.

"There are no rough patches in my book," Shakespeare blurted out suddenly.

Rudy reiterated that yes, it had probably been a poor choice of words on his part; all he had meant to say was that all the manuscripts they published, even those from their very best writers, could always benefit from a little editing. Like I said, it was funny watching them bob and weave, trying to deal with my monkey. They were used to dealing with human writers, not furry little long-tailed creatures who could barely see over the top of the conference room table.

The second topic of interest we discussed was the marketing plan they envisioned. This was Mollie's area of expertise, and she said, "People are going to want to see Shakespeare for themselves, so we think the best way to make this happen is for him to appear on TV talk shows. We'd like to have Shakespeare do as many as possible."

I could tell Shakespeare liked this—the idea of becoming a TV celebrity—by the expression on his face.

"Everyone will be talking about you," Mollie said. "You will be a household name."

This was exactly what I was trying to avoid, but Mollie was right that we'd have to get Shakespeare into the public spotlight in order for his book to sell. Right now, no one even knew who he was. Once they saw him talking, laughing, and telling stories on their TVs, he'd be real, not just a zoological oddity. And once he was real, people would want to know what he had to say. I asked Mollie, just out of curiosity, whether she saw any book signings in Shakespeare's future, and she said the events were fun, but in her opinion they didn't do a lot to help. And Shakespeare, being as remarkable as he was, might attract too many people, more people than could be managed. When Mollie said this, it occurred to me how difficult our lives were likely to become, living with this bona fide celebrity. Mollie said that while we were on the talk show circuit, Fisher & Sons would provide security to protect Shakespeare from the public, but when the talk shows were over, it would be up to us to ensure his safety. I turned to Shakespeare and asked him if this was truly the route he wanted to go, having all these fans chasing after him, and I could tell he wasn't the slightest bit daunted. He just nodded his head and grinned.

"So I'm going to be famous," Shakespeare said to Mollie. "Everyone will know who I am?"

"Yes, they will."

"I like the idea."

"You may find it very annoying," I said.

"No, I'll like it. I'll definitely like it. Who doesn't want to be famous?"

"And all this fame opens the door for a second book," Mollie said.

"A second book?"

"You can write your autobiography."

"He's only five years old," I said. "What five-year-old writes an autobiography?"

Mollie ignored my question and said to Shakespeare, "An autobiography would sell like crazy. Everyone is going to want to know everything about you, from your early days as a baby in Marty's house to your life as a superstar."

"A superstar?" I asked.

"I think he'll be a superstar," Mollie said.

A superstar indeed. I hate to admit this, but Mollie was absolutely right. Once the book was released, and once we started doing the talk shows, Shakespeare was an immediate hit. The book started selling like crazy, breaking all sorts of sales records. When we were finished with the talk shows, we came back home to Corona del Mar. For the next several months, our lives were unbearable. People were constantly coming to the door, wanting to talk to Shakespeare, wanting to meet him in person.

There were news reporters, journalists, authors, and lots of crazy fans. The fans were the worst. They wanted photos of themselves standing with Shakespeare, autographs in their copies of his book. They wanted him to read things they'd written and get his opinion—maybe help them get published by pulling some strings. Some of them just wanted to talk to him, about all kinds of things, about current events, sports, and the arts, even about their personal problems. I mean, they didn't even know him, but they felt a connection, like they were somehow close friends. And if I hadn't known better, I'd say some of the female fans actually wanted a romantic relationship with him—yes, with a monkey. It was pretty weird. I'd never been around a celebrity before, and I was amazed at how all this happened. This lunacy went on for months, and then it finally began to die down, not completely but enough so that our lives became manageable again, moderately manageable anyway.

Then something happened that I had not expected at all. We got a call from a movie producer named Adolph Nelson, who wanted Shakespeare to star in a movie. He was producing a fourth version of *A Star Is Born*, except this variation would feature a monkey as the star. It was such a bizarre idea that I laughed when I heard it. When Adolph first began pitching the idea, I thought the call was a gag. But then I realized the man was serious, and I listened patiently and politely. This movie was going to be created specifically for Shakespeare. In other words, if Shakespeare said no, there would be no movie. The idea was that a famous American mystery writer would learn of a monkey like Shakespeare and purchase him from the original owner for himself. Although very successful, this author was a drug addict and alcoholic, on a path of self-destruction. But he wanted to teach this monkey to be a successful writer like himself, and when the monkey moved in with him, he worked to teach him everything he knew about the craft. He would introduce the monkey to publishers and editors and other writers he knew. The monkey would go on to have this amazing and successful career as a writer, thanks to the author, but while the monkey was enjoying this success, the author would continue his decline into his drug addiction and alcoholism. At the end of the movie, the author would die a tragic death from suicide. After I heard Adolph's pitch for this movie, I told him that I'd discuss the proposition with Shakespeare, that we'd give it some serious thought. And when I told Shakespeare about it, he told me he'd already seen two of the three other versions of this movie.

"It's clever," he said. "I think I'd like to do it."

You know, letting Shakespeare write and publish a book was one thing, but letting him star in a movie was another. Now he'd be hanging around all those movie types, and I wasn't sure this was what I wanted for him. Who knew what kind of influence they'd have? And already his studies with Dr. Barney and the professor had been delayed because of the book deal and all the talk shows we had done. Now we were talking about how many more months of putting aside his academics, and just to make a silly movie? On the other hand, acting in a film was likely to be an experience he'd never forget, a once-in-a-lifetime opportunity from which he'd surely learn a lot. And I knew how he loved movies; I remembered how he used to watch them every night on the sofa while I was sleeping. He was only five years old, yet for a monkey he was fully mature. And who was I to tell an adult monkey how to run his life? We discussed the pros and cons of the movie offer on and off for several days. We discussed them between ourselves, and we talked about the matter with Sarah. Finally, Shakespeare came to the conclusion that yes, he would like to be an actor. He wanted to give it a try. I asked if it would be all right with him for me to be with him during the filming, and he agreed to this. He wanted to be independent, yet he still wanted me by his side. In fact, he also wanted Dr. Barney and the professor to come. I guessed the three of us would serve as a kind of security blanket.

The project was to be filmed in Hollywood, so the four of us rented a house nearby while Sarah remained home in Corona del Mar. She was still very busy with school. It had been painful leaving her back at home while we did all those talk shows, and it was going to be equally hard to be away from her during the filming of Shakespeare's movie. The good thing about the movie, however, was that the set was only an hour or so away from home, so we'd be able to drive down to see Sarah on the weekends. When the filming started, Sarah was finishing her last undergraduate term, and the workload was intense. But the weekends were ours to enjoy, and we had a lot of fun taking day trips, eating out at restaurants, and sometimes seeing movies. Often we'd just hang around the house together. I was lucky to have found someone like Sarah to be in my life, for she never tried to mold me into something I wasn't. And she never complained about Shakespeare, even though my life revolved around him more now than ever. She had known Shakespeare was part of the deal when she married me.

The film shoot took about four months. I have no idea whether this is considered especially fast. I do know that the producer wanted to get the movie done and distributed as soon as possible, while Shakespeare was still a popular commodity. By the time the film made it to the theaters, Shakespeare was six years old. I can't even describe how excited he was when the film opened in our local theater. He wanted to go see the public's reaction, but of course when we took him to the theater, there was no way of disguising him. Everyone immediately knew who he was and crowded around us, asking for autographs and hoping to get pictures of themselves with Shakespeare using their camera phones. When the movie started, everyone took their seats and left us alone. We watched with the rest of the audience, and to be honest, the movie was pretty well done. Shakespeare had me get him a big bucket of popcorn, but he ate only about a third of it, his eyes being much bigger than his stomach. When the movie was over and the lights came back on, the whole crowd broke out in applause, knowing Shakespeare was still there. It was funny, how proud I was of my little monkey. I think Sarah felt the same way, very proud. We felt so important just being by his side, being the people who were closest to him and who would go home with him that evening. It was truly one of the more memorable evenings of our lives, and all we did was pay admission and sit through a movie.

It was after the movie that I began to fully appreciate just how popular Shakespeare had become. As Mollie had put it, he was a superstar. I don't know why it took so long to finally sink in for me. And I haven't even told you yet about all the fan mail. We were receiving a lot of it every day. Shakespeare was dedicated to reading every letter he received, and though he was still spending time on his studies with Dr. Barney and the professor, we decided to let him set aside three hours each day to read and respond to his mail. Most of the mail was very positive, but some of the letters were mean and malicious. And some were just sad. But Shakespeare responded to all of them, even the unpleasant ones. One letter he received was from a ten-year-old boy in South Carolina. According to Shakespeare, in the letter the kid said that Shakespeare had inspired him. I don't know why the kid felt inspired by a monkey—I never did get to read the actual letter—but that's how he felt. The boy had been diagnosed with a terminal brain tumor, and he spent hours in his hospital bed each day, hoping to get well. He had included with his letter a photo of himself; he was a very good-looking child, almost pretty. Shakespeare came to me with the photo in his hand and told me to charter a jet to take us to South Carolina, to see the boy. "I want to see him in person. I want to talk to him." I agreed to do this, knowing it was important to him. He said he didn't want anyone to know where we were going; the visit had to be a private affair. "I'm not doing this for any publicity. I just want to talk to the boy."

A week later we were in South Carolina, and we drove to the boy's hospital in a rental car. When we arrived, the boy's parents met us in the hallway. They thanked Shakespeare for coming and assured him they'd told the boy nothing about the visit. Shakespeare then went into the room alone while the rest of us waited in the hallway. I have no idea what Shakespeare said. None of us heard a word of the conversation. He had been in the boy's room for over an hour when the door finally opened and Shakespeare walked out.

"How'd it go?" the boy's mother asked.

Shakespeare told her only that she had a wonderful son and should be proud. We left the hospital and went back to the airport, and Shakespeare didn't say anything during the entire drive. We boarded the plane and flew back to Orange County. During the flight Shakespeare said only one sentence: "I'm a very lucky monkey, to be living this life." I never did ask Shakespeare what he and the boy talked about, and he never offered to tell me. I did receive a call from the boy's parents letting me know the boy had died, and when I told Shakespeare, he had no outward reaction. He just went to his room and shut the door. It occurred to me that I'd been living with him for over five years, and not once had I seen him cry. Could Shakespeare cry? I had no idea.

It's funny how you can live with someone for a long time and suddenly realize there are things you just don't know about him or her. This was sometimes the case for me with Shakespeare. I guess you could also say it was true with Sarah. I mean, for all the time we'd been married, Sarah's plan following college had been to become a writer. She didn't just want to write ordinary novels; she wanted to write something that would make people stand and take notice. This was her dream, and I honestly couldn't imagine her doing anything else. But there was something about her I didn't know, something I guess even she didn't know. When we were first married, I had turned one of the bedrooms at our house into an office for her, and she had initially used it to do her schoolwork. It was a perfect room with a great little window that looked out over the garden in our backyard. The plan was for her to use this room for her writing when she graduated from school, and that's precisely what she did, spending months in there working at her computer, presumably typing the words to the next great American novel. But I would discover after the sixth month that she was getting nowhere, that she hadn't written a thing. She'd start a project, write the first few chapters, and then abandon the idea. Then she'd start another project and do the same thing. She did this over and over, so that after six months of effort, she had produced absolutely nothing. She finally came to me and revealed that she no longer wanted to be a writer. I was shocked, for I'd had no idea this was going on.

I'd like to be able to tell you I helped Sarah, but it was Shakespeare who actually came to her rescue. We were eating dinner and talking about her problem when Shakespeare said to her, "You should be an editor, not a writer."

"An editor of what?" Sarah asked.

"An editor of anything. You love to read. You love to critique. Isn't that what you did all those years in college? You need to be an editor."

"I wouldn't even know where to begin."

"Only because you haven't been looking. You've been looking for something to write. You should have been looking for something to edit."

"He has a good point," I said.

"I can get you a job as an editor," Shakespeare said.

"You can?"

"As sure as I like bananas."

"Where?" I asked.

"Isn't it obvious?"

"Actually, no."

"With my publisher, Fisher & Sons. We'll get Rudy to hire her."

"How will you do that?" Sarah asked.

"We won't give him a choice."

I laughed at this. "You can't just walk in and demand that Rudy hire her."

"I can if we have leverage."

"Such as?"

"My new book."

"You're going to write another book?"

"It's already written."

I had no idea what Shakespeare was talking about. "When have you found time to write another book?" I asked.

"I've been working on it every day. You just haven't been paying attention."

"What's the title?"

"I don't know yet."

"What's it about?"

"It's about everything."

"You're not making any sense."

"I've been thinking about this idea for weeks. We'll compile the letters I've been receiving from fans and add all my responses. I've saved every one of them on my laptop. I have a record of every piece of fan mail I've received and every reply I've sent. We'll pick and choose the best, put them all together, and voila, we'll have a best-selling book. I'm sure Rudy will like this. In fact, he'll be thrilled."

"You're sure of this?"

"I'm positive."

"Yes, it might work."

"But we give the project to Rudy under one firm condition."

"That he hire Sarah?"

"Exactly."

"I don't know," Sarah said.

"And her first project will be to edit this book. She can help me put everything together."

"It's perfect," I said.

"Rudy owes us. He knows it. His company made a fortune off my first book."

"Aren't their offices in New York?" Sarah asked. "How will I work for them?"

"You can work here out of our house," I said. "Since when do you need to be in a physical office to edit books? You might have to fly out there once in a while to meet with authors, but we can come with you. I like visiting New York."

"So do I," Shakespeare said. "Let's call Rudy tomorrow."

"You don't think Rudy will be resentful?"

"At what?"

"At being forced to hire me?"

"Rudy's a team player," I said. "Besides, once he sees what you can do, he'll be thanking us for bringing you to him."

"Yes, he'll be thanking us," Shakespeare said. Then he jumped up and down on his chair and clapped his hands. I know I said he'd matured, but he still did this when he was especially excited.

Nebraska

Sarah's parents had been out to California several times since her twenty-first birthday, but we'd never made it back to Nebraska to visit. We felt it was time to do this, so the three of us packed our bags and boarded a chartered jet. The trip wasn't just for Sarah; I wanted to see where she had grown up. And I was hoping to meet a few of her old high school friends. She'd told me stories about them, but I'd never met any in person. I thought the trip would be fun. I'd never even been to Nebraska, or anywhere else nearby. In fact, except for New York, I'd never been anywhere east of Arizona.

Tom met us at the airport in his gigantic Ford pickup truck. Wow, what a beast this thing was, much larger than anything he'd actually ever need. You'd think he was a farmer or construction worker, not just the owner of a simple hardware store. Judy hadn't come with Tom; she was at the house waiting for us. Tom and Shakespeare had grown fond of each other during Tom's last few visits to California, and Tom now called Shakespeare Bill, as in William, as in William Shakespeare. Tom looked in his rearview mirror so he could see Shakespeare in the back seat. "Bill," he said, "have you been taking good care of my daughter?"

"Oh yes," Shakespeare said.

"And has Marty been behaving himself?"

"He's a good husband."

"That's what I like to hear."

"Did you know Shakespeare got Sarah a job?" I asked.

"Did he now?"

"Yes, Daddy, he did," Sarah said.

"And how'd he do that?"

"He got me a job working for his publisher. I'm now an associate editor for one of the most reputable publishers in the country."

"You're okay with her working?" Tom asked me, as if he expected me to have a problem with it.

"Yes, I'm okay with it."

"Your mom will be happy to hear about this. She's been worried about you having nothing to do."

"I have plenty to do."

"And how about you, Marty? Are you still working for that scholarship fund?"

"Yes," I said. "They keep me busy."

"And what about Bill? Do you still have that doctor and professor coming over to the house?"

"They come over."

"Good, good," Tom said. Seemingly pleased with the answers, he turned on a country music radio station.

It was about a twenty-minute drive from the airport to Sarah's parents' home. Their neighborhood was just as I'd envisioned, a tract of nice little plain-Jane houses, each with its own front lawn, trees, and assorted flower beds. There was nothing out of the ordinary. Tom pulled his truck into the driveway, and we all jumped out and walked to the front door. Judy was there to greet us, holding the door open. She had a great big smile on her face and an apron around her waist. "How was your flight?"

"Everything went great," Sarah said.

"I need to use the bathroom," Shakespeare said, raising his hand.

"It's down the hall and to the left."

"Thanks," he replied, and he ran through the house and down the hallway, closing the big bathroom door behind him.

"I'll have dinner ready soon. I hope you're all hungry."

"I could eat a horse," I said.

"The place looks exactly the same as it did when I left for school," Sarah said. She was looking around at the inside the house.

"We haven't changed a thing," Tom said.

"That picture on the mantel is new," Judy pointed out.

Sarah walked over to the fireplace and picked up the framed picture. It was a family shot of all of us, including Shakespeare, from one of the times they had visited us in California. Sarah showed the photo to me. It had been taken at the beach.

"I remember that day," I said. "I remember the guy who took the picture. That was before Shakespeare was famous, when we could walk down the beach without attracting a hundred people."

"The good old days," Sarah said.

"Yes," I agreed.

Having finished in the bathroom, Shakespeare appeared from the hallway. "When's dinner?" he asked.

"It's just about ready," Judy replied.

"I'm starving."

Judy had cooked chicken pot pies for us, not the little factory-produced ones from the freezer section of the grocery store, but real, full-sized, homemade chicken pot pies. Everyone was in a good mood at the table, and we talked a lot while we ate. Tom had made Shakespeare his own booster seat so that he could eat with us at the table. Shakespeare got a big kick out of this, and Tom told us he'd made two of them, one to keep at their house for our visits and one we could take home with us. "Now Bill can sit down when he eats, like a regular person," Tom said.

I thanked Tom for making the seats, and so did Shakespeare.

"Samantha called a couple hours ago," Judy said to Sarah. "She wanted to know if you were here yet, and I told her no. I told her you'd be arriving soon and you'd call her when you got here."

"I'll call when we're done with dinner. We're going out with her tonight."

"I think she's looking forward to seeing you. She sounded excited."

"Sam and I haven't seen each other for five years. I wonder if she looks the same."

"Oh, she does. I saw her a couple months ago, at the grocery store. She's the same lovely girl. We talked a little, and she told me she's still working at Jack's Café as a waitress. She doesn't have a steady boyfriend, but she has her own apartment. She said she's saving up for a car. Where are you going tonight?"

"Don't know yet."

"Do any of your other friends know you're here?"

"Sam's the only one I called."

"Maybe she told them."

"Maybe," Sarah said.

"I wonder whatever happened to Richard," Tom said. "Are you going to see him?"

"No, of course not," Sarah said.

"You had such a crush on him," Judy said.

"He was a nice kid," Tom said. "Wasn't he going to work for his father?"

"Yes, last I heard."

"So there've been other men in your life?" I asked jokingly.

"Oh, she had quite a thing for Richard," Judy said. "But she couldn't seem to get him interested in her. The only time he came over here was to pick up something from Tom for his father once. Sarah thought he'd come over to see her."

"Oh, Mom."

"I like this chicken pot pie," Shakespeare said, changing the subject.

"Yes, it's great," I agreed.

"I thought you boys would appreciate a little home cooking. It's one of Tom's favorites."

"I'll admit it," Tom said. "Your mom spoils me with her cooking."

When we were done with dinner, Sarah gave her friend Samantha a call, and they decided we'd pick her up and go out somewhere. Tom said we could take his truck, which was a little daunting since I'd never driven anything so monstrously big. Tom said it drove just like a car, except that it took up a little more space on the road. "You'll get used to it," he told me, handing me the keys.

We then left the house. It turned out that Samantha lived in an apartment building on the other end of town. The building was kind of run-down and looked like it'd been built thirty or forty years ago by someone who didn't care what it looked like. But this was typical of Sarah's hometown. Things weren't new and shiny like they were in California, and they lacked style. Apparently, Nebraska was where all the less talented architects moved after graduating from college, or maybe people just didn't care what their buildings looked like. In either case, this was the impression I had.

We walked up to Samantha's porch and rang her doorbell. She

answered, and she was even prettier than Sarah had described. She was wearing a tank top and jeans, and her blonde hair was half tied back in a ponytail and half falling about her lovely face. She had the most marvelous blue eyes and a wonderful casual air about her. It was easy to like this girl, and I could see why she and Sarah were friends. The first thing she noticed, of course, was Shakespeare. "So this is the little monkey," she said.

"This is Shakespeare," Sarah said.

Samantha kneeled down to Shakespeare's level. "I've been wanting to meet you."

Well, if monkeys could blush, Shakespeare's face would've been bright red. I could tell he was immediately in awe of this attractive girl. "Hi," he said.

"I saw your movie," said Samantha.

"You did?"

"Everyone in town has seen it. Everyone knows who you are."

Shakespeare said nothing, and Samantha stood up and spoke to all of us. "Where should we go tonight?"

"I don't know," Sarah said.

"Why don't we go to the high school? We can sit on the front steps, like old times. Maybe we can grab a six-pack of Coke from the grocery store. We can sit on the steps and catch up. How long has it been? Five years?"

"Yes," Sarah said.

"So this is your husband. You told me his name, but I forgot it."

"My name is Marty."

"Yes, Marty. I always knew Sarah would bring home a winner."

"I don't know about that," I said. I was acting demure, but I actually liked the compliment. I looked forward to getting to know Samantha better.

"I see you brought your daddy's truck."

"Yes," Sarah said. "Marty's driving it."

"Do they have trucks like that in California?"

"Not many," I said.

"Well, let's go, shall we? No reason to hang around this dump."

"Okay," Sarah said.

As we walked toward the truck, Samantha said to Sarah, "I'm just so happy you're here. I can't believe we're together again. You should come back here more often."

"I should," Sarah said.

We hopped in the truck, with Sarah and me sitting up front and Shakespeare and Samantha sitting in the back. We stopped at the grocery store and bought some Cokes and a bag of potato chips and then drove to the high school. No one was there, and I parked the truck along the sidewalk. We walked to the front of the school building and sat on the steps. It was an ugly old school and looked more like a strip shopping center without any tenants. There were flower boxes on each side of the staircase, but there were no plants or flowers in them. "This is a nice spot," I said, trying to be polite.

"Sam and I used to sit here all the time, talking. It kind of became our place."

"We'd spend hours here," Samantha said, "mostly talking about boys."

"Open the chips," I said.

"Here," Sarah said. "Open them yourself. You're the one who wanted them."

All this time, Shakespeare was seated beside Samantha, looking up at her. He was usually more talkative, but something about Samantha had him tongue-tied. If I hadn't known better, I'd have thought he was smitten with her. He just sat there staring. She didn't seem to mind.

"Sarah, do you remember Mr. Barkley?" Samantha asked.

"Of course I do. He was our American history teacher."

"Guess who he's marrying?"

"Who?"

"Nicole Manchester."

"Are you serious?"

"Who's Nicole Manchester?" I asked.

"She was in our class, a cheerleader."

"Did they know each other in school?" Sarah asked.

"Of course they did."

"I mean, did they really know each other?"

"What do you think?"

"So how old is he now?"

"He's in his late thirties, at least."

"How weird."

"Do you remember Nicole's little brother, Bobby? He had all those freckles on his face."

"Sure, I remember him."

"He married Sally Paxton."

"The girl with the lisp?"

"Yeah, that's her. She works at the grocery store now. She's a cashier. She still has the lisp. You should hear her try to talk to the customers. They all pretend not to notice."

The group was quiet for a moment, and then Sarah asked, "What ever happened to Richard?"

"Ah, the old flame," I said. "Sarah's parents warned me about him."

Samantha laughed and then said, "He works for his father. He looks like he's aged twenty years. Isn't holding up too well. You're lucky you never got serious with him."

"Do you remember when I tried to get him to drive me home from that party at Melissa Atherton's house?"

"Yes, I remember that."

"What happened?" I asked.

"We were all at a party," Sarah said. "It was during our senior year, and Richard was there by himself. For some reason he hadn't come with any friends that night. Usually, he was with his buddies, but that night he was alone. Sam and I concocted this perfect scheme to have Richard drive me home from the party. Sam and I had come in her father's car. But I needed to make it appear she couldn't take me home, so we lifted the hood of the car, and with a wrench Sam found in the trunk, she disconnected the cable from the battery. We then closed the hood and went back to the party. When eleven thirty rolled around, we hung out in the front yard, waiting for Richard to leave. When we saw him saying good-bye to Melissa at the front door, we ran to the car and made it look like we were trying to start it.

"As Richard walked by, we said hi to him. 'What are you girls doing?' he asked. We said we were trying to start the car, but the engine wouldn't turn over. We told him that Sam had called her dad but that she couldn't get a hold of him. We also told him I had to get home, that I was late for my curfew. I asked Richard if he could please give me a ride. Rather than give me a ride, the dope told Sam to unlatch the hood, and she did. He lifted the hood and looked at the engine. 'Your battery isn't connected,' he said. 'The cable has come loose.' He then attached the cable and tightened the nut with his hand. 'Try it now,' he said. Sam hopped in the car and turned the key, and of course the car started right up. 'You should probably get a wrench and tighten it more, or it will probably come loose again.' Richard shut the hood, and I just stood there staring at him. 'Thanks,' Sam said. 'Yeah, thanks a million,' I said. Richard said it was no problem, and he smiled and walked away. He was completely clueless."

"He used to be so handsome."

"He was an idiot," Sarah said.

"Do you remember Andy Briar?" Samantha asked.

"Sure, I remember Andy."

"He was my first crush."

"I didn't know that."

"That's because I never told anyone."

"I don't remember you even going out with him."

"I never did."

"Where is he now?"

"He moved to San Francisco."

"When did he do that?"

"Right after we all graduated. He was gay."

"How do you know?"

"He told me."

"He told you? When?"

"Last year. I was working, waiting tables at Jack's, when Andy came in to the restaurant. He was with another man, a very attractive man. He'd come to visit his family. They sat near the window, and I stepped up to take their orders. 'Do you remember me?' I asked, and Andy said 'sort of,' which I figured meant no. I told him my name and then said I'd had a crush on him in high school. He laughed and said, 'It wouldn't have done us much good. Didn't you know I was gay?' I told him I had no idea, and I think I blushed. I don't know if I was embarrassed that he was gay or embarrassed that I'd had a crush on him. I guessed that this man he was with was his partner, and the scene suddenly felt strange to me. I mean, I'm as open-minded as the next girl about this sort of thing, about people being gay, but the idea of Andy kissing and fondling this man he was with made me feel uncomfortable. I guess it's one thing to accept gay people in general, but another to have them sitting right before your eyes. Anyway, I served them their lunches and said good-bye to Andy when they left. I noticed Andy had left me a rather measly tip, next to nothing. Are gay men cheap in general, or was it just him? I don't know, but I wished I hadn't seen him that day. I used to have such nice memories of Andy."

"He could've at least tipped you well," Shakespeare said.

"You'd think so, wouldn't you?"

"If you waited on me, I'd give you a big tip."

"No offense, but do they even allow you into restaurants?"

"Yes, some of them."

"Did I tell you I liked your movie?"

"I think so," Shakespeare said.

"I think you're a good actor. You did a really good job. What was the name of the monkey you played?"

"Able."

"Yes, Able the Monkey. He was very likable."

"Thanks."

"Do you have a girlfriend, Shakespeare?"

"No, I don't."

"Don't Marty and Sarah let you bring home girl monkeys?"

"I don't like them."

"You don't like girl monkeys?"

"They're dumb. They can't even talk. They don't even know how to use a toilet. I like people instead."

"You poor thing."

"I get to meet lots of nice people."

"But no girlfriend."

"You could be my girlfriend—you know, while we're visiting."

Samantha laughed. "Yes, I'll be your girlfriend."

Shakespeare liked this idea, perhaps more than Samantha realized. I could tell he liked this girl, and he smiled at her, wanting her to smile back at him.

Instead she looked at Sarah and asked, "You know who else I liked in high school?"

"Who?"

"Gabe Hardy."

"I remember Gabe. Didn't he take you to the prom?"

"Yes, I thought I might have a chance with him. His dad was a doctor. He had a good family."

"What ever happened to Gabe?"

"He's living with Nancy Rogers. They're not married, but they're living together. They have a one-year-old baby."

"Oh my."

"You know what he told me on prom night? He said I was the prettiest girl in the school. He said he loved my eyes. He didn't say he loved me, but he said he loved my blue eyes. He said he'd wanted to go out with me ever since he was a sophomore, but he couldn't get up the nerve. He thought I'd turn him down, so all that time he'd kept his distance. Then he said he'd realized school was about to end and he'd have to either ask me to the prom or regret it for the rest of his life. So he finally got up the nerve, and of course, I said yes. I'd always thought he was such a good-looking boy. And he seemed to have nice manners and a decent sense of humor.

"But do you know what he tried to do to me on prom night, when he drove me home? I never told you about this. Instead of driving me to my house, he drove us to the cornfields, to a little dirt road where he parked and turned off the lights. When I asked him what we were doing there, he just said, 'What do you think?' Then he reached over to put his arms around me and tried to kiss me. I tried to push him away, but he just said, 'Come on.' He did this about three times in a row and then put his hand on my leg and tried to slide it up under my prom dress. I told him to stop, but he just kept saying, 'Come on.' He was kissing me and saying it at the same time. I wasn't sure what to do. I didn't want to hit him, since he'd been so nice to me all night. I didn't know how to tell a boy I liked him but didn't want to have sex. Finally, I put my hands on his chest and shoved him back hard. 'You have to stop,' I said. 'I don't want to do this.' I looked him right in the eyes. I could tell I'd hurt his feelings, and for a moment he just stared back at me, his lips all wet from kissing me. Then he said he was sorry and started the car back up. 'I thought you liked me,' he said. I told him I did like him but that I just didn't want to get physical, not that night. Maybe it was a mistake. Maybe I should've let him have his way. I honestly don't know. It's not like I didn't think he was attractive, but it just didn't seem right at the time. He drove me home, and neither of us talked. When we reached my house, I said good night and told him I'd had a nice time at the dance. He didn't say a word, and I closed the car door.

"The next day was brutal, since he was in my chemistry class. It seemed like we both spent the entire hour avoiding eye contact with each other. I felt bad about that evening for weeks, until I discovered what he'd said to his friends; he told them the two of us had gone all the way. At first I was going to confront him, but I thought better of it. I decided to just let it slide, you know, like water under the bridge. What would be the point? Who would believe me? It would be my word against his, and he wasn't known to be a liar. In fact, he had a great reputation. Fortunately, his lie never made it beyond his circle of friends; none of them felt inclined to tell anyone else."

"You never told me about any of this," Sarah said.

"I was embarrassed."

"It wasn't your fault."

"No, I know that now."

"How many other things haven't you told me about?"

"I don't know."

"I thought we told each other everything."

"It's easier to talk about now that we're older, now that it doesn't mean so much. When we were younger, everything seemed so important, like life-or-death."

"Yes, it seemed that way."

"I'm glad I was never a girl," I said.

"Me too," Shakespeare added, and everyone laughed. Then he said to Samantha, "If I was your boyfriend, I'd take good care of you."

"You are my boyfriend, remember?"

"Oh yeah," Shakespeare said, smiling. "Well, you're safe with me."

Everyone laughed again, and then we continued to talk, sipping our Cokes and eating potato chips. We stayed on the steps talking until around midnight. By then, Shakespeare was sound asleep, with his head in Samantha's lap. I hated to wake him up, but we couldn't very well stay there forever.

"I guess we should call it a night," Sarah said.

"It's been fun," Samantha said.

"Yes," I agreed.

I picked Shakespeare up and carried him to the truck, where I put him on the back seat. We then drove back to Samantha's apartment. It was a quiet drive, and there weren't many cars on the streets. By the time we dropped Samantha off, Shakespeare was awake. We said good-bye to Samantha, and I drove away.

Shakespeare leaned forward from the back seat. "She's beautiful, isn't she?"

"What?" Sarah laughed.

"I mean, for a human. She's considered beautiful, isn't she?"

"Yes, she's an attractive girl," I said.

"I like her."

"I like her too," Sarah said.

"I mean, I really like her a lot."

"And she liked you."

When we returned to California, I noticed a change in Shakespeare's mood. He wasn't depressed, but he was very pensive. There was definitely something on his mind, and it turned out to be Samantha. I figured he was experiencing his first crush on a girl, a girl who just so happened to be human. Sarah and I talked about this when Shakespeare wasn't nearby, trying to figure out the best way to deal with the situation. Neither of us came up with a good idea. In the meantime, Shakespeare asked us to get him a photo of Samantha that he could put on the wall of his room. We weren't sure whether we should say yes, and then Shakespeare asked for even more—he wanted Samantha's mailing address so he could write her a letter. What kind of letter would he write? Shakespeare certainly wasn't stupid. He had to know that pursuing a close relationship with Samantha was futile. But love makes people do and think strange things, and I honestly think Shakespeare believed he was in love with her. Sarah and I decided that we'd speak to Shakespeare together. We sat down with him on the front-room sofa.

"We need to talk to you about something," I said.

"So talk," Shakespeare said.

"I'm not sure how to say this without hurting your feelings."

"Just say it. I won't get hurt. I know you'd never do anything to hurt me."

"It's about Samantha."

"Oh, Samantha," he said, and his cooperative mood seemed to change.

"We don't want to hurt you," Sarah said.

"Then say what you have to say."

"You need to stop thinking about her."

"Stop thinking about her?"

"Maybe not completely," I said. "But we think you might be thinking about her a little too much."

Shakespeare thought for a moment and then said, "I don't really see how this is any of your business."

"We care about you," Sarah said.

"Yes, we do," I agreed.

"Maybe I don't want you to care about me."

"I don't believe that," I said.

"No, you're right. But I don't want you telling me whom I'm allowed to think about. What if I told you two to stop thinking about each other?"

"That would be different," I said.

"Different how?"

"We're both human beings."

"So monkeys and humans can't care for each other?"

"That's not exactly what we're saying."

"Then what are you saying?"

"We're saying your affection for Samantha may be more intense than you can handle."

"That doesn't make any sense."

"When she said she'd be your girlfriend for a night, she was just kidding around."

"Kidding around? As in playing a joke on me?"

"No, as in kidding around," Sarah said. "Like mutual kidding around, being playful."

"The way friends do," I added.

"Of course. I knew that," Shakespeare said. He said this so confidently, but did he really mean it? Or was he just trying to save face? "You're telling me something I already knew."

"We weren't sure if you knew," I said.

"And we don't want you to get hurt."

"Do I sound hurt?"

"I don't know," I said.

"I think you guys have too much time on your hands." Shakespeare then stood up and started to walk out of the room.

"Where are you going?" I asked.

"To my room. I have a lot of studying to do. The professor gave me a ton of homework for this week." He then went to his room and closed the door behind him.

"How do you think we did?" I asked Sarah.

"I think he's hurting."

The Ninth Letter

S hakespeare brooded for days. And there's nothing worse than a brooding monkey. Monkeys should be jubilant and playful, but he was disinterested and morose. We knew why he was unhappy, but we didn't dare talk about it. He spent most of his time in his room working on his studies, trying to forget Samantha. Then, like the sunlight bursting out from behind a storm cloud, he shone again. It was such a sudden change, and I never did figure out what prompted it. But he was now happy and inquisitive and full of energy. Yes, he was back to normal. He seemed to have come to his senses, like so many of us have to do, accepting his lot in life and possibly realizing it wasn't such a bad lot after all.

Meanwhile, I got another letter from a man named Evan Johnson. I haven't yet told you anything about Evan for I'd been keeping his correspondence to myself, even keeping it from Sarah. I was the only person who knew about his letters, which I'd been receiving for the last several years. He'd also tried to call me several times, but I always told him I didn't want to talk and hung up. I didn't want to speak with him, and I didn't want to write him back.

Evan Johnson's letters were printed on UCLA letterhead. They were very official-looking and were meant to be taken seriously. Evan was a professor at the university, and he was interested in Shakespeare. He wasn't just a little interested, but a lot interested. In fact, he was sort of obsessed with my monkey, and he wanted Shakespeare to come to the university to be observed and educated. According to Evan, the university was where Shakespeare should be. The school had so much to offer, with all its facilities, professors, and departments. He said that what I was trying to do with Dr. Barney and the professor was admirable but that a university setting would improve Shakespeare's growth tenfold. This letter was the ninth I'd received from Evan; I had thrown all the others away. As always, I read the letter in its entirety, curious to see whether there was anything new.

Dear Mr. Anderson,

I am writing again about your remarkable monkey. You haven't responded to my previous letters, or to any of my phone calls, but I'm not going to throw in the towel. I'm going to keep writing and calling, hoping you'll eventually come to your senses and realize what's best for your animal. You must understand that your monkey isn't just a casual oddity, but a true wonder of science, a once-in-a-lifetime spark of intelligence that deserves to be nurtured and explored in the best and most advanced environment. While I can see why you're motivated to take on this responsibility yourself, there are things we can do here at the university that far exceed your capabilities. I know you only want what's best for Shakespeare, and I know you wouldn't deliberately do anything to hold him back from achieving his full potential. But you are depriving him of something inarguably important and beneficial. As I've explained in my previous letters, putting Shakespeare under our care would not mean divorcing you from his life. On the contrary, we would be willing to work with you in all ways possible to ensure that you maintain a good and loving relationship with him, including regular visits to your home, outings with you and your wife, and whatever else makes you comfortable during his stay here. Our goal is not to take your marvelous monkey away from you; rather, our goal is to help both of you.

I understand that right now you have Shakespeare under the guidance of a local psychologist and a professor from a community college. That's a good start, but think of what he'd be able to learn under the tutelage of some of the finest minds in the country. That's what we offer here at the university, some of the country's smartest men and women. I'm confident we can work something out with you, if only you would respond to my attempts to reach you. Think of what's best for this animal—and what's best for you. Please call me so we can discuss this matter further.

This letter from Evan wasn't much different from his previous letters. It was the same message, with slightly different wording. The university wanted more than anything to get its hands on Shakespeare. UCLA wasn't the only university that had approached me, but it was certainly the most persistent. My fears about sending Shakespeare to a place like UCLA were powerful and probably well founded. I didn't want Shakespeare to become an academic institution's guinea pig, poked and prodded by medical doctors and PhDs, constantly tested and analyzed. And that's exactly what they would do. They didn't really want to educate or care for Shakespeare; they wanted to perform a sort of living autopsy on him and find out what made him tick, what made him capable of thinking like a human being. I myself wasn't concerned with what made him tick or think; I was determined to see that he led a rewarding and challenging life without other people's meddling. I didn't want everyone sticking their noses into every facet of his business. Shakespeare was like a little person to me, and to my way of thinking, he deserved to be happy like the rest of us.

After reading this latest letter from Evan, I set it down on the kitchen counter and moved on to my other mail. There were about eight fan-mail letters to Shakespeare, which I set aside for him. There was a bill from the electric company, an explanation of our health care coverage for a doctor's visit I'd recently made, and a flyer from a local real estate broker. Meanwhile, Sarah had been working in her office that afternoon on Shakespeare's latest book, the compilation of fan letters he'd talked Rudy into publishing. Sarah had been working hard on the project for days as its editor. She came into the kitchen to ask me a question. Actually, she had several questions. She wanted to know what I thought of three particular letters that Shakespeare wanted included in the book. She felt they might be too controversial and wanted a second opinion.

"Can you read them and give me your thoughts? I can't decide whether they're appropriate."

I followed Sarah into her office, and she pulled the first letter up on her computer. It was from a young girl in Phoenix who wanted Shakespeare's thoughts on the possibility of getting an abortion. She wrote,

> This is kind of silly, isn't it? Writing to a monkey for advice? But a lot of the kids at my high school have read your book, and I read it too. And I saw your movie. I think you're very smart, not just for a monkey, but I mean really smart. I think you can help me, so I'll tell you my situation. Last week I discovered I was pregnant, and I can't decide what to do. I've always been against abortion, I guess because my parents say they're against it, and so does our church. Abortion is murder, isn't it? Would you call it murder, taking a baby's life for the convenience of its parents?
>
> But now that I am pregnant, I'll be honest with you. I don't want to give birth to this baby, and I certainly don't want to be responsible for raising it. I'm too young. I'm only seventeen years old. I mean, sure, I'm old enough to get pregnant, but I'm not old enough for the responsibility that goes along with having a child. I'm sure of this, so I'm now considering an abortion. I have no idea how to go about getting one, but I know a girl at school who did this, and she seems to be doing fine. Is it really murder to end a pregnancy when it's unwanted? Would I be committing a horrible sin if I went through with this procedure? You are not a human being, and you are not committed to one side or the other. Like you said in your book, it's pointless to pick sides. But that's what people seem to do. All they do is fight and argue without really caring how the pregnant girl feels. I just need a rational and moral opinion from someone who is thoughtful and intelligent, not someone who is on one side or the other. So I guess I'm asking you, what do you think I should do? Should I get an abortion? I know you're probably very busy, but the sooner you can

write back to me, the better. Your opinion will mean a lot to me, and I need to make a decision.

"So what did Shakespeare have to say?" I asked.
"Read his reply. It's right here."
"Is he pro-abortion?"
"No, I wouldn't say that."
"Does he think she should keep the baby?"
"No, he doesn't say that either. Just read." Sarah had me look again at her computer monitor, and I saw what Shakespeare had written to the girl.

> My dear, you are debating whether it's appropriate for you to kill your unborn child. To kill or not to kill— that seems to be the question. Listen, is it any wonder you're struggling with this problem? Is it any surprise you're having difficulty making up your mind? Just look at the violent world around you, at the way things are, at the way they've always been. People say life is sacred, yet what do they do? They arm themselves to the teeth. Do you have any idea how many handguns and rifles are owned by your neighbors? Do you know how many billions of dollars, francs, rubles, yen, and pounds are spent worldwide just to give governments the ability to kill? It's a human obsession, this killing thing. Yes, I know, humans have this lofty and incontrovertible idea that life is sacred, yet how much weight does this assertion actually carry? I say the proof is in the pudding, and for the pudding, all you have to do is watch the six o'clock news for a daily accounting of just a tiny fraction of the killings that take place each day. It's one adult versus the other, people who are old enough to know better, killing as if there were no other way to resolve their differences. This is the sad example they set for a young girl to follow, the model you are given to imitate. How do young people like you learn to behave and address their own problems if

not by carefully watching and following in the footsteps of their elders?

And here lies the crux of your indecisiveness, for what happens to a child's attitude in the midst of all this killing? For sure, something very precious is destroyed, a basic respect for human life, not just lip service on the subject, but real, heartfelt respect shown for other breathing beings. In your letter you speak of abortion like you're trying to decide what color to paint your toenails, and you don't even mention the actual alternative available to you. You simply ask whether you should get an abortion, as though this is the only question needing to be answered. But there is another road you can take; you can carry the pregnancy to term, deliver your baby, and give it up for adoption. If you do this, no one has to die. There is no murder being committed, and you will not be saddled with the onus of raising a child. True, you will have to suffer a very embarrassing nine-month ordeal, but isn't this the price you should pay for being careless with your lovemaking, and isn't it a very small price to pay in lieu of knowing for the rest of your life that you deliberately killed an unborn child?

You asked for my opinion, and I'm telling you exactly what I think without taking sides. I'm neither pro-life nor pro-choice. I am simply looking at your situation and trying to come up with the best possible course of action. Do I believe in God? Do I believe that life is sacred or that killing is a mortal sin? I honestly don't know how I feel about these questions, for I'm just a monkey and not a God-fearing or churchgoing human being. But I'll tell you what I do intuitively know: that it's wrong to take a life when there's another way to handle things. If you don't feel this way, go ahead and get the abortion. Go ahead and kill your baby. People kill other people every day, and your decision will hardly be indefensible. There will be many others of a like mind to keep you company and console you. You can put a notch in your gun handle and carry on with your life as though nothing happened. It's done all the time, and you'll hardly be the first. You won't be breaking any new ground. Just keep in mind that whatever you decide, you will have to live with it for the rest of your life.

After reading Shakespeare's response, I looked at Sarah and said, "It does sound a little harsh. I wonder what the girl thought when she read it?"

"Do you think he was wrong?"

"Not necessarily wrong. Just a little harsh."

"Do you think people will get upset when they see a monkey writing like this to a seventeen-year-old girl?"

"I don't know."

"I think this book should be entertaining. I don't think it should incite anger."

"It's hard not to get people riled up when you're talking about abortion," I said. "It's just one of those topics."

"Maybe I should exclude the letter."

"Maybe, but on the other hand, his reply reveals his morality. People might like that."

"Well, which is it? Leave it in or take it out?"

"You're the editor."

Sarah rolled her eyes. I wasn't being too helpful. "Well, maybe you can help me with this one." Sarah then pulled up a second letter up on her screen. It was from a black man in Atlanta who'd read Shakespeare's book and wanted his opinion on prejudice. He wrote,

> I'm a college-educated black man with a wife and two children. I have a job with a major construction company as a project manager, and I truly enjoy my work. I make a good living at this and like to think I lead a responsible and respectable life. I read your book about taking sides and have some questions for you. I thought your book was intelligent and thoughtful; otherwise, I wouldn't be writing to you. I mean, seriously, who writes for advice

from a monkey? But I think you and I have something in common. I am not a stereotypical black man, and you are not a stereotypical monkey. Perhaps you can understand what it's like to be judged by appearances. Do you have any idea how hard it is to be accepted as a literate and responsible man in the world today when your skin is black? I feel I'm accepted by no one, not by whites because I'm black and not by fellow black people because they think I'm trying to act white. I probably have it a lot harder than you. I mean, everyone knows who Shakespeare is. Your reputation always precedes you. But everyone does not know who I am until they get to know me, and that takes time and effort. Everywhere I go, I have to prove myself, to whites and blacks alike.

You can't imagine the ridiculous prejudices I have to overcome on a daily basis. All I want is to be viewed as a human being, given the benefit of the doubt. Yet everywhere I go, these prejudices precede me. I work in the construction industry, a field that is notoriously racist. I know what I'm doing, yet people resent taking orders from me, and they question my every decision. White people think I'm more interested in basketball and hip-hop music than I am in doing my job, and black people call me an Uncle Tom. But I'm just an individual. In your book you write that people should stop taking sides and see each other for what they are. Yet is this really possible with the way people think? I guess my question is, what can I do? And I don't mean as a black man. I mean as an individual. What can I do to change the way people think when they see me, or hear me, or have to deal with me? In your book you identify the source of the problem as man's propensity to take sides, and you say this needs to end, but you don't say how. So tell me, how do we do away with prejudice? How do we change the way people think? How will I ever be viewed as what I am, rather than as what others think I should be? How will I ever been seen as me?

"This question doesn't seem controversial."

"But read Shakespeare's answer."

"Is there something wrong with it?"

"Just read it."

I continued to read. Shakespeare wrote back to the man as follows:

You are on the right path. You may not realize it, but you're doing what you should do. One of the mistakes you're probably making is thinking there's anything you can do to end prejudice. So long as there are people of different colors and different nationalities and speaking different languages, there will always be prejudice. What you humans don't seem to realize is that the steps you often take to end prejudice only make it worse. Do you want to know one of the biggest missteps black people have made? It's been banding together and organizing into a force. It was a huge mistake, taking sides like this, thinking there was strength in solidarity. Do you see what this has done to the individual black man and woman? It has virtually destroyed any chance they have of ever being judged on their own merits. When a non-black man first meets you, he sees you as a member of the black team, not as an individual. And it isn't necessarily his fault. That many blacks call each other brothers and sisters definitely doesn't help the situation. They're not really brothers and sisters, are they? They're individuals, or at least they'd be better off thinking of themselves as such. When you hear a black man call another a brother, he may as well be sticking a knife in his friend's back.

People seem to think that by joining together, they can somehow achieve fair treatment, but nothing could be further from the truth. By taking a side like this, by saying 'we are all of a like mind,' they've ensured the very prejudice they're trying to overcome. Now when a white person sees a black man, he thinks of him as one of those black men, not as an individual. The only real way to fight prejudice is through individuality, being oneself, not being a part of a larger and badly stereotyped group. Freedom from prejudice does not come from taking sides. This freedom comes from individuality. You should guard against groups and their spokesmen. You should embrace the individual man and woman. That's how I'd answer your question. Don't try to change the minds of others. Just work on yourself and try to stand out. Be what you are.

"What do you think?" Sarah asked.

"It makes sense to me."

"You don't think it's a little racist?"

"Not at all. I mean, it might go against conventional wisdom, but it isn't necessarily racist."

"You don't think it's out of line for a monkey to tell a black man to refrain from calling other blacks brothers and sisters?"

"I don't know. Maybe a monkey is the perfect person to come out and say it."

"Maybe."

"People say united we stand, and divided we fall. But they also say birds of a feather flock together. It's not a 'united we stand' thing anymore. It's a 'birds of a feather' thing. It's not as out of line as it sounds."

"So you think I should leave this letter in?"

"You're the editor."

"That's what you said about the last letter."

"It's what you're getting paid for, to be the editor. Why are you asking me to do your job?" I smiled when I said this, not wanting to make Sarah mad. I think she was a little miffed that I wasn't taking a stand but also pleased that I was leaving the decision up to her.

"Okay, let's look at one more," she said. "This is a more recent one." Sarah pulled up the third letter, and I started reading.

This fan hadn't written about sensitive issues like abortion or racism. She was just a kid who had sent a short fan letter and asked for an autograph. She wrote,

I am eight years old. My name is Megan. I think you're a cute monkey, and I think you're smart. I know you wrote a book, but I'm probably too young to read it. And I know you made a movie, but my dad said I can't see it until I'm older. But I have seen you on TV, and I think you're funny. You make me laugh. Sometimes I wish I was a girl monkey so I could marry you. Can you please send me your autograph? I love you.

"That's it?" I asked.

"Read what Shakespeare wrote."

"Did he send her his autograph?"

"Just read what he wrote."

I looked at the monitor. There were two letters. The first reply was short, and I read it quickly.

Dear Megan, thanks for your kind correspondence. I have enclosed an autographed picture of me, and I hope you like it. The picture makes me appear more handsome than I actually am. You know, you don't need to be a monkey for the two of us to be good friends. And I'd like to think of us as friends. I have enclosed a second letter for you to read. It's intended for you to look at when you're older, so give it to your mother or father to save. Have them promise to give it to you on your fourteenth birthday.

So that was the first letter. The second one was much longer.

Okay, so you're fourteen? Happy birthday, Megan! I hope you got some nice gifts, and I trust you're doing well. I wanted to tell you about a boy I met named Michael, but his story wasn't exactly appropriate for an eight-year-old girl. So I'm having you read this now. Michael wrote me a letter years ago, back when he was still alive. He died shortly after he wrote the letter. I was lucky enough to see him before he passed away, and I was able to talk to him. He was in a hospital in South Carolina, suffering from a brain tumor. We talked for over an hour about his letter and about his life. He wrote to me because I was a monkey, and he said I'd inspired him. This was the reason I flew to South Carolina to see him—because I'd inspired him, and I felt I owed him a visit after I read his letter.

It turned out Michael longed to be a girl. When I first saw what he'd written, I thought it was a prank. But the more I read, the more I realized the kid was on the level, pouring his heart out to me. But why me? It was because I was a monkey. It was because if anyone would understand him, it would be me. This is how he saw it. He asked me if I felt weird being so freakishly smart while living in a monkey's body, and I had to say yes, that it was sort of weird, sometimes even intolerable. Then he asked me if I'd rather be a human, and I had to tell him the truth: that I'd never really longed for this. I told him that I thought humans were kind of ugly and that I wouldn't want to look like one. I mean, they were attractive in an odd sort of way, but still kind of ugly. Well, he told me he seriously still wanted to be a girl. I had no desire to be a human, but I could relate to such a desire. I learned at a young age that I was very different from other monkeys. They were stupid, and they lacked manners. They didn't wear clothing, they ate with their hands, and they threw feces when they were angry. They were kind of disgusting little animals. But I was different. Michael wanted to know what my secret was: how did I deal with being so different? This was what he wanted from me, an answer. Now, I was only five years old at the time, not exactly the wisest person Michael could have sought advice from. But I'll tell you what I told him. It's something I tell myself every day, and it's something I now want to impart to you.

I say, count your blessings, Megan. It's as simple as that. People say it over and over, but it never seems to sink in. Count your blessings, and everything in life will just fall into place. Remember what you wrote to me? Do you still want to be a monkey so we can get married? I doubt it. You might be surprised at how many letters I get from people like you, wishing for things they'll never have. You wished you were a monkey. Do you still wish for things you can't have? I think all of us do this. Do you sometimes wish you had different parents? I certainly do. Do you look in the mirror and wish you were prettier or that you had different hair or that your eyes were a different color? Do you wish you were richer or smarter or had a better sense of humor? The next time you look at yourself in your mirror, while brushing your hair or applying your makeup or putting on your earrings, remember that years ago there was a young boy in South Carolina who would've given anything to just be you, just as you are with all your flaws, real or imagined. He just wanted to be a girl. He would've given anything, Megan. I told him to count his blessings, and I'm telling you to do the same now. Of all the advice I'm capable of giving, this is the best I have to offer. It keeps me in the game. It makes me feel like my life is worth living. This is my birthday gift to you. Sure, it's dusty, hackneyed, and often repeated, yet somehow I find it's always relevant and shiny new. I say it to myself every morning of every new day.

When I finished reading, I asked, "Why wouldn't you want to print this letter? It's very positive. I like what it says."

"I was thinking of Michael's parents."

"What about them?"

"Maybe they wouldn't want others knowing their son wanted to be a girl—you know, that their son was transgender. Maybe they didn't even know about it themselves."

"That's a good point," I said.

"I guess I can contact them."

"That would probably be a good idea."

"You met them," said Sarah. "What were they like?"

"They seemed like nice people."

"So what should I say to them?"

"Just tell them the truth."

"And if they want everything kept secret?"

"Then don't print the letter. I'm sure Shakespeare will understand."

I suddenly heard Shakespeare's voice behind me. "What's this?"

I turned to see him standing in the doorway. He had a piece of paper in his hand. It was the letter from Evan at UCLA. I had left it on the counter, forgetting to throw it away. "It's a letter," I said. "I think it's from a professor."

"At UCLA?"

"Yes," I said.

"He says this is his ninth letter."

"Are you reading my mail?"

"He says he's also tried to call you?"

"Yes, he has."

"When were you going to tell me about this?" Was Shakespeare angry? Oh yes, he was angry. And he wanted answers.

Darling Little Girl

It had been weeks since Shakespeare found the letter from Evan, and during this time Sarah had been working like crazy on his new book, toiling in her office night and day. She was taking her first project as associate editor for Fisher & Sons seriously. She wanted to prove herself to Rudy, to show him that hiring her hadn't been a mistake. She finally had everything together, a completed manuscript of all the fan mail she'd carefully selected from Shakespeare's files and all of his entertaining replies to the letters. Rudy and Sarah decided to name the book *Fan Mail*, and Rudy wanted the book to be published as soon as possible. All they had to do now was iron out a few details and collect release forms from the letter writers. I looked over what Sarah had done and liked what I saw. It included a little bit of everything, letters from children, teenagers, adults, and even some seniors. Shakespeare's responses were entertaining and well written, as though he'd had this book in mind the whole time, as though it had always been a part of his plan.

If you're wondering about the letters from and to Megan, they were included. Sarah had gotten a hold of Michael's parents, and they were okay with the story about their son being published. Michael had told them everything before he died, so they already knew about his desire to be a girl. Sarah's call did not upset them, and they were happy to have Michael be a part of Shakespeare's book. They truly loved Shakespeare and told Sarah to thank him again for coming all the way out from California to visit Michael during his last days. They also asked Sarah to inform Shakespeare that Michael had died not as a boy, but as a little girl. They had bought him some makeup, a wig, a girl's wristwatch, and a pair of fuzzy slippers to wear in the hospital. They also started calling him Michelle instead of Michael, as per his request. His mom said he had made a darling little girl and that he had passed away with a smile on his face, holding his mom's hand. "He was in such a good place after Shakespeare visited," she told Sarah. "He was talkative and upbeat. He was at peace with the world, knowing he was keeping no secrets. We loved him, and we were so proud of him."

When Sarah told me about Michael's last days, the story made me want to cry. But I'm not a crier. Instead, I just shook my head and said, "Well, I'll be darned."

It's true that Shakespeare was angry with me for not having shown him Evan's letters or returned any of the professor's phone calls. He said that I had no right to be ignoring Evan, that the offer to go to UCLA affected him, not just me. I apologized and told Shakespeare he was probably right to be upset, but I explained my reasoning and told him I didn't think the idea of going to a university was a good one. When he told Dr. Barney and the professor about the offer, I figured they'd back me up. So I was surprised when they didn't agree with me; they thought we should seriously consider sending Shakespeare to college. They told me this in the kitchen while I was making a bologna sandwich for lunch and while Shakespeare was in his bedroom working on an assignment, giving them the opportunity to share their feelings with me in private.

"He's a lot smarter than either of us," the professor told me. "It's becoming obvious."

"There are limits to what we can do with him," Dr. Barney added.

"Maybe there's someone else we can recruit to assist you guys," I suggested. "Can we find someone else to come to the house and work with you, someone who specializes in gifted students? Does he really need to go off to a university? I like the idea of him staying here where I can keep an eye on things."

"Maybe you need to let go," Dr. Barney said.

I thought about this and asked, "Do you think I'm being too possessive?"

"You're feeling like any parent would at the prospect of losing his child," said Dr. Barney.

"Yes," the professor said. "Maybe it's time to push Shakespeare out of the nest, to let him fly on his own, you know, so he can do his own thing."

To be honest, I'd never given this idea much thought. I had just assumed he'd always live with Sarah and me, until he died.

"It's not like he's a pet," Dr. Barney said. "He isn't like a cat or a dog."

"No, he isn't a pet," the professor agreed.

"But he's a member of our family. And no offense to either of you, but I don't trust all those academic types at the university. Shakespeare may be fascinating to them, but they won't love him and look out for him, not the way Sarah and I do and not the way you do. He's safe here at home. At least while he's here, we always know he's loved and safe."

"I have an idea," Dr. Barney said.

"What's that?"

"Why not have the professor or me go with him?"

"To the university?"

"One of us could live with him there."

"Or both of us," the professor said.

"Yes, or both of us," said Dr. Barney.

"We'd have his back. We'd be like guardians or bodyguards," Professor Wild said. "We'd protect him. They wouldn't be allowed to do anything to him without our approval. Do you think they'd agree to this?"

"I think they'd agree to about anything. They just want him at the university, at any cost. I think if I required them to stand on their heads and whistle the national anthem, they'd agree to do it."

"I'd be willing to go with him," Dr. Barney said.

"So would I."

Shakespeare and I hadn't talked about the letter from Evan since he found it on the counter. So I asked them, "How does Shakespeare feel about going to UCLA? You guys are around him all day. Has he talked to either of you about it? He only told me he was angry that I didn't tell him about the offer. He never told me how he felt about the idea of actually going there."

"Oh, he wants to go. He doesn't want to tell you because he thinks it will hurt your feelings."

"You shouldn't have kept those letters from him. Now he knows you don't want him to go. This is the reason he's not pressing the issue."

"Darn," I said, and that was all I said. I had nothing else to add. The thought of Shakespeare leaving made me feel sad. I couldn't imagine how empty the house would be without Shakespeare. It would be just Sarah and me, and our long-tailed companion would be gone. There'd be no more banana peels to pick up, no more music from his CD player in his bedroom, and no more late-night swinging in the front-yard trees. I thought back to the day I first brought Shakespeare home, when he was just a curious little monkey, before he could even talk. He had grown up so fast and now was apparently ready to leave our house to go to college. To college! It was unfair how quickly the time had passed. Did he want to leave? The expression on my face must have shown how I was feeling, for Dr. Barney came closer and put his hand on my shoulder.

"It hurts, doesn't?" he asked.

"Yes," I replied.

"We all love him."

"Yes, we do."

"Are you going to finish making your sandwich?"

"Oh … yes," I said. At some point I had stopped preparing my lunch. I had a loaf of bread in my hands and an open package of bologna on the kitchen counter. I went to work on the sandwich and said, "Maybe I should give Evan a call."

"Who's Evan?"

"Evan Johnson. He's the guy at UCLA who's been pestering me. I guess it wouldn't hurt to talk to him, to see what they have in mind."

"It'd be a good idea," Dr. Barney said.

"I think it'd be far out," the professor said.

"Yes," I said, "it'd be far out." Then I laughed. The professor always amused me with the way he talked, like he was still a teenager back in the sixties.

The two men went back to Shakespeare's room and continued with his lessons. I looked for the letter Evan had written, found it in my office, and gave Evan a call. I have to tell you the truth—making this call upset my stomach. But I knew it was the right thing to do for Shakespeare. When Evan answered the phone, I introduced myself, and he was clearly elated to hear from me. I told him that I wasn't agreeing to anything, that I just wanted to explore our options and possibly meet at the campus, where he could show us around and give his pitch to Shakespeare. "It'll be up to him," I said. "I'm not going to force him to do anything. If he really wants to do this, he'll tell us so."

"That's fine," Evan said.

"And if we do decide to go ahead, there will be some conditions."

"That's understood."

"Shakespeare means the world to us. As you know, he's very special. We're going to want to be sure we're doing the right thing."

"We'll work with you however we can."

"Can I ask you a question?"

"Sure," Evan said.

"What exactly is your job at the university?"

"I'm the executive vice chancellor and provost."

"Wow," I said.

"Shakespeare is one of our top priorities."

"I guess so."

"He's going to be our Ishi."

"What's an Ishi?"

"It's a who, not a what."

"So who is it?"

"Ishi was a man. He was an Indian."

"An Indian?"

"This was well before your time. In fact, it was before mine. He helped put the University of California at Berkeley on the map. Ishi sparked the imaginations of millions. He was considered the last living so-called wild Native American in the United States, and everyone was curious to learn everything they could about him. They found Ishi in the wilderness, foraging for food, and they brought him into town. People flocked in to see the lone Indian, and he was a genuine sensation. This was in the early 1900s. Several professors at UC Berkeley saw a terrific opportunity to protect him and learn from this living national treasure, and they coaxed him into coming with them, with the professors then providing a nice place for him to live, debriefing him, and teaching him the ways of the modern world. Books and articles were written about him, and people couldn't get enough of it. Your monkey isn't the last of a kind like Ishi; better yet, he's the first of a kind. At least, he's the first as far as we know, for there's no record of any monkey in the world even coming close to his intelligence level. Has your doctor or professor even tested his intelligence? Do you know what his IQ is? That's one of the first things we'd do—test him for his IQ."

"Dr. Barney tested it. It came out at 156."

"Unbelievable."

"It's high, isn't it?"

"It's high even for a human being. For a monkey, it's astronomical. It's hard to fathom."

"I don't want Shakespeare treated like some sort of genius freak."

"We won't treat him like a freak. We have several bona fide geniuses here at the university, and I can assure you they're not treated like freaks."

Although I was still a little anxious about the idea of sending Shakespeare to UCLA, my conversation with Evan was a good one, and it made me feel better. I told him I'd talk to Shakespeare to see if he was interested in visiting the campus, although I already knew what his answer would be. After hanging up the phone, I went to Shakespeare's bedroom and opened the door.

"Sorry to interrupt," I said.

Shakespeare, Dr. Barney, and the professor all looked up at me to see what I wanted.

"I need to talk to you about something. I especially need to talk to Shakespeare."

"What is it?" Shakespeare asked.

"I called that guy at UCLA."

"You called Evan?"

"Yes," I said.

"And?"

"He'd like to meet with us, at the campus, to show us around."

"Are you serious?" Shakespeare asked.

"Yes," I said. "I think we should do this. I mean, at least we should look into it, right?"

Shakespeare ran up to me and hugged my leg. He said, "I really want to do this."

"I know you do."

"This is so cool," the professor said.

"Is it groovy?" Shakespeare asked the professor, still hugging my leg.

"Yes, it's groovy."

Later that day I called Evan again. I set up a visit to the campus later in the week, and he said he'd send a car to pick us up. It was a crummy drive, the trek between LA and Orange County, so I told him a ride would be great. I had no desire to do the driving myself. I suspected we were going to be treated like VIPs, and I'm not going to lie: I liked the idea of this.

At dinner that night I broke the news to Sarah. She was surprised that I was moving forward with this idea and said, "Are you really thinking of doing this?"

"Everyone seems to think it's for the best," I said.

"No one asked me."

"Well, what do you think?"

"I think if Shakespeare wants to do it, it's an excellent idea. Does Shakespeare want this?"

"I do want to do it," Shakespeare said. "I really want to go to college." He was exuberant, wide-eyed, and talking with his mouth full.

With her question answered, Sarah said, "Well, then I guess that settles it."

"I still have many details to discuss with the school," I said.

"I'm sure you do."

I told Sarah when our meeting with the school was scheduled, and she asked if she could come along.

"I don't have any problem with that," I said.

"Are Dr. Barney and the professor coming?" Shakespeare asked.

"Do you want them to come?"

"Yes, I want everyone to come."

"Fine," I said. "We'll all go together."

It would be several days before we went to the campus, and during that time Sarah continued going back and forth with Rudy, tweaking Shakespeare's manuscript. Sarah told me Rudy was crazy about the book, and she said Mollie wanted to put Shakespeare back on the TV talk show circuit, to get the book noticed, to get it on everyone's shopping list. This talk show thing had been fun the first time around, but now it just seemed like it would be a lot of work. I asked Sarah if she thought it was necessary to make all these TV appearances again, and she said Mollie believed it was. She thought we should have faith in Mollie's expertise.

"If you don't want to do this, I will," she said.

"No, I'll go ahead and do it."

"Can I tag along?" she asked.

I didn't see why not, and we decided to go as a family. I asked Sarah when Mollie wanted us to start, and she said as soon as the releases were all collected and the book was printed. Shakespeare had been a big hit the first time he appeared on the talk shows, and there was no reason to believe the shows wouldn't be even more interested in him now. Surely, they'd do whatever was needed to fit him into their guest lists. So it appeared that soon we'd all be on the road, promoting the new book. At first it made me feel exhausted just to think about it, but then I grew excited. With Shakespeare possibly going to UCLA, this might be our last hurrah as a family.

You know, besides Shakespeare, the only animal I had ever lived with was a cat named Simba. This was back when I was a kid and my parents were still alive. I loved that cat. He wasn't skittish or aloof like other cats. He had a great personality and was attached to me. When Simba was a kitten, he'd play with me for hours on end, and when he grew older, he'd always choose to sit with me, like we were best pals. When my parents and I would get comfortable on the sofa at night and watch TV, Simba would sneak onto my lap and curl up to sleep. When I looked down at him, he would look up and meow at me, as though trying to say something. I always wondered what he was trying to say. He was so happy living in our house. It was my job to feed him and give him water, and I always made sure he had plenty of both. Then when I was ten years old, Simba disappeared. We always let him out of the house during the day, but he didn't come home that night. Just like that, the cat was gone, and we couldn't find him anywhere. My mom and I printed up "lost cat" flyers and put them in all the neighborhood mailboxes, but no one ever called. We also went to the animal shelters, thinking someone might have found him and dropped him off, but he wasn't there either. He was just gone.

For months I thought about this poor little cat, lost and all alone, meowing for food at strangers' doors, looking for water wherever he could find it, getting thinner and thinner, perhaps even growing ill. Simba was probably so confused, wondering what had happened to us and why we hadn't found him. He was probably thinking back to how good he'd had it, living in our house, sitting in my lap while I watched TV. It was torture thinking about Simba like this, and it put me in a terribly sad mood. Now this mood was coming back to me as I thought about Shakespeare moving out of our house. I was going to lose him, my good buddy; all those wonderful years we'd spent together would be just memories, sad memories, and Shakespeare would no longer be living in our house. Just like Simba, he'd be gone for good.

Those were the sorts of feelings I had whenever I thought of Shakespeare going to UCLA, and the feelings just got worse as the day of our visit approached. I'll tell you what I did to try to make myself feel better: I played a lot of tennis at the club, at least two matches a day. I tried to work the anxiety out of my system, to get myself thinking about something else. When the matches were over, I'd hang out in the clubhouse bar and chat with the other members. I'd try to get them to talk about their lives so I could forget mine for a while. One of the conversations I had was with a guy named Artie Howser. Artie was older than me, married with one son, and his son had just moved out of the house to attend college out east. He had made great grades in high school and had aced his SATs, so he could have picked any school, but he had chosen MIT, clear across the continent.

"It's like he wanted to get as far away from us as possible," Artie said. "I'm really going to miss him. Do you have any kids?"

"No," I said.

"Are you married?"

"Yes, I'm married."

"Do you plan on having kids?"

"Not in the near future."

"Well, you're still young."

"We have a monkey."

"A monkey?"

"His name is Shakespeare. Perhaps you've heard of him? He was in a movie."

"Oh, Shakespeare, yes. The talking monkey?"

"Yes, that's him."

"So you're the monkey guy."

"Yes," I said. "I'm the monkey guy."

"I heard that you played tennis here. I never knew your name, but I've heard of you."

"Shakespeare wants to go to UCLA."

"He's going to college?"

"That's the plan."

"A monkey going to college? To UCLA? Well, I'll be darned," Artie said with a laugh.

"Actually, right now we're just going to check the place out."

"Are you going to miss him?"

"He isn't gone yet."

"Oh, he will be. Just be glad he isn't going out east. We'll be lucky if we see our son Thanksgiving or Christmas. He promises he'll visit, but just watch—he'll have an excuse not to come. I've talked to other parents, friends of mine in the same boat, and they say that's the way it is. You raise them and love them, and the next thing you know, they move out of the house and break your heart."

"I guess so," I said.

"Is it true what they say about your monkey? Can he speak five languages?"

"No, he only speaks English."

"I heard he can do calculus."

"Yes, he can do that."

"Does he go to a school now, like a high school?"

"Actually, he's been homeschooled."

"Of course. I guess it wouldn't work out too well, having him in a high school. He'd probably be too big a distraction."

"Probably."

"How about college? What's he going to do there? Is he going to attend classes?"

"I doubt it. He's probably going to have private lessons, like he does now."

"Do they charge the same tuition as they charge the other kids?"

"No, there's no tuition."

"A free college education at UCLA? Wow, you're so lucky. My kid's education at MIT is going to cost me a small fortune."

"Yes, I guess I'm lucky he's a monkey."

Artie thought for a moment and then continued his questioning. He had a lot of questions. "Didn't your monkey also publish a book a while ago?"

"Yes, it was a best seller."

"Did it make a lot of money?"

"Yes, quite a bit."

"Where does the money go? Does he have his own bank account?"

"I set up an account for him in my name."

"What does he spend money on?"

"Nothing, really."

"Christ, I've got to tell my wife about this. We should've had a monkey. We could've saved ourselves a bundle of money."

I liked Artie. I didn't tell him this, but he was nearly as inquisitive as Shakespeare.

When the morning came for us to be driven to the UCLA campus, Shakespeare woke me up at seven, jumping up and down on the bed, wanting me to get ready and come have breakfast. Dr. Barney and the professor were already at the house, and Sarah was cooking for all of us in the kitchen. We all had breakfast together, and everyone was chatty and excited, like we were going on some grand vacation. Shakespeare could barely contain himself.

"It's here!" he shouted. He was at the front window, looking out toward the yard. Parked in the driveway was a big black SUV, and out climbed its driver, a young man dressed in a dark suit and tie. His shoes were black and shiny, and the SUV was sparkling clean, as though it had just been run through a car wash. The kid had a very handsome face, like a model, and he appeared to be several years younger than me, probably in his early twenties. He rang the doorbell, and Shakespeare answered it.

"Let's go!" Shakespeare called to the rest of us.

Sarah grabbed her purse, and we all headed toward the front door to leave. "I'm Marty," I said to the kid.

"My name is Hopkins," he said, reaching out to shake my hand. "I'll be your driver. So this must be Shakespeare." To Shakespeare he said, "I know a lot about you."

Shakespeare smiled at Hopkins and then said, "I call shotgun."

"I think he wants to sit in the front seat," I said to Hopkins.

"That's fine with me."

"Well, I guess this is it," I said. I locked the front door, and we all climbed into the SUV, heading to UCLA.

Albert

Hopkins turned out to be quite the talker. It didn't interfere with his driving, but he talked the whole way to Los Angeles, mostly to Shakespeare. He had learned several days earlier that he'd be transporting Shakespeare, and so he had taken the time to read his book in advance, wanting to be well versed in Shakespeare's interests. It wasn't like he spent the whole drive talking about it, but he started off by telling Shakespeare, "I read your book."

"Did you?" Shakespeare asked.

"I thought it was interesting, the way you used humankind's love of war to explain how we all relate to each other on a daily basis. Those are some pretty profound thoughts for a monkey. Tell me, did you come up with these ideas all by yourself?"

"Yes, I did."

"Do you think other monkeys see humans the same way you do?"

"I don't think other monkeys think much at all."

"They must think something, right?"

"Generally speaking, monkeys are stupid. They can be trained to do tricks and some useful tasks, but that's about it. They seem smart compared to other animals, but they're actually quite stupid." Shakespeare paused and then said, "They're like many humans."

"Do you think I'm stupid?"

"You don't sound stupid. But then, I don't know you that well."

"I got good grades in high school."

"Did you?"

"I decided not to go to college."

"Why not?" Shakespeare asked.

"It was too expensive. And you don't have to have a college education to be a success. There are lots of successful people who never went to college, or who did go but dropped out."

"That's probably true. Of course, you don't have to be that bright to be a success. It just depends on how you define success."

"Do you think you're a success?"

"I'm only six years old. It's a little early to tell whether I'm a success."

"You wrote a book, and you made a movie. The movie did well at the box office, didn't it? And your book was a best seller. I'd say those are successes."

"They were successes only because I'm a monkey. My book and movie probably would have gone unnoticed if I were just another human being."

"I've been thinking of writing a book."

"Oh? What about?"

"It would be a novel about Albert Einstein. I think it's a novel idea for a novel." Hopkins laughed at his little play on words and then asked, "Do you want to hear my idea?"

"Why not?"

"Okay, the title would be *The Secret Children*. It would be about a clandestine government project in the 1930s in which Einstein is convinced to donate his semen to an agency that has searched all over the world and found a pool of women who are themselves exceptionally bright and talented but incapable of having children because their husbands are sterile. This agency's doctors work their way into the couples' lives, convincing them to become pregnant by artificial insemination. The couples are promised sperm from donors of an intelligent and healthy stock but aren't told the actual donor is Einstein. A handful of these women go on to become pregnant with the offspring of Albert Einstein. The happy couples still have no idea who the actual sperm donor was, nor do they know that this government agency will be tracking their children for the rest of their lives. Then about forty years following the births of the children, the main character of the story reveals the truth to the families. That's as far as I've gotten with the story, but what do you think? Don't you think it'd make for an interesting book?"

"It would be interesting," Shakespeare said. "What would the children be like?"

"They could all be different. They could be both men and women.

One could be a very successful musician, while another could be a wealthy businessman, or maybe a doctor or a lawyer. One might just be a housewife. That would be one of the girls, obviously. One could be an alcoholic or a drug addict, living on skid row. Who knows? There are all sorts of possibilities. And it would be interesting to see not only how they turn out but also how the revelation that they're the offspring of Einstein affects them when they are given the news. Do their attitudes change? Do their lives change? Do they suddenly have profound regrets about the lives they've led? Or do they just stay the same?"

"You seem to have given this a lot of thought."

"I have."

"Have you written anything down?"

"Nope, it's just in my head."

"You should start writing."

"You think so?"

"Of course. What's stopping you?"

"I actually think it's a good idea," Sarah said, joining the conversation.

"She should know," I said. "She's an editor."

"Are you?" Hopkins asked.

"I am."

"And you like the idea?"

"I think it's worth pursuing. Do you know how to write?"

"Of course he knows how to write," Shakespeare said. "Who doesn't know how to write?"

"I mean, as in being an author?"

"I don't know."

"You should take some courses," Sarah said. "There are some good classes you can take at community college where you can learn the fundamentals. There are lots of things you'll need to know."

Hopkins seemed surprised by our interest in his story, and he was quiet for a moment, taking it in. Then he said, "It's not my only idea."

"You have another idea for a book?"

"Actually, it's an idea for a song."

"A song?"

"A country-western song."

"What's this idea?"

155

"I'm thinking of a song about a couple of rodeo cowboys. The first cowboy is gay, and he falls in love with the other. Problem is, the other cowboy isn't gay at all, so the first cowboy's love goes unrequited. This goes on for several years, until the gay cowboy comes up with an idea to rectify the situation. He decides to have a sex change operation and turn himself into a cowgirl. As a cowgirl he plans to seduce the cowboy of his dreams. This plan works for a while, until the straight cowboy discovers what is going on and ends the relationship. It's a sad song, with the gay cowboy losing his love and stuck being a girl, something he never actually wanted to be. I know of no country song that even comes close to approaching this subject, but surely it's relevant in this day and age. It's a brave new world, right? I'm thinking of lyrics using the words 'transgender' and 'pretender.' It's a good rhyme."

"Have you written any of the lyrics?"

"No, not yet."

"Do you have any music for it?"

"No music either. It's just an idea. I'm good at coming up with ideas. Do you think I could sell this idea to a country song writer?"

"Maybe."

"Ready for another one?"

"Another what?"

"Another idea."

"Sure, go ahead," Shakespeare said. He seemed to enjoy listening to Hopkins talk.

"Do you like art?" Hopkins asked.

"Yes," Shakespeare said. "I like it a lot."

"This is my idea for a painting. Do you know what memes are?"

"Of course."

"My idea is to paint memes. I'm not talking about people, landscapes, or still lifes, but actual memes. Of course, you'd need to have people and landscapes and inanimate objects as props. But the focus would be on the meme, in its purest form, brought to life by the skill of the artist. I think there's beauty in memes. It wouldn't be something surreal, or abstract or concrete, but something elusively fascinating, captured on canvas like a jar full of fireflies. Am I making any sense to you? I know it sounds kind of weird, but really it isn't. Not when you think about it. I mean, memes are real, aren't they?"

"Have you tried to do this?"

"No," Hopkins said.

"Why not?"

"I don't know how to paint. I can't even draw. I can barely draw a stick figure. But someone could do this, someone who knew what they were doing."

"I like you," Shakespeare said.

"You do?"

"Yes, I think I do."

"People say I drive them crazy. They think I'm kind of weird, coming up with all these ideas."

"That's because most people are uncomfortable with creativity. They want the same thing over and over. It's just the way most humans are. They get comfortable with the status quo, and they don't like changes. Are you going to be my regular driver?"

"I don't know. I just got this job. I don't know what they have planned for me."

"What did you do before this?"

"I was delivering pizzas."

"Where?"

"In Westwood. Mostly to college kids. They eat a lot of pizzas."

"This job suits you better."

During the rest of the drive, Shakespeare and Hopkins continued to talk about Hopkins's ideas while the rest of us sat quietly in the back, listening. Occasionally, one of us would chime in, but for the most part we were content to let this former pizza delivery boy and Shakespeare converse between themselves. When we arrived at the campus, Hopkins parked the SUV alongside a sidewalk in front of a building and ran around the car to open the doors for us before we had a chance to unlatch them ourselves. He took his job as our chauffer seriously, and opening our doors was a part of his job. A man was waiting for us at the curb, and Hopkins introduced us to him: this was Evan Johnson. He then hopped back in the SUV and sped off.

Evan had us follow him to his office. I noticed that he had to duck when he walked in through his doorway, for he was surprisingly tall. For some reason I'd imagined him as a smaller man when I spoke with him on the phone, but he was well over six feet, taller than any of the rest of us. He looked like a giant next to Shakespeare, and Shakespeare looked up at him like he'd never seen a human so tall.

"Just how tall are you?" Shakespeare asked.

"Six-eight," Evan said. "And yes, I played college basketball. I was on the team years ago."

"Were you any good?"

"I was okay. I could hold my own."

"Do you have any trophies?"

"I have a few."

"I like trophies," Shakespeare said. "Someday I'm going to win some trophies."

"I don't doubt that for a minute," Evan laughed. He then looked around at the rest of us and said, "Why don't you all take a seat and make yourselves comfortable?"

The office was impressive, with all sorts of framed diplomas, certificates, and awards hanging on the walls. There were bookcases filled with old books, and the room was filled with antique furniture, featuring lots of leather upholstery and carved wood. The chairs were solid and comfortable, and the floor was covered with a plush pile carpet. It seemed more like a successful attorney's office than a college administrator's lair. I could tell Evan was proud of this office just by the way he moved about in it and by the way he took a seat behind his massive desk.

"I like your office," I said.

"Thanks."

"I like walking on your carpet," Shakespeare said. "It's squishy."

"Yes, it's squishy."

"So what's on the agenda?" I asked.

"First I'd like to talk to you all for a few minutes, so that you can get to know me and understand what the university has in mind for Shakespeare. Then I'd like to take you on a tour of the campus and have you meet some of the professors Shakespeare will be working with. Last but not least, I'd like to show you where Shakespeare will be living when he moves here. We've prepared an apartment for him. Of course, we've done this without his input, so if he wants any changes, we can certainly make them. But I think he'll like what we've done."

"You've already prepared his living quarters?"

"Yes, I guess we have."

"Aren't you getting ahead of yourself?"

"I'd like to think we're optimistic."

"I see."

"If you'd like, we can skip the apartment and just look over the campus."

"No, I want to see my apartment," Shakespeare said. "I want to see where I'm going to live."

I think Evan knew Shakespeare would say this. He smiled and said, "It's up to you." I agreed that we would take a look at the apartment.

Evan then went on to talk a little about himself and about the university, how the school would be committed to providing Shakespeare with the best possible academic program. "We're offering him an education in everything from art to science. We'll allow him to pick a major, just like any other student. We'll provide him guidance, but his choice of a major will be left up to him. We don't envision him going to classes with the other students; instead his studies will be one-on-one with our best professors. We think this will be the best way for him to learn without distracting or being distracted by the other students. We envision him earning an undergraduate degree, perhaps even a master's or a doctorate to go along with it. This will be up to him, how far he wishes to go up the collegiate ladder, but no matter what happens, he'll always be welcome to stay with us, even after he has earned his degrees. We want this to be his new home, which isn't to say the rest of you won't still be involved in his life. You'll be welcome to come up and visit him anytime, and we'll drive him down to your place in Corona del Mar for visits as often as you wish. We know you all have a special bond with Shakespeare, and we'd never do anything to destroy that bond. You've become his family, and here at the university, we think family is important."

I looked at Shakespeare after all this talk and asked, "Well, what do you think?"

"Who will my driver be?" he asked.

"Your driver?"

"The person driving me to Corona del Mar and back. Who will be my driver?"

"Whoever is available, I guess."

"I want it to be Hopkins."

"Hopkins?"

"The guy who drove us here today. I want him to be my personal chauffer."

"That can be arranged."

"I like Hopkins."

"Yes, he's a likable young man."

"And the professor and the doctor. I want them here with me."

"You mean living on the campus?"

"They don't have to live on the campus," I said, clarifying Shakespeare's request. "But they do need to be put up somewhere nearby. We want them involved in everything you do. And we want them to have the power to stop anything you're doing with Shakespeare if they feel it's inadvisable or inappropriate. They'll be here to look out for his interests while I'm not here."

Evan thought about this and said, "I guess that can be arranged."

I continued, "What the doctor and the professor say to your people will be followed. If they say they don't want something done, then it won't be done. Of course, I'll have the final say. You can appeal any of their decisions to me."

"Okay, we can agree to that."

"And if we ever decide we don't like the way things are going here, Shakespeare will be allowed to come home with no objection from you or anyone else at the university. He'll have the right to leave this place anytime he chooses, and for any reason."

"Yes, that's fine. But he won't want to leave. I'm quite sure of this. He belongs here." Evan looked over at Shakespeare and smiled.

Shakespeare smiled back at him, seeming impressed with Evan's willingness to go along with our terms. It was like I thought: the school was willing to do just about anything to get him living on their campus.

"Shall we tour the campus?" Evan said.

"Let's do it," Shakespeare said.

The six of us stood up and left the office, and Evan led us on his guided tour. It took the better part of the day. We met with several of the professors the school planned on having work with Shakespeare, and they were affable and kind to Shakespeare, going out of their way to be polite. The longer this tour went on, the more comfortable I began to feel about Shakespeare living here; it wasn't anywhere near as ghoulish as I'd anticipated. The truth was that it would have been wrong for me to hold Shakespeare back from the opportunity that was being offered by the school, and certainly he would never be challenged at our little home in Corona del Mar the same way he would be challenged here at the university. He needed something like this in his life, and he deserved it. Our final stop on the tour was Shakespeare's apartment, which had been designed by a team of architects in the university's facilities department and which was located in the life sciences building. It was mostly just one huge room. But it was really huge, big enough to ride a horse through. It had everything Shakespeare could possibly want; there was a kitchen and eating area, a private bathroom, a clothes closet, a library filled with books, a sleeping area with a bed and a nightstand, and a TV area with a sofa and big-screen TV. There were shelves filled with puzzles and games, a large whiteboard on the wall, and several workstations and many chairs. On one wall was a large black-and-white photograph of a monkey in a space suit that caught Shakespeare's attention, and he walked over to it. "Who's this?" he asked.

"That's Albert," Evan said.

"So who is he?"

"Albert was the first monkey to travel into space. He was a hero."

"A hero?"

"Yes," Evan said. "A true American hero."

"Where'd you get the picture?" I asked.

"From NASA. We had it blown up and framed."

"Did he live through his mission?" Shakespeare asked.

"No, he died."

"So they sent him up and he died?"

"Yes."

"Better to kill a monkey than to kill a man—is that the way they looked at it?"

"I guess so."

"What kind of monkey was he?"

161

"I think he was a rhesus."

"So they killed him." Shakespeare thought for a moment and then asked, "Can you take the picture down? I don't think I like it."

"We can do whatever you wish."

Shakespeare wasn't noticeably moved by the photo of Albert; he just wanted it taken down. I suspected that he saw no reason to be reminded of how Albert had allowed himself to be taken advantage of and killed just because he was a stupid monkey. He was nothing like Albert. No, there was a new kid in town, and his name was Shakespeare. He was not a guinea pig or a mine canary. He was an animal to be reckoned with.

He looked around at the rest of the room, and I could tell by the expression on his face that he liked everything else he saw. "It's like my room at home, except it's twenty times bigger. And it's all mine, right? This is all for me?"

"All for you," Evan said.

Shakespeare walked over to the big TV and put his hand on it, looking at me. "TV," he said. "Do you recall that, Marty? It was one of my first words."

"Yes, I remember that."

"Now I'll have my own TV."

"Yes," I said.

"Does this window open?" Shakespeare asked, looking at the window near the TV.

"I think so," Evan said.

Shakespeare stepped to the window and opened it. He poked his head outside and looked around. There were several large trees just outside the building, and I knew what he had in mind. "This is going to work out perfectly," he said, bringing his head back in. "What do you think?" he asked me.

"About what?"

"About this apartment."

"If you like it, I guess I like it."

"I think it's wonderful," Sarah said.

"Yes, very cool," the professor said.

"I'd like to live here," Shakespeare said.

Evan smiled. "That's what we wanted to hear. Like I said, anything you want changed, just ask and we'll change it anytime. Your wish is our command. We want you to be comfortable."

"I think we should talk about this more," I said. "Maybe at home tonight." But I was wasting my time, trying to slow things down. Shakespeare was obviously sold on the idea of moving out of our house and occupying this spacious apartment.

"What's to talk about?" Shakespeare asked.

"Nothing, I guess."

"I think Shakespeare will be very happy here," Sarah said.

"We at least need to work out the living arrangements for the doctor and professor," I said. "Where will they live? Will you find apartments for them?"

"We won't be that picky," Dr. Barney said.

"The place where I live in Orange County isn't anything to write home about," the professor said. "It won't take much to please me."

"I'm sure we can find something satisfactory for both of you. I'll get my people right on it."

"I guess we've seen enough," I said.

"It's getting late. You'd all probably like to get headed back home."

"Yes," I said.

"I'll get your ride for you."

"It's going to be Hopkins, right?" Shakespeare asked.

"Yes, it will be Hopkins."

Evan made a call on his cell phone and set up our ride, making sure Hopkins would be our driver. When we got back to the main building, Hopkins was waiting for us at the side of the road. We all said good-bye to Evan, shaking hands and promising to work out all the details soon. We climbed in the SUV, and Hopkins shut our doors. He then hopped into the driver's seat and stomped on the accelerator, and off we went toward the freeway. I think everyone was tired from talking all day, and it was quiet for a while.

Eventually, Hopkins turned his head to speak to Shakespeare, who was sitting up front again. "You want to hear another idea of mine?" he asked.

"Sure," Shakespeare said.

"It came to me while I was waiting to take you guys home. It's for another book. I'd call it *Monkey Business*."

"Is it about me?"

"Sort of."

"Is it about a monkey?"

"Yes, it's about a monkey."

"Can the monkey talk?"

"Oh yes, he can talk. But he doesn't go to college, not like you. Instead, he starts his own business. He becomes an entrepreneur."

The Ugly Duckling

We decided to keep Shakespeare from moving to UCLA until after he'd completed all his talk show appearances. There was no reason to rush things, and according to Mollie, the talk shows were a priority. Shakespeare went along with this plan, even though I knew he was dying to move into his new apartment. We started doing the talk shows around two months after we met with Evan, beginning in New York and winding up in Los Angeles. When we were done, we all spent several weeks relaxing at our house in Corona del Mar, and when we finally told Evan we were ready, he sent Hopkins to the house to pick Shakespeare up in the SUV. We boxed up all of Shakespeare's things, which consisted primarily of his clothing; he'd accumulated a lot of clothes over the years, and he wanted to bring all of it with him. He also packed up some other minor items, but there wasn't much he needed since the apartment had been fully outfitted by the school. Evan had sent us an inventory of the apartment's contents so that we'd know what was appropriate to bring. Once everything had been loaded into the SUV, Sarah and I said good-bye to Shakespeare. It was a tough afternoon, to be sure. I did my best not to cry, but I could feel myself wanting to sob. When the SUV finally sped away, and I went back into our empty house, I broke down and bawled like a baby.

So Shakespeare was now just about seven years old and living at UCLA, starting his studies with the professors there. It seemed so weird that he could have grown up so quickly and that he was now out of our house. I wished I'd done more with him while he lived with us, rather than having had him spend so much time with Dr. Barney and the professor, but hindsight is twenty-twenty, no? What was done was done. We still had his weekend visits to look forward to, and he came to visit us every Saturday and Sunday, Hopkins being his faithful driver. I can't even tell you how good it made me feel to see that black SUV pull up into our driveway each Saturday morning, knowing that Shakespeare was sitting in the passenger seat, riding shotgun. Hopkins would open the door for him, and he would jump out and run into our arms, after which we'd have two full days together. They say absence makes the heart grow fonder, and in this case it was certainly true. Shakespeare was the light of our lives.

When he was home, we talked about all the things he was learning at school, and it reminded me of the way I'd felt when I first went to college, discovering there were so many subjects to explore, so many books to read, and so much information to process. It's funny, but what really seemed to interest Shakespeare wasn't math or science, for example; it was the study of human beings. Does this surprise you? It was a little curious to me that a monkey would find humans so intriguing, but that's exactly the way it was. It turned out that anthropology, psychology, sociology, and history were his favorite subjects. But he liked other topics as well. He had no idea how he'd ever be able to pick a major.

In the meantime Shakespeare's book was selling like crazy, not at record levels like his first book, but well enough to make it another best seller. The fan mail Shakespeare was now receiving was a little overwhelming, and being very busy with his schoolwork, he needed someone to help him answer the letters; he just didn't have time to answer all of them himself. So Evan found a student at the university who was interested in getting to know Shakespeare and who wanted to write his responses. The student's name was Becky Carlson, and she was a sophomore majoring in English literature. Evan worked out an arrangement with the girl, paying her per word to write Shakespeare's replies, and each day she met with Shakespeare for several hours to go over the mail and then wrote letters back to all who'd written. Some of Shakespeare's fans just wanted autographed photos of him, and some didn't require much of an answer at all. Often all Becky had to do was write a note thanking the letter writer for his or her thoughts and wishing him or her the best. But some of the letters were more involved and required lengthy responses. Although Becky wrote all the responses, Shakespeare read them first before she sent them out, sometimes making changes and sometimes just leaving them be, and he personally signed all of them. It was kind of deceptive, sending out these letters as though they actually had been written by Shakespeare, but his time was now precious, and this was the only way he felt he could pay proper attention to his fans and still concentrate on his studies.

Shakespeare came to like Becky a lot, and one weekend he asked if he could bring her home to meet us. Of course, we said yes, and Sarah and I both looked forward to getting to know her. Sarah prepared the guest room for Becky to sleep in, and Hopkins brought them to the house on a Saturday morning. Becky was not exactly a gorgeous girl; in fact, she was kind of ugly. Her eyes were too close together, and her nose was too large for her face. Her teeth were surprisingly discolored for a girl her age, and when she smiled, it was actually kind of disconcerting how yellow her teeth were. Her hair was like straw, tied back in a stiff ponytail, and she was a little overweight but wore loose clothes to conceal her shape. But when she spoke, her appearance became a non-issue, for she was eloquent and intelligent, and it was no wonder Shakespeare enjoyed spending time with her. We all sat down to dinner that Saturday night, and she talked to us a little about her classes at the university. Then she said, "I don't have a great deal of experience with people, but unlike most I've met so far in my life, Shakespeare has a true moral compass."

I liked hearing this, and I think Sarah did too. It's always nice to know the person you've raised from a baby to a young adult has turned out well in the eyes of another. I'm calling Shakespeare a person, and he was a little person, wasn't he? I don't think the word "person" is inappropriate when used to refer to our monkey because he was so much more than a run-of-the-mill simian. Yes, "person" was the perfect word to describe him. Maybe he was not a human being, but he most certainly was a person.

Becky continued, "Has Shakespeare told either of you about his idea for his next book?"

"No," I said.

"What is it?" Sarah asked Shakespeare.

"It's just a germ of an idea right now."

"We'd like to hear it."

"It's going to be titled *Life and Death in America*. It's going to be my monkey's-eye view of how people view life and death in this country. I have a lot of ideas, but I haven't written anything down yet."

"It sounds interesting," I said.

"It will be amazing." There was a twinkle in Shakespeare's eye when he said this.   I wasn't sure what more to say, so I said nothing, and we were all quiet for a moment.

Then Sarah broke the silence, changing the subject. "So where are you from?" she asked Becky. "Are you a native Southern California girl?"

"Oh no," Becky laughed. "Do I look like a Southern California girl? Actually, I'm from Seattle."

"Did you grow up there?"

"Yes, I did. Born and raised."

"What are you doing here in Southern California? What made you pick UCLA?"

"Good school and no rain. I had to get out of the rain."

"It rains here sometimes," Sarah said.

"But not very often," I added.

"It's nothing like Seattle."

"Do you like California? Do you go to the beaches here?" asked Sarah.

"No, not ever."

"Don't you like the beach?"

"I don't like the waves. The sound depresses me. All that heavy power, churning and pounding for no reason. I don't know why; it just depresses me."

"Marty used to take us to the beach," Shakespeare said. "Remember our walks on the beach?"

"I do," I said.

"I used to pick up shells and feathers. I used to bring them home."

"You kept them in a box in the backyard."

"Yes, I remember that."

"Those years were fun," I said.

"I liked being a little monkey and going to the beach with you. I liked growing up here in Corona del Mar. I had a fun childhood."

Then Sarah asked Becky, "What about your parents? I mean, what do they do for a living?"

"My father is a medical doctor, a podiatrist. My mother is a stay-at-home mom."

"Do you have any brothers or sisters?"

"I have two younger brothers. They're still living with my parents. One is seventeen, and the other is fourteen. They're both in high school. They're mostly interested in sports. I'm kind of the black sheep of the family, liking to read the way I do. No one else in my family likes to read. They read a little, but not nearly as much as I do."

"My parents live in Nebraska," said Sarah. "They don't read much either. Did you know I studied English literature in college, like you?"

"Yes, Shakespeare told me. He said you are now an editor for Fisher & Sons."

"Yes, Shakespeare got me the job. I love what I do. Do you have a favorite author, Becky?"

"You mean other than me?" Shakespeare asked.

Everyone laughed.

"Of course," Sarah said. "I mean other than you. We all know you're our number one."

"I used to like Hemingway an awful lot," Becky said. "At least I thought I liked him until I met Shakespeare. Hemingway seems a little depressing to me now. Ever since I met Shakespeare, I've tried to avoid depressing things. He has taught me to look for the good in life. He's changed my attitude." Becky turned to look at Shakespeare, and he stood up in his chair.

"I need to go to the bathroom," he said. He then jumped off the chair and ran down the hall to take care of his business.

"Isn't he wonderful?" Becky said.

"Yes, we like him," I said, smiling. I liked that Shakespeare had had such a positive influence on this young girl.

"I've never known anyone like him."

"He's one of a kind," I said.

"I'm so glad he came into my life. I wasn't exactly miserable before I met Shakespeare, but I wasn't happy either. He's shown me how to be happy. He's shown me how it feels to be right with the world. Do you know what I mean by this? Do you know the children's story about the ugly duckling? Did your parents read this story to you when you were kids?"

"No," I said.

"I'm familiar with it," Sarah said.

"My mom used to read it to me over and over. It was written by Hans Christian Andersen, and it was one of my favorite fairy tales. I believed in it, and it gave me hope. It's about an ugly little duckling who is abused and ridiculed by the others because of his awkward looks. But eventually, it turns out the little bird isn't a duckling at all. He matures into a graceful and lovely swan. I was a dopey-looking child, just like the ugly little duckling. I could relate to his predicament. And I always dreamed I would one day grow up to be a magnificent swan, just like the ugly duckling did. That was my dream, but the day never came. I'm still no beauty, not even close, not like so many other girls my age. There's nothing I can do about it. I can try to use makeup and fix up my hair, but I am what I am, a pudgy young woman with a big nose, naturally yellow teeth, and dry, scratchy hair. Few boys are interested in me, and even fewer girls are interested in being friends with me. I've always felt a little sorry for myself, but then I met Shakespeare. He saw something in me that I didn't see; he saw me for who I was, and he made me feel good about myself. He made me feel like I was a lovely swan after all, and he taught me to count my blessings. None of us has everything we want in life, yet each of us has so much. And I have enough, enough to make me happy."

"What did I miss?" Shakespeare said. His voice startled all of us. He had returned from the bathroom and was now approaching the dining room table.

"We were just talking about you," Becky said. "About how you've helped me."

Shakespeare jumped up into his chair. "Everyone's always talking about me."

"You like being the center of attention, don't you?" I asked. "You knew we'd be talking about you."

"I guess I did at that," Shakespeare said with a laugh. He looked around at all of us, making a silly face. He then picked up his fork to go back to work on his dinner.

Something about Becky became clear to me over the rest of that weekend, something Sarah noticed as well. The girl liked Shakespeare a lot, perhaps more than just as a good friend. I mean, she really adored him, the way a girl might like a boy romantically. It was the way she talked about Shakespeare, the way she looked at him, the way she admired him and hung on his words. "If I didn't know better, I'd think she was in love with him," I told Sarah.

Sarah said the girl certainly seemed sensible enough to know better than to fall in love with a monkey. I saw things a little differently but pretended to agree with her. What eventually would happen between these two would be hard to believe. I'll admit, even I was surprised.

In the months that followed, Shakespeare continued to do well at the university. I spoke with Dr. Barney and the professor often, and they both thought the school was doing an excellent job. In fact, they felt their presence was no longer needed in Los Angeles, and they told me they were thinking of returning to Orange County. "There just isn't much for us to do here," the professor said. "Evan seems to have everything well under control, and we haven't seen the school do anything we'd consider inappropriate or against Shakespeare's best interests."

I told them if they felt that way, I saw no reason for them to remain. I too was comfortable with the way Shakespeare was being treated and was confident that he was in good hands. When they told Shakespeare they were planning to move back home, he didn't raise a fuss at all. He was fine with the way things were and didn't feel he needed them to look out for him any longer. It was a sad day when they finally did make the move, for they had played such a significant role in Shakespeare's life. But circumstances change, and life marches onward. The professor and Dr. Barney moved back home while Shakespeare stayed in school.

Dr. Barney started his psychology and tutoring practice up again, and it didn't take him long to procure new young clients. He was now well known in Orange County for his work with Shakespeare, and although obviously no one else needed help with a talking monkey, parents did like the idea of bringing their children to a doctor of such renown. The professor also got his old job back at the community college. He was something of a celebrity on the campus because of his work with Shakespeare, and the students were thrilled when he showed up to teach their classes. He told me he was going to write a book about his years with Shakespeare. I told Sarah about this, and she immediately contacted the professor, thinking that Fisher & Sons would be the ideal publisher and that she would be the perfect editor. Rudy liked the idea, saying that it would serve Shakespeare well to keep him in the public eye, maintaining his value. Shakespeare, of course, was working on his own book about life and death in America, but he was very busy with his schoolwork, and there was no telling when he'd actually be done with the project. So keeping Shakespeare in the news while he worked on his book was important to Rudy; he didn't want anyone forgetting about him.

As it turned out, Shakespeare didn't need any help staying in the news. He took care of this on his own, or should I say with the help of Becky. Shortly after the end of his first year at UCLA, Shakespeare and Becky dropped a bomb on everyone. And I do mean everyone. They first made the announcement to Sarah and me at our house in Corona del Mar, on one of the weekends they visited us. They couldn't wait to tell us about their decision, and when Hopkins pulled up in the driveway, the two of them ran up to the front door holding hands. "We have something we need to tell you right away," Shakespeare said. "It's something urgent."

I had no idea what they were going to say.

"What is it?" Sarah asked.

"Everyone needs to sit down."

We all walked into the front room and took our places on the sofas. "So what's so tremendously important?" I asked.

"Show him," Shakespeare said to Becky, and she held out her left hand, her ring finger fully extended. On the finger was a big diamond engagement ring.

At first, Sarah and I were confused. "Becky's getting married?" I said.

"To who?" Sarah asked.

"To me," Shakespeare said. "We're going to tie the knot next month."

"The two of you?" I asked.

"Oh," Sarah said. She looked like she'd just been kicked in the stomach.

"How can you do that?" I asked. "You're a monkey. She's a girl."

"It's all worked out."

"What do you mean it's all worked out?"

"Thank the state of Nevada."

"Nevada?"

"We're going to get married in Las Vegas."

"Can a monkey get married there?"

"The state of Nevada said they'd do it. Just for Becky and me, they said they'd issue a license. We're going to be husband and wife."

"Are you sure you understood them correctly?" I asked.

"I talked to them too," Becky said. "It's what they promised. They said they'd do it for us. We're going to get a letter from the governor to take to the marriage bureau."

"I think they're doing it for the publicity," Shakespeare added. "But who cares? So long as they do it. I'll be the first monkey ever to take a human wife. Becky will be my wife, and I'll be her husband."

Ordinarily, I wasn't one to darken Shakespeare's dreams. Very seldom had I ever told him he couldn't do what he wanted, especially if it was important to him. But had he really thought this through? A capuchin monkey married to a very human girl? I was used to Shakespeare doing some amazing things with his life, but this? The idea of him getting married to Becky took me by complete surprise. I didn't know whether I should be supportive or put my foot down and try to prevent the whole thing from taking place. Then I thought, why not? Why shouldn't Shakespeare be allowed to get married, and why not to Becky? If he loved her, and she loved him, who was I to prevent this union? And who was anyone else to interfere? But it was so weird, wasn't it?

I couldn't believe the next thing I said. "I think this is great news."

"You do?" Sarah said.

"I do."

"Have you told Becky's parents about this?" Sarah asked.

"Not yet," Becky said. "We were going to call them tonight."

"You're going to tell them over the phone?"

"Yes," Shakespeare said.

"Don't you think you should tell them in person?" Sarah asked.

"We're both too busy to fly up to Seattle."

"Have they even met Shakespeare?"

"They met him the last time they came down to visit," said Becky. "They said they liked him."

They might have liked him, I thought, but no doubt they had no idea that Shakespeare was about to become their son-in-law, a long-tailed, little husband to their daughter. Certainly, they had never expected their daughter to marry a monkey. They would probably throw a fit. One could only imagine. My guess was that they would be on the first flight to Los Angeles in order to meet with their daughter in person and put an end to this crazy plan, and I turned out to be right.

Becky's parents arrived at the airport the next morning, rented a car, and drove directly to the school. But they did not see Becky; instead, they asked the school for my name and address and drove down to my house. They wanted to confront me, the owner of this audacious monkey. They had it in their minds that I could and would control this situation. When they arrived at my house, they rang the doorbell, and I answered.

This was the first time I had met Dr. and Mrs. Carlson. They were both in their midforties, and they looked their age. Dr. Carlson was dressed in a suit and tie, and his wife wore a blouse, slacks, and lots of costume jewelry. They were a nice-looking couple, what you'd expect of a doctor and his wife. I invited them into the house. Sarah was gone at the time, out grocery shopping, so I had to face these people by myself. Neither of Becky's parents looked anything like her; they were both so nicely put together, trim and physically fit, every hair in place, well-proportioned. There's not much I can say to describe them other than to say they were handsome. In fact, they were extraordinarily handsome. Becky's mom seemed friendly enough, but Dr. Carlson's demeanor was all business. I asked them to take a seat on one of the sofas in the front room, and I sat down across from them.

The doctor's posture was awkward and rigid, as though he couldn't possibly make himself comfortable. "We have a problem," he said.

"Do we?" I asked.

"Surely you know about our daughter and your monkey?"

"That they're planning to marry?"

"Yes, that."

"I found out yesterday," I said.

"Well, so did we."

"You could've knocked us over with a feather," Mrs. Carlson said.

"We're expecting you to put a stop to this," said the doctor.

"Me?"

"Shakespeare is your monkey, isn't he?"

"Yes, he's my monkey."

"You need to put the brakes on this."

"I don't think I can. In fact, I don't think I should."

"You're kidding, right?"

"No, I'm not."

"We're wasting our time here," the doctor said to his wife. He started to stand up.

"Wait," I said. "Just hear me out."

"You have something to say?"

"I do," I said.

The doctor sat back down. His wife put her hand on his forearm, seemingly hoping to calm him. I don't want to give the impression that the man was outright mean or angry. I mean, he seemed a little of both, but he was also something else. He was frightened. Yes, it was fear I saw in his eyes, fear of everything that might happen should his daughter go through with this crazy marriage—for who knew what would happen? Not just to the doctor and his wife but also to their sons and most importantly to Becky. I had thought about this a lot since hearing the announcement the day before, and I did have something to say to Becky's parents.

I said, "You used to read a fairy tale to Becky when she was a child called 'The Ugly Duckling.' She told us about this story, how important it was to her. Can I be honest with you? I'm not sure how you're going to take this, but I have to tell you how I see this situation and what it means to your daughter. Becky isn't exactly what you'd call a knockout in the looks department. I don't mean to say she's ugly, but by her own admission, she isn't exactly being fawned over by all the boys at college. She isn't asked out on dates. She spends a lot of time alone. Boys show little interest in her, and the same goes for other girls she'd like to be friends with. She's lonely; are you even aware your daughter is lonely? Do either of you know what it's like to be lonely, to be the one who is always left out? Do either of you know what it's like to be the ugly duckling that never grew into a swan? I can tell by your good looks that you don't. You have no idea. The girl has been heartbroken, I think—that is, until she met our monkey. Shakespeare has changed her life. She told us this. She didn't just hint at it; she came right out and said this to us. You should know that Shakespeare has a good soul, and he will treat your daughter well. I think he loves her, and I believe she loves him. I think we all need to keep our minds open and accept the future these two have planned for each other. You need to give Shakespeare a chance. I think if you do, you will see your wonderful daughter experience the chance to become the magnificent swan you promised she would be when you read to her, when you filled her with hope and promise for a fulfilling future. With Shakespeare as her husband, she can become that swan."

The doctor just stared at me for a moment. It was hard for me to tell what he was thinking. I noticed his wife squeezing his forearm with her hand, again trying to calm him. Finally, he said, "This is crazy. Shakespeare is a monkey. Okay, he can talk, and maybe he's a nice guy. But he's still a monkey, and no one will be better off if our daughter marries a monkey. If you won't stop this marriage, I will."

Cupid's Arrow

S arah and I packed for the trip, loaded the car, and were on our way. I
drove us through the annoying Southern California traffic toward the
desert, toward the barren state of Nevada and its crown jewel city. It was a
Friday afternoon, probably the worst time we could've picked to make the
drive, for the freeways were packed with cars. There were people on their
way home from work, others on their way to the desert to play in the dirt
over the weekend with their noisy motorcycles and ATVs, and of course,
many like us who were just on their way to visit Las Vegas. Becky and
Shakespeare had had the right idea; they had left with Hopkins as their
driver earlier in the morning, missing all this bumper-to-bumper traffic.

I looked over at Sarah in the passenger seat as she thumbed through a
magazine. "Do you think Becky's parents will show up?" I asked.

"I don't know," she said.

"For Becky's sake, I hope they do."

"I wouldn't be surprised if they stayed at home, especially after
everything her father did to prevent the wedding."

"He was not an easy man. I did my best to talk to him, but I don't
think he listened to me. I mean, I think he listened, but he didn't want to
hear what I had to say."

"You said the mother seemed reasonable."

"Yes, I think Mrs. Carlson could've been talked into coming if it were
up to her. She seemed like a rational person, but I also got the impression
that she was the sort of wife who, after all was said and done, would do
as she was told by her husband. And I think Dr. Carlson would rather see
Becky marry a child molester or a drug addict than marry a monkey. If
Becky's mom actually talks him into coming, it will be a miracle."

Sarah looked deep in thought for a moment, still thumbing through her magazine. Then she said, "This is pretty weird, isn't it? Did you ever think we'd be driving to Las Vegas to witness Shakespeare getting married?"

"Not in a million years."

"No," Sarah said, "not in a million."

"In all this time, the idea of Shakespeare getting married never even crossed my mind." Changing the subject, I said, "This drive is making me drowsy. I'm going to stop for a cup of coffee."

"I'd like one too."

"The sign said there's a Starbucks ahead."

"Ah, Starbucks. They're everywhere. It's like they follow me around."

I pulled off the freeway at the exit and drove to the Starbucks, which was in a small shopping center. We got out of the car and headed toward the entrance. It was hot outside, and the wind was gusting, sending debris and litter flying everywhere. God, how I hated the wind; my hair was now a windblown mess. I pushed open the door for Sarah, and the two of us walked into the busy store while I combed my hair back into place with my fingers. Sarah used the restroom while I placed our orders with the kid at the cash register. When we got our drinks, we returned to the car and sped off. The coffee was hot, so I let it cool off in the cup holder before drinking it.

As we got further out of California and closer to the Nevada border, the heavy traffic began to clear, and the drive became a little easier. "Are you nervous?" Sarah asked.

"I suppose I am, a little."

"Shakespeare has been like a son to you."

"Yes, it's kind of weird, but I guess you could say that."

"Did escrow close on the house yesterday?"

"Yes, just as planned."

"So they can move in after the honeymoon?"

"There shouldn't be a problem."

"It was good of you to help them find a place to live so close to the campus."

"Actually, it was Evan who found the house."

"But you got the wheels rolling."

"Yes, I did. I just couldn't see Becky living with Shakespeare in that crazy apartment. It was designed as a bachelor pad for a monkey, not as a place to settle into with a new bride. He'll keep the apartment for his writing and studying, but that's all. Evan said he'd be fine with that."

Sarah continued to thumb through her magazine and then switched to a new one. She'd brought a whole stack of magazines for the trip. She asked, "Do you know who all has been invited to the wedding?"

"Shakespeare went through the list with me several days ago. Didn't he already tell you?"

"He told me a few of the names," Sarah said. "He said the professor and Dr. Barney were coming and that Evan would be there. I asked him if Rudy could come, and he said that'd be fine, so I invited Rudy. He should've flown in to Las Vegas from New York yesterday. He should already be there. Also, my parents are arriving sometime tonight from Nebraska. And Shakespeare wanted Hopkins to be there as well. He still likes Hopkins a lot."

"He told me they also invited one of Becky's old high school teachers. Becky was one of her favorite pupils. I don't think Becky had any close friends her own age, so this teacher is probably the only person from her past that she invited, other than her family. I think her name is Ruth Atkins."

"Not a lot of people have been invited. It's going to be a small group."

"Yes," I said.

"I think that's how they wanted it. They don't want it to be a big deal."

"No, it will be a big enough deal when the press and public get wind of it."

"I can only imagine," said Sarah.

"I can see the headlines now."

"What do you think is going to happen?"

"What do you mean?"

"How are people going to take it? Are they going to applaud Shakespeare and Becky for their bravery and stand behind them, or will there be a torrent of outrage and anger?"

"Probably a little of both," I said.

"It could be the most famous marriage of the twenty-first century."

Sarah was right. I don't think she was exaggerating. Other celebrity marriages would pale in comparison, for who ever would have imagined a twenty-year-old human woman marrying a seven-year-old monkey? People would be talking about this event for years, about how Becky, once just a simple girl attending UCLA, had married a rich and famous simian in Las Vegas. She would be easily as well known as any Kardashian, and people would want to know everything about her, every little detail of her life, every bit of minutia. Shakespeare and Becky would be on the front pages of newspapers, on the covers of magazines, and all over the six o'clock news. Everyone would want to learn more; they'd want to know everything about this sensational couple.

As Sarah and I approached Las Vegas, the sky was turning dark, and we could see the glow of the city in the distance. It was still hot outside, and we had the windows rolled up and the air conditioner on, blowing cool air into the car. I'd been to Vegas several times in my life, but this would be Shakespeare's first encounter with it, and I wondered what he'd think of the place, with all its crazy flashing lights, noisy and confusing casinos, and throngs of adults acting like adolescents. I think if he actually had known what Las Vegas was like, he might have had second thoughts about getting married there, or maybe not. Maybe it didn't matter to him, so long as he was getting married. I mean, that's what was important, not the ambiance of the surroundings, just getting married. And the governor had written them a letter, hadn't he?

Sarah and I checked in to the Mirage. It was a decent room, and they didn't overcharge us for it. We had dinner downstairs at one of the hotel's restaurants and then watched a pay-per-view movie on the TV before going to bed. The next day, the day of the wedding, we took a cab to the little chapel. The place was called Cupid's Arrow, and it was right on the strip, near several other similar wedding chapels. We were not the first to arrive, for Dr. Barney and the professor were already there, and so was Rudy. We went into the chapel and took our seats and waited for the rest of the guests to arrive. I looked around at the place while we waited, and I have to be honest: it looked a little like a nineteenth-century whorehouse with all its Victorian woodwork, red and pink curtains and drapes, and fancy velvet upholstered chairs. The room smelled floral, not like real flowers but like some sort of flower-scented air freshener. It was too sweet to be the aroma of the real thing; besides, there were no real flowers in the room. There were several bouquets, but they were obviously made of silk, and they were dusty and looked like they'd been there for years.

As we waited, the guests trickled in, and recorded organ music played in the background. Finally, it looked like everyone had arrived—well, everyone except for Becky's family. At five o'clock sharp the ceremony began, and Shakespeare and Becky walked into the room. There were two chairs facing each other at the front of the room, and Becky sat in one while Shakespeare stood on the other, so that they could face each other eye to eye. The minister and his wife then entered, and the organ music was turned off. There was still no sign of Becky's family. The minister began to greet the guests, and just as he did, Dr. Carlson, his wife, and Becky's two brothers walked into the room. I couldn't believe they had actually shown up, and I nudged Sarah and smiled at her. When Becky saw them, she grasped Shakespeare's hand, motioning toward them with her eyes. He smiled when he saw them taking their seats, and it was like everyone in the room sighed a deep breath of relief at once.

The minister spoke to us for about twenty minutes, reading from several pieces of paper Shakespeare had written on. Then the couple exchanged vows, and the minister asked if they would be faithful, obey, stay with one another in sickness and in health, and so on and so forth.

Becky cleared her throat and said, "I do." But Shakespeare seemed off in another world, standing on his chair in a daze.

"Well, do you?" the minister asked.

"Oh, I do, I do," Shakespeare said, coming to his senses, and everyone laughed—everyone, that is, except for Dr. Carlson.

Becky's father had sat stiffly through the entire ceremony, dour-faced and still as a statue. I felt sorry for the guy. For him the whole thing must have seemed like Chinese water torture. His wife might have talked him into coming, but he obviously rather would have been somewhere else, just about anywhere.

After the ceremony we all went to the top of Mandalay Bay for dinner. Shakespeare had made reservations, and they put a bunch of tables together for our group. When we all had arrived, the hostess led us to our seats and handed out our menus. There was no booster seat available, so Shakespeare stood in his chair at the head of the table, and Becky sat in the first chair to his right. It was a happy and loquacious group except for Dr. Carlson, who was still moping, finding it difficult to be the slightest bit festive.

Sarah's dad noticed the doctor's mood and tried to cheer him up by telling a joke. "Hey, Doc," he said. "Have you heard about the psychiatrist and proctologist opening a clinic together?"

"No, I haven't," Dr. Carlson said.

"They're calling it Odds and Ends."

Everyone laughed at the stupid joke except for Dr. Carlson. He managed a polite smile, but that was all.

"I know another proctologist joke," Dr. Barney said.

"Let's hear it," the professor said.

"It's not a dirty joke, is it?" Sarah asked.

"No, it's not dirty."

"Go ahead and tell it," I said.

"Okay, so there's this guy who has a glass eye," Dr. Barney said. "He likes to pop it out of its socket and poke it into his mouth in front of his grandkids, pretending to eat it, pretending to gulp it down. They always get a gross kick out of this, but one day the guy accidently swallows the eye for real. He hopes to pass it in his stool later on, but the eye plugs his bowels, and now he's constipated. So he goes to see the proctologist to get the eye dislodged, and the doctor bends the guy over and looks up his rear end with his scope. He sees the eye looking back at him, and says, 'What's the matter, pal? Don't you trust me?'"

Again, everyone laughed, everyone except for Dr. Carlson. It seemed like nothing was going to make him budge from his mood, so instead of trying to cheer him up, everyone just ignored him and began talking to each other. The guests chatted mostly about the ceremony and about how much they liked what Shakespeare had written.

"It was very moving," Judy said, and Sarah smiled approvingly at her mom.

"I thought it was beautiful," said Ruth, Becky's high school teacher.

"Shakespeare has a way with words," Sarah said.

"He always has," I said.

"Is that why you named him Shakespeare?" Mrs. Carlson asked. "Because of his ability to write?"

"No, actually, I named him Shakespeare before he'd said or written a word."

"But it was so auspicious," Shakespeare said. He was beaming.

"Yes, I suppose it was at that."

"Who ever would have thought a monkey would become one of our best-selling authors?" Rudy said.

"And a famous actor," Shakespeare said. "Don't forget about my movie."

"Who could forget?" I said.

"He was in a movie?" Becky's youngest brother asked.

I was a little surprised that he'd never heard of the movie; I thought everyone was familiar with it. "Oh yes, the movie came out last year."

"So he's an actual movie star?"

"A regular Hairy Grant," I said. This got a few laughs. "We're still getting offers from Hollywood, but Shakespeare turns them down. He wants to get his college education, don't you, Shakespeare?"

"I do," he said.

"And he wants to write another book."

"I'm working on one now."

"What's it about?" Mrs. Carlson asked. She was trying very hard to be nice, compensating for her husband's unfriendliness.

"Life and death in America."

"It sounds so serious," Mrs. Carlson said.

"It's not such a serious subject."

"Isn't death serious?"

"I'm not sure I'd describe it as serious. Life is like an ear of corn; it's only so many inches long, from one end to the other, from birth to death. It starts, and it stops. The fact that an ear of corn has two ends doesn't make it a serious topic; it just makes it an ear of corn."

The professor laughed.

"Did you guys teach him this?" I asked.

Dr. Barney said, "He comes up with this stuff all on his own."

"I wish I'd come up with that one," the professor said. "I'd like to take credit for it."

"So would I," Dr. Barney said.

"Speaking of corn, I'm getting hungry," Shakespeare said. "Where's our waiter?"

"I don't know."

"I'll go find him." Shakespeare hopped down from his chair and went off in search of the waiter. It didn't take him long to find him, and he came back pulling on the man's hand, bringing him toward the table.

"Your little friend tells me you're all ready to order," the waiter said to us.

"Yes, we are," I said.

The waiter proceeded to take all the orders. He was a very friendly fellow in his midforties. He wasn't particularly handsome, but he had an animated personality that made up for what he lacked in looks. I liked his black hair, which was parted straight down the middle, something you didn't see often anymore. This hairstyle gave him an old-fashioned appearance, like some happy guy right out of an old barbershop quartet, and all he was missing was the waxed handlebar moustache and garter on his sleeve.

Shakespeare was the last of us to order, and he asked for a bowl of fruit and a packet of saltine crackers. The waiter said he didn't think they had any saltine crackers, so Shakespeare asked that he just give him a small plate of the croutons they used for their salads.

"Very well, sir," the waiter said. It was amusing to see how respectful the waiter was to Shakespeare, the way he called him sir and treated him like a celebrity. He then asked for a photo of himself standing beside Shakespeare. I took the shot for him using his cell phone. "My wife isn't going to believe this," he said. "She's one of your biggest fans."

"And you're not?"

"Oh, of course, I'm a fan too."

"Have you read either of my books?"

"I don't like to read. But I saw your movie. Are you going to make another movie?"

"Maybe."

"So what are you folks doing here in Vegas?"

"We're on a secret mission," I said.

"I think we can tell him," Shakespeare said. "He has a trustworthy face."

"Can you keep a secret?" I asked the waiter.

"Oh yes, I can certainly keep a secret."

"It won't be a secret for long," Becky said. "Soon it will be all over the news."

"But how would you like to be the first to know?" I asked.

"I'd like that," the waiter said.

"Okay, here it goes. We're here for Shakespeare's wedding."

"His wedding?"

"Yes, he just got married."

"To whom?"

"To me," Becky said.

"He married you, a human? You two are married?"

"That's the general idea."

"Oh, wow."

"Are you surprised?"

"Yes, I guess I am. I mean, I didn't think a monkey would be allowed to marry a human. Is it all legal? Did they give you an actual marriage license?"

"Yes, they did."

"How does that make you feel?" Shakespeare asked.

"What do you mean?"

"Are you offended or angry? Or are you happy for us?" Shakespeare asked. "People are going to take sides, like they always do. Which side will you be on?"

"I guess I'm happy for you. I guess if that's what you two want, then it's okay with me."

Then Shakespeare asked the weirdest question. He looked the waiter right in the eye and said, "What do you think of us having sex?"

The question surprised all of us, and the waiter's face turned a little red. "Having sex?"

"Do you think it's okay? I mean, between a human and a monkey?"

"I don't know. Is that what you're going to do? How will you do it? Actually, no, don't tell me. It's none of my business."

"No, it isn't your business. But it's an interesting question, isn't it?"

"I think you're embarrassing him," I said.

"Too many people think marriage is all about sex," Shakespeare said. "But it's only a small part of the big picture. There are so many more things to marriage than sex."

"Yes, of course."

"I wouldn't mind a little sex," Becky said. I was surprised that she said this. She was more open about the subject than I would have expected.

185

"It's something we'll have to work out," Shakespeare said.

This was something I'd always liked about Shakespeare, his willingness to talk about whatever was on his mind. It could sometimes be embarrassing, but I think it was better than the alternative—refraining from talking about subjects just because they caused a few red faces. People always knew where they stood with my monkey, and people were always aware of what he was thinking.

The rest of the evening at the restaurant went well. I think we all liked our dinners, except for Sarah, who said her filet mignon was kind of tough. Hopkins made a toast to the married couple, and everyone clinked their glasses. Evan also made a toast, and so did I. Hopkins took lots of pictures with his cell phone, almost to the point of being a pest. The conversation then broke up into three groups, so that Sarah and I found ourselves talking primarily to Shakespeare, Becky, and her brothers, while Hopkins talked to the professor, Dr. Barney, and Mrs. Carlson. The guests at the other end of the table made up the third group. There was a lot of laughter, and everyone was having a good time. When we finally decided to call it a night, we went down the elevator together and then broke up to go our separate ways.

When Sarah and I arrived at our room, we changed into our pajamas and got comfortable on the bed. I turned on the TV and looked for a show to watch. I came across the local news, and to my surprise, there was a photo of Shakespeare filling the screen. I turned up the volume to hear what was being said. The newscaster, a man, announced that Shakespeare had been married in Las Vegas this evening, and then the photo switched to another shot, one of Shakespeare and Becky leaving Cupid's Arrow and getting into Hopkins's SUV. The photo surprised me. I didn't remember any photographers lurking outside the chapel, and I wondered how someone had been able to get the photo.

"The bride is Becky Carlson of Seattle," the newscaster said. "We understand that she's a twenty-year-old student Shakespeare met at UCLA. Her parents, Dr. and Mrs. Carlson of Seattle, were also at the wedding, along with a small group of assorted friends. We don't have any other details on the marriage but will bring them to you as soon as we get them."

The studio camera then switched to the man's female co-anchor. She laughed and said, "Now I've seen everything."

Leroy McNabb

"Do you think I've put Becky at risk?" Shakespeare asked. He was holding a letter in his hand, and we were sitting in the front room of his house. Becky was at school, attending classes, and I had come to visit at Shakespeare's request. He'd said it was important, so I had canceled my tennis match that afternoon and driven up to Los Angeles right away. This was about four weeks after the wedding in Las Vegas, and Shakespeare was worried about this particular letter. Becky and Shakespeare had received many angry and life-threatening letters since the wedding, but this one troubled him more than the others.

"Read it to me again," I said.

"Here," Shakespeare said. "You can read it for yourself. I don't want to read it again. I've already read it five times."

I took the letter in my hand and read from beginning to end. It was creepy, written by someone who clearly wasn't quite right in the head, and it outlined all the writer's reasons that Shakespeare shouldn't have been allowed to marry Becky. He went into great detail about the unraveling of the moral fabric of America, how we were condoning promiscuity and homosexuality and now even bestiality and how we were all doomed to become one giant red, white, and blue Sodom and Gomorrah. According to the letter, Shakespeare's wedding was a gross abomination, a blatant act of heresy that needed to be rectified, and the writer stated in no uncertain terms that he was up to the task of making things right. The writer identified himself as Charlie but said this wasn't his real name. Charlie said he would take whatever action was necessary to break up Shakespeare and Becky, even if it meant killing one of them. Charlie then went on to make it clear that he had been stalking them, mentioning all the things they did during their days, where they were at each hour, where they ate their meals, and even what bathrooms they used at the university. Like I said, it was creepy to think this man was so obsessed.

"Have you noticed anyone following you?" I asked.

"Never," Shakespeare said. "But I suppose I should keep my eyes open. And so should Becky. This guy sounds determined. This is more than a typical piece of hate mail; I think it's serious."

"We should call the police."

"You think so?"

"Yes, I think it'd be a good idea."

So that afternoon I called the police, and two detectives came to the house. One was named Connors, and the other was Eagleton. Detective Connors was a heavyset fellow with bushy eyebrows and a head full of messy brown hair. He had small, piercing eyes, and his clothes were wrinkled, as though he'd slept in them. Detective Eagleton, on the other hand, was nicely dressed in well-pressed clothes and very neatly groomed. Eagleton's features were ordinary, with nothing much to distinguish him from anyone else. I let the two men into Shakespeare's house, and the four of us sat in the front room. Shakespeare offered them something to drink, but they said they were fine.

"So let's have a look at this letter of yours," Connors said.

"It's right here," Shakespeare said, and he handed Connors the letter.

Connors held the letter so that Eagleton could read along with him at the same time. When they were done reading, Connors placed the letter on the coffee table. "Have you noticed anyone following you?" he asked.

"No one," Shakespeare said.

"How about your wife? Has she noticed anything unusual?"

"She's never mentioned it."

"Has she seen this letter?"

"No, I just got it this morning."

"Charlie is stalking the two of you," Connors said. "Stalking is illegal. So is making death threats."

"Do you think you can arrest him?" I asked.

"I could if we knew who he was. But we can't very well arrest a ghost. Our success with this will depend on what Charlie does from here on out. He'll need to make a mistake—do something to reveal himself. We'll take the letter and envelope to our crime lab. Maybe they can come up with something, a fingerprint or some DNA. But unless we come up with some more evidence than the contents of this letter, there isn't much we can do."

"So what does Shakespeare do in the meantime?" I asked. "What should his wife do?"

"They should be careful," Eagleton said.

"Yes, and be on the lookout," said Connors. "If you think you spot this Charlie character, call us. Don't try to apprehend him yourself."

"That's it?" I asked. It was a little disappointing that the police weren't offering to do more. I asked if they could provide an undercover cop to follow Shakespeare and Becky for their protection, but Connors said they weren't in the bodyguard business; if I wanted this sort of service, I would need to hire a private eye.

"Odds are that it's just an empty threat, that Charlie is just trying to scare you," the detective said. "We've seen this sort of thing before, and it seldom amounts to anything serious. If this guy really wanted to kill you or your wife, he'd probably just do it. He wouldn't warn you with a letter."

Shakespeare heard what the detective said, but it didn't make him feel much better about the threat. When the detectives left the house, Shakespeare and I spoke more about the situation, and he decided that he needed to tell Becky about the letter. He didn't want to alarm her over what might be nothing, but she deserved to know what was going on so that she could keep her guard up, just in case Charlie was for real. Shakespeare also wanted to find a private eye for protection. Neither of us had any idea how to go about finding a good private eye, so we looked on the Internet and tried to locate someone who would be appropriate. We found one person who advertised himself as a bodyguard, among other things, and Shakespeare had me give the guy a call. His name was Jason Epstein, and he told me he'd take on the project, but he didn't want to meet us in person, thinking Charlie might be watching. Instead we arranged everything over the phone, and Jason said he'd immediately put his team to work shadowing Shakespeare and Becky, to try to find out who Charlie was. We hoped Jason and his team could gather enough evidence so that the police could arrest the man. This felt weird, like we were now involved in some movie thriller, trying to catch a bad guy before he caught us—or before he caught Shakespeare or Becky, I should say, for no threats were ever made against my life.

Three months following the letter's arrival, during which time Jason Epstein continued working to find Charlie, Sarah and I were trying to get used to Shakespeare's new life. Things were much different now that Shakespeare was married. He no longer came to visit us every weekend the way he used to because he now had his own life with Becky. He was also very busy with school and even busier working on his new book. His goal was to complete the book before he turned nine, and he was now just about eight years old. It occurred to me that we'd never thrown a single birthday party for him, since I had never had a precise date for it. When I got him, all Vern had told me was that Shakespeare was roughly a year old.

Sarah suggested we make up a birth date for him and throw a little surprise party. I thought Shakespeare would get a kick out of this, so we picked a date and decided to call it his birthday. Sarah got a cake and some party favors, and we invited the professor and Dr. Barney over and then asked Shakespeare and Becky to visit our house that night, ostensibly just for dinner. When they arrived with Hopkins, we all jumped out to the front porch and shouted, "Happy birthday!"

I think Shakespeare was truly surprised. "How do you know today's my birthday?"

"We just made it up," I said.

"It should be close," Sarah said.

"I think this is wonderful," Becky said.

"Yes, thank you," said Shakespeare.

"Let's have some cake," I said.

We stepped into the house, and Sarah went into the kitchen. She took a moment to light the candles and then returned to the dining room with the cake. If Shakespeare had been a little younger, I think he would've jumped up and down and clapped his hands, but he was older now and did a better job containing his excitement. Sarah set the cake down on the table, and Shakespeare climbed up on a chair and blew out the candles. Everyone applauded him.

"Did you make a wish?" Sarah asked.

"Of course," Shakespeare said. "You don't think I'd blow out the candles without making a wish, do you?"

"I'll bet he wished for world peace," the professor said.

"Something like that," said Shakespeare.

"Ha," Dr. Barney laughed.

"I think it's funny how humans are so vehement about celebrating their birthdays," Shakespeare said.

"It's tradition," I said.

"It's more than that."

"In what way?"

"As in how important it is for you to keep track of the years. Keeping count of the years is so important to humans. Counting the number of years is more important than the quality of the years themselves. Human beings are counters. Other animals don't do this."

"So who wants a slice?" Sarah asked. Everyone said they wanted some, and Sarah served it up.

"How's the book coming?" the professor asked.

"Yes, how's the book?" Dr. Barney repeated. Neither the professor nor the doctor had seen Shakespeare since the wedding, and both were curious to know how he was progressing with his book.

"It's coming along well," Shakespeare said. "Right now, I'm writing a chapter about hypocrisy. It's going to be a long chapter. I might have to break it up into several parts. When it comes to life and death, Americans are relentless hypocrites. It's incredible, the way they say one thing while doing the opposite."

"Is that true?" I asked.

"Oh, you can bet on it."

"Our cynical little monkey," the professor said, smiling at Dr. Barney.

"It isn't cynicism," Shakespeare said.

"What is it then?"

"I'm just being honest. I'm telling it like it is. What is it people in this country like to say about life? They like to say it's sacred, right? It's the one thing everyone seems to agree on—that life is sacred. Yet what do people actually do? They kill and kill, and then they kill more. I don't know how to state it any more succinctly or honestly. If human beings are anything, they are killers. They kill by the thousands, by the millions, and they take lives from the living like no other species on this planet. They kill themselves, and they kill others. They kill both men and women, they kill their young, and they kill their unborn, not by accident and not just every once in a while, but steadily and purposefully. Do you have any idea, for example, how many abortions take place in this country every year?"

"No," I said.

"Nearly a million. A million killings every year for what? For convenience?"

"Do you consider abortion murder?"

"Who said anything about murder? I'm just talking about killing."

"So you're against abortion?"

"No, I'm not against it. Myself, I don't care either way whether a woman aborts her child. I'm just trying to call a spade a spade. Abortion is killing. You may think it's justifiable, or you may think it's horrific, but it's still killing. And every year people in this country kill twice as many unborn babies as there were soldiers who died in the Civil War. Every year this happens, as surely as the earth circles the sun. Do you see the hypocrisy here?"

"I guess I do."

"I say, go ahead and abort your babies, but don't turn around and claim life is sacred."

"But life is sacred, isn't it?"

Shakespeare didn't answer my question. Instead he asked, "Do you want to hear more hypocrisy?"

"I guess so," I said.

"How about war? Now we're not talking about unborn fetuses. Now we're talking about all kinds of living, breathing people, all different ages, from all walks of life."

"Okay."

"Americans love a good war, don't they? They pretend to believe that war is hell; that's what they like to say. Yet they send their young and able-bodied youth off to kill and die like they're sending them down the street to play baseball with their friends. It's an unbelievable thing. Young men and women in the prime of their lives, actually just beginning their lives, barely old enough to drink or smoke, are sent off to fight in the wars caused by their elders. I can't even fathom this. Why in the world would anyone want to send his son or daughter off to war? It makes absolutely no sense to me, no matter how I try to justify it, no matter what kind of spin I put on it. Sure, there are times it is necessary to fight, but these times are few and far between. The truth is that when it isn't even necessary to fight, humans go to war. Americans love to do this. They manufacture causes, rationalize excuses, and kill others and allow their own children to be killed. They take sides and dig in their heels, flying their flags and blowing their bugles. Americans just can't get enough of it.

"We live in a killing culture. If you're having difficulty believing this, just look at the movies we watch. Look at the advertisements and trailers. How many of these involve some actor holding a gun? Does life imitate art, or does art imitate life? Does it even matter anymore? Clearly, this country is obsessed with handguns and rifles, with people shooting at each other, with people taking each other's lives, not just far away at war but here at home on our own soil, American against American. You look to your Constitution and pervert the right to bear arms for a well-regulated militia as the right to bear arms, period, not to defend the country, but to shoot at each other. It's amazing how so many Americans have interpreted the Constitution this way. And gun proponents would have you believe that the more guns we pump into society, the safer everyone will be. It's crazy, isn't it? Americans are desirous of a safe existence, yet they're also obsessed with having the ability to kill each other, at close range and long range, at any distance. And I'll tell you something else. It's ironic that so many right-wingers in this country are so antiabortion, while at the same time so pro-gun. It's also ironic that those who condone killing unborn babies are often vehemently against their fellow Americans carrying guns. The hypocrisy works both ways. The hypocrisy is rampant.

"What is it about killing other human beings that Americans find so irresistible? They do say life is sacred, but they can't seem to help themselves. They've just got to kill. Shouldn't they be shocked and outraged by this behavior—I mean, really shaken up over all this violence? Where was the outrage when we flew halfway around the world to wage war on Iraq? Do you know how many civilians were killed in this crazy war to find weapons of mass destruction that didn't even exist? Nearly as many innocent civilians were killed in Iraq as were killed by the atomic bombings of Japan. I don't think most Americans know this, and I don't think many of them even care. Americans were put into an emotional frenzy when three thousand people died in the World Trade Center tragedy, yet the deaths of over a hundred thousand Iraqi civilians at the hands of our government barely registered a raised eyebrow."

"You make humans sound so evil," I said.

"It has nothing to do with being evil. Killing is just something humans do. I guess what amazes me isn't that humans like to kill, but that they like to pretend not to like it. They say it's a cardinal sin; then they do it anyway. They claim to believe that killing is wrong, while at the same time killing. All you have to do to end the hypocrisy is say killing is okay. But humans will never say this. They think if they say killing is okay, everyone will just start killing each other."

"Isn't this true?"

"I don't know. Is it?"

"Seems to me there need to be rules."

"It's funny, isn't?"

"What's funny?"

"The smarter an animal is, the more it needs rules to behave. You'd think it would be the other way around—that with intelligence, an animal would inherently understand why it is important to behave properly, yet this isn't true, is it? The smarter the animal is, the more it needs rules to guide its behavior, because being smart apparently predisposes it to act badly."

I was amazed, and yet I wasn't amazed. I mean, I knew Shakespeare was smart, but I was now so impressed by how he was able to analyze and talk about complex things. It would've been impressive if he'd just been a young man in college, but a monkey?

I wanted to hear him speak more about his book, about all his ideas, but Sarah said it was time to open presents. All of us had something to give him, including Becky and Hopkins, who had been told about the birthday idea several days earlier. Shakespeare was the only one who'd been surprised by our little party. Sarah led us into the front room. The rest of us had finished our cake while Shakespeare was talking, but Shakespeare still had some left to eat, so he brought his plate with him and set it on the coffee table. "Can I have some milk to go with this?" he asked.

Sarah went to the kitchen to get him a glass and then handed out party hats to everyone, colorful paper cones with elastic strings to go under our chins. We all put on our ridiculous hats, and Shakespeare got a big kick out of this. I could tell by his demeanor that he was truly enjoying himself.

Hopkins handed him his first present. "This is from me," he said.

"From you?" Shakespeare laughed. "What could it possibly be?"

"Open it," Hopkins said, perched on the edge of his seat. He couldn't wait for Shakespeare to see what he'd bought.

Shakespeare carefully unwrapped the present and held it up for everyone to see. It was a hardbound book of interviews conducted with Bob Dylan over the years. "You said you were interested in him," Hopkins said. "Remember when we were talking about him?"

"Yes," Shakespeare said. "People call him a genius, and I'm always interested in reading about geniuses. I've heard some of his songs on the radio. Thanks for this, Hopkins."

"You're welcome," Hopkins said.

"Open mine next," Becky said. Her colorful party hat and big nose made her look sort of like a clown, and I stifled a chuckle. She handed Shakespeare her gift, and he proceeded to unwrap it.

"Well, I'll be darned," he said. It was a kit for making sushi, something I never would have thought to give Shakespeare. To think I had lived with him for so many years, and I had no idea.

"You like sushi?" I asked.

"Love it," Shakespeare said.

"I've been taking them to a little sushi bar on Hollywood Boulevard," Hopkins said. "It's one of his favorite restaurants."

"Now you can make your own at home," Becky said.

"Yes, I can't wait."

"Here," the professor said. "This is from Dr. Barney and me."

Shakespeare took and unwrapped their gift and opened the top of the box. Reaching inside, he removed a big golden trophy cup with a heavy white marble base. On the base was an engraved plate, which Shakespeare read aloud. "Shakespeare, World's Best Capuchin," he said. Then he laughed.

"You said you always wanted a trophy," Dr. Barney said.

"Now you have one," the professor added.

"Yes, a trophy!" Shakespeare exclaimed. He held it high over his head and did a little dance. "I'm a champion," he said. "Shakespeare, the world's best capuchin!"

We all laughed.

"I know exactly where I'm going to put it when we get home, on the mantel over the fireplace in our front room."

"What a terrific gift," Becky said.

"Here's the last one," Sarah said, handing him another present. "This is from Marty and me."

"Another book?" Shakespeare asked, feeling through the wrapping.

"It's sort of a book. Open it."

Shakespeare tore off the paper, tossing the wrapping aside. He looked at the present curiously. It was a photo album Sarah had put together with pictures of all of us, from when I first brought Shakespeare home from Vern's up until the day he left for UCLA.

"We wanted you to have something to remember all those years by," Sarah said. "We went through all our photographs and picked out the best for you."

"Wow," Shakespeare said.

"Do you like it?"

"I love it," Shakespeare said. He was thumbing through the photo album, looking at the pictures. "We had such good times here."

"Yes," I said. "I think we did."

"So many memories."

"This is going to make me cry," Sarah said.

"Time to change the subject," Hopkins said, not wanting to interrupt but not wanting to see anyone cry. "Did you tell Marty and Sarah about Charlie?" he asked Shakespeare.

"Charlie the letter writer?" I asked. "What about him?"

"Jason knows who he is," Shakespeare said.

"You're kidding."

"One of Jason's guys spotted a man following Becky. He'd kept a low profile for a while, but apparently he thought it was safe to start stalking us again. He was following Becky from her midday class to the library, and after she went into the library, he went home. Jason's man followed him in his car, and he got his home address and license plate number. Turns out his name is Leroy McNabb. Jason said he was going to turn the information over to the detectives so they could pay a visit. I think once he knows the cops are onto him, he'll stop what he's been doing."

"The creep," Becky said.

"He should go to jail," Hopkins said.

"I just want this Leroy character to leave us alone. He doesn't need to go to jail. I'm not going to press charges," said Shakespeare.

"I thought you wanted him arrested," I said.

"I've thought about it. He's a human being."

"That's an excuse?"

"He just did something stupid. No one got hurt. If the police locked up everyone who did something stupid, the jails would be overflowing into the streets."

"You really see it that way?"

"I do."

"You're a better man than I."

"That's the thing. I'm not a man at all. I'm a monkey. If you were to ask me if that makes me better than you, I would have to answer in some ways no. But in other ways, yes."

Saint Michael's

Was life sacred? And if life was sacred, didn't that imply the existence of God? And where did Shakespeare stand on the subject of God? You're probably more than just a little curious to know the answer to this last question. Well, so were many of Shakespeare's fans. You might be surprised at how many letters Shakespeare got asking him about his religious beliefs. Up until recently, Shakespeare and Becky had responded to these inquiries with harmlessly evasive replies, dodging the questions. But now Shakespeare wanted to set the record straight. He felt he owed his fans the truth, so he devised a plan.

Six weeks after we celebrated his eighth birthday, Shakespeare told me his intentions. He wanted to take a few weeks off from working on his book to write an article describing his monkey's view of God and religion. When he discussed this with me, I warned him to be careful. I told him people were funny about religion, and in my opinion, they'd be especially sensitive to having a monkey lecture them on the subject of God. I mean, who in their right mind would want to be told how to think about this subject by a monkey?

Nevertheless, Shakespeare wrote the article, and he found a home for it in the *New Yorker*. I didn't know how many people read the *New Yorker*, but I knew the magazine was, compared to others, highly respected for the quality of its articles. But respected by whom? Was it respected by the average television-obsessed citizen of this country, the average working stiff, the average God-fearing, churchgoing man or woman? This was not likely. It was more likely respected by intellectual types who were far and few between. America isn't exactly known for its abundance of intellectuals. Anyway, the article was printed, and it was a sensation. And when I say it was a sensation, I don't mean in a good way. Bits and pieces of it were pulled out of context and broadcast on TV and reprinted in newspapers and other magazines, with the apparent intention of eliciting outrage from the general public. Yes, the article created a quite a stir, written by an upstart monkey who now not only dared to marry a human but also dared to challenge humans and their faith in God. The article had the audacity to put forth Shakespeare's reasons for being a Godless atheist. An atheist of all things! It was unbelievable. It was like poking a stick into a beehive.

Everyone suddenly had an opinion, and most of them were not in Shakespeare's favor. Americans dug in their heels and took sides, probably the exact thing Shakespeare didn't want to happen. He had only wanted America to see his viewpoint, a thoughtful and honest attempt to seek the truth. I don't think he had any intention of stirring up so much controversy, pitting Americans against each other and, worse yet, pitting many of them against him. One of his most vocal critics was the current affairs talk show host Ned Freeman. Freeman's show, *America Live*, was broadcast live every evening and had millions of loyal viewers. Freeman began talking about Shakespeare in nearly every show. His criticism was sometimes scathing and other times humorous but in a ridiculing way. He never called Shakespeare by name; he always called him America's Godless Monkey. Freeman went on every evening about America's Godless Monkey and his heresies, and Shakespeare watched every show. He became obsessed and wanted to appear on *America Live* as a guest, thinking if he could assuage Freeman, he could win over the minds and hearts of everyone else. Shakespeare was not used to being in a position where so many people disliked him. He knew that the marriage to Becky had certainly created some friction between himself and the public, but now with this anti-God thing going on, with his having told everyone he was an atheist, the uprising against him was getting out of hand. He knew something had to be done.

Six weeks after the article was published in the *New Yorker*, Freeman finally agreed to have Shakespeare on his show. The show was broadcast every weekday evening from its studio in Los Angeles, so getting there would be easy. It was only about a twenty-minute drive from Shakespeare's house. I asked Shakespeare if he wanted Sarah and me to come for support, but he said no, this was something he had to do himself. He didn't even want Becky to come, so she stayed home. He had Hopkins drive him to the studio for the Thursday evening broadcast. I don't know what happened when he arrived, or anything about how he was treated by their staff, except for what Hopkins told me. Hopkins said they were accommodating and polite. I do know for sure what I saw on the actual show, when Shakespeare was put in the live hot seat. Ratings for that evening's show went through the roof because everyone wanted to see what Shakespeare and Freeman would say to each other. I would learn later that it was Freeman's highest-rated show.

I'll recount for you some of what was said because it reveals a lot about Shakespeare and what he was up against after having written his *New Yorker* article. Freeman started the interview by saying to the camera, "We have him with us here today as promised, America's Godless Monkey, a.k.a. the genius capuchin of UCLA, a.k.a. Shakespeare. Welcome to *America Live*."

"Thank you," Shakespeare said. "It's a pleasure to be here with you."

"Is it really a pleasure? You're here to talk about your recent article in the *New Yorker*, where you denounced God. You've caused quite an uproar."

"Among some, I have."

"Granted, there are a few fringe atheists who agree with what you wrote. But let's be honest: you've angered a lot of people."

"Yes, that seems to be the case."

"So you're here with some explaining to do."

"Yes, I'd like to explain."

"Maybe you can explain this. In your article you wrote, 'God did not create man, but man created God.' You wrote that, didn't you?"

"Yes, I wrote that."

"You go on to say, 'God is an invention, like a simple machine, like a wheel and axle or an inclined plane. The invention of God makes tasks easier for humans to complete, in this case the task of thinking. Humankind is always striving for easier ways to do things.' Is that what you wrote?"

"Yes, I did."

"And you really believe this?"

"I do. The concept of God allows humankind to avoid being bothered with difficult questions. Humans are able to think more clearly without having to constantly wrestle with bothersome unknowns. The idea of God allows for an ease of thought, the same way a simple machine allows for ease of work."

"So God is an invention?"

"Yes, an invention of humans."

"For ease of thought?"

"Yes, precisely."

"And you know this for a fact? You want your readers to accept this from you as a fact?"

"Well, it's my opinion."

"As a monkey."

"Yes, as a monkey. But whether I'm a monkey or a human being is irrelevant."

"Is it?"

"Yes, I think it is."

"Do you know how many people in America believe in God? And I'm talking about humans, not about you and your banana-eating relatives. Tell me, Shakespeare, how many Americans believe in God?"

"I don't know. A lot, probably."

"Over two hundred million adult Americans believe in God. Are you telling me that you know better than two hundred million Americans? You, a monkey, think you know more than the rest of us?"

"I do have my opinion."

"But would it be fair to say you're outnumbered?"

"Yes, that would be fair."

"Tell me, what makes you so special? What makes you think you can grasp something the rest of us are incapable of understanding?"

"But you are capable of understanding."

"Then why don't we understand? Why hasn't everyone read your article and said, 'Wow, this monkey's really onto something. I think he's right about this. By golly, there is no God'?"

"Most people haven't read the article."

"No?"

"Most people have only heard parts of it quoted out of context."

"So it's the media's fault you're misunderstood?"

"Yes, to a degree."

"You think if everyone read the entire article, they'd all suddenly change their minds and agree with you? Do you actually believe this?"

"Probably not."

"Then what are you saying?"

"I'm not sure, exactly."

"I thought you came on this show to explain yourself and change some minds."

"I did."

"Well, then change my mind."

"But your mind seems already made up."

"No, I've changed my mind before. I've changed my mind about a lot of things. They say you have a high IQ, so at least give it a try. Put some effort into this and see if you can change my mind."

I think Shakespeare could sense that Freeman was being sarcastic, so instead of accepting his challenge, he said, "They called Galileo a heretic. They said he didn't know what he was talking about."

"You're comparing yourself to Galileo?"

"No, I'm just saying certain beliefs can be contrary to conventional wisdom but can be accepted as true, given more time."

"How much time do you need? You know, this is only an hour-long show." Again with the sarcasm.

Shakespeare said, "Do you believe man was created in God's image? Isn't that what the Bible says?"

"Yes, I believe that."

"Then how do you explain me?"

Freeman laughed. "Oh, you're something altogether different."

"A man in God's image?"

"No, just a monkey. A very smart monkey, I'll grant you that. But I'd say some wires got crossed somewhere, as they do for a pair of Siamese twins, or a hermaphrodite, or a child with microcephaly. No offense, but you belong in a circus freak show."

This hurt. When Freeman said this, I saw something change in Shakespeare's eyes. I could tell he suddenly wished he'd never agreed to go on this show, and for a moment he looked like he was going to cry. He wasn't angry; he was just hurt, like he'd been betrayed. Freeman broke for a commercial, and just before the cut, the camera zoomed in on Shakespeare's unhappy face.

Sarah put her hand on my shoulder and squeezed. "This isn't going well," she said. "We should've talked Shakespeare out of doing this."

"I tried," I said.

"What did he think was going to happen?"

"He thought he'd have a chance to explain himself."

"Didn't he know what this man is like?"

"He knew."

"Then why go on his show?"

"Overconfidence, I suppose. He's used to talking to people who admire him, not people who dislike him. All these years, we've deliberately sheltered him from men like Freeman. That was probably a mistake."

"I wish there was something we could do."

"What's done is done," I said.

The rest of the show didn't go much better than the opening segment. I wanted to turn it off, but I watched the entire thing. Freeman had a rebuttal for every point Shakespeare tried to make. He made Shakespeare look like a self-absorbed fool. What is it about faith and religion that defense of them can come across so righteously, even though they make no logical sense? I agreed with almost everything Shakespeare had to say, but unlike Shakespeare, I'd always known better than to make these feelings known. It was because he was a monkey, I guess, that he didn't know when to keep his mouth closed. I should've done a better job coaching him to stay away from this sort of controversy, and I felt partially responsible for the way this show went. When it was over, I wanted to drive up to Los Angeles to talk to Shakespeare, to console him, to tell him things would be okay, but he probably just wanted to be alone. Besides, he had Becky. She was his wife, and it was now her job to cheer him up and support him, not mine.

I did call Evan after the show and asked him if he'd watched. Yes, he'd seen the entire thing, he said, and he was sorry things hadn't gone better, but he'd expected things to go as they did. "I tried to talk Shakespeare out of doing the show last week, but he insisted on meeting with Freeman."

"I tried too," I said.

"He thought he could handle it."

"He has a lot of self-confidence. He's not used to things going against him."

"You want to know what he needs?"

"A therapist?" I asked.

"No, your monkey needs a publicist."

"A publicist?"

"All celebrities have them. He needs someone to coach him on how to get along with the public and someone who can now do some damage control."

"Like a PR person?"

"Yes," Evan said, "a PR person. They're called publicists."

"I wouldn't even know where to look."

"Neither would I. But I know who can help you find a good one. What was the name of that producer Shakespeare worked with when he made his movie?"

"Adolph Nelson."

"He'd know the name of a good publicist. He probably knows lots of them. You should ask him. And I'd do it sooner rather than later."

So the next day I called Adolph and got the name of a publicist he promised was the best in the business. Her name was Hillary West, and her office was in Beverly Hills. I was told she didn't come cheap, but she knew what she was doing. At first Shakespeare wasn't thrilled about meeting the woman, but he eventually gave in and decided to see her. I told him he needed to take this matter seriously if he wanted to rescue his good standing with his fans and keep from becoming a pariah. When I said the word "pariah," he just stared at me, sort of bewildered.

"Do you really think it's getting that bad?" he asked. I said I did, and we scheduled a meeting with Hillary.

When we walked into her office, her face lit up. "So this is Shakespeare," she said, reaching down to shake his hand. "Ah, we're going to whip things back into shape for you. When I get done, you're going to shine like a brand-new copper penny."

I think Shakespeare took an immediate liking to this woman. She'd used the right words on him—being a monkey, he'd always liked shiny things. He sat down to listen, showing no signs of resistance. He wanted to hear everything she had to say.

Hillary was probably in her forties. She had a fresh and youthful face, bright red lips, and lots of rouge, yet she also gave the impression of being someone who had a lot of experience and who was serious. She was not a thin woman, although I also wouldn't call her fat. I'd say she was about eight inches shorter than I was, but she didn't go through the trouble of wearing high heels to make herself appear taller. She seemed to have no qualms about her appearance and was comfortable just being who she was. What really stood out about Hillary, however, wasn't any particular physical feature; rather, it was all the costume jewelry she wore, on her wrists and fingers, around her neck, and hanging from her earlobes. The jewelry tinkled and rattled as she moved, like she was made of wind chimes. When she got herself comfortable behind her desk, Shakespeare and I sat in chairs across from her. We were both startled when she slapped her hand down on the desktop.

"Will you trust me?" she asked.

"We've been told we can trust you," I said.

"I've looked into your situation. You folks have a problem."

Shakespeare said nothing. I said, "What do you think the problem is?"

"The way I see it, you've made two mistakes."

"Two?" Shakespeare asked.

"First, you married a human. Who's ever heard of a monkey marrying a woman? Right off the bat, you've alienated a whole group of people. I mean, same-sex marriages are one thing, but animals marrying humans? Many will never forgive you for this."

"But we love each other," Shakespeare said.

"Is he for real?" Hillary asked me.

"Yes," I said. "They do love each other."

"Do you think people care?"

"Do they?"

"No one cares whether you love your wife. They care that your wife is a human. And humans and monkeys don't belong together, not as husbands and wives. It's like a man marrying his bitch dog or some lady marrying her tomcat. It just isn't done. I mean, you've done it, but it just isn't done. You're asking an awful lot of your fans, to accept this as normal."

"So what's the second mistake?" I asked. I knew the answer, but I asked anyway.

Hillary looked at Shakespeare. "You're a self-proclaimed atheist."

"That's it?" Shakespeare said.

"I can tell you from experience that the public hates atheists. Personally, I don't know why. But I also don't know how to say it any clearer. Mess with their belief in God, and you may as well jump in front of a moving train."

"Is it that bad?" I asked.

"Yes, it's that bad."

"So is there anything we can do?"

"What's your mail been like?"

"My mail?" Shakespeare asked.

"Your fan mail. What kind of fan mail have you been getting recently? What's the ratio? How much of your mail is now hate mail?"

"We've been getting a lot of angry letters," Shakespeare admitted. "A lot more than usual, ever since the *New Yorker* article."

"Well, we're going to change that."

"How?" I asked.

"Do you trust me?"

"I do," Shakespeare said.

"Just do what I say, and we'll turn this thing around. There's nothing we can do about your marriage. I guess that's now a done deal, so I'm not going to ask you to get divorced. But there's a lot we can do about this God-versus-atheist thing. And there's a lot we can do to promote an image of you people will like. I take it you don't want to be hated?"

"No, I don't want to be hated."

"Will you do what I say?"

"I think so."

"Good, I think we're getting somewhere already. Just do what I say. Hillary knows what's best."

"What do I do?" Shakespeare asked.

"First, don't talk to anyone in the press. Refer all their questions to my office. Just tell them to speak to your publicist until you get the hang of what we're trying to do. Second, you're going to need to make a statement to your fans."

"A statement?"

"We need to defuse this atheist issue."

"I can't tell the public I believe in God. It would be dishonest. I don't want to be a liar."

"You won't have to be a liar. Give us a couple days to come up with something. We'll write the statement for you. We're very good at what we do, and we won't make you say anything you don't believe."

"Okay."

"I have an idea, and I think it will work. I need to make a couple calls before I tell you what it is. But if it's to work, you need to trust me. Yes, we need to start bringing back your fans. We need those who've abandoned ship to climb out of the water and get back on board. And we need those who've remained loyal to feel like they've done the right thing. Don't get me wrong—we won't be able to convince everyone, but there's no celebrity in the world who's loved by everyone. You're always going to have detractors. There will always be people who hate you and hold you in contempt. That's the price you pay for being famous. Are we on the same page?"

"Yes," Shakespeare said. "I think so."

"And you, Marty?"

"Yes, it all sounds good to me."

"Then let's make it so."

And with that, we concluded our first meeting with Hillary. She said she'd be in touch in two or three days, and we walked out of her office. When she did finally call, Shakespeare and I were excited to learn what she and her staff had come up with. I read the statement they'd prepared, and I had to admit I was impressed. They'd written a short but very carefully worded speech for Shakespeare to read to the press. According to Hillary, the reading would take place on the steps of Saint Michael's Cathedral in downtown Los Angeles, home of the nationally loved and celebrated Father Ernest Birdsong. The father had agreed to be there with Shakespeare, and he too would have some words to say. The idea was to make it appear that Shakespeare had the support and blessing of the father, that the two of them were good friends despite Shakespeare's atheism. So how had Hillary arranged this? I asked her that very question.

Hillary laughed and said Father Birdsong owed her a large favor. "I got the father out of a very difficult jam several years ago," she said. I didn't pry, so I didn't have any more details than that, nor did I need to have them or even want to know.

It was ingenious really, making Shakespeare appear to be friends with one of the country's most respected men of the cloth. I could only imagine what sort of jam this guy had been in and what Hillary had done to help him out of it. The press conference was held as promised at noon on a Saturday, on the church steps, and there was a huge turnout of reporters and cameramen. Father Birdsong took charge of the event, saying a few encouraging words about Shakespeare to start things off and then turning everything over to the infamous monkey.

There was a chair for Shakespeare to stand on so that he could read his statement at the podium. He climbed onto the chair, unfolded the paper Hillary had prepared for him, and proceeded to read. "First, let me thank my good friend Father Birdsong for arranging this press conference here on the steps of his beautiful cathedral."

Hopkins and I were both in the audience to watch, and we did so with anticipation. Becky, however, had stayed at home per Hillary's instructions. Hillary didn't think it was a good idea to have Becky there, reminding the public of Shakespeare's marriage.

Shakespeare held his paper and continued with his statement. "I've called you here to apologize for any statements I may have written or said recently that offend those of you who have faith in God. I have come to realize I was careless with my words, and I'm sorry for that. It was never my intention to cast God or any of his followers in a discouraging light; I was only trying to express my own personal beliefs. In this country we are all allowed to believe or not believe in God as we see fit, and one side of the issue should never disrespect the other. Freedom to believe in the God of our choice, or not to believe in a God at all, has always been a cherished freedom that makes this country so great. I have nothing but the highest admiration for the churches and many religions of this country, and I hope those of you who are believers will accept this heartfelt apology."

When Shakespeare was done speaking, he remained standing atop his chair, and Father Birdsong stepped up to the podium again. The father smiled and said to Shakespeare, "I think I speak for everyone across the country when I thank you for your sincere words. You're a good person, Shakespeare, and it's good to know we can all be such good friends." The father then reached out and shook Shakespeare's hand, and the two stood side by side to pose for some pictures.

I looked over at Hillary, who was also in the audience, and she winked at me and smiled. Hopkins whispered to me, "Jesus, Marty, that was awesome."

The event then turned into a question-and-answer session, and most of the questions from reporters were directed at Father Birdsong. He continued to do everything possible to convey his warm feelings for Shakespeare, and he was very believable. You never would have guessed that he was doing all this as a favor for Hillary. The father was such a polite man and an articulate speaker; it was no wonder he was so widely respected and admired all over the country. What he actually thought of Shakespeare and his atheism, I had no idea.

It was amazing what this little press conference did for Shakespeare's image. In the weeks that followed, the angry letters dwindled to almost none at all, and even Ned Freeman began to let up on his contentious rhetoric. Shakespeare's *New Yorker* article eventually slipped out of the news completely, and for the time being, my monkey was back in the public's good graces. People loved him again. They forgave him for being an atheist, and they even seemed to accept Becky being his wife. Hillary had done her job and had earned every cent we paid her.

Mint Jelly

The day had finally come. Nearly a year had passed since the press conference at Saint Michael's, and Shakespeare had finally completed the manuscript for his new book. He had kept the original title, *Life and Death in America*. He gave Sarah and me each our own copy to read, and he also mailed one to Rudy in New York and one each to the professor and Dr. Barney. Shakespeare was now nine years old, and Becky was twenty-two, soon to be graduating from college. I was thirty-one, and Sarah was twenty-six.

Life had been relatively uneventful since the press conference, and Shakespeare had been staying out of trouble, spending his time working on his book and on his studies. The book, of course, had been his primary focus, and he was very proud of it. He told me it was the best thing he'd ever written, and was it ever long. The manuscript was over a thousand double-spaced pages and nearly six inches thick. It made his earlier books look like pamphlets! It took me the better part of two weeks to read the entire thing, and when I was done, I actually felt out of breath. Sarah finished reading her copy just a day after me.

"What did you think?" I asked.

"It's amazing," she said.

"Do you think Rudy will publish it?"

"I'm sure he will. Aren't you?"

"I don't know."

"I don't understand. Do you think there's something wrong with it?"

"It's different, isn't it?"

"It was written by a monkey."

"I realize that."

"Shakespeare isn't human. You have to remember he sees the world differently."

"I'm not saying I disagree with anything he wrote. It's just a little bold."

"But his logic is sound."

"Remember all the trouble he got into when he wrote that article about his atheism?"

"Of course I do."

"Well, that was logical."

"What's the alternative? That he write something which makes no sense?"

"Of course not."

"Then what's the problem?"

"I worry about him."

Should I have been worried? Was I concerned about nothing, or was Shakespeare throwing himself in front of a moving train again, like Hillary said he'd done with the *New Yorker* article? Was this book too outspoken for the average reader? And did it go too far? Or was he just writing the truth as he saw it, as any bright English-speaking monkey would? What exactly was my problem with it? Didn't he have a perfect right to express his opinions?

I knew from experience that Shakespeare had to be careful. He was famous and influential, and people paid close attention to everything he said. It is a strange relationship that the public has with celebrities, the way they love to love them but also love to hate them. Celebrities are always under a microscope, and every word they utter is examined, weighed, and analyzed. And why? Is there a reason for this? What does it matter what a famous person thinks about anything? Some neighbor down the street might have the most bizarre thoughts and opinions known to man, or he may agree with everyone else about everything, but who really cares? He's just so-and-so down the street. But my monkey was another story, and all that he said and wrote seemed to matter to everyone. Well, almost everyone. I'm sure there were people who couldn't have cared less about what he had to say, but they were few and far between.

This intrigued me, the way people paid such close attention to celebrities, and it always amazed me the close attention they paid to Shakespeare. Was this important? Well, it was important to me. I'd always wanted him to go as far as possible, and I didn't want him constricted by our human mores. Yet what I hadn't anticipated was the way he'd be treated. The public could not have cared less about my monkey's individuality; instead, they just wanted him to be one of them, to think like them, to feel like them. They wanted him to conform and confirm: to conform to the status quo and to confirm that this status quo was right and righteous. Why are humans like this? Why do they look to their brightest thinkers to agree with them, to come up with nothing new or extraordinary? Isn't this what we all do? We insist on convention and cringe at change. We seem to like things just the way they are, no matter how upside-down they might be.

So should I have been worried? Shakespeare's book was hardly earth-shattering. Or was it? It did present a lot of new ideas. At least they were new to me, and I figured they'd be new to others. It was a monkey's view, a fresh, unfettered, logical look into the way Americans see and treat life and death. If someone had asked me personally whether he'd written anything shocking or subversive, I would have had to answer no. But I could still see how this book could spell trouble.

Take his chapter titled "Loving Death," for example. The title of the chapter alone was odd, for who in their right mind could love death? I was sure this would make a few people angry, maybe even many. "So why do men hate death?" he wrote. "Without death, their lives would be nothing." According to Shakespeare, death made life worth living; in fact, death made life possible. He said we should all love death as much as we love life. He said that humans strove to achieve things when there was a reason to do so and that death was the ultimate motivation. The more the threat of death was taken away, the less people appreciated their lives and the less they felt like the clock was ticking. Death was what caused humans to do things, not life. Life alone, without worry about death, would be vacuous and pointless. According to Shakespeare, without death hanging over their heads, life would have no meaning for humans at all. Motivation meant everything. When people were poor, they strove to earn money. When people were sick, they worked to get well. When they were sad, they made an effort to get happy. When they were cold, they tried to warm themselves up. And when people were faced with dying, they did everything possible to take advantage of the time they had left. Shakespeare wrote that the more humans did to keep death at bay in general, the more they were cheating themselves out of the fruits of life.

Does this make any sense to you? I think it was a sound argument. But people would hate it because it required that they love death, and who in their right mind would want to love death, either theirs or anyone else's? Who was going to be happy when the doctor told them they had a month to live? Who was going to smile when a loved one died in a car accident, reminding surviving family and friends how short life could be, proving that death was always lurking right around the corner? But the truth was, there was no reason to run unless you were being chased, and the closer death was to your heels, the faster you were going to move your feet. And it was a good thing for people to keep their feet moving, to stay on their toes. It was a good thing humans all had to run from death; otherwise, they'd never appreciate and take advantage of their lives. Have you ever talked with anyone who had a near-death experience? Didn't such people always relate how the experience had made them appreciate every little aspect of their lives? Even the smallest things suddenly had such great importance, and even the simplest realizations were succinct and profound. Forget life after death. And forget the spirit world or the idea of reincarnation. Death is death, as it should be. It's the end of life, and it's a good thing. People should love death as much as they love their own mothers, maybe even more, Shakespeare argued.

So would this make people angry, being told to love death more than their mothers? I thought so, and not just a little bit angry. I thought it would make them a lot angry. It presumed that death was a final ending, not a stepping-stone to another life. It was amazing, all the means people invented for life after death— heaven and hell; ghosts and spirits; people coming back as others, or even as animals. I thought it was funny that people would rather come back to earth as a dumb animal than face the prospect of never coming back at all. Yet did anyone really believe this nonsense? They said they believed it, and they paid it a lot of lip service. They got angry when you contradicted these beliefs and explained to them what death actually was. They didn't like these fantasies being taken away from them, yet they were just that, weren't they? They were desperate little fantasies. If people really believed in life after death with their hearts and souls, would they be so upset when a loved one died? Would they be so afraid of dying themselves? I didn't think anyone actually believed they were going to live on after their heart stopped beating, after they stopped breathing, and I think everyone knew deep down that death spelled the end. But I didn't think they wanted to be told this, especially not by a monkey. Who wanted a monkey bursting his bubble? Who wanted a monkey telling her that everything she really suspected about death was true, that it was so empty and final, for what would this mean? It would mean no matter what you did with your life, it wasn't enough. You had your chance, and you blew it. You could've done so much more! Odds are, if you were like most Americans, you spent most your life working at a job you didn't particularly like, watched a lot of TV, and spent a lot of time sitting in traffic. I thought that's how it was for most of us. People would be angry with themselves for squandering their lives, but they'd want to kill the messenger rather than themselves. They'd want to punish Shakespeare.

Can you imagine loving death? That's what Shakespeare was asking us to do. Death was the ultimate yardstick of human tragedy. Isn't that how we measured all the bad things that happened—by how many people died? How many people died in a plane crash, an automobile accident, a fire, a explosion, a capsized ship, or an act of terrorism? This is the ultimate number, the death count. How many people died in World War II versus World War I, how many unborn babies were killed by abortions, how many civilians died annually in the war on terror, how many smokers had been killed by cancer? Death was the ultimate tragedy, the ultimate consequence, and the ultimate crime. Was there a crime any worse than taking another's life? There were a thousand ways you could make the lives of others miserable, but kill someone, and you received the ultimate sentence—death by lethal injection, electrocution, or hanging by the neck or maybe, if you were lucky, spending the rest of your life in prison. Death was as serious as it got for us humans. Shakespeare was right to say humans were terrified of death. But they hated it when they should love it. They feared it when they should appreciate it. Without all this stinking death, life would be like a sun that refused to set, a day that refused to turn to night, a tedious story with no denouement, droning on forever with no end in sight. There was such a thing as too much of a good thing, wasn't there? We should be thankful for the Grim Reaper's scythe. Shakespeare wrote, "We should love death as much as we love life itself, for it gives our existence shape and mass, the way a potter's capable hands mold art from clay."

Do you buy any of this? What about the person who might argue, "Okay, so if death is such a good thing, how about I kill you right here and now? Will you thank me for giving your life shape and mass?" And I think that's a fair question. Shakespeare wrote the following answer: "We should be grateful to death because it makes life precious. And because life is so precious, we should do everything in our power to keep it from succumbing to death." I thought this made a lot of sense, in a strange sort of way. I mean, I really had to think about it for a while to embrace it. But it did make sense, and the more I thought about it, the better it sounded. We needed to love death but avoid it at all costs.

There was, according the Shakespeare, yet another reason for humans to love death. In this same chapter, Shakespeare wrote about reproduction, the great giver of life. He explained how dying made reproduction possible, how death was an essential part of the equation. None of us would be here were it not for death. Death made for life! What would happen if life forms continued to reproduce and create new life without the lives of the old ending? The world would be overrun with living critters and plants, choking and smothering each other, competing for scarcer and scarcer food sources. It would be a disaster.

Death has allowed the old to give way to the new. The old falls to the earth and decomposes, rotting and providing nourishment for new life to flourish. This is how all of us came to be, with the old giving their lives to make way for us, breathing life into the new generations, and over and over again, the new generations then grow old themselves, dying and making a place for the next generations. Death is essential in this process. The death of our own parents and grandparents is the prerequisite for our own lives, for our chance to be children, adolescents, parents, grandparents, and then corpses ourselves. We should love death because it allows us to live. Death is the very reason we're breathing, the reason our hearts beat and pump blood, the reason we have our place in the world, the means through which we're given life.

Do you fear death? You probably should. But do you resent death? Well, you probably shouldn't. You should fear death and love it simultaneously. Is it hard to love something that is tracking you down and trying to take your life? Of course it is, and it's one of the great ironies of life. Can you love a tiger that's gnawing at your throat? Can you love a high-powered rifle aimed at the back of your head? If you're trapped in a burning house, can you love the fire that's about to consume you?

In his manuscript, Shakespeare wrote, "You can fear death and try to stay alive, but when death finally wins, and it will, give it a big smile and say thanks for your life." I read this line to Sarah, and I asked her what she thought.

"So no more black armbands and tears," she said.

"No," I said.

"It's hard to imagine."

"No one will ever go for this. People love wallowing in their sorrow and self-pity. Taking this away from them would be like stealing."

"Do you think Shakespeare is wrong?"

"Wrong, no. I don't think that's the word for it. Inhuman might be more like it."

"Inhuman?"

"Because he's a monkey. Because he doesn't buy into the human grieving thing. I think people like to grieve, or they wouldn't spend so much time doing it every time someone they know dies. They wouldn't do it when they worry about their own eventual demise. But Shakespeare is right. Grieving over the dead is like crying over a sunset, as though it's the last time the world will ever see the light of day. Sure, one day is over, but there will always be that day to remember, and there will be plenty more days coming to replace it."

"So long as the world turns."

"Yes, so long as the world turns. And when the world stops turning, a sun will rise elsewhere, on some other planet, in some other galaxy. And death will be as much a blessing to that world as it is in ours—for death begets life, always and forever."

Yes, I actually said that to Sarah. I was starting to sound like Shakespeare with all this lofty talk about appreciating death. The big question here, however, wasn't whether I bought into this line of thinking but was whether the general public would agree or would just think Shakespeare was full of it. You have to really think about this stuff in order for it to make good sense, and people as a rule aren't all that fond of thinking. People want to believe death is bad and life is good, plain and simple. It's a tidy way to look at things, and it puts everyone on the same page. It's a wonderful thing when a baby is born, but when someone dies, it's time to cry and lament, time to put on our sad faces and deliver somber words, as surely and mechanically as workers on an assembly line. And it was my opinion that anyone who challenged this human ritual was begging for trouble—especially if that person happened to be a know-it-all monkey. It was one thing to be a monkey who has difficulty with God; it was wholly another to write a book that worshipped death.

It took Rudy only three months to get the book on bookstore shelves. He had pushed hard to get it edited and printed as quickly as possible because he wanted to have it available for Christmas. It came out in October, in plenty of time for the holiday season, and the publisher anticipated record sales. Shakespeare hadn't been in the news since the press conference with Father Birdsong, but Rudy had waged a large media campaign to create interest in the book and to get people thinking about Shakespeare again. There were no talk shows this time since Shakespeare said he didn't want to do this, but there were ads everywhere, and Fisher & Sons had sent out press releases and advance copies to all appropriate critics and influencers. I was told that on the day the book was made available for purchase, stores could barely keep up with the demand. I learned this later, but I wasn't actually around that day to see it. Neither were Sarah, Shakespeare, or Becky. The four of us had decided to miss all the hoopla and had gone to a cabin in the remote mountains of Big Bear. We wanted some privacy, to be away from everything, and the cabin retreat was a perfect place for us to get away.

The cabin belonged to Evan, who used the place to get away from things. It sat on five acres of pine trees and boulders, and he had loaned it to us for three weeks. There was no TV, no radio, no Internet, and no telephone service. There was no newspaper delivery or any mailbox. The four of us had left our cell phones back at our houses so we wouldn't be disturbed, and it was great being away from things for such a long time. I couldn't remember ever having been so out of touch with civilization for any time even approaching three weeks, and neither could anyone else. The timing of our trip was intentional, to avoid all the tumult that would surround the rollout of Shakespeare's book. Only Evan knew we were in the cabin, and we were sure he wouldn't tell anyone. For three weeks we were safe and secluded, without a care in the world. We spent a lot of time indoors, reading and talking, sitting around the fireplace, sometimes playing board games. We took walks in the woods, but we tried to be careful, not wanting anyone in the other cabins to spot Shakespeare. Becky and Sarah went into town for groceries a few times, but that was the only contact we had with people. Shakespeare would sometimes climb the pine trees that surrounded the cabin. He'd get way up high in them, and I'd shout for him to be careful. "You're kidding, right?" he'd say, laughing. I guess it was funny to him, me worrying about a monkey falling out of a tree.

One night at dinner, Sarah brought up Shakespeare's book. We humans were having lamb chops, green beans, and boiled potatoes while Shakespeare ate a banana and a big orange slice of cantaloupe. We'd all promised at the outset of this vacation that we wouldn't talk about the book, but we were running out of things to discuss. Besides, the book was on everyone's mind, whether or not any of us wanted to admit it. It was the reason we were all up at the cabin. "What do you think the critics are saying?" Sarah asked. "I'm dying to know."

"We said we wouldn't talk about it," Becky said.

"But don't you want to know?"

"Of course I want to know."

"Everyone's going to love it," Shakespeare said. "I'm sure of it."

"He's always so confident."

"It's the best thing I've ever written."

"Don't be surprised if some people don't like it," I said. I hated to be an Eeyore, but it was how I felt.

"You can't listen to them," Becky said.

"There'll always be that group," Shakespeare said.

"What group?" I asked.

"That group of people who don't like me."

"Like Ned Freeman?"

"Yes, like him," Shakespeare said. "I could write a thousand-page ode to the magnificence and loving spirit of the almighty God, and he still wouldn't like me."

"There are a lot of people just like him."

"But they're not my audience."

"Who exactly is your audience?"

"Animal lovers."

I laughed at this. "Yes, animal lovers do like you."

"Young people look up to him," Becky said. "He has a big following on our campus."

"Young people tend to be more open-minded," Shakespeare said.

"Older people are more set in their ways," Becky added. "New ideas intimidate them."

"How old is Ned Freeman?"

"Probably in his forties."

"I'd like to see Ned Freeman's face when he reads your chapter about terrorism."

"He'll probably bust a blood vessel."

"That chapter is going to make a lot of people mad," I said.

"You think so?" Shakespeare asked.

"People in this country don't see us as terrorists."

"Well, if it walks like a duck and quacks like a duck, then it probably is a duck."

"I'm just saying."

"Human beings are such amazing creatures," Shakespeare said. "It's a lot more interesting studying human beings than it is studying any other animal. They take themselves so seriously, yet their behavior is nuttier than any zoo cage full of wild monkeys. Why do people think monkeys are so fun to watch? They ought to watch themselves. Humans are the true comedians on this planet. Humans are hilarious."

"That may be your opinion," I said. "And it may be my opinion too. But I don't think other people believe they're as funny as we do."

"That's one of the things that makes them so funny. They're funny precisely because they don't know they're funny."

"Do you think we're funny?" Sarah asked. "Marty, Becky, and me?"

"You're different."

"How are we different?"

"Okay, I take it back. You're funny too."

"Are we?" Sarah laughed.

"If you only knew," Shakespeare said.

"You're a racist," I joked.

"I suppose I am. But I do love you guys."

"We know you do."

"Like a master loves his slaves," Becky said.

"Oh, not like that at all."

"Then like what?"

"It's hard to explain."

"Listen to him," I said. "He writes a thousand-page book about life and death, but he can't explain his love for the three closest people in his life."

"That's true," Shakespeare said.

"Funny, isn't it?" I said.

"Yes," Shakespeare said. "It is sort of funny."

"Pass me another lamb chop," I said.

Sarah passed one to me, and I cut into it with my knife.

"Do you ever think about the animals you eat?" Shakespeare asked.

"What do you mean?"

"I mean, do you ever wonder what they were like? Did they have names? Did they have any friends? Did they have personalities?"

"I've never thought about it," I said.

"How do they kill them? Does anyone know? Do they shoot them in the head? Do they slit their throats?"

"I don't know," I said.

"I don't know either," Sarah said.

"Don't ask me," Becky added.

"Why don't human beings eat monkeys?" Shakespeare asked.

"Maybe they do, in other countries," I said.

"Do you think they do?"

"I'm just guessing. I don't really know."

"I'm glad I'm a vegetarian," Shakespeare said. "No blood on my hands."

"No," I said, "there's no blood on your hands. But you're a monkey, and you'll never appreciate just how great it is to have a really fine piece of meat. Ah, the spoils of death. This lamb really hits the spot. Now can someone pass me the jar of mint jelly?"

Living Proof

When we returned from the cabin in Big Bear, we discovered that all hell had broken loose. Shakespeare's book was being talked about everywhere, and people were not the slightest bit pleased with it. It wasn't just Ned Freeman who was squawking; everyone seemed to have something disparaging to say. Overnight, Shakespeare had turned from the monkey in the good graces of Father Birdsong to a demon, to the Antichrist. He was not a pariah, not just yet, for being a pariah would have meant people were avoiding him, and they were doing anything but that. "Did you hear what he wrote about this?" was the question of the hour. "Did you hear what he said?"

I would've been curious to know how many of these people had actually read Shakespeare's book. I suspected most of them were getting their information from critics, newscasters, and talk show hosts. I'd always thought it was an awfully long read for the average person, and the public didn't do much reading, especially when it came to thousand-page books. They were probably getting their information from TV and the morning papers, or even from family and friends. But this didn't stop them from having strong opinions, even if the opinions had been given to them by others. "This is what happens when you give a monkey free rein to write a book," one lady said on the evening news. I thought, *Actually, this is what you get when you tell the truth to morons.* The only people who seemed to get anything positive out of the book were the fringe elements of society who would accept any opinion so long as it went against the status quo. And of course, there were the college students, who were probably siding with Shakespeare just to spite their bourgeois parents. Jeez, what a mess this was. It was much worse than I'd anticipated. Although I had expected some problems, I hadn't foreseen anything like this.

My first inclination was to call Hillary, to see if there was something she could do, but I didn't want to call her without talking to Shakespeare first. Becky called me before I could even pick up the phone, and she sounded worried. She said Shakespeare was getting death threats again, now more than ever, and although she thought calling Hillary was a good idea, something needed to be done right away to protect Shakespeare from the kooks and crazies. I'd never heard this kind of fear in her voice before, and I asked if she could put Shakespeare on the line. When he picked up, I said I was going to call Jason, our private eye, and ask him to send one of his men to their house. With one of Jason's employees there, we'd all be able to sleep easier.

Shakespeare said Hopkins was already there with Becky and him, spending the night on the couch, but if I thought it was necessary, I had his permission to send over one of Jason's guys. "This whole thing is getting out of hand," he said. "I've never seen such a fuss made over a stupid book. Now I wish I'd never written it."

We continued to talk, and I got Shakespeare's permission to call Hillary, to see if there was something she could do to quell the outrage. He had always liked the woman, and I knew he would say yes. She'd worked her magic before, and perhaps she could do it again—maybe get good old Father Birdsong involved again. Who knew what she'd come up with, but certainly she could think of something. This was precisely what she did for a living, and it was what we paid her for.

When I called, she said she'd been trying to reach me. "Where the heck have you been?" she asked, and I told her about our trip to Big Bear. She said, "Listen, I need to speak with you as soon as possible."

"I take it you've been watching the news?"

"The news?"

"All the turmoil over Shakespeare?"

"Oh, that's not why we need to talk. It is, and yet it isn't. I've got a problem."

"What kind of problem?"

"We need to talk in person."

"In your office?"

"No, I'll meet you at your home."

I didn't want to drive all the way to Beverly Hills, so I said, "That sounds great."

"Can you meet this afternoon?"

"I have a tennis match scheduled."

"Can you cancel it?"

"I suppose I can."

"I'll leave now. It'll take me a little over an hour to get there. You haven't talked to a reporter from the *LA Times* named Jeffrey Thompson, have you?"

"No, why?"

"I'll explain when I get there."

Hillary hung up the phone without even giving me a chance to say good-bye. It was sort of weird, the rush she was in and the way she had abruptly ended the call. Now she had me wondering just what was so important that she had to meet me right away, and at my home rather than in her office. I didn't have the slightest idea what she wanted to talk about.

I sat down on the sofa and opened the morning paper, which I hadn't read yet. I just wanted to kill some time before Hillary arrived, but I found myself reading the opinion section. I knew I should have avoided it, but I read it anyway. There was a full-length editorial about Shakespeare written by a man named Jacob Arnold. He was complaining about Shakespeare's views on the sixth commandment, a topic to which Shakespeare had devoted an entire chapter in his book. Shakespeare had pointed out that the commandment ordered people not to kill, when anyone with half a brain knew that killing was not only sometimes acceptable but also often necessary. I'm leaving out a lot, but let's just say Shakespeare wrote that the commandment was flawed. Obviously, people often had good reasons to kill, so how could a perfect God write such a flawed rule? God was perfect, wasn't he? Or maybe not. Maybe God was no more perfect than the rest of us. Or maybe he didn't even exist and hadn't written the commandments at all. Maybe they had just been written by some dumb human, or maybe they had been written by Moses. Or maybe they had been written by some mischievous stone cutter with his hammer and a chisel. It was such a long time ago, so who really knew who had written them or where they had come from?

This outraged the author, Arnold, and he said it was obvious

Shakespeare didn't have the slightest idea what he was talking about—anyone with a third-grade education knew the commandments had been written by the finger of God. "What the Bible says goes," he wrote. "What are you going to believe in, the misguided conjecture of a monkey typing on his toy word processor or the divine word of God?" I guess that said it all, didn't it? Shakespeare was a mere monkey, and God was God.

When Hillary arrived, I let her into the house, and we sat in the front room. Sarah had been working in her office, but she came in when she heard us talking. She asked what Hillary was doing here, and I explained what was going on. She looked over at Hillary and said, "Shakespeare could use your help. I'm glad Marty called you."

"That's nice," Hillary said, "but you may not be so glad I came over when you hear what I'm about to say."

"What's the problem?" I asked.

Sarah took a seat beside me, and Hillary sort of shook her wrists, adjusting her many bracelets. Then she took a deep breath. "It's a long story," she said.

"Well, start at the beginning."

"I need to go back nine years."

"Nine years?" I said, surprised. "I thought this was about Shakespeare. You've only known him for about a year."

"Shakespeare is only a small part of the story."

"Okay, well, go on."

"Nine years ago was when I started my agency. I was trying to get my foot in the door with a few famous actors and actresses, doing my best to make a go of it. It was rough going, getting started, because no one knew who I was. Then through a friend of a friend, I hooked up with Father Birdsong. He was my first major celebrity client. Everyone knew who the father was, and he needed a publicist to handle his routine affairs with the press. He hired me, and I went to work for him immediately. It was a pretty easy gig, until she happened."

"Until who happened?"

"Julie Garner."

"Who's Julie Garner?"

"Julie was one of Father Birdsong's parishioners, a lovely young girl who attended the father's sermons every Sunday with her mother. Julie and her mother lived together in a nice little house in West Hollywood, and there was no dad in the picture. It was just the two of them. Julie's mother had divorced the dad right after she gave birth to Julie, and he moved to Alaska. So now comes the problem. I'm not sure how it happened because the exact details were never given to me, but Birdsong got Julie pregnant. Julie told her mother about the pregnancy as soon as she found out. She also told her that the baby's father was Birdsong, yet for a while they told Birdsong nothing. It was a serious problem because Julie was only sixteen, and the last thing she needed in her life was a baby to take care of. About two months into the pregnancy, they decided to tell Father Birdsong. I'll bet he turned white as a ghost. He immediately called me since I was his publicist, and he figured I'd know how to handle the situation. I said I didn't know what to do, and he said, 'The girl needs to get an abortion.' This surprised me since I knew the father had been railing against abortions for years. According to Birdsong, abortion was murder, and I didn't see how he could condone such a thing, especially for his own child. But we thought about it hard, and neither of us could think of any other realistic way out. Allowing a sixteen-year-old girl to carry his child to term was out of the question. That would mean a baby in the world with his DNA, evidence of what he'd done, and people would also demand that Julie tell them who had fathered the child. And we weren't sure whether Julie could keep her mouth shut. She was just a kid. One wrong word from Julie, and the father's career could be over. So she had to get the abortion."

"What happened?"

"I arranged with the girl and mother to go to a doctor we could trust. Father Birdsong agreed to pay for the procedure, and we gave the girl's mother the money. The girl and mother also agreed to stop going to the father's sermons. The goal was to split them up, with no chance of them seeing each other again. In addition to paying for the abortion, the father agreed to pay a large sum of money for their trouble. This was with the condition that the mother would use the money to pay for Julie's college education. After this, neither Birdsong nor I heard a peep from the daughter or mother for years, until just eight months ago. The mother had remarried, and the daughter was still single, and both were still living in West Hollywood, in the same house. They had fallen on hard times, and Julie and her mother decided the best way out of their financial woes was to seek more money from Birdsong. They decided to approach him and ask not for a huge sum but for enough to keep them comfortably afloat. Unfortunately for Father Birdsong, the mother's new husband overheard the two talking about the blackmail scheme. He was furious. Instead of discussing the matter with the mother and daughter, he went straight to the *LA Times*. He went behind his wife's back since he knew she wouldn't want the scandal to go public. Now you're probably wondering what sort of chance this man would have against the word of Father Birdsong. But there's one thing I haven't told you. Julie never had the abortion. She never even saw the doctor."

"She had the child?"

"It was a boy. He's now eight years old."

"And he's living in West Hollywood?"

"Yes, with Julie, her mother, and the stepdad. He's been living there all this time. When the stepdad went to the *LA Times*, the paper put an investigative reporter named Jeffrey Thompson on the story. He's been poking around a lot, asking lots of questions. I think he's been able to get samples of the boy's DNA and of Birdsong's as well. I think he knows the boy is Birdsong's son, and doing the math, surely he's figured out Julie was sixteen when the child was conceived. I don't know what the statute of limitations is for statutory rape, but never mind the criminal charges. If any of this story gets out to the public, charges or no charges, the father is in serious trouble. Do you see?"

"Yes," I said. "He has a big problem."

"And so does Shakespeare."

"What does any of this nightmare have to do with Shakespeare?"

"Everything. Remember I told you the father owed me a favor, and that's why he came out in public and supported your monkey? Do you think Father Birdsong would've held that press conference for any other reason? He didn't even like Shakespeare, but he owed me, and he owed me a lot. He thought I'd made a huge problem go away for him, and so he helped me with Shakespeare; he got us out of our own jam by saying all those nice things, the way he thought I'd gotten him out of his jam."

"So now Shakespeare is connected."

"Yes. If Thompson puts all this together, Shakespeare is going to find himself connected to all of it. Never mind his offensive book and all the crazy things he wrote—now he's going to be part of a full-fledged celebrity scandal. There won't be anything I can do to clear his name because I'll be a part of the accusations; we're all going to be on the same sinking ship. Remember, we're talking about a man of the cloth and a sixteen-year-old girl. The public will be livid."

"Have you talked to Thompson?"

"I've been avoiding him."

"But you think he'll call me?"

"I'm sure of it."

"What do I do?"

"If he asks you if you know anything about Birdsong doing a favor for me or me doing one for him, you just say no. You tell him you know nothing about any favors."

"You want me to lie for you?"

"I want you to lie for yourself. I want you to lie for Shakespeare."

"Isn't it illegal to lie?" I wondered if this was a stupid question, but I asked it anyway.

"It's only illegal to lie under oath. Hopefully, I'll be able to keep you out of a courtroom."

"Jesus," I said.

"If this whole thing gets out, the difficulties you're having now with the book will seem like nothing by comparison."

Sarah said, "So your problem has become Shakespeare's problem, and he didn't even do anything." She sounded a little angry.

"I'm sorry about this."

"You should be."

"I need to tell Shakespeare," I said.

"No," Hillary said. "The less he knows about this, the better."

After we were done with our meeting and Hillary had left the house, Sarah and I debated whether we should tell Shakespeare what was going on. I could see Hillary's point about not telling him anything, for the less he knew about things, the less he'd be held accountable. But I couldn't remember ever lying to Shakespeare about anything, except for when I hid Evan's letters, before Shakespeare went to UCLA. That was a lie, wasn't it? Keeping UCLA's offer from him for such a long time had been a lie. I felt terrible about that lie, and it hadn't gotten me anywhere. All it had done was make Shakespeare mad, and he had ended up going to UCLA anyway. No, lying to Shakespeare was not a good idea. I felt we needed to tell him about Hillary and Birdsong, and Sarah agreed. I was beginning to not like Hillary so much, and I had an uncomfortable feeling about her, considering what she had done with the father and that sixteen-year-old girl and the way she was now asking me to lie for her. Just what kind of woman was this?

I called Shakespeare that evening and told him I needed to meet with Becky and him. When he asked me why, I told him that it was important and had something to do with Hillary.

"Are we hiring her again?" he asked.

"No," I said. "It's not that."

"Then what is it?"

"She's done something you need to know about."

"I don't understand."

"You will," I said.

"I'll come down there. I'm tired of being cooped up in this house. I'll have Hopkins drive me tomorrow morning."

"Bring Becky with you," I said.

"Why Becky?"

"She needs to hear what I have to tell you."

"I think she has classes tomorrow morning."

"Tell her to skip them. This is important."

"Okay, we'll see you tomorrow."

When I hung up the phone, Sarah was staring at me. She said, "I think we're making the right decision, telling Shakespeare."

"So do I," I said.

"I wonder how he's going to take it."

"I have no idea. He's been under a lot of pressure because of his book. This is probably the last thing he needs, something else to worry about."

"What are we going to tell that reporter?"

"Thompson? I haven't decided yet. It depends on what Shakespeare has to say. I'm going to leave it up to him. It's his life we're talking about. It will affect you and me, but not nearly as much as him. And it will affect Becky. She should have something to say about it. We need to respect their wishes."

The next morning Shakespeare and Becky arrived at our house. Hopkins drove them, so he was there too. Hopkins was like family now, so I didn't see any reason he shouldn't be allowed to sit in on our conversation. I started at the very beginning and told them the entire story about Hillary, Father Birdsong, and Julie. When I was done talking, they all sat quietly, staring at me.

Finally, Shakespeare said, "I feel sorry for Hillary."

"You feel sorry for her?"

"Yes, I do."

"Even knowing how much trouble she's probably gotten you into?"

"People aren't perfect, Marty."

"You might not recover from this."

"But I've done nothing wrong."

"The public won't see it that way."

"So what is she asking us to do?"

"She wants us to tell the reporter that she never mentioned anything about Father Birdsong owing her a favor."

"Actually, she didn't ever mention it to me."

"But she did to me."

"Then you're the only one she's asking to lie."

"I guess you're right."

"So what do you want to do?"

"I'm asking you."

"I want you to do what you think is right."

"It will affect you."

"This situation is going to affect me no matter what you say. People are going to believe what they want to believe."

"What would you do if you were me?"

"Fortunately, I'm not you. I don't have to decide. And I'll be fine, no matter which way you choose to go."

"I know what I'd do," Hopkins said.

"What would you do?" I asked.

"I'd tell the reporter the truth."

"So would I," Becky said.

"Even if it means causing Hillary so much trouble? It's going to make her look pretty bad."

"She isn't your problem," Hopkins said. "She's a big girl, a grown woman, and she can take care of herself. She's responsible for her actions, not you. We have enough to do, dealing with Shakespeare's book. We don't need to add lying about Hillary to our list of problems."

I looked over to Shakespeare to see if he agreed, but he didn't indicate his opinion one way or the other. Then I looked at Sarah, and she smiled at me.

"You're going to do what's right," she said. She knew my answer before I even said it.

"Okay, I'll tell the guy the truth," I said. "I'll tell the reporter what Hillary told me."

"You're making the right decision," Sarah said.

Shakespeare said, "Like I said, I feel sorry for Hillary."

"I'm not sure I do," I said. "She's in a tough spot, but she shouldn't have asked me to lie for her. That was going too far."

"What do you think is going to happen?" Becky asked.

"To Hillary?"

"No, to Shakespeare."

"I don't honestly know."

"I do," Shakespeare said. "It'll be like pouring gas on a fire."

Two days later, I got the call from Jeffrey Thompson, wanting to meet and discuss Hillary. He wanted us to get together over lunch at a restaurant in Newport Beach, not far from my house. "It'll be on me," he said, and I agreed to come.

We met at the restaurant, and Thompson had the hostess seat us way in the back, away from the rest of the people at a table where we could talk without being overheard.

Thompson was a tall fellow and probably about my age, in his early or midthirties. He had long hair, not long like a hippie, but long so that it nearly reached his shoulders. It was uncombed and wavy and went along well with his clothing, which looked like it had been purchased from a Salvation Army thrift shop. Nothing went with anything else. He wore a hodgepodge of styles and colors, and his shoes were worn and seemed way too big for his feet. It was comical really, the way this guy didn't care about his appearance, but when he spoke, he was clear and deliberate. He sounded very intelligent, and I liked that. And he didn't seem to have any animosity toward me, not the way some people did who knew of my relationship to Shakespeare.

"I'm glad you agreed to meet with me," he said. "Do you know why I wanted to talk?"

"I think I do. It's about Hillary West and Father Birdsong."

"Yes. She must have contacted you."

"We talked."

"Am I going to get any straight answers?"

"I think you will."

"That's good to know. I've been trying to get a hold of Hillary for weeks, but she's avoiding my calls."

"She doesn't want to talk to you."

"You know this?"

"She told me. And she told me what you wanted."

"Yet here you are."

"I've thought a lot about this. She'd prefer I kept quiet, but I'm going to tell you the truth."

"I appreciate that."

"So go ahead and ask your questions."

"Fine, here's my first. Are you aware that Father Birdsong has a child?"

This surprised me. I hadn't expected him to ask me any direct questions about the father. I figured he'd only ask about my relationship with Hillary. "What do you know about this?" I asked.

"I thought you were going to answer my questions."

"What do you know?" I asked again.

"Okay, I'll tell you what I know. Then will you answer my questions?"

"Yes," I said.

"I know that the father got a girl named Julie Garner pregnant eight or nine years ago. She was only sixteen at the time, and the father had Hillary talk the girl into getting an abortion. He paid the girl and her mother some money, and that was supposed to be the end of it. But it wasn't. It turned out the girl never got the abortion, and she gave birth to a son, a boy who still lives with her in West Hollywood. I learned all this from Julie's stepfather, and it all checks out. Right now Julie and her mother are trying to get Birdsong to pay them more money, to keep them quiet. Have I told you anything you don't already know?"

"No," I said. "I knew all this."

"I've been working on a story about Father Birdsong for several years now. Julie wasn't the first parishioner he'd had a tumble with, and she wasn't the first who was a minor. I know of three others the father had similar relationships with, but Julie is the only one who has living proof."

"Living proof?"

"The little boy and his DNA."

"Oh, of course."

"Apparently, Birdsong had a thing against using protection. Imagine the arrogance of this man, taking the risk of getting these girls pregnant. The other three girls got abortions, arranged for by your friend Hillary, so it's just their word against Birdsong's. But Julie, her case is different. Her little boy is living proof the father had sex with her when she was only sixteen."

"Have you talked to Julie?"

"She won't talk to me. Only her stepfather has been willing to talk."

"What about the mother?"

"She won't talk either."

"But these other three girls? They've all talked to you?"

"Oh yes. And they're willing to come forward. They're even willing to testify in court. They want to stop Father Birdsong from doing this again to other young girls."

"Wow," I said.

"Yes, wow. How much of this story did you already know?"

"I only knew about Julie. Hillary told me about her a couple days ago. I didn't know anything about the other three. She said you'd be looking for me, to talk about Julie. She didn't mention the other victims. I don't think she knows you're aware of them."

"Did she tell you what to say?"

"Yes, she did. I mean, she asked me not to tell you something."

"And what was that?"

"That Father Birdsong owed her a big favor."

"That's how she got the father to stand behind your monkey, isn't it?"

"Yes, he owed her one."

"She said a big one."

"Yes, a big favor."

"Did you have any idea what the favor was in exchange for at the time she got Birdsong to help with Shakespeare?"

"Not then, no. I mean, I get it now. But I had no idea at the time. If I'd known what she'd been doing for Birdsong, I probably would've found Shakespeare a different publicist."

"I think I believe you."

"I'm telling the truth."

"Can I get you on record, saying everything you've told me?"

"I suppose so," I said.

Thompson removed a small tape recorder from his coat pocket and pressed the record button, setting it on the table between us. We went through everything we'd talked about for a second time, and he recorded everything I had to say. As I spoke for the recorder, I remembered what Shakespeare had said—that this was going to be like pouring gas onto a fire.

Aisle 6

Everything that was happening to Shakespeare was very upsetting for me; I didn't want people disliking my monkey. But things were pretty bad, and I was sure they were going to get worse when Thompson's article was published, exposing Birdsong and Hillary, tying Shakespeare to their unsavory schemes. When the article finally did come out, everyone rallied against Shakespeare, even more so against him than against Birdsong or Hillary. It seemed they were just itching for another reason to pick on him. Never mind all the hate mail and negative talk on TV and in the newspapers; the UCLA alumni and students' parents were the ones causing the biggest problems, pressuring Evan to eject Shakespeare from the campus. They wanted to take away his apartment and figure out a way to make him leave the school for good.

Evan called me and told me the trouble he was having with these people, and I didn't know what to say. I don't think Evan wanted Shakespeare to leave, but the pressure was too great to ignore or dodge. No one wanted the school associated with such a problematic and reckless monkey any longer, so right before Christmas, Evan asked Shakespeare to leave. Evan had grown to like Shakespeare a lot, and I knew it hurt him to do this. We boxed up Shakespeare's things from the apartment and took them to his home. There was nowhere to put anything inside the house, so we stored it all in the garage. It was a sad thing, seeing all the stuff Shakespeare had accumulated at school now boxed up and soon to be forgotten, soon to be collecting dust, a phase of his life that had so unfairly ended. Shakespeare was now a virtual prisoner in his own house, with nowhere to go other than down to our place in Corona del Mar, since there was wasn't anywhere he could show his face without being recognized.

Becky had bought a car for herself, so she and Shakespeare no longer needed Hopkins to drive them around in his SUV. Hopkins stayed on the school's payroll as a driver, now taking others to and from the campus but stopping and visiting Shakespeare whenever he had free time. Becky was not asked to leave the school, and she stayed on to finish her final semester. She was looking forward to graduating soon and being done with the place. In addition to going to school, she took charge of all the household errands, for she was able to go out in public without much of a fuss. Most people didn't even recognize her as Shakespeare's wife. It was only Shakespeare who drew the attention and ire of the public, so he stayed home where it was safe while she went out. He had few visitors during these months. Hopkins, of course, was one of them, and a few of the college professors came over, but not very often. I don't mean to make it sound like Shakespeare had no friends, but for the most part he was avoided. I guess now it was safe to say that he'd finally become kind of a pariah, with so few people wanting anything to do with him. Things were nothing like they had been in his heyday, when he was so popular.

So did Shakespeare become bitter? Amazingly, no, he didn't. Nor did he give up. He decided to write another book, which Rudy agreed in advance to publish. It was to be titled *A Monkey's Apology*, and Shakespeare told me the opening sentence of the book would read, "I apologize from the bottom of my heart for letting America down." When he read this sentence to me, I wondered what the heck he was up to, for I knew he wasn't one to lie about his opinions or change his mind just to be liked and forgiven by others. I knew he had a lot of integrity, something I'd always admired. He said the next two sentences were "I have upset a lot of people, and I never meant to do that. I love human beings, and I love this country." I asked him where the book would go from there, and he told me he was keeping it a secret until the manuscript was completely done. He didn't want any input from me or anyone else; he wanted to write the book all on his own, which was typical of Shakespeare. He had always been so independent, another thing I'd always admired about him.

Whether or not you agreed with the things Shakespeare did, said, or wrote, you did have to admire his honesty and his fierce individuality, although maybe "fierce" isn't the right word here. Was he really fierce? No, not really. He was gentle, loving, and forgiving. He was all those things you'd expect of a good Christian, yet he was a self-professed atheist. You know, I'd always believed one could be a good person without believing in God, and Shakespeare was proof of this. Not only was he not a God-fearing Christian; he wasn't even human! But he had a good heart and a kind disposition, and he was amazingly honest. It was frustrating, knowing that he was such a better person than people were giving him credit for. In fact, I'd say he was a better person than most of his critics; many of those who were complaining about him wouldn't know a good Christian if they were face-to-face with one, nose-to-nose. A lot of people wrote and said some very nasty things about my monkey, yet I don't remember him ever losing his cool or wanting to take any kind of retaliatory action. A lot of people didn't like him at all, but they could've learned a lot from him, if only they weren't so closed-minded.

Shakespeare continued to work on his new book while Becky finished her final semester. It was getting close to his tenth birthday when he told me about his haunting premonition. I need to tell you about this because it truly bothered him. It wasn't a specific event he feared, the sort of thing you could put your finger on; instead, he just had a gnawing feeling that something was about to go terribly wrong. "Something very bad is about to happen," he told me. "I can feel it coming, like an oncoming train."

I suppose, in hindsight, I should have paid closer attention to this. Instead, I told him to relax and said that if anything was going to go haywire in his life, it already had. I mean, seriously, what else could go wrong? And he was safe, wasn't he? It was not like he was exposing himself to any sort of trouble. He remained in his house practically 24-7, day and night, out of public view, protected by Jason's bodyguard. Yes, we still had a bodyguard at his house, twenty-four hours a day, always on high alert. Who knew what some crazy person might be capable of doing or when such a person would make his or her move? So we had security in place. I thought Shakespeare was worrying about nothing, and that's what I told him.

"You can say whatever you want," he said. "I still feel like something truly awful is right around the corner, just waiting to happen."

When Shakespeare's tenth birthday rolled around, we decided to have another birthday party for him at our house. We thought it might cheer him up to know that there were still people who loved him and wanted to pay him tribute. After all, a birthday party is a sort of tribute, isn't it?

You celebrate another year of a person's life, and you wouldn't bother to celebrate it unless you loved the person and his or her life had value. We invited all of Shakespeare's close friends and family to the gathering. Of course, Sarah and I would be there, and so would Becky. The professor and Dr. Barney promised to come, and even Evan said he would drive down from Los Angeles. Rudy promised to fly out from New York, and Hopkins would come down with Becky and Shakespeare. Sarah invited her parents, and Tom and Judy said they'd come for sure, all the way from Nebraska. Becky asked her family to come, and at first they said no. But her mom later changed her mind and decided to come with the two brothers. Dr. Carlson remained in Seattle, saying he had work to do, but I think all of us knew the real reason he stayed home. He still couldn't stand the sight of Shakespeare, now more than ever after the Birdsong and Hillary fiasco. And he was still angry that his daughter had married a monkey. I didn't think he'd ever get over the marriage, not in a million years; it was a shame that he carried such a powerful grudge.

We all got together at our house, and I borrowed a couple of outdoor patio tables from neighbors, which we put together in the backyard to accommodate us all. I barbecued hamburgers, and Sarah and Becky prepared the rest of the food. It was quite a feast, and everyone was in good spirits, even Shakespeare, who truly seemed to be enjoying himself.

"It's great that all of you came," he said. "I love my family, and I love my friends. I wish every day could be like this."

"Every day should be like this," Sarah said.

"I'd like to make a toast," I said, raising my glass of iced tea. "Here's to the most misunderstood monkey in America."

"Yes, that's me," Shakespeare said, smiling. "Hopefully, my new book will rectify that."

"Always the optimist," the professor said.

"You're writing another book?" Evan asked.

"Yes, and Rudy said he'd publish it."

"I did say that," Rudy said.

"What's it about?" Evan asked. "I thought you were done writing books."

"It's an apology."

"An apology from someone who owes none of us an apology," Becky said, a little bitterly.

"No, actually, I do owe America an apology," Shakespeare said.

"I think he's got something up his sleeve," I said. "That's what I think."

"Have you read any of it?" Dr. Barney asked.

"He won't let me look at it."

"It's top secret," Shakespeare said.

"Have you seen it?" Sarah asked, looking at Becky. Perhaps as his wife she might know more than the rest of us.

Becky shook her head no. "He doesn't want me telling him what to write or influencing him. He won't even let me take a peek."

"I liked your last book," Mrs. Carlson said.

"You read it?"

"Of course I did."

"Did you read the entire thing?"

"I read most of it. I don't know what all the fuss was about. I thought it was fascinating."

"What was your favorite part?"

"What you wrote about terrorists. I'd never looked at terrorism the way you described it. I know that what you wrote made a lot of people very angry, but I thought it made sense."

"Sounds like you have a fan," I laughed.

"See, not everyone hates me."

"I think it's interesting how Americans are so quick to call others terrorists," Mrs. Carlson said.

"Yes," Shakespeare agreed.

"While we're one of the worst."

"We need to look at ourselves in the mirror," the professor said. "People in this country need to look at themselves, long and hard."

"I also liked what you wrote about killing farm animals," said Mrs. Carlson. "I mean, I didn't like reading about how many animals we kill and how badly they're treated in the process. But it opened my eyes. It seems so wrong to kill so many of them, just for their meat."

"Don't look at me," Shakespeare said. "I'm not eating a hamburger. The burgers are for the rest of you. As you can see, I'm eating fruit, nuts, and lettuce. I get along just fine on this."

"Yes," I said. "There's no blood on Shakespeare's hands."

"All this killing," Mrs. Carlson said. "It just can't be a good thing."

Becky's oldest brother said, "Well, I happen to like eating hamburgers."

"So do I," her younger brother said.

"I like them too," I agreed.

"But it isn't the act of eating that's the problem," Becky said. "It's all the killing. That's the problem, all the killing. I'll bet if any of you spent any significant time in a slaughterhouse, you'd have some trouble enjoying your hamburgers."

"Maybe, maybe not," I said.

"Humans are an odd lot," Shakespeare said. "They love eating meat, yet they claim to hate all the killing required to put it on their plates. And the killing goes on and on. Humankind is against it, yet they're for it. Humans are such hypocrites."

"People don't like to be called hypocrites," I pointed out.

"Yes, I learned that the hard way."

"And people don't like to be called killers."

"No, they don't. And they don't like to be called terrorists, either. I learned that too. People don't mind doing all kinds of awful things, so long as you don't point it out to them."

"Are you sure you can't tell us about your new book?" Mrs. Carlson asked. "I have to tell you, I'm now very curious."

"The truth is I don't know what I'm going to write. I've started, but I don't know where I'm going with it, not exactly. I just know I need to write it. It's important that I apologize."

"But for what?"

"For upsetting so many people. I never intended to make so many people mad at me."

"If they're mad at you, it's their problem," Evan said. "Let them be mad. In my opinion, you didn't do anything wrong."

"But I did."

"Did you? What would you do differently, given the chance to do it over again? All you did was tell America the truth. Would you lie?"

"I wouldn't go back and lie. But maybe I could've phrased things differently. Maybe there was a better way of getting my points across."

"Or maybe it's just because you're a monkey," I said. "Maybe they don't want to be told the truth by a monkey. Monkeys are supposed to swing from tree branches and eat bananas, not write books about humans and their hypocrisies. You might have overstepped your bounds from their perspective."

"Maybe."

"It's something to think about."

"Can we change the subject?" Shakespeare asked.

"Of course we can," Sarah said. "It's your party."

"How about it, Hopkins?" Shakespeare said, looking over to him.

"How about what?" Hopkins asked.

"What's on that mind of yours? Any new crazy ideas you'd like to share?"

"Maybe," Hopkins said.

"Come on, out with it. You're always thinking of something clever. What's the soup du jour?"

"Okay, how about cars?"

"What about them?" I asked.

"Do you think cars are alive?"

"Alive?" I said. I think I must have smiled when I said this. I mean, honestly.

"Yes, alive. I mean, maybe they're not plants or animals, but to my way of thinking, they're definitely living things. They're in a class of their own, but just as alive as you or me. I was thinking about this on the way here while Becky was driving. Shakespeare was in the passenger seat, and I was in the back, watching Becky drive the car and work all the controls. Then I got to thinking about how lively and complex a car actually is, sort of like a human being, with a nervous system, skeleton, outer skin, and many interior organs. It has its own veins and arteries, twisting and turning throughout its body, carrying gas, oil, and coolant to where they need to go, and it consumes air and fuel and expels waste in the form of exhaust. It breathes and swallows just like a person; it moves forward and backward, and it can get ill or injured and require medical attention to heal. It starts off in life all shiny, new, and young and ages over time and finally dies, just like a human being, from a baby to an old man to a corpse. Have you ever thought of a car this way? They're such interesting creatures made of metal, rubber, plastic, and glass, some made with a touch of leather and some with a touch of wood, inhaling air and slurping up gasoline."

"Ah, but can a car reproduce?" the professor asked. "All living things are able to reproduce."

"Are they? What about a mule? Isn't a mule a living thing? I don't think a mule can reproduce. And what about a man who's had a vasectomy? He can't reproduce, so did the vasectomy kill him, or is he still just as alive as he always was, just unable to reproduce? I don't think a living creature has to be able to reproduce in order to be alive."

"But is a car born?"

"Of course it is. It's born in a factory. It's put together piece by piece and given life. It grows a chassis and axle and wheels, and from the chassis sprouts an engine, radiator, and battery, and from that grow seats, a steering wheel, and a dashboard. It develops a protective skin of steel, plastic, and chrome trimmings, dotted with glowing headlights for eyes and equipped with an antenna for catching useful radio signals. And over time it evolves, mutating into newer, improved models, with intriguing new shapes, colors, and accessories. Each generation of car is better suited to the environment than the previous generation, more efficient, more adept, and safer. It's a clear and indisputable example of natural selection and evolution. Even Charles Darwin would be impressed."

"But a car can't operate without a man or woman to drive it."

"And?"

"Well, how do you account for that?"

"In a word, symbiosis."

"Are you kidding?"

"Not at all. There are lots of living creatures that depend on other living creatures to function and stay alive, even to reproduce. So a car requires a person to make it work? Mistletoe also requires a host tree branch to grow, and blossoms require bees to pollinate them. Look up symbiosis on the Internet; there are all kinds of good examples. Cars are just a terrific example of living creatures depending on each other, each helping the other to stay alive."

"But a car can't think," said one of Becky's brothers.

"Neither can a tree," Hopkins replied. "Isn't a tree a living thing?"

"I guess so."

The professor laughed and said, "Then I guess if you really buy into all this talk about cars, you'd also have to call something like a toaster a living thing."

"A toaster?"

"It too is made in a factory. It has a framework, guts, and a skin. A human is required to operate it, just like a car. It feeds on electricity and bread and excretes slices of toast. According to your train of thought, it's a living thing, and we eat its waste."

"I never thought of that, but yes, you're right. I can accept that. A toaster is a living thing."

"Hopkins, you're one of a kind," Shakespeare laughed. Then to the rest of us he said, "You've got to love this guy!"

"My morning slice of toast will never taste the same," I said.

"Toaster poop," Dr. Barney said, and everyone laughed.

We all continued to talk and eat and have a lot of fun. When we were done with our meals, Sarah brought out Shakespeare's birthday cake for dessert. Then Shakespeare unwrapped his presents, and finally, at around ten, the party broke up, and everyone left.

"I think Shakespeare enjoyed himself," I said to Sarah.

"Yes, so do I," she said.

"It was a good idea, throwing a party for him."

"Yes, it was."

Then the day after the party, it happened. Shakespeare's premonition came true and in a big way. He was told about the incident before the rest of us, by the police officers who visited his house. Most others heard about it later on the evening news, but Sarah and I got a call from Shakespeare shortly after the police visit. I'd never heard him sound so distraught. He wasn't angry; he was just terribly sad. Seldom did Shakespeare cry, but he was sobbing as he spoke that day. He said that he'd called Hopkins to come over to keep him company and that Hopkins was on his way. I'd never expected anything like this to happen, and the tragedy took everyone by surprise. The TV news was having a field day with the event, and the reporters were all starting to show up at Shakespeare's house. What a horrible day this was. I wondered if we should've seen it coming.

Earlier in the day, Shakespeare had noticed they were out of toilet paper. It wasn't Becky's normal day to go grocery shopping, but she had to get the toilet paper, so she hopped in her car and drove to the grocery store. She grabbed a grocery cart and pushed it up and down the aisles. There was nothing out of the ordinary at first, and she went about her business as usual. She was in aisle six, grabbing some dishwashing soap and laundry detergent, when she must have felt the muzzle of the man's revolver pressed against the back of her head. No one knows what the man said to her before he pulled the trigger, or whether he said anything at all. There was a loud pop as the gun went off, and Becky's head jerked forward just before she crumpled to the floor. A witness said people in the store were screaming and running for cover, thinking they might be the next victim. But no one else would be shot because it was Becky and Becky alone that the killer had been after. Right after the murder, the shooter tried to run away, but a young college student hustled after him, tackling him and knocking the gun out of his hand. He then pinned him down and yelled for the others to call for help. This young man, it turned out, was on the UCLA wrestling team, and he had no problem keeping the shooter down until the police arrived. Several people ran to help Becky, but she was already dead. They didn't show any photos of Becky on the TV news, but they did include a shot of all the blood on the floor, a picture of the gory crime scene they felt compelled to broadcast for their viewers.

After Shakespeare's call, Sarah and I immediately got in the car and started the drive to his house. My hands were shaking, and there was a pain in my stomach. When we arrived, there were reporters and cameramen everywhere. They all wanted to get a comment from Shakespeare, but Hopkins had been keeping them at bay. As Sarah and I walked up to the house, one of the reporters stepped in front of us, holding his microphone to our faces and asking us to say something. I shoved him out of our way and went to the front door, where Hopkins let us in. Once inside the house, we slammed the door shut. "Jesus," I said to Hopkins. "How's Shakespeare taking all of this? This is crazy."

"He's a little overwhelmed."

"Where is he?"

"He's in the family room. He's watching the TV."

"Do they know anything about the shooter?"

"Yes, they've identified him."

"And?"

"It was Leroy McNabb. Do you remember him?"

"Like hell," I said.

"He finally made good on his threats."

We walked to the family room, where Shakespeare was seated on the couch, watching the news on the TV. "They keep showing this shot of her blood on the floor," he said. "Do you see what it says? 'Famous monkey's wife murdered.' They say the shooter was Leroy McNabb. How could he actually do this? What did Becky ever do to him? What did either of us do to deserve this? So we got married. Isn't that all we did? Since when is it a crime for two people who love each other to get married?"

"It isn't," I said.

"Do you think this was my fault?"

"Of course not," I said.

That's what I told Shakespeare, and I believed what I said. But in the days that followed, there would be others who would argue otherwise and hold Shakespeare responsible for the murder.

One of Shakespeare's biggest problems after the murder was Dr. Carlson, who blamed Shakespeare for everything. And he made sure everyone was aware of his opinion. He wasn't the slightest bit shy about talking to the media, and he welcomed every news reporter who asked for an interview or a comment. What I would have given just to shut this guy up and keep his rants out of the news.

Vanishing Act

I looked at Shakespeare, who was angry with himself. "He's wrong," I said, referring to Dr. Carlson, who was on the news again.

"I don't want to talk about it."

"Surely you know he's just upset."

"I know that Becky's dead."

"Because of one crazy lunatic."

"And I did nothing to stop him. I had a chance to press charges, and I did nothing. I really don't want to talk about it."

I decided not to argue. I gave Shakespeare his space, and I didn't bring it up again. In fact, we didn't talk about it for months. Instead, when we did talk, we discussed other things of little significance—the weather, politics, and sporting events.

Everyone deals with grief in his or her own way, and Shakespeare's way was to keep quiet about what had happened and work on his book. The book became his primary focus, consuming all his time. Whenever I called him, he'd speak to me for a while and then say he had to get back to work. We invited him down to Corona del Mar several times, but he didn't want to come. Sarah went up to Los Angeles every so often to help Shakespeare with his grocery shopping and other errands, but he didn't talk to her much either. He just said thanks and then went back to work, writing.

Then I got a phone call that took me completely by surprise; it was Vern. I hadn't talked with Vern since taking Shakespeare to his house for that unsuccessful reunion with his parents. I'd always wondered why Vern had never called since that reunion, especially after Shakespeare became so famous. Surely, he had learned of my monkey's astonishing talents and had followed what had been going on in our lives. But he had never called.

"Vern, how the heck are you?" I asked.

"I'm fine, Marty," he said.

"No doubt you're calling about Shakespeare."

"I am," Vern said.

"Have you been following him in the news?"

"Oh yes, I've been paying attention. Seems like I sold you quite a remarkable monkey."

"Why haven't you called before now? I thought I'd hear from you years ago. Actually, I thought you might want to take Shakespeare back. To tell you the truth, I was a little worried about you laying claim to him since you never did give me a written receipt."

"Oh no," Vern said. "I have all the monkeys I need. I told you that when I sold him to you."

"Yes, you did."

"I need another monkey like I need a hole in the head. I have my hands full."

"Ha," I laughed.

"I suppose you have your hands full too."

"You're right, I do."

"I told you Shakespeare was smart the day you took him from me. Didn't I tell you that?"

"Yes, you did."

"You know, your friends at UCLA have been a real pain in my neck."

"They have?"

"They finally decided to leave me alone."

"What were they doing?"

"Calling me over and over. They wanted to get their hands on Shakespeare's parents. They wanted to breed them, to see if they could create another Shakespeare. And they wanted to do all these crazy tests on them. I told them to go fly a kite, many times. That guy over there, Evan? He doesn't like taking no for an answer. He's been very persistent, calling me all the time."

"Evan was contacting you?"

"Yes, that was his name."

"He never told me anything about this."

"Maybe he didn't want you to know."

"When did he stop calling?"

"Not long ago. I told him I was going to tell my attorney to sue the school if they didn't stop harassing me. I had to threaten them."

"I had no idea."

"I don't even know an attorney, nor do I have the money to hire one. I was bluffing, I guess. But the bluff seemed to work. Evan finally stopped calling. So how's the little fella doing?"

"Not too well."

"It's a shame about his wife."

"Yes," I said.

"I knew something like this was going to happen. It didn't surprise me at all."

"It didn't?"

"Monkeys are a lot of trouble, Marty. I should've told you when I sold Shakespeare to you. You should've been warned. And the smarter they are, the more difficult they are. You bought yourself a world of mayhem on the day you took Shakespeare off my hands. Mind you, I had no idea how smart the little fella actually was, but I did know he was smart. And I knew he was going to be a handful."

"So why are you calling me now?"

"I guess I was just curious."

"Curious about what?"

"About how Shakespeare was doing. He's been through an awful lot. I haven't seen anything in the news about him lately. Are they finally leaving you alone? I guess I just called to see if he was okay."

"He's focused," I said.

"Focused on what?"

"On writing another book."

"Good Lord. Do you think that's such a good idea?"

"It's what he wants to do."

"So what's this book about?"

"He says it's an apology. He wants to apologize to the public for his last book."

"And you believe him?"

"Shouldn't I?"

"Have you seen any of what he's written?"

"He won't let me look at it."

"I see. So you're not really sure exactly what he's doing."

"No, I suppose not. He says it's a secret. Do you think I should be concerned?"

"Just be careful. Monkeys are natural-born troublemakers. They have a knack for really stirring things up. And they're very impulsive. There's no telling what they'll do next. Don't be surprised if he opens a whole new can of worms."

"Jesus," I said.

"Just make sure you read the manuscript before he gets it published."

"I'm sure he'll have me read it first."

"Make sure of it."

I continued talking with Vern for about an hour, telling him stories about Shakespeare, about our life together. I could tell Vern got a big kick out of this, learning so much about his smart little monkey. When we were done talking, Vern thanked me for my time and wished me luck dealing with Shakespeare during this difficult period. After I hung up the phone, I thought about the conversation. I didn't really buy into Vern's belief that Shakespeare was a natural-born troublemaker. Sure, I guessed monkeys could be mischievous, but I had never felt he'd intentionally gone out and tried to cause all the problems that came his way. All he'd ever wanted to be was honest and thoughtful, but for some reason, honesty and thoughtfulness weren't too highly regarded. Perhaps they never have been, and maybe they never will be. Maybe Shakespeare had been a little too bold, but I didn't think it was fair to blame him for his current rough situation, not entirely anyway.

I got another interesting call a couple days after I spoke with Vern. This one was from Adolph Nelson, the movie producer, and he wanted to know whether Shakespeare would be interested in starring in another movie. This surprised me, given Shakespeare's current standing with the public, but when I asked Adolph about this, he laughed and said, "Famous people sell movies, whether the public loves or hates them. Never underestimate the raw power of celebrity."

I asked Adolph what the movie was about, and he ran through the entire plot: Biff is a talking money who is adopted by a middle-class family in the suburbs near Los Angeles. Biff is to be a family pet, bought mostly to benefit the children, to give them a unique animal to play with and enjoy.

But it turns out Biff is quite a character. He's well behaved while around the adults, but when the parents are out of the picture, he drinks, smokes, and cusses like a truck driver. He's nasty with the girls and terribly mischievous. His debauchery and desire to cause trouble make him a horrible influence on the kids, getting them into all sorts of crazy situations. The film is a humorous litany of his lewd acts and misadventures, which end when the parents realize just what kind of monkey Biff actually is. Despite the kids' objections, they decide to sell Biff to a medical research company that wants him for experiments. On the way to the company, the family recalls some of their favorite stories about Biff, and just as they're about to drop him off, the parents have a change of heart and decide to keep him. "Do you promise to behave?" the father asks.

Biff agrees and then winks into the camera and smiles, saying, "A promise is a promise, but never trust a monkey." The film ends as one of the daughters says, "I love you, Biff," and gives him a big hug. Adolph wanted to title the film *The Bad Monkey.*

"It sounds like an excuse for a lot of raunchy humor and R-rated gags," I said.

"Yes, basically, that's what it is."

"And you think Shakespeare will like this?"

"Do you think he will?"

"Not really," I said.

"Can you run it by him?"

"I can, but I think he'll say no. This Biff character is kind of an idiot."

"He's an antihero. Actors love playing antiheroes, don't they?"

"I don't know. I don't know any actors."

"You know Shakespeare."

"I do know him."

"Then talk him into it. He'll have a ball. He needs something fun in his life, and this movie will be a lot of fun. We have a great scriptwriting team, and there'll be a lot of great stuff. Honestly, with everything that's gone wrong in his life recently, he'll enjoy this. It'll be good for him."

"Maybe."

"Will you ask him right away?"

"It'll need to wait."

"For what?"

"He's in the middle of writing a book. He won't want to be bothered with this until he's done."

"When will he be done?"

"Soon, I think."

"Then you'll ask him?"

"I will."

Although the movie sounded kind of ridiculous, Adolph might have been right about Shakespeare needing to participate in something frivolous. And who knew what it might do for him and the public? Combined with his new apologetic book, it might actually help win back some of his popularity, something I knew he wanted. I mean, I knew he didn't want to become something he wasn't, to be false or dishonest, but I was sure he wouldn't mind being loved again, for everyone loves to be loved, right? No normal person wants to be hated. In fact, the more I thought about the movie, the more I liked the idea, and I decided I wouldn't wait for Shakespeare to finish his book. I would let him know about Adolph's offer right away, and I would do my best to sell the idea.

The next time I spoke with Shakespeare, he said he was nearly done with the book. I told him about Adolph's movie and asked if he'd be interested in it. After listening to me patiently, he said I'd have my answer soon. "Your answer will be in the book," he said. I asked him what he meant by this, and he just repeated himself: the answer to my question would be in the book, and it would be obvious. Shakespeare was usually more up-front with me, and I wondered what was with all the mystery. Why not just answer my question with a simple yes or no? I would learn the reason when I read the book.

When Shakespeare was done writing the book, he gave me a copy of the manuscript to share with Sarah. He also sent a copy to Rudy. We were the only people to see the book prior to its publication. It was about three hundred pages, and I read it over a couple of days. Most of it was what I had expected, with many detailed explanations of the statements he'd made in his previous book. He wasn't making any excuses or backpedaling on any issues; he just wanted to make it clear why his opinions were valuable. He wanted the public to know he wasn't just being critical for the sake of being critical. He was just trying to help. But then came the shocker, the final chapter of the book. It made the blood rush from my head. It caught me completely off guard and put me into a panic.

Rather than try to paraphrase what he said, I'll give you his final three paragraphs verbatim.

> I wonder if any of you can fathom what it's like to be a monkey. I'm not talking about being a run-of-the-mill monkey, but a monkey who is like me. Through no fault of my own, I was born with an agile and creative mind. I see things in the world that for some reason humans have a hard time recognizing. You may disagree with this, but I think it's true. I believe I have this special knack. And I think it's one of the reasons I've been so misunderstood and disliked; I don't fit neatly into a defined category of thought that's acceptable. When I wrote my book about life and death in this country, I had no idea it would cause such a stir, but there's no escaping the fact that I made a lot of people angry. Perhaps a monkey is just able to see things more clearly than a human being. I know this sounds a little arrogant, like I have a high opinion of myself, but I think it's true. So much of how humans think and come to conclusions is clouded and twisted by denial, prejudice, emotion, misguided faith, and an astonishing lack of logic, and as a result the most intelligent animal on the planet finds itself tangled in a trap of falsehoods and hypocrisies.

> So yes, this book is an apology, but perhaps not quite the apology you expected. I've tried to do a better job describing my views and explaining how they might be taken to provide humans with a better life, to help them get along better. I think I could've done a better job of this in my previous book, and for not doing that, I do apologize. But if you were expecting me to apologize for my actual opinions, you are probably pretty disappointed, having come to the end of this book and having received no such apology. No, I do not apologize for my opinions,

for they were all carefully calculated and well thought out in a search for the truth. Being a monkey, I had no reason to take sides on any issue, sides that humans have devised; I had only a desire to see and report on things as they actually are. As a result it seems that I didn't make just a few people mad; instead, I got under everyone's skin. Think of it, the nerve of this banana-eating, long-tailed monkey telling humans what they should do, how they should treat each other, and how they should see things. I understand this anger, I guess. It seems I've annoyed the very people I was trying to help.

I think I've said enough to last a lifetime, and I'll be writing no more books or magazine articles. I have a passion for writing, but enough is enough. It's time for me to move on and leave you people alone. The following announcement will probably please a lot of you: I am leaving, period. I am going away, and you will not be able to find me. Even my closest friends will not know where I am. I leave behind the books I've written as my contribution to your society, but it's your society, not mine. I am a monkey and not a man. And it's time I starting living like a monkey, enjoying my life and putting all this madness behind me. Live and let live—isn't that what they say? So with that in mind, I now say good-bye and wish you all the best.

When I read these words, I immediately called Shakespeare to talk him out of leaving, but there was no answer. I quickly had Sarah read the end of the book too. "What do you make of it?" I asked her. "Do you think he's gone? I called his house, and there's no answer."

"We should drive up there," she said.

"Where would he go?"

"I have no idea."

"If he really left, how will we ever find him?"

"I don't know," Sarah said.

I had a terrible feeling I'd never see my monkey again. Shakespeare wasn't one to say one thing and do another. If he said he was going to leave, he meant it. And he was clever enough that finding him might prove impossible. Sarah and I hopped in our car and drove up to his house in Los Angeles. When we got there, we rang the doorbell, but there was no answer. I turned the doorknob, but it was locked. Sarah had her key with her, so she unlocked the door, and we stepped inside. We both called his name, but he didn't respond. We checked every room in the house, many of them twice, and it was clear Shakespeare was nowhere in the house. He'd left most of his clothes in the closet, but his little suitcase was gone. Also gone was the emergency stash of cash that he kept in a safe in his bedroom. The safe door was wide open, and nothing was inside. I now knew for sure that Shakespeare had left and without even saying good-bye.

"This is a nightmare," I said.

"Where's Jason's man?" Sarah asked.

"Good question."

"Isn't he supposed to be here?"

"Yes, someone is always supposed to be here."

"Call Jason."

And that's exactly what I did. Jason picked up the phone, and when I asked where his man was, he told me Shakespeare had sent the man home that morning, telling him he was no longer needed. I told Jason that Shakespeare was missing, and he asked if he'd been kidnapped. I said no, that he'd just left on his own. Jason said that he had thought it was odd when Shakespeare sent his man home, and I told him he should've called and told me. I suddenly felt like blaming Jason for the entire vanishing act, but I stopped myself. It wasn't Jason's fault. It wasn't anyone's fault.

During the following weeks we got the police involved in the search for Shakespeare and also asked Jason to pool his resources and help. Neither group turned up even the smallest clue. Days went by, then weeks, then months, and there was no sign of Shakespeare anywhere. At first his disappearance was in the news, a great mystery worthy of the public's attention, but as weeks passed, everyone lost interest. Rudy decided to publish Shakespeare's book as promised, but by the time it became available for purchase, no one seemed interested, and sales were very disappointing.

It was about four months after Shakespeare left us that I got a call from the Los Angeles police. At first I thought they were calling to report that they'd found my monkey or uncovered a clue as to his whereabouts, but that wasn't the reason for the call. They were calling because someone had set Shakespeare's house on fire, and the fire department was at the scene trying to put it out. "You should probably come up here since you're the owner of record," the officer told me.

I told Sarah what had happened, and the two of us drove up to the house. By the time we got there, the flames had consumed the entire place. The house looked like something from a war zone, like it had been struck by bombs. The firefighters were working on containing it, making sure the flames didn't spread to the adjacent houses, but the house itself was a total loss. I found the captain and asked him if he knew what had started the fire, and he said he guessed it was arson, but he couldn't say for sure until after the investigation. He asked if I had any idea who would do such a thing, and I told him there were probably a lot of possibilities. "Shakespeare wasn't very well liked," I said.

"We're aware of that. But no recent threats?"

"No," I said.

"Everything he owned is gone," Sarah said.

"It'll be like he was never here," I added.

"Sorry, folks. We did our best. Whoever set this fire knew what they were doing."

"We probably shouldn't have left the house vacant for so long," I said. "We should at least have taken his things out of it."

"You thought he might come back," said Sarah.

"It was a possibility."

"Well, he won't be coming back now," the captain said. "Not to this house."

I think that's when it hit me that Shakespeare wasn't returning, not ever. I finally accepted what had been so hard to accept: that he was gone for good. I think Sarah felt the same way, for she started crying during the drive home. "He's truly gone," she said. "We should give up the search. We should put an end to all this. We're not going to find him."

"I think you're right," I agreed. I felt like crying too, but I held it back.

The months that followed were sad and empty; it was so weird not having Shakespeare in our lives. He'd created a lot of worry and anxiety with his antics, but he'd also brought us a lot of joy. In a way, his life had defined ours, and Sarah and I missed him terribly. Ten months after Shakespeare's disappearance, Sarah and I found ourselves talking in bed, and Sarah brought up the idea of our having a child, something I hadn't thought of much while we had Shakespeare. I mean, the idea had crossed my mind, but I'd never taken it too seriously. We'd had our hands full with my monkey. But now with Shakespeare gone, this idea of having a child seemed like it might be a good one. We talked about it off and on over the following month. Then Sarah stopped taking the pill, and within only a year she gave birth.

Just like that, we had ourselves a pooping, drooling little newborn baby boy whom we named Tyler William Anderson, Tyler because we both liked the name and William after William Shakespeare. One day we'd have to tell Tyler he was named in part after a monkey, and at first he might not like it. But once we told him all about Shakespeare, I expected he would feel honored. At least that was the plan.

Long Gone

When I first purchased Shakespeare and brought him home, he had been able walk and climb like a trooper and soon was saying words. On the other hand, there was Tyler. I have to be honest—I was surprised at how utterly helpless and annoying human babies were. I mean, seriously, he couldn't do anything on his own, other than suck, poop, and cry. I think the crying was the worst part of the whole baby experience. I couldn't wait until he grew up enough to understand the simple words "be quiet!" I didn't mind changing diapers so much, or feeding him or rocking him to sleep, but listening to his crying was intolerable. I didn't remember Shakespeare ever crying at all. But Tyler would cry in the morning, in the afternoon, and in the wee hours of the night. And often he'd cry over nothing, just seeming to cry for the sake of crying. Everything would be perfectly fine, and he'd just start bawling for no apparent reason other than to pointlessly fill our ears with this incessant din of unpleasantness.

I could write chapters and chapters about Tyler. Despite all the crying, it was a joy to watch him grow during his first years. Eventually, the crying subsided, and he just became a whole lot of fun. The older he got, the more time I spent with him. I have to admit that I wasn't much of a baby-loving person, but I truly loved it as Tyler bloomed into a little boy. I seemed to be living a second childhood with him, and though I was his father, together we did many of the things little boys do together. God, what fun this was! But this story isn't about Tyler and me; it's about my monkey, Shakespeare. So as much as I'd like to tell you about Tyler and my time with him, I'll try to stay on topic and stick to Shakespeare.

Considering that he left us, you might think there'd now be little for me to write about Shakespeare, but you'd be wrong, for although he was gone, he was still very much in our lives. He'd had a great influence on all of us, and we weren't prepared to let his memory slip away. For example, we continued to celebrate his birthdays, even though he was never around to join us. Sarah and I would invite everyone to our house, and we'd have dinner and cake, reminiscing and telling stories about him and speculating on where he was. I liked these birthdays because they brought back a lot of good memories, and they also allowed us to stay close as a group and catch up on what we all had been doing since the last time we met.

It was on Shakespeare's sixteenth birthday that we invited the usual crowd to our house, just as we did every year. I should mention that a few changes had occurred in the group since Shakespeare left us. First, Mrs. Carlson and Becky's brothers no longer came to the parties. I think ever since Becky's murder, Mrs. Carlson just wanted to put Shakespeare and the rest of us out of her mind, pretending the whole thing had never happened. Although I would have liked to have her and the boys there, I didn't blame her for staying away. Also, I now invited Vern to these parties, and he always showed up. He had become a lively part of the group, and everyone there seemed to like him. Vern was in his seventies now but still very energetic and talkative. I'd started inviting a couple of Shakespeare's professors from UCLA to join us too. One was a philosophy teacher named Edward Cable, and the other was a sociology professor named Edith Bowers, and they had liked Shakespeare a lot. They always drove down from Los Angeles with Evan. Both had had a lot to do with encouraging Shakespeare to write *Life and Death in America*, and they'd had high praise for the book when it first came out, unlike many of their peers. They'd also reached out to me to express their concern when Shakespeare ran off, something not many people did. For most people it had been good riddance.

It was hard to believe Shakespeare was living out on his own, now sixteen years old, residing who knew where. It seemed like just yesterday that I'd brought him home from Vern's. So much had happened over the past sixteen years, but in an odd way, it felt like no time had passed at all. It's strange how life sometimes feels this way, isn't it? Some days seem to go on for years, and some years seem like just a few days. With Shakespeare time had seemed to go by so fast.

Anyway, everyone we had invited showed up for the sixteenth birthday party, making twelve of us. I barbecued hamburgers on my grill, and Sarah prepared the rest of the meal in the kitchen. We served all the food to our guests while Tyler was napping in his room. He had had a busy morning playing with Dr. Barney and the professor, and Sarah figured a nap would do him good.

"So what do you think Shakespeare's doing right now?" the professor asked. "Never mind where he is. What the heck is he doing now?"

"Probably writing another book," Hopkins said.

"I doubt that," I said. "He said he was all done writing books. He made that pretty clear."

"Probably not done reading them, though."

"Yes," I said. "I can see him reading now, curled up on a sofa somewhere with a great big book in his lap. How he loved to read."

"Or maybe he's watching an old black-and-white," Sarah said. "He liked that old movie channel on TV."

"I say he's watching a pirate flick," the professor said. "He loved those old pirate flicks."

"Do you think he's still here in California?" Judy asked.

"In California?" I said. "Maybe. He did seem to like it here."

"He could be anywhere," Hopkins said.

"True enough."

"Do you think he suspects we still celebrate his birthdays, without him being here?"

"I doubt it."

"Do you think he'd be happy to know?"

"Yes, I do," I said.

"So do I," Sarah said.

"He liked being the center of attention," the professor said. "And he especially liked to be listened to. When I try to guess where he might have gone, it's hard for me to imagine him living like a hermit somewhere, shut off from the world."

"I doubt he's shut himself off from the world," Vern said. "The way I figure it, he's probably on the Internet."

"On the Internet?"

"Posing as a human."

"Yes," Dr. Barney said. "I'll bet you're right. He always liked posting things on the Internet. He liked the anonymity. Good call, Vern. I think that's where he now is. I'll bet he's in some chat room right now, talking up a storm."

"It makes sense," Tom said.

"No one would have any idea who he actually is. No one would even guess he's a monkey."

"And he could say anything he liked."

"He'd be just another person with a computer and keyboard."

"And driving the other people crazy."

"With his logic."

"Yes, with his logic."

"He had such an awesome mind."

"Did I ever tell any of you about my five rules of freedom?" asked Professor Cable, the philosophy teacher. No one said yes, so he continued. "I was teaching Shakespeare about the concept of freedom, and we got around to discussing my own views on the subject. This was one of my favorite topics, freedom. People use the word a lot and talk about it like they know what it means, but few of us actually take the time to think much about it. Anyway, I came up with my five rules for freedom, a litmus test for determining whether a person is actually free. I was very proud of this list and had worked on it for a couple years. I thought this list was so profound as to deserve a book of its own, and I wrote a book. One afternoon I brought the manuscript over to Shakespeare to get his input. I thought he'd be impressed, and he placed the stack of papers on his desk and began to read. But instead of being impressed, he stopped after the first page and handed the big manuscript back to me. 'You've got this all wrong,' he said. I asked how he knew this, since he'd read only one page, and he said, 'There are no such things as rules for freedom. Once you require a set of rules, a person is no longer free to do as he or she pleases. You're saying the person must obey your rules. Your rules negate freedom right off the bat.' Well, I wanted to throw the manuscript in his face, but I thought about what he'd just said, and he was right. He then told me not to waste any more of my time because freedom simply could not be defined, not by anyone—because once you wrote a definition, any definition at all, you put bounds on what freedom was, and a person could rightly ask himself, 'Am I free to act outside of those bounds?' Do you see what he meant? It's a word that by definition has no definition."

Professor Wild laughed.

"That sounds like Shakespeare," I said. Everyone was quiet for a moment, thinking. "Anyone else?" I said. "Any memories to share?"

"Do you remember that summer when we took him to the Grand Canyon?" Sarah asked me.

"Of course," I said.

"You took him to the Grand Canyon?"

"He'd seen pictures of it in books and wanted to see it for himself. He caused such a stir at the restaurant. Everyone there wanted autographs and photos of themselves with him. We were barely able to eat our dinners. I think the people were more excited about seeing Shakespeare than they were about seeing the national park. He was very popular back then. That was when the public loved him. Those were such good times."

"Do you remember what Shakespeare said about the Grand Canyon?" asked Sarah.

"Yes, he said it made him feel small."

"I think the word he used was 'insignificant.'"

"Yes, insignificant."

"He said it was the most amazing thing he'd ever seen."

"We should've taken him on more trips," I said.

"I took him on a few trips in Southern California," Evan said. "But mostly to museums."

"I didn't know that," I said.

"I'm sure I told you."

"I remember him telling you," Sarah said.

"I took him to the Museum of Contemporary Art, to one of the locations in Los Angeles. It was pretty funny."

"What was funny?"

"His reaction."

"Didn't he like it?"

"It was like the opposite of what you described for the Grand Canyon. We looked at every piece on display, every Miro and Lichtenstein and Pollock and whoever. I mean, Shakespeare really looked at the works with interest, spending several minutes examining each piece, taking it all in. I think people there knew who he was, but they were very respectful, not crowding around him or harassing him for photos or autographs. It was a different crowd than the sort of people you find at national parks. Then when we were about to leave, some lady who worked at the museum came up to Shakespeare and looked down at him, smiling. She asked, 'So what do you think of our collection?' Shakespeare looked at me, as if to get my approval to say something, and I nodded my head, telling him to go on. He looked at the woman and said, 'The emperor has no clothes.' That's all he said to her, and I could tell she wasn't sure whether to be offended or just laugh. She chose to laugh, pushing the exit door open for us, and Shakespeare and I then walked back to my car, where he said, 'I feel so superior.'"

"Superior to what?" Judy asked.

"Just superior."

"I think I know what he meant," the professor said.

"So do I," I said.

"That was the last time I took him to see any modern art."

"Probably a wise decision," I said.

"Do you remember the evening we took him to the symphony?" the professor asked me. "They were performing a Mozart concerto that night. It was before we could take him anywhere."

"Yes, when you rented that wheelchair?"

"Ha," the professor laughed.

"I thought that old hen was going to lay a couple eggs right then and there."

"What happened?" Evan asked.

The professor recounted the story about how he and Shakespeare had shown up for the concert in a wheelchair, how he'd told the ticket lady that Shakespeare was his service animal.

"A service animal," Evan laughed. "That's pretty good."

"It worked, and they let us in. I cited the Americans with Disabilities Act. They decided not to violate the law."

"Did Shakespeare like the concert?"

"He loved it."

"Some monkeys like music," Vern said. "One of my monkeys likes country western."

"Which one?" I asked.

"Matilda, Shakespeare's mom. Whenever I play country music in the house, she howls, like she's crying, like she understands the lyrics."

"Has Shakespeare ever met Matilda?" Evan asked.

"We tried to get them together," I said.

"They didn't get along," Vern added.

All of us were quiet for a while as we ate our hamburgers. Then I heard the dog barking from the neighbor's backyard, over and over again. It had probably been barking the entire time we were talking, but for some reason I just now noticed it, the endless stupid barking of their dumb dog. The barking reminded me how dumb most animals were—all except for my monkey, Shakespeare, who was not only smart but probably too smart for his own good. Why did he have to be so smart?

"This may sound selfish," I said, "but sometimes I wish Shakespeare hadn't been so bright. It would've been nice just to have a normal monkey, a creature who didn't write books or appear on talk shows or make movies. I would've been fine with a monkey I could love and call my own. I would've liked a monkey who didn't find it necessary to run away, a monkey who would have been happy living here with Sarah and me for the rest of his natural life. Christ, I really wonder where the heck he went. Don't the rest of you?"

Everyone nodded their heads, and Sarah put her hand on my forearm. I think she thought I was going to cry, but I wasn't. I wasn't sad. I was done with my crying. I was just wishing things had been different.

"I know what Shakespeare would tell you," Dr. Barney said.

"What would he tell me?"

"To count your blessings."

"Amen to that," Vern said.

Tyler appeared in the doorway behind me, rubbing his eyes and yawning. He had just woken from his nap. He noticed the empty chair next to Sarah, his place at the table that she had saved for him. He climbed up into the chair and began looking things over. We'd all stopped talking, and Tyler said, "So do I get a hamburger?"

"Of course you do," Sarah said. "We were waiting for you to wake up."

"It doesn't look like you've been doing much waiting. It looks like you've all been eating."

Everyone laughed.

"Here's your burger," Sarah said, and she slid a big hamburger onto Tyler's plate. It was a good-sized patty with an oversized bun. "You want me to cut it up for you?" Sarah asked.

"No, no cutting. I'm not a baby, and cutting is for babies."

"He's no baby," I said.

"No, I'm no baby," Tyler agreed. He grabbed the hamburger with both hands and lifted it to his face, opening his mouth wide.

"You sure you don't want me to cut it?"

"No, no cutting," he said, still holding the burger at his mouth.

"That hamburger is bigger than you are," Dr. Barney said to Tyler.

Tyler ignored the comment and took the largest bite he could manage, but he barely nicked the thing. He got a mouthful of bread since his teeth hadn't even reached the meat. But he was proud of himself for having refused the cutting. "See?" he said. "You didn't have to cut it up for me."

"Bravo!" the professor said.

"Can I please have some milk?"

"Sure, I'll be right back," Sarah said, and she went into the house for a glass of milk. When she returned, Tyler was working on his second bite, and everyone was gawking him. He was very serious about eating this burger, and for some reason everyone at the table wanted to watch.

"It's not polite to stare," Tyler said without looking at anyone in particular.

"Tyler's right," Sarah said.

"You're a comedian," I said, laughing.

"I'm not a comedian."

"Do you even know what a comedian is?"

"I'm just a boy," Tyler said emphatically. "I don't want to be a comedian." Tyler then chewed and swallowed his second bite and finally asked, "So what is a comedian?"

"It's someone who makes people laugh."

Tyler grabbed his milk and drank the entire glass, rather quickly. He put the glass down on the table, looked at everyone, and then belched loudly. Most of us laughed, and Tyler laughed too. He was pleased that he'd made us laugh. "I guess I am a comedian," he said.

"We don't belch at the table," Sarah said.

"I couldn't help it."

"If you need to burp, leave the table and burp somewhere else."

"I bet I can burp louder than you," Vern said to Tyler, winking at him.

"Sure you can. You're bigger than me."

"That's true," Vern said. He then held his belly, swallowed a throat full of air, and let out a belch that actually startled Sarah.

"Honestly," Sarah said, making a face.

"Listen to this," the professor said, and he moved his head around weirdly. He too swallowed some air, opened his mouth, and belched five times in a row.

Tyler got a big kick out of this and laughed out loud. "How did you do that?" he asked.

"You're all impossible," Sarah said.

"If Shakespeare were here, he'd put you all in your places," Dr. Barney said.

"You're right," the professor said. "He was the king of burps. He could belch louder and longer than anyone I've ever known. He could even pronounce words and sentences when he burped. I once saw him burp an entire haiku poem."

"You're kidding," Vern said.

"I think he had to take two breaths, mind you, but he managed to do it."

"I remember that," Dr. Barney said. "We were having lunch at the university cafeteria. There was a group of women sitting at the table next to us. They all stared at us, spellbound."

"Disgusted is probably more like it," Sarah said.

"Anyway, it was pretty funny."

"Let's change the subject," Sarah said, pretending to be angry. She wasn't really angry, but she did want to talk about something else.

Tyler went for his third bite of his hamburger, and still he could barely get the thing into his mouth. He did manage to gnaw off another piece, but he complained, "All I'm getting is bread."

"Tyler," Hopkins said, "do you know whose birthday we're celebrating today?"

Tyler chewed and swallowed his mouthful of bread and then said, "It's Shakespeare's birthday."

"Yes, but do you know who Shakespeare is?"

"He was my dad's monkey."

"He knows," I said.

"Do you know what kind of monkey he was?"

"He was a smart monkey. Dad told me he knew how to talk. I was named after him, my middle name."

"So do you know why he isn't here with us?"

"Because he had to leave."

"Do you know where he is now?"

"Where?" Tyler asked.

"Actually, none of us know."

"It's a secret?"

"Yes, it's a secret. He doesn't want any of us to find him. He wants to be left alone."

"Why?"

"Because people weren't being very nice to him."

"Why not?"

"Because he told them the truth."

"He got in trouble for telling the truth?"

"Yes," Hopkins said.

"Is that true?" Tyler asked me.

"How about we have cake?" I said to Tyler. I was deliberately changing the subject, not being in the mood to explain to a four-year-old how a person could get in trouble for telling the truth. "Are you ready for some cake?"

"I've barely eaten my hamburger."

"I feel like eating cake."

Tyler looked over at Sarah. He asked, "Can I have cake without eating my dinner?"

"It's a party," I said, pleading Tyler's case.

"Oh, why not," Sarah said. "I'll go get it."

"I want to help," Tyler said, and he followed Sarah into the house and to the kitchen, where they stuck the candles into the cake and lit them. When they returned, the candles were all aflame, and Tyler asked who was going to blow them out.

"Why don't you do it?" I said.

"Can I?"

"Go for it," I said, and when Sarah set down the cake, Tyler took in a deep breath and blew out all sixteen candles.

"Good show," Vern said.

Sarah began slicing up the cake, and Tom said to me, "Seriously, Marty, where do you think he went?"

"You mean Shakespeare?"

"Of course I mean Shakespeare. You knew him better than all of us. Where do you think he went?"

"Maybe he joined a circus."

"A circus?" Tyler asked.

"No, seriously," Tom said again. "You've had years to think about this. Where do you think he is?"

"I wouldn't put anything past him."

"And?"

"I just don't know."

"We looked everywhere," Sarah said. "Both the police and our own private investigator searched for months."

"If he doesn't want to be found, you're not going to find him," the professor said. "And he doesn't want to be found. I think that's obvious."

"It just amazes me that he could just vanish into thin air, without leaving a single clue, without eventually making a mistake."

"Any ideas, Hopkins?" I asked.

"For this one, no. I have no ideas."

Costa Rica

S everal weeks after we celebrated Shakespeare's sixteenth birthday, I got a series of afternoon calls while in the middle of a tennis match. My cell phone was in my tennis bag, which was on the bench at the side of the court. I ignored the first three attempts to reach me, but when I heard the fourth, I figured I better stop and answer my phone. I told my tennis opponent to wait while I ran to get it, but by the time I got to my bag, it had stopped ringing. The missed call was from Sarah, so I called her back. She picked up right away and sounded out of breath when she answered, which I thought was odd. "You just called me four times," I said. "What the heck is so important?"

"We got a letter from him," she said.

"A letter from who?"

"From Shakespeare."

"Are you sure?"

"Of course I'm sure."

"What does it say?"

"You need to come home and read it."

"Wow, I'll be right there," I said.

I told my tennis opponent that I had to leave, that I had a personal emergency to attend to. In no time, I had packed my tennis bag and was running to my car. I backed out of my parking space and sped toward home, and when I got there, I ran to the front door and entered the house. Sarah was in the front room, smiling at me.

"Where is it?" I asked. "Where's the letter?"

"It's in the kitchen, on the counter."

"What does it say?" I asked, but I wasn't expecting an answer. I was already on my way to the kitchen, where I found the letter and the envelope

267

it had arrived in. I first looked at the envelope; it was addressed to Sarah and me, and though there was no return address, it did have a surprising postmark. "Costa Rica?" I said.

"Just read the letter," Sarah said.

"Yes, of course."

"He wants to see us."

"He does?" I asked, and I held the letter in my hands to read it. It was definitely his handwriting.

Dear Marty and Sarah,

You're probably surprised to be getting this letter from me. As I'm sure you have guessed from the postmark and stamps, I am living in Costa Rica. I have been living here since I left California. Life has been very good for me. I am doing well, and I hope you are doing well too. I would like to see both of you. If you are not still mad at me for running away, and if you would like to see me, please come to Costa Rica this summer and meet me at the Four Seasons Hotel on the Papagayo Peninsula, in the northwest part of the country. I will look for you sometime during the first week of July on the hotel beach. When you come, pick a spot where there are no other people. The north stretch of the beach isn't usually too crowded, so this should be easy for you to do. Just throw down a couple towels and enjoy yourself under the sun. I will be checking the beach regularly, and if you're there, I'll find you. It's important that you don't tell anyone about this and that you bring no one else. I'm trusting you to keep the entire contents of this letter secret. And I ask that you keep my whereabouts secret as well. I love both of you and look forward to seeing you soon.

"Wow," I said.

"Yes, wow," Sarah said.

"I wonder what he's doing there, way down in Costa Rica of all places."

"July is only a month away."

"Yes," I said. "We'll need to plan."

"What will we do with Tyler?"

"Don't you want to bring him with us?"

"He said he just wanted you and me. I don't think he wants us bringing anyone else."

"Obviously, he doesn't know we have a son," I said. "But I guess you're right; we should respect his wishes. We'll leave Tyler here."

"My parents can watch him while we're gone. I'll call them this week to set things up. They can come out here and stay at our house. I'm sure they'd love being with their grandson for a week or so. It'll be a perfect vacation for them."

"What are we going to tell everyone about our trip? Your parents are going to ask why we're going down there all of a sudden. And others will ask too. Why are we going to Costa Rica? What should we say?"

"That we're going on our own vacation."

"I guess that makes sense."

"Lots of people vacation in Costa Rica."

"Wow," I said. "I can't believe we're going to see him. I wonder what kind of life he's been living. I wonder what he's been doing all this time."

"It sounds like he's happy."

"Yes, he sounds happy. That's a good thing."

"So now we wait for July," Sarah said.

It seemed like it took forever for July to roll around. Finally, it was time for us to leave, and all our things were packed and ready. Sarah's parents were at the house to watch Tyler. I can't even explain how excited I was; I felt like dancing on the ceilings, like doing a crazy upside-down jig. We had a limousine take us to the airport, where we boarded our plane to Costa Rica. When we arrived, we hired a driver to take us to the Four Seasons Hotel on the Pacific coast. There was lots of interesting tropical scenery on the way, but I didn't pay attention to any of it. And neither did Sarah.

"You're going to like Costa Rica," our driver said, but we weren't listening to him. Our minds were on Shakespeare.

As we pulled up to the resort, Sarah squeezed my hand.

"Here we are," the driver said. "This is a very nice hotel. It's one of our finest. I'm sure you're going to like it."

"Thanks for the lift," I said, and I paid the man and gave him a generous tip.

The driver was right; it was a nice hotel. In fact, I wondered what Shakespeare was doing at such an upscale place. What was he involved in that he could afford hanging out at such an expensive hotel? He'd left California with a pretty decent stash of cash—I didn't remember exactly how much we kept in the safe for his emergency fund, but it was substantial—but it wasn't enough for him to have lived at a place like this for all these years, not even close. Besides, Shakespeare surely had spent most of the money just getting here without being noticed. He would've had to pay some people off. He would've had transportation expenses. It wouldn't have been a cheap thing to do, making it down here without being noticed.

That evening we ate dinner at one of the resort's restaurants, and I asked the waiter if he knew of a monkey living at the hotel. He laughed and said that lots of monkeys lived in Costa Rica and that if we looked carefully, we would see some of them in the trees the next day. Clearly, the guy didn't get what I was talking about, so I dropped the matter. When we were done eating dinner, we went to the gift shop for some room snacks. I asked the cashier the same question I'd asked the waiter, about a monkey staying at the hotel, and she gave me the same answer. It didn't appear anyone knew what I was talking about, and Sarah said I should just wait until the next day.

"We'll wait at the beach like he told us to do," she said. "He said he'd find us. He didn't tell us to look for him."

I sighed impatiently but agreed she was right. We went to our room to watch some TV, and eventually we went to bed.

The next morning I got up at dawn. I made a cup of coffee using the little coffee maker in the room, and then I woke Sarah. "Let's go," I said. She asked what time it was, and I told her. She said to hold my horses, so I let her sleep another hour. I turned on the TV and watched the news for a while. Finally, I couldn't stand it, and I woke her up again. "What the heck are we waiting for?" I said. "He could be out there right now, looking for us."

Sarah laughed, and this time she got out of bed.

We had breakfast in one of the restaurants, grabbed some towels for the beach, and began walking north up the coast just as Shakespeare had instructed. It was already warm out, but there weren't many people on the beach. We found a spot far from the hotel where there wasn't anyone around at all, and we waited. Sarah had brought a book to read, but I spent all my time looking up and down the beach for Shakespeare.

"You know, looking for him isn't going to make him get here any faster," Sarah said.

I heard a rustle in the tree branches overhead, and at first I didn't think anything of it. But then I realized what it might be, and I looked up. It was Shakespeare! He was hanging from a branch with one hand, swinging back and forth playfully. "Marty!" he exclaimed. He dropped from the tree to the sand.

"It's you!" I said.

"Of course it's me."

"I was wondering if you were coming, if you were actually going to find us."

"Shakespeare!" Sarah exclaimed, dropping her book to her lap.

"Let's get a good look at you," I said.

"To heck with that," he said. "Give me a hug!" He jumped into my arms and hugged me around my neck with his long arms. Then he gave me a kiss on the cheek and jumped over to Sarah to do the same.

Sarah was laughing with joy. "I can't believe it's actually you."

"In the flesh."

"You live here at the Four Seasons?" I asked.

"I do," he said. "Well, more or less."

"I asked around for you. I asked about a monkey who lived here, and no one seemed to know what I was talking about."

"There are lots of monkeys living here," Shakespeare laughed.

"There are?"

"We live outside."

"You mean you live in the trees?"

"Did you think I had a room here?" Shakespeare asked, laughing. Then he said, "Sit tight a minute. I want you to meet my family."

"You have a family?"

"Just wait here. I'll go get them," he said, and off he went. He climbed back into the tree and leaped to another tree and then another. He was gone for a minute, and then he returned to the tree branches above us with four other monkeys. They crawled carefully toward us, staying up in the tree, moving very slowly, as though they were afraid of us. They were looking down, curiously.

"They're not going to jump down to meet you," Shakespeare said, "but I wanted you to see them."

"Just a minute," I said, and Sarah and I stood up to get a better look.

Shakespeare introduced us to the four monkeys one by one. The first was Tillie, his wife. The second and third were his children, Veronica and Blake. Shakespeare introduced the fourth as Tillie's older brother, Eddie. "I gave them their names," Shakespeare said. "Tillie and Eddie didn't have names until I met them. Obviously, I gave Veronica and Blake their names when they were born. They don't understand English, but they do respond to their names. I think they like having names. So what do you think? Don't I have a handsome little family?"

"Oh yes," Sarah said.

"Do they know who we are?" I asked.

"They know you're my friends."

"But they won't come down out of the tree?"

"They're kind of shy."

"When did you meet them?"

"I met Tillie when I first came here. I liked her right away and made her my wife. Her brother kind of came with the deal. He doesn't get along well with others, but he behaves himself when he's with us. We had Veronica two years ago and Blake three years ago."

"And you say you've all made this your home, around here at the hotel?"

"Here and there. But yes, we try to stay around the hotel. It's a good food source for us. People sometimes leave food out, trying to feed us. They like to watch us eat. And the restaurant dumpsters are always full of good things. They throw away a lot of perfectly good food."

"So you eat out of dumpsters?"

"Not always, but often."

Shakespeare jumped down from the branch, and Sarah and I sat back down on our towels. The four monkeys hurried away, scampering back into the cover.

"I'm glad we got to meet your family," Sarah said.

"Sorry they're not more social."

"There's something different about you," I said, changing the subject.

"Yes, I'm different. I'm happier."

"No, I mean different about the way you look."

"Healthier, maybe?"

"No, that's not it. Yes, I know what it is. You're not wearing any clothes!"

"Well, I would look pretty silly wearing a jacket and tie, jumping from tree to tree."

"I guess you would. It's just that it used to be so important to you, dressing well."

"Not anymore."

"Obviously not."

"My priorities have changed, Marty. I'm a real monkey now, no longer pretending to be a human."

"Is that what you were doing, pretending?"

"Something like that."

"I have a question for you."

"Go ahead."

"How the heck did you get down here from California? We were looking all over for you. Seriously, Shakespeare, we had the police searching everywhere, and we even hired Jason to look."

"I had an excellent plan."

"You must have had help."

"Oh, I did."

"Well, who helped you?"

"Promise you won't get mad at him?"

I thought about this and said, "Yes, I guess I can promise that."

"It was Hopkins who helped me."

"Hopkins?"

"In fact, he put together the entire scheme. It was my desire to leave, but he devised and handled everything. Most of what needed to be accomplished had to be done by a human. There was no way I could do it all myself."

"All this time, he's told us nothing."

"I told him to tell you nothing. He was just doing what he was told."

"So he lied to us?"

"Yes, he lied."

"He's always seemed so trustworthy."

"He has been trustworthy, to me," Shakespeare said with a smile. Of course, he was right.

Then I asked, "Do you have any idea what you did to Sarah and me, how we worried about you? It was awful."

"Sorry about that."

"You at least could have told us where you were going," Sarah said.

"You would've tried to stop me."

"Yes, maybe we would have."

"I had to make a clean break. It had nothing to do with you guys. I just didn't belong. I knew you loved me, and I knew everyone else cared about me. But I no longer belonged with any of you. Things had turned ugly, and they were getting worse every day."

"We could've fought for what was right."

"But what was right?"

"A lot of what you were saying was right."

"For a monkey, maybe."

"I don't understand what that means," Sarah said.

"Neither do I," I said.

"Do you really need me to explain?"

"Yes, I think we do."

Shakespeare took a deep breath and stared at us. He wasn't frustrated, but he seemed a little surprised that we needed an explanation. "Human beings are not monkeys," he said. "Can we agree on that?"

"Of course," I said.

"Do you know what makes humans different from monkeys? In fact, do you know what makes humans different from all other animals?"

"Intelligence?" I said.

"Yes, that's a factor. But that's not the primary difference. What really makes humans different from other animals is their aversion to honesty. Human beings dislike honesty more than anything else. The truth can be very annoying, and humans don't like being annoyed."

"You don't think humans seek the truth?"

"Sometimes they claim to seek the truth, and sometimes they actually do look for it, but only once in a while. Most of the time, it isn't the truth they're after. What they usually seek is a means of proving what they want to believe is true. There's a big difference between wanting to understand reality and simply wanting to confirm what one desires reality to be. Is this making sense?"

"I think so," I said.

"I'll give you an example. I'll take an example right out of my book. Humans believe killing is wrong, no? Isn't this the sixth commandment for Christians?"

"Yes," I said.

"And it's a commandment, right? It isn't just a hint or a suggestion; it's a loud and clear order from God carved in stone. Yet humans kill all the time. There are thousands upon thousands of deaths at the hands of men and women every year. The vast majority of Americans are Christians, yet they can't seem to restrain themselves from killing each other. Do they admit to what they are, and do they tell the truth? No, what they do is quite the opposite. They employ euphemisms and respectful titles to describe themselves, at times going so far as to call each other heroes, and they come up with a litany of justifications and excuses for their behavior, never mind the law of God. It's all a lie. Everyone is lying."

"Everyone?"

"At one time or another. They lie by killing, or they lie by condoning it. And yes, I mean everyone. You know, I don't happen to agree with the sixth commandment, so I'm not saying it's wrong to kill. There are lots of good reasons to take another's life. But I'm saying it's one thing to kill honestly and another to pretend you're not really killing. Humans kill like no other animal on the planet and then pose as a peace-loving species. Humans refuse to admit what they are: killers. The human species is not honest with itself."

"So what else do humans lie about?"

"You really need me to tell you?" Shakespeare said, laughing. Obviously, he'd been thinking about this subject, and I hadn't. "How about God?"

"People lie about God?"

"God is a lie."

"I'd agree with you if you questioned the existence of God, but how is he a lie? Isn't this more an issue of one's beliefs, whether or not one has faith?"

"Listen, Marty, faith is one of humankind's biggest and most blatant deceptions, a real whopper. It's the mother lode, a grand lie to outdo all lies. After all, what do you think faith is? It's nothing more than a deliberate self-deceit devised to provide pat answers to difficult if not overwhelming questions. Humans would rather have faith in something, no matter how ludicrous and unsupportable it is, than carry on not knowing. Not having all the answers is intolerable."

"You don't mind having no answers?"

"I don't mind at all. I'm a monkey. What do I need answers for?"

"Aren't you at least curious?"

"Of course I'm curious. But being curious is a far cry from needing to lie to yourself."

"I can understand that," Sarah said.

"When I first realized how smart I was, I felt like I was a human being. I believed I could relate to humans, think on their level. Intelligence is a wonderful thing, and I knew I had it. But the more I used it, the more I realized I wasn't human at all. I don't like being deceitful, and I don't care for fooling myself, not about anything. No, I am not the slightest bit human. I'm a monkey with a talent for thinking, but to expect myself to get along in a world filled with lying human beings was to deny what I am. It's just another lie."

"It surprised me when you left us. It seems like such a waste, you now living like this."

"Only because you're human. Look at it this way, Marty. If you had an exceptional talent for climbing, would it be fair for me to expect you to survive like a monkey, to live here in the trees with me and my family? Is that what you would want to do?"

"I suppose not."

"I didn't just sit on my hands when I lived with you. I did make a contribution. I wrote several books, and they're all available for purchase. People are welcome to read them whenever they want if they desire to learn what I had to say. It's not like I was silent. And maybe some of my ideas will take hold in the future. But just between you and me, I think it'll take a human to make this happen. People just don't like being told how to think and behave by a precocious simian who knows how to write. The truth is, I made a lot of people very angry, trying to fit in, trying to get my viewpoints across. I'm not one of you. I never was, and I never will be. I am a monkey."

"I think what he's saying makes sense," Sarah said to me.

"I don't like it," I said.

"Just because you don't like something doesn't mean it won't be so. Ha! You're such a human!"

"I guess I am."

"Try to be honest," Shakespeare said. "Try to think like a monkey." He laughed after he said this, the way a monkey would laugh. Then he sat on the sand, getting himself comfortable. "So enough of all this," he said. "Tell me what I've been missing. What's been going on back home? How has everyone been doing?"

"We have a child now," Sarah said.

"A human child!" Shakespeare's face lit up, and he clapped his hands. "Is it a boy or a girl?"

"A little boy. He's four years old," said Sarah.

"We sort of named him after you," I said.

"After me?"

"His middle name is William."

"How nice. I like that."

"We thought you would," Sarah said.

Honestly, Shakespeare was beaming. I'd never seen him so happy. We spent the rest of the morning talking about things back home, about how everyone was doing, about the books Sarah had been editing lately, about the birthday parties we had thrown for him. I think Shakespeare appreciated the updates, but none of what we told him made him show the slightest inclination to change his mind and move back. It occurred to me that he meant every word he had said, that he truly was his own person, a mature and honest adult, making his own decisions and living his own life.

When we ran out of things to talk about, Shakespeare said, "I've enjoyed this immensely. Let's do it again. Let's meet again next year, same time and place."

"That would be great," I said.

"I guess I should get going."

"Yes," I said. "So should we."

"No hard feelings?"

"No, of course not," I said.

Shakespeare stood up. He gave Sarah and me each a big hug. He then shrieked and ran to the tree trunk. "Until next July!" he said. He waved good-bye, climbed up the trunk, and scurried away through the branches to find his family, and with that, he was gone.

Sarah and I folded up our towels and walked back to the hotel. I felt happy and sad. I was happy that we'd had a chance to finally see our monkey but sad that it had lasted for only a couple of hours. It just made me realize how much I missed him.

When we got back to the room, we called the airline to change our flight. We had no desire to stay any longer in Costa Rica and just wanted to get back as soon as possible to the place we called home. "To each their own," I said to Sarah.

She nodded and smiled. "I wonder how my parents are doing," she said. "Tyler can be a handful."

"I'm sure they've been doing fine."

"I can't wait to get home."

"Same here," I said.

Set Point

A year has passed since we met Shakespeare in Costa Rica. It's now July again, and Sarah and I are getting ready to go for our second rendezvous. We're bringing some photographs with us this time, mostly of Tyler but also of everyone else, pictures we took at Shakespeare's last birthday party. We're looking forward to hanging out on the beach, hearing what's new, and telling Shakespeare what's been going on with us. Truth is, not a lot has happened since we last met. When Shakespeare lived with us, there was never a dull moment. Now that he's been living in Costa Rica, life has been interesting, but it's nothing like it once was.

I was able to fit in a tennis match yesterday afternoon, playing against an architect named Henry Ackerman. Henry is a bachelor about my age, and he has his own firm called Ackerman & Associates. I've been playing tennis against Henry for many years. I don't care much for the guy; he's a little too self-centered and full of himself for my taste. He's always talking about his latest projects and how important they are. He designs strip shopping centers all over Southern California, which honestly aren't that important, but listening to Henry, you'd think he was designing high-rises for multinational corporations and real estate tycoons. He always talks about his firm using the word "we," saying "we did this" and "we did that," when the truth is the firm consists of Henry and a single part-time draftsman. He doesn't even have a secretary. Yes, it's just a one-and-a-half-man operation, but to talk to him, you'd think he had a whole floor full of busy employees cranking out mountains of drawings. I guess if he weren't so annoying, he'd be amusing, but he grates on my nerves every time I talk to him. When he isn't bragging about work, he's talking about his new Porsche. And when he isn't chattering about his Porsche, he's recounting all the details of his latest expensive vacation. My guess? Henry has more debt than Greece, financing his car and his trips all over the world. Orange County is kind of a strange place, full of characters like Henry; they're a dime a dozen.

Here's the truly annoying thing about Henry: he's a pretty darn good tennis player, apparently better than I am. In all the years I've played against him, I haven't managed to win a single set. I don't know if I have some kind of psychological block against beating this guy or if he's truly as good as he seems. It's hard to believe he could be so much better than I am, considering how much I play and practice and given all the lessons I've taken. I mean, I consider myself to be pretty adept at the sport, and I'm able to beat most of my opponents at least once in a while. Yesterday, when I was playing against him, I finally had him cornered in a tiebreaker, and I thought I had a chance to break the spell. It was my advantage, and all I had to do was win the point, and I would win my first set against him. My initial serve to him was out by a mile, but my second serve was strong, and it was right on the line. But not according to Henry. He said the ball was out. The ball was out? You've got to be kidding! I told Henry he was wrong. I had won the set, and the bastard wasn't going to give me credit for it. We argued for a couple of minutes, and I mean really argued. Eventually, I let him have his way, and I conceded to his call. We continued to play, and of course Henry beat me in the end.

When I came home, Sarah asked me how things had gone, and I told her I'd finally beaten Henry Ackerman. In my mind I had won, and I wasn't lying. That serve had been on the line. I knew it, and Ackerman knew it. We both knew the truth, the truth as I'd wanted it to be.

And that brings me to the here and now. Sarah and I are waiting on the porch for the limousine to take us to the airport, to fly to Costa Rica for a second time. Soon I'll be with Shakespeare, telling him this story about how I finally beat Henry. As Shakespeare would say, I'm such a human. And it's so true, that I'm a human. That tennis match meant a lot to me, and I can't wait to see him again, so I can tell my story. He'll listen patiently, giving me the benefit of the doubt, my dear simian, my remarkable little monkey.

Printed in the United States
By Bookmasters